FORGIVEN

SHEILAH FLETCH

Comfort PUBLISHING

For information, address Comfort Publishing,
296 Church St. N., Concord, NC 28025.
The views expressed in this book are not necessarily those of the publisher.

First printing

Book cover design by
Colin L. Kernes

ISBN: 978-1-936695-03-4
Published by Comfort Publishing, LLC
www.comfortpublishing.com

Printed in the United States of America

*I would like to dedicate this book to the first love
of my life Jesus Christ in thanksgiving for the gift of my
God loving and God fearing husband of forty five years
Dr. Andy Fletch. Andy you were like a midwife in birthing
'Forgiven'. You encouraged, took care of the electronic
details and faithfully prayed with me. How blessed is a
woman who has a husband willing to pray with and for her!*

Chapter One

"Max, Max!"

Startled, the man turned his head towards the voice that hoarsely whispered his name...and to the hand shaking his shoulder.

"Max, wake up! Shhhh! Be quiet."

Max stared wide-eyed into the face of Philip, his cell-mate.

"Be quiet, Max! You're shouting in your sleep. Don't draw attention to yourself. Murph's on tonight!"

Max nodded numbly "Thanks, Philip."

As Philip returned to his bunk, Max realized he'd woken in a cold sweat. "Damn! Get control of yourself, Carron!"

He'd been dreaming and he knew exactly what. The dawn would usher in his long awaited release.

"Six long years in this place for something I never did... Six damn years!"

Anger seethed within him.

"With no record, it should have been less than two years... Could've even been probation. No! Six years, why? Justice?... His Honor, Jack Walters going to prove himself?... Show himself so tough? No compromise... and..." But, Max knew why.

"Hell, if my name had been Maxwell Kerr instead of Massimiliano Carron, my sentence would have been probation...But no! My family is Sicilian, connected to Mafioso names, so six years it was! I could have appealed it except for that pact I made with Pop. Regrets?" He let out a deep sigh. "No, but then, in here, as some citizens would say, my ancestry was not so detrimental."

1

A faint smile crossed his lips, tightening quickly as he recalled his dream...no, rather nightmare! His stomach twisted and his anger flared again. Most of the guards were decent. Sure, they demanded respect, but they still treated you as human. Then there were those few, like Murph. He and his little core of followers coughed up legalized brutality, and Murph was on tonight.

"Thank God, Philip shut me up." Max chuckled softly to himself. Then his vivid nightmare again flashed across his mind. In the dream Murph and his cronies had burst into his cell forcing him into that sickening, humiliating strip search. Why? Just to provoke him, sucker him into retaliating, perhaps delaying his release. *"Bastards!"* He had resisted striking back and that was why Philip caught him shouting in his sleep.

Max checked his watch...3 a.m.

"Christ, please keep me awake and quiet, and keep Murph occupied elsewhere. He should be off duty by 6. Then let me get out of this damn place!"

Now wide awake, Max began to go over the plan he had formulated and refined over the past six years. The more he had tried to let it go, the more the idea would return.

"Why the hell had that damn judge given him six years?"

He just couldn't shake that question. He knew his father would want him home immediately, to soothe his mother's pain. In fact, his mother' pain was the ache in his own heart. Her pain was his pain. There was such a strong bond between them. He might resemble his father but inside he knew he had his mother's heart.

A lump formed in his throat as he recalled her gentle face. *"Damn!" He missed her so much! She loved her family, especially him. Not a mean bone in her body, always putting others' needs ahead of herself!*

Max allowed his mind to travel back...back to his mother. It had been so long since he'd last seen her. In his world, mothers didn't visit their sons in jail. So, she wrote him letters, but all would be censored, by his father. No real sharing, just she loved him, missed him, was praying for him. In his mind's eye he could see her warm smile.

He laughed to himself, *"Oh yeah, and can I ever see her strong determination! She sure is pure Sicilian."* His eyes moistened, *"but is she ever a real lady!"* From aristocratic blood he'd always been told.

Max drew a deep breath as his thoughts turned to his father. To his knowledge, his father wasn't Mafioso, but he sure knew plenty who were. Pop was a successful businessman, referred to by many as Don Carron. Not the Mafia Godfather, but definite Godfather, to many in their close knit Italian community. It was a sign of respect.

"Respect?" Max nearly choked on the word. He shook his head sadly. How he longed to earn his father's approval. But the harder he tried, the more it seemed to elude him. Maybe when he returned home things would be different? Perhaps his sacrifice for the family's sake would at last garner his father's favor. All he could do was hope. He knew his father would also hate the Honorable Judge Walters, but would bide his time waiting for an opportunity to repay.

Max's jaw tightened, "But, damn, this is not my father's life! It is mine. It is my battle, not his!" he snarled under his breath. Then, like a broken record his mind returned to that haunting question. *"Why the hell did he give me six years? With no prior arrests, or convictions, why did he do that to me?"*

This "why" burned a hole in his gut, but it would not be for long. He had already formulated the plan to get his answer. Eagerly he eyed the clock again, 6a.m. had arrived! Freedom awaited him.

"Amazing, when a guy's charged up emotionally, just how fast time goes," he mused. He heard the shift changing. For the last time, he would need to fit into the routine...get up, wash, shave, dress, then file into breakfast.

"Thank God! No Murph harassment."

He almost felt disappointed. Then, to his surprise, many of the inmates gave him knowing winks, even some of the guards wished him good luck. Emotionally it began to dawn on him, soon, very soon, this place, for him, would be history.

He growled to himself, *"Good riddance to a bad memory, a very bad memory!"* Sitting at breakfast, beside his cellmate, he whispered, "Next spring, Philip, I'll be here to pick you up. I won't forget. April 7th it's your turn!"

Philip acknowledged Max's promise with tears in his eyes, and mouthed the words "Thanks...do be careful, Max. Good luck!"

The two men had formed a special bond when Philip had entered prison. In fact it was Lobsinger, the guard, who'd seen to it that Philip had ended up as Max's cellmate.

Philip had committed a white collar crime. At five foot eight, his slender build, horned rim glasses and receding hairline had him marked for bullying, or worse.

One thing about "Lobi" (as the inmates had nicknamed the guard; behind his back, of course), was that he had a good sense of the internal dynamics of the prison. He really tried to be fair with everyone. Max had found favor in Lobsinger's eyes. Philip would need a protector to survive and Max would make a good one. Fortunately the two men had connected quickly, and through his relationship with Max, Philip had managed to gain the respect of the other inmates.

"Yeah," Max thought, *"most of the guards honestly work to ensure that incarceration alone, plus the stigma of a record is the only punishment. Lobi is just such a correctional officer. I respect him for that, and somehow, I feel the respect has been reciprocated."*

Max's thoughts were interrupted by a hand on his shoulder. Looking up, he was surprised to discover the hand belonged to Lobsinger.

"Well, Max, *today* is your day!" the guard smiled warmly, "I suspect you've counted off each day for six years, to arrive at this one. So, when you finish breakfast, take a shower, and you'll find your new civilian clothes on your bunk. After you're dressed, I'll come to your cell to escort you to the warden's office. There you'll be debriefed and receive the official release documents."

"If you don't mind, I'd like to go to Mass first."

Lobsinger laughed, "Max, I have to tell you that we've got a pool going about when you'll enter Seminary. You never miss a Mass. Okay, go to Mass, keep your routine and then prepare for release."

Max pondered the guard's remark, walking to the Chapel, *"Was his desire a sign, even a call, to the priesthood?"* After all, he experienced such a peace at Mass, whether it was conducted in English or Latin. He always had, even as a boy.

"But priests, Max, "Ol' Boy," don't carry guns, and you know your one love, one enjoyment is your gun!"

In his mind, he could even see the gun, heavy but well balanced, a perfect fit for his hand. The initials J.D. were etched on the butt, reflecting the gun's previous owner. Even more than holding it, he loved shooting it. He sighed softly.

"Not only can I see you, J.D., I can feel you...I love the thrill of rapidly shooting a target, and hitting the mark every time! Damn, six years without that joy! Walters, you and I need to talk. We WILL talk! Whoa! I almost forgot, that is why I am going to Mass."

During his incarceration, Max had taken the time to read and reread the Bible. He had discussions with the Chaplain and the Priest, and both agreed. The Bible did say that *"each man should take all of his thoughts captive, and give them to Christ."* It also said that, *"if in all our ways we acknowledge God, that he will direct our path."*

"Well," Max almost spoke out-loud before catching himself, *"I need all the help I can get to pull off my plan, so here I am."*

He entered the Chapel, genuflected, crossed himself, and sat down in the pew. It was a familiar routine for Max, but actually talking to God, as if God was in the room, wasn't! For the first time in his life, he felt self-conscious as he knelt before the altar.

Everyone else might think he was nervous about his pending release from prison. In fact, given Max's Sicilian ancestry, prison scuttlebutt suggested his lengthy jail term resulted from a falling out with somebody high in the Italian community. Some even speculated that his father was the person in question. That being the case, people could surmise his chapel time was motivated by real fear.

Whatever anyone else thought, had they been able to enter his thoughts, they would have been shocked to hear this muscular, six foot one convict, earnestly praying with the sincerity of an altar boy.

"Jesus Christ, I'm asking you to help my quest to meet this Walters guy. You promised if I'd ask that you would direct my steps, and Big Guy, I really need some help on this one!"

He paused briefly, unsure what should come next, then he recalled his school boy teaching and concluded "In the name of the Father, Son, and Holy Ghost" crossing himself as he breathed an audible "Amen." There it was done. Now, he could leave!

He grimaced as he dressed in the prison-supplied clothes. These were a far cry from the tailored, designer suits to which he was accustomed. He smiled for soon that too would be rectified.

The next hoop to jump through was the formal visit to the Administration Office to pick up his personal belongings. These included his wallet, ID, Driver's License, all renewed, thanks to Pop, and of course, the traditional money for the one-way bus ticket home. No one would be here to pick him up. Everyone would remain at home, waiting to greet him.

To Max's surprise, Warden Blackmore met him at the office entrance. The man appeared as austere as his surroundings, impeccably dressed in a dark blue suit with a baby blue silk tie that accentuated his steel blue eyes. It seemed, to Max, that those eyes bore right into his very soul. Blackmore carried himself with an air of authority. His very demeanor said, *"Don't mess with me!"*

Still Max had considered the warden, an O.K. guy, albeit a no nonsense guy! From Max's perspective the warden had always treated him fairly.

Blackmore extended his hand to Max. "Mr. Carron, may I see you for a few moments in my office?"

He then lead Max into a spacious office, whose rich mahogany furniture, and plush carpet sharply contrasted with the bleak prison furnishings, Max had experienced.

However, it wasn't the warden's office that grabbed Max's attention, it was his words.

"Mr. Carron! It had been six very-long years since he'd ever been addressed as Mr." As Max figured it, *"Mr. Carron, implied respect...And boy, did that feel good!"*

He had expected the usual 'school boy' lecture, "hope you've learned your lesson, keep your nose clean." However, Blackmore's next words caught him off guard.

"Max, I wanted to thank you for pushing me to allow you to take post-graduate courses. Your diligence to your studies served both you and the penal system well.'

"Professor Brown's support and praise of your work has encouraged us to begin an experiment, in which advanced courses will be offered to other select inmates. So Max, congratulations for your pioneer work."

Max's eyebrow raised, as he thought, *"congratulations? Thank you? In all my 34 years, those are words that I rarely heard. Pop always had conveyed that I could do better. Somehow, it wasn't just Pop, but even in our Italian community, it seemed their expectation was that I was capable of more."* He grunted inwardly, *"And, as for the non–Italian community, their attitude seemed to be that I was never capable of any good!"*

He had to admit 'congratulations, thank you,' felt good. Inside he was experiencing a warm glow just like Mama's words of praise had always sparked within him. But these words had come from a man, a man in authority!

"So, here are your Harvard transcripts, Max" Blackmore continued, "Even if you can't go to the bar, they should help you find meaningful employment."

After that Max received the traditional pep talk the 'seasoned' inmates had told him about, and the final handshake.

For the first time in over six years, Max felt good about himself. So engrossed in his thoughts, he almost collided with Lobsinger as he stepped out of the Administration Office. The guard had rushed to the office, Philip in tow, with the hope of meeting Max before he left.

"Max," Lobsinger grinned, "Philip wanted to say Good-bye". With that he stepped aside to allow the two men the rare opportunity to privately share their farewells.

"I will be here for you, Philip, when you're released. I promise!" Max whispered in his cellmate's ear, as he gave the man a hug.

Philip stifled his tears, "Thanks, Max, for all you did to keep me safe. Not to mention, all of the ways you helped me gain acceptance with the others. I won't forget that, ever! Now, God bless, and good luck, Buddy!"

There it was again...*'Thanks?'* He was being thanked. Once again, he felt warm inside. Then it was over, he was being escorted to the prison entrance. At last, he was on his way to freedom!

As he heard the front gate clang shut behind him, Max turned and glanced back at the prison with its formidable grey walls and barbed, curled wire on top. He shuddered.

"It looked like a tomb when I got here. It was a tomb when I entered. It still is a tomb!" His jaw tightened, "With all of the hopelessness, the despair, the brokenness, and yes, the perverseness in there...did I die in prison? Is there any part of me that still lives?"

He gazed upwards. It was then that he noticed the blue skies and the sunlight. He loved feeling the warmth of the sun's rays upon his face. It was wonderful! Looking across the street he could easily see the park. Squirrels scurried through the grass, which was just starting to green. Spring crocuses had already popped out of the ground, dotting the bland landscape, here and there, with bursts of vibrant color. Fresh buds speckled the tree branches everywhere, once again offering the promise that new life was poised to break forth.

A grin stole across his face, flinging his arms high, he shouted to the empty street, "I did survive! Max is back in town!"

Max could have called a cab to get to the bus station. However, he had predetermined the approximate time needed to walk to the bus depot. He knew he had ample time to get there. So, even before he left the prison, he had decided that he would walk, if the weather was good. It had rained the night before and the spring rains were washing away the grit of winter. There was a freshness in the air. Songbirds were returning. He started to identify the various chirps and twitters. Chickadees, sparrows, robins and cardinals blended into a spring symphony that seemed to mirror the song in his own heart.

"Yeah, everything is just like me. As I get away from here, the grit will wash from my soul, allowing me to sing once more! "

Suddenly, a car raced by Max, as if it had deliberately targeted the large, mud puddle near him, at the side of the road. The timing was perfect. Max was doused with a deluge of dirty water. Pent up anger surged within him, his dark brown eyes flashed menacingly at the car. It screeched to a halt about twenty feet away from him, and the window rolled down.

"Suit looks good on you, Carron, especially with the mud. You remind me of a drowned sewer rat."

The retort was followed with raucous laughter from within the vehicle.

"Murph!" Max recognized the voice immediately. He had anticipated his challenge to come inside the prison, but not on the outside.

The car doors slowly swung open. Out stepped Murph and two of his henchmen. Max froze, every nerve in his body was on red alert. The trio of men strode toward him, fists clenched, sinister smirks on their faces.

Chapter Two

As the sleek black limousine drew up under the canopy of "Chez Marie", the smartly dressed doorman stepped forward, stretched forth his white gloved hand and opened the passenger door.

His effort was rewarded not only with a benevolent tip but also by a gracious smile from the stunning young woman who emerged from the vehicle.

"Henri, Comment allez vous?"

Before the man could respond, his benefactor broke into laughter. "Sorry, Henry, just had to practice my French! Simply asking how are you doing?"

The doorman broke into a toothy grin, his white teeth a sharp contrast to his black face. "Had me worried for a moment, Ms. McDonald, some customers actually expect everything to be authentically French. 'Fraid that lets me out, lived all my life in Washington."

"Seriously though, Henry, I do want to know how you are doing? Did your son get that football scholarship at Penn? He did! Wonderful... you won't need my tip then." She grinned impishly at the man, "Don't worry, Henry, I was just kidding, but I am really glad at your son's good fortune. Please extend my congratulations to him and your wife."

Turning to the limo, she poked her head back into the car and with the authority of a five star general directed, "Alice, please be back at exactly 1:30 p.m. I have to be at the State department by 2:00."

Even before the limousine door closed, M.K. McDonald had made her entrance into Washington's popular French restaurant. All heads turned, especially those of the men.

Dressed in a tailored pin stripped pant suit, with matching leather pumps, she moved with the grace of a model. The austerity of her outfit was softened by the gently flowing lines of her chiffon blouse. Its pastel green color perfectly accentuated the wearer's striking red hair and sparkling green eyes.

With her rosy cheeks and ivory complexion, the woman was radiantly beautiful, elegantly feminine, no denying it. Yet she carried herself, as many might imagine, Joan of Arc would have done. Her poise and demeanor clearly reflecting the fact that she was the competent and successful CEO of a large global corporation. As she approached, the maître d beamed in recognition.

"Mam'selle McDonald, how good it is to see you again. I have your table for four at the window."

He gestured toward the young lady already seated.

"Mam'selle Walters is already here."

The cute effervescent teenager jumped up in greeting the moment she was spotted.

"Kaye, I'm so glad you could come, and do I ever need to talk to you before Daddy gets here!"

Kaye looked lovingly at the pert blonde before her. Tiffany, at five foot three, clearly had inherited her mother's height. Though not quite as petite as Marnie Walters, Tiff was, none the less, physically fit. Round in the face, her most striking feature was her big blue eyes, which right now were being used to woo Kaye to her cause.

"Ahha, so this is a conspiracy meal you've drawn me into Tiffany?"

The young woman threw her head back and giggled, her pony tail bobbing up and down.

"Well, sort of... I figured you'd help me win my case... And as you know, being the daughter of a Supreme Court

Justice is not very easy!" She feigned a pout.

Kaye leaned forward in mock horror and whispered, "Surely, Ms. Walters, you can't be asking me to join a plot against a judge of our country's highest court?"

Tiffany sat ramrod straight in her chair, folded her arms across her chest and without cracking a smile responded.

"I'm afraid, Ms. McDonald, that is indeed what I am requesting. You know, better than anyone, how protective Daddy is of me."

Kaye laughed, "Well, I know how protective you think he is. You and I both know how deeply he cares for you."

Tiffany frowned, "Yes, I know that, Kaye! But I'm finished with my freshman year at college and I've just discovered the most, absolutely, exciting summer work opportunity. In fact, participating in it will give me a major course credit!"

Kaye eyed Tiffany skeptically, " Really? Please explain."

"It's an archeological dig in Mexico, and my Professor said that it's open to ten students.'

"They prefer seniors, but for exceptional students they will entertain, as candidates, even those entering their sophomore year." Tiffany leaned across the table, "Kaye, I am fascinated by archeology. In that subject, I am ranked at the top of my class."

Kaye furrowed her brow. "Sounds like an excellent academic opportunity, Tiffany. Why do you think your father would oppose your participation?"

"It's a full sixteen weeks, Kaye. That means I won't get home for the summer, which means there will be no time with Mummy or Daddy! With Crissy off working on her Masters in California..." Tiffany sat back and sighed, "Let's face it, I'm the last chick to leave the nest. In my Psych class they taught about the various stages of life." By now her big blue eyes were beginning to moisten, "Kaye, we learned it can be really hard for parents when their kids leave...I don't want to cause my parents grief...But, Kaye, I really do want to go on this dig!"

Kaye feigned a cough and put her hand over her mouth. It was all she could do not to laugh. She tried to act if she was pondering her reply. Finally, she cleared her throat.

"Tiff," she began, "I know spending time with you is very important to your parents. You are correct your parents do miss your sister, Crissy...But I also know they are proud of both their daughters' accomplishments...And... and they do expect you to become independent adults."

Kaye folded her hands on the table, smiled, her own eyes now moist. "Know what else, Tiff?"

The young co-ed shook her head.

"You lucked out in the gene pool. You inherited your mother's compassionate heart and your father's academic drive. So... Ms. Tiffany Walters, I am honored that you have asked me to support your proposal to your father. I will listen as you plead your case to him, and if I can run interference for you, I will."

At that, she raised her hand, "I, Kaye McDonald, solemnly do pledge to support Ms. Tiffany Walters' archeological dig pitch to her father."

Both broke out in laughter, "Look, Tiffany. Here comes your adversary now. And it looks like he's brought some back-up support with him. Isn't that Special Agent Epstein with him?"

Tiffany's eyes widened, "Kaye, how could he know?"

Kaye's lilting laughter burst forth...some called it music from the Emerald Isle. It was one of her most endearing traits.

"Tiffany, I'm sure Epi is here just for the free meal. Have no fear! Be strong and courageous my fearless warrior as you set out to battle your father."

Jack Walters was approaching fifty. A star quarterback in his younger days he had managed to maintain his athletic physique. At six foot two, broad shouldered and square jawed, Jack cut an imposing figure. But it wasn't simply his physical features that impressed others. The man exuded confidence. Born and raised in Idaho, Walters had the work ethic of a western farm boy...which meant he worked long and hard. He had graduated cum laude, first in his class, at Harvard and his mind, like fine wine, had only improved with age.

Slightly balding, Walters wore his hair close cropped and sported a neatly trimmed moustache. He was the type of guy that people rose in his presence, both in, and outside the court room.

In sharp contrast to Walters was his dinner partner, Special Agent Bernard Epstein. Epi, as he was known by most everybody, bore a striking physical resemblance to the frumpy T.V. Detective character, Colombo. And like Colombo, the man was constantly underestimated, but not by those in law enforcement... and definitely not by Jack Walters.

Jack's blue eyes twinkled as he drew near the two women. "It's obvious the two of you are enjoying each others' company. I hope your laughter was not directed at us?" he said as he gave Kaye a peck on the cheek.

"Oh, Jack, you are just so perceptive!" Kaye retorted, laughing.

The last thing Tiffany wanted was to have this luncheon deteriorate into a mere social outing. She had an agenda, which she was determined to ensure got addressed. She bounded over to her father warmly embracing him. "Daddy, thank you so much for coming!"

Tweaking his daughter's nose, Jack jested, 'Tiffany, a judge must always attend court, and when you summon Kaye to assist your case, I know it has to be important."

"Ah! Yes, Your Honor," Kaye mocked in an Irish brogue "I can see how serious you take this summons ensuring you are accompanied by FBI Agent Epstein as your witness. Top- o'-the-mornin' to ye, Epi," she laughed, as she extended her hand to the younger man.

Epi threw up his hands and returned the banter. "I confess. I was enticed to accompany His Honor when he invited me to have lunch with his self and two charmin' ladies."

"Epi," Kaye replied, eyeing him seriously, "you haven't got a drop of Irish blood in ye. You're incapable of dishing out blarney. The only reason that you and Jack came is because you knew "Chez Marie's" food is excellent, plus I'd be picking up the tab."

"There you go, Epi" Jack intoned. "Just like I told you. Look how quickly she cuts to the chase. Indeed, it was a tremendous loss that law-enforcement and the judicial system took when Ms. M.K. McDonald rejected us in favor of a business career."

Almost sadly, Kaye smiled and sighed, "Sometimes, who or what we are is not our choice, often life just chooses for us. The only choice left for us to decide is whether to make the best or worst of our circumstances."

She paused, her eyes closed momentarily and when they reopened those green eyes neither sparkled nor twinkled but bore a striking resemblance to cold hard jade. Raising her right hand she said resolutely, "And I, dear lady and gentlemen, have chosen to make the best of what life gives, so help me God! And, I assure you that is a prayer, not a courtroom tag on to placate you two gentlemen."

The waiter now stood before them, temporarily suspending their conversation. With Kaye and Jack interpreting the French menu for Epi, the four ordered their lunch.

"So" Jack began "what is the reason that my freshman daughter orchestrated this luncheon?

Tiffany quickly commenced to lay out the offer to be part of the University's summer archeological Aztec dig in Mexico. She was careful to naturally stress all the pros, and discreetly minimize the cons.

Judge Walters wrinkled his brow and peered over his horned rimmed glasses at his daughter with that analytical gaze that attorneys and their clients dreaded.

"Crumb! The courts only get him for a few days or weeks." Tiffany groused to herself. *"I have to live with him!*

Thank God for Kaye! Without her, I'm sure my case would be hopeless."

In fact, before Jack could reply Kaye had jumped into the fray. "Epi, it is good you came to lunch. You can tell us, what are the safety issues, in the area of Mexico where this dig takes place, not only for Americans, but for someone with Tiff's background?"

"I can inquire for you, but off the top of my head, right now I think it is a very secure area. It might be wise though, Tiffany, if you did go with an altered identity. I'm certain that could be arranged with the University and your professor."

At this turn, in conversational direction, Tiffany's jaw dropped. She stared at her father, whose focus had instantly shifted from her to Epi.

"Would the Bureau take steps to ensure my daughter's safety?" Jack queried.

"Of course!" Epi said "It's to our advantage to be as proactive as we can. It helps to ensure that no high-profile kidnapping or murder of an American citizen takes place anywhere."

Tiffany looked surprised at the change in concerns being expressed. She had expected parental rejection purely because his little girl was flapping her wings. But, Hey! The conversation was now speaking of adventure. Something the high-spirited, Walters girl just loved.

Tiffany tried to frame her request in the most adult way she could. Inside, she was bouncing up and down, wanting to scream, *"Wow! Oh Yeah! What an experience!"*

To her credit she succeeded, as she asked simply, "So, Daddy, can I put in my resume to the archeological department?" And it produced the desired response.

"Yes," her father said slowly, "provided both the FBI and CIA agree. Epi, can you start the ball rolling?"

Epi did agree, and Kaye laughed, "Congratulations, Tiffany! You've now stepped on the bottom rung of adulthood. You engineered this whole proposal with absolutely no need of my rather extensive, international and Bureau expertise."

Tiffany's face lit up like fireworks on the fourth of July. Her big, blue eyes sparkled with enthusiasm as she described the archeological dig site. It was obvious, Judge Walters' daughter would be a good addition to the team, and a very good student of ancient Aztec culture. All three adults were duly impressed by her knowledge. It was great dinner conversation and refreshingly not related to the work-a-day cares of all three.

Abruptly Tiff stopped, furrowed her brow and looked at Kaye.

"Lord," Kaye thought *"you look exactly like your Dad!"*

"Kaye, I never thought to ask you...Those horrid phone calls you got last year, have you ever received any more?"

All eyes were now on Kaye, who seemed much more subdued. She closed her eyes. Did Jack detect a slight grimace?

Kaye sighed, trying to smile. "Nope, Detective Nancy Drew, no new contacts...Those other ones were quite enough, Thank you very much!

"Kaye," Epi interjected "Please, let us know if they should resume. You need to know it's not uncommon for psychopathic perps to play this game. They initiate contact with their intended victim. The victim notifies police. Wire taps are set up. Nothing comes from it. Then, several months, usually a half-year later, the perp resumes the calls. However, now the victim is too intimidated to call the police, for fear of being embarrassed again. It messes with people's minds and emotions."

Kaye gave a hollow laugh, then responded "You can say that again, but it's not only mental and emotional games regarding the calls. It's the insinuations that ensue from staff, and supposed friends. These are mostly unspoken thoughts, though they are occasionally said out loud. I was absolutely stunned when someone – who shall remain nameless – suggested to me that it probably was my subconscious desire to have a lover. They volunteered to set me up, and even suggested I was "sex starved". All I could think to say was "Thanks but No Thanks!" I don't think that I personally understood the words, "humiliation" or "mortification" until that moment."

Jack registered shock at her revelation. Mouth agape, eyes filled with compassion, he exclaimed, "Kaye, I had no idea you were subject to such trash!"

"Well, Your Honor, welcome to the world of cut-throat big business. Although I do suspect that you may put up with as much back stabbing in the "halls of justice" as we do in our corporate world."

Epi looked at her intently. "Kaye, I know that was a horrid experience, but there is the possibility that those phone calls were more than a malicious malcontent. Psychos are real in my world. They toy with a victim, much like a cat does with a mouse. They play these games to put everyone off-guard."

He continued, "Their primary strategy is to make their prey afraid to be humiliated again. This is combined with their ability to influence law enforcement officers to believe that the entire scenario is only the victim trying to get attention. When all their plan is successfully in place, they will strike suddenly."

Epi shook his head, " Kaye, everyone looses, especially the victim. But, believe me, it leaves behind many traumatized friends and lawmakers. They are the ones who have to deal with the fact that they failed to protect. So, Kaye, promise us that you will trust us. Don't be afraid to notify us, even if it happens three or four more times. Guys like this need to be stopped!"

"Thanks, Epi, for your words of encouragement." Kaye smiled, wryly.

"Kaye," it was now Jack's turn to plead, "Epi is speaking wisdom. You know Dave and I..."

"Me too!" chimed in Tiffany.

"Yes," Jack continued, "all of us believed you. Please, promise us that you will confide in us, should these calls start again."

Kaye looked at them all...her eyes meeting theirs. She could feel their concern for her. She didn't doubt either the sincerity or wisdom behind Epi's words. They were her friends and yes, she did trust them. But none understood that it was not them she needed to guard against. As CEO of Kayleen Enterprises, investors needed full confidence that the captain of their financial boat was psychologically sound. Her role was to ensure the confidence of those investors was not undermined!

She crafted her words carefully and couched them in Irish wit. "I do believe your love, and I thank ye for it. That's precisely why I'm picking up the luncheon tab. I know the Bureau, the Justice Department and certainly freshman students are not as financially well-heeled as big business."

Playfully, she continued, "I promise to notify you immediately, if the calls return. Should I fail to do so, I shall, most certainly, be devoured by the Leprechauns!"

Her cheerful demeanor paid off. The others began to laugh and she could see they were relaxing. She had won over her audience, as only she could. She shook hands with Epi, then planted a kiss on Jack's forehead. Immediately she warned him to wipe off the lipstick, before His Honor returned to the courtroom. Turning to Tiffany, she gave her a hug and a firm admonishment to *"Go get 'em Tiger, and enjoy Mexico,"* then off she swished. No one else saw her eyes roll heavenward, or heard the prayer of her heart – *"Precious Jesus, only you know I promised to confide in them with all my toes and fingers crossed."*

The others may have been at ease, but M.K. McDonald's own heart had been stabbed with fear. She knew those calls had resumed once more!

Chapter Three

"Thought you might like a lift to the bus, Max? Course now that you're all wet and dirty I couldn't have you sit on the seat" Murph mocked.

Max felt the hair on the back of his neck standing on end just like his Pop's old Rottweiler. Rapidly he tried to assess his options. No way did he want to get in their car.

"Could he outrun them? Maybe? Could he take them? Yes, but at what cost?" Max could see the headlines, *"Released inmate takes it out on former prison guard, fortunately two other guards just happened along to save the day."* The only other option was to let them beat the snot out of him.

The sneer on Murph's face told Max this legal bully had also calculated all the options. However, all four men were so intent that none noticed the blue sedan that had quietly pulled up behind them.

"Too bad, pretty boy, that the prison scrap you were in broke your nose." Murph drew back his right fist ready to smash Max in the face.

"Max, so glad I saw you! Hi Murph, fellows, you guys must have wanted to catch Max to say good-bye too?"

Max breathed a sigh of relief, quietly adding under that breath, "Thank you Mary, Mother of Jesus." He turned and with a smile replied, "Mr. Lobsinger, sorry I didn't get a chance to say good-bye before I left."

Lobsinger extended his large hand in a warm grip that Max readily accepted. "Say, Max, I'm going right by the bus station, would you like a lift?" Looking apologetically to Murph and the other guards, he continued, "I guess you fellows had the same thing in mind, but hey, there are three of you. There's more room in my car."

Murph just scowled "Fine, Bob, you take him. Farewell, Max, better not return!" and he gave a hollow laugh as he retreated to his car, accompanied by his two lackeys.

As Max got into Lobsinger's car he stole a quizzical glance at his benefactor.

"Yes, Max, we were suspicious Murph would try to take it out on you. Warden Blackmore suggested I follow."

"But, if you know they're rotten apples, why aren't they axed?"

"We're working on it, Max. Everything takes time. We are unionized, and rightly so, but it means everything must be documented. Sorting out the apples takes time. There are "bad ass" guards who harass inmates and there are inmates looking to axe good guards."

"Meanwhile guys like me get caught in the cross fire." Max stared glumly at his wet, dirty suit. "Their car doused me pretty good. I'm afraid your seat will get wet. I feel like a kid that's wet his pants!"

"No worry, Max." Lobsinger chuckled. "I can assure you my family has ensured this car is well endowed with stain! However, if you want to do your part to nab these bullies, give me a signed written report of their threats, and I will ensure it is used in the investigative process."

"Mr. Lobsinger"...

"Max, you can call me Bob. We are on equal footing now."

"Okay, Bob, what happens if I do tell my side of the story, and give you a signed statement? What does that mean for me? I don't want to stay here in this place any longer. I want to be on that 1 p.m. bus."

"Just tell me what happened. Write it down, sign it, and I'll take it to Warden Blackmore. It will be awhile before we build a case of sufficient magnitude to warrant dismissal. Only then, you might be called. In all probability, you could swear out an affidavit in your own city with the D.A.'s office there."

"One more question...If I give you this written complaint, what assurance is there that those creeps won't take it out on any of the prisoners who associated with me?"

"You mean like your cellmate, Philip?"

"Yeah, not just Phil, but definitely him included," Max replied.

"Max, I can assure you, that the warden's office will closely monitor the situation. They will be watching for anything that could be construed as third-party reprisal."

Max eyed Lobsinger, and said, "In that case, I'll be glad to document what just happened to me." So, he detailed the deliberate soaking and subsequent threats of violence.

Max readied himself to get out of the car and enter the station. Suddenly, Lobsinger turned to him and said, "Max! Look me in the eye."

As Max returned the gaze, Lobsinger continued, "I have three questions, Max. First, you were sent up for drug trafficking. Did you do it?"

"No!" Max said quietly, "I didn't."

"Second question then... "Did your father know you didn't do it?"

Max drew a deep breath, and quickly replied, "Yeah, he knew."

"Okay, third question then... Are you in any trouble with your family when you go home? You know what I mean? Worse trouble than what Murph, and company, were going to give you?"

Max's jaw dropped. He looked at Lobsinger in total disbelief. His brow wrinkled, "What?"... Then he began to laugh. "No! None at all! Absolutely none!"

Nodding his head in response to Max's reply, Lobsinger leaned towards him. The guard stared intently at him, in what Max imagined was almost a fatherly gaze. Then he reached out, put his hand on Max's shoulder and gently said, " Good, Max! Then there's no pressure on you to do anything you shouldn't. You've got tremendous potential. Don't blow it! Good luck and may I never see you again."

Lobsinger extended his hand and shook Max's firmly. As the car door closed, the guard waved a final good-bye and drove away.

That warm feeling inside returned to Max. He couldn't explain it. In fact, it puzzled him.

This man had been paid to guard him, yet it seemed to Max that this guard cared for him like a friend would.

"How could people in such antagonistic roles be friends?" Max pondered as he purchased his one way ticket to Cleveland.

From Cleveland it was assumed that he'd transfer to Chicago. The Cleveland bus was only half-full so he had a seat all to himself, privacy at last! As the bus rumbled down the Interstate, Max savored his new freedom. A freedom to do what he wanted, when he wanted! He felt like a little kid with a new toy, exploring its potential. He got off the bus.

No more bus rides! *"Thank you!"*

He exchanged the Chicago transfer for cash and used some of the money to hail a cab. The Cleveland Hilton was his destination. Cleveland might not be the world's biggest tourist center but to Max, every scene was exhilarating, even the guy sweeping the sidewalk. All spoke of unrestricted movement, a mobility, that for six years, he'd been denied. He got a brief glimpse of Lake Erie. Unexpectedly memories of Lake Michigan...Chicago cascaded through his mind. He bit his lip and willed his longing for home to vanish. He could not, would not let his feelings circumvent his plan!

He entered the ornate hotel lobby and walked up to the registration desk, totally unashamed of his disheveled looking suit. To the quizzical look of the desk clerk, he simply smiled and said, "Tangled with an automobile generated, mud puddle splash. I believe you have a reservation for Mr. Massimiliano Carron?"

"Yes, Sir, it's prepaid and is for two nights. You are in suite 834 which is a non-smoking room."

As she handed him the key, Max noticed she'd checked his left hand ring finger before offering an alluring smile. He politely returned her gaze and left.

He grumbled to himself, "Girls are not on my agenda and never were!" He rolled his eyes, "How could they be? With a Sicilian father like mine, who expected me to shepherd my younger sister, I had a full-time job! At least I did until six years ago."

Max's countenance softened, as he thought of Sophia. More specifically, he focused on all that his prison term had bought her.

Turning the key to his room, he chuckled, "Oh Yeah! I am free, not only from prison, but also from babysitting my vivacious little sister." Turning on the light, he drank in the opulence of his accommodation. "Sure beats a cramped prison cell, old boy!"

He explored the spacious bathroom and then spied the spa, complete with mirrored walls.

"Bill and Lou, sure knew what their boss needs" he mused. He went to the bar fridge but came away disappointed with the beer, wine, liquor. They were all there, but not what he craved, which was a vintage bottle of his favorite Sicilian wine. He closed the fridge.

"So, Maxie, you'll just have to be satisfied with the spa!"

He whipped off his clothes, leaving them where they fell and gave a little snort.

"No longer do I have someone hovering over me demanding I keep my clothes neat, folded and in the place they demand!" He gave a punch with his fist, "Yes, freedom!"

He filled the whirlpool with water as hot as he could stand. Then he decided to reconsider the wine. No Sicilian, not even Italian wine! Californian would have to do.

Sitting in the spa, the water gently massaged his body. He'd had an emotionally charged day, now sipping the wine, he sensed his tension slowly ebbing away.

"Six years! Lord, that demanded great self-discipline on

my part."

Max threw his head back and groaned. "In the pen, a guy would be mincemeat if he ever showed his emotions or exposed his true thoughts. As for expressing your wants," he pursed his lips, "not happening! Sheesh, until now, I never realized how much I had to practice self-control. That was work, big time! No wonder I feel exhausted."

For the first time he noted the ceiling to spa mirrors that surrounded the tub on two sides. He stood to admire his physique, and began to grin, "Not bad, old boy, not bad. Abs are looking great." He flexed his biceps and nodded his approval. "Legs look good, too, Maxie. So, self-discipline wasn't all bad, at least in the prison gym." He let out a low whistle. "Using control there has paid big dividends."

Content, he sat back down in the spa, poured another glass of wine, raised the glass and to his mirror image shouted "Salute!"

In the midst of his revelry, he suddenly thought of his Aunt Louisa, and was seized with panic.

"Cripes! She's sure to be at it even now! Making a list, checking it twice…That woman has Santa Claus beat by a mile and a half! She never could stand single, Italian men… 'They otta be coupled with a nica young, Italian girl' she'd say. Her idea of 'nica', compared with a guy's, was usually further apart than L.A. is from New York."

He smiled to himself "For 28 years, I managed to avoid her marital net. I was always off, shadowing Sophia, when Aunt Louisa orchestrated her infamous 'get-together' dinners. And you, Your Honor," Max looked into the mirror and raised his wine glass as a salute, "made avoidance of Aunt Louisa feasible for another six years! So…" he sighed, "I get to postpone the inevitable reunion with Aunt Louisa, for a few more weeks. In the meantime, Max, better start thinking of new avoidance strategies!"

A flare of resentment shot through him. "It's not like I hate girls. I don't. I enjoy female company. I just don't get this male/ female attraction hula-ballou." He snorted, then pondered, "Nonetheless, somehow in my ethnic background if a guy wasn't chasing skirts, everyone would think the boy was not all right...Horrors! Even worse! Maybe he could be gay!" Those thoughts actually began to pique him a little.

"Jesus Christ! Yes, Jesus, I'm not swearing here." He clarified his position, to whom, he wasn't entirely sure. He paused a moment, eventually deciding the listener must be his mirrored reflection.

So, he continued, "Yes, I am praying! Jesus, as I read the Bible, you never chased after females or males. Yet, both were attracted to you. Yes, and people of all ages and different races too." He frowned, then questioned, "Why does everybody have to make such an issue about a single guy?'

"To be honest, it seems that I feel the same way about sex as Scrooge did about Christmas." Max laughed out loud. "That's right ... Bah Humbug!"

A quiet thought popped into his mind, *"But Scrooge changed!"* That sudden change of perspective caught him off guard.

"Yeah, well I won't!" He replied emphatically.

Startled, he looked at himself in the mirror. "Sheesh! Now I'm talking to myself. Maybe prison had more effect on me than I imagined?"

At that point, another thought darted into his head, and he continued his conversation with the mirror. "Right! If a guy is born into an Italian community, the only one allowed to be neutral about sex," He lifted his hand and wagged a finger at the mirror. "No, expected to be neutral...is a priest!"

A sly smile crossed his face, "Hmm... Maybe I could pretend to be a priest, and escape the sex and marriage thing altogether!"

A deep belly laugh erupted, so once more he raised the glass this time to himself, "Salute!"

That's when he noticed how wrinkled his flesh was

becoming. He decided now was the time to vacate the spa. He climbed out, dried himself off, flopped on the bed, and grabbed the remote.

"Hey, bonus time! It's the Stanley Cup hockey playoffs, and the Hawks are in!" Immediately, he was lost in the game.

Next morning, he rose early. Letting his fingers do the walking in the "Yellow Pages", he discovered what sounded like a good, Italian men's clothing store. He set out in search of new 'digs.'

He wasn't boasting. The truth was that he had a physique tailors loved. Clothes fit with only minor alterations, all of which could be done on the spot. He selected two suits, one a black pin stripe, the other a dark navy, and a camel sports jacket with black slacks. He rounded out his wardrobe with several complementary shirts, matching ties, a couple of mock turtlenecks and of course socks and underwear. Italian, black leather loafers completed his shopping spree.

He had indicated that he wanted to wear some of his purchases and was brusquely denied. *"Until, of course you have paid!"* was the response of the salesperson.

In fact, that individual had been very inattentive to Max during the entire selection period. Max clearly understood the clerk's aversion, as he grumbled to himself, *"Lucky for you, Bud, I can recognize quality, Italian clothes and I'm in need of a complete wardrobe. However, if I wasn't in a hurry and better knew this town, you'd never get my business."*

He strode to the till and under the clerk's skeptical eye swiped his credit card. It was all he could do not to laugh when the purchase approval came through. That approval ushered in an immediate attitude adjustment in the clerk. "Which outfit did he wish to wear? By all means use this change room. The adjustments will be but a moment."

He thought, "Too late guy, your judgment of me was just too obvious. You did not earn my favor!"

He chose the camel jacket, black slacks with a burgundy mock turtleneck. A pair of black, leather loafers completed his 'new look'. He smiled as he perused himself in the mirror *"...Plus, silk underwear feels great,"* he mused.

Exiting the change room, he grabbed his purchases and headed for the street. The sales clerk came running after him with the clothes the prison had issued.

"Give them to Goodwill," he instructed and quickly left. He was a brand new man... back where he had left off six years ago!

As Max entered the expansive hotel lobby, the desk clerk signaled he had a message for him. The clerk leaned across the reception desk and apprehensively whispered that two men had inquired of him. Since he had not responded to the page, they had indicated they would wait for him in the lounge. "Sir, those gentlemen were rather large, and very..." the clerk paused searching for the most discrete word to use.

Max raised his eyebrow and said softly, "Intimidating?" The clerk smiled weakly and nodded his head.

"It's okay, they're family," Max said reassuringly. He smiled pleasantly, thanked and tipped the clerk. He took his purchases to his room and then headed for the lounge.

His eyes filled with tears, when he saw them. He had to chuckle to himself though. *"No wonder they freaked out the desk clerk. Bill and Lou really do look like Hollywood stereotypic mobsters. But, both are like marshmallows. "*

They hadn't noticed him, too preoccupied, *"...probably with the racing form, unless they've had a major transformation in the past six years. Something I highly doubt!"*

He snuck up behind them, slowly and quietly. In the gruffest voice he could muster, he growled, "What are you two doing here loitering in this bar?"

It worked. Their short Sicilian fuse had been ignited. They leapt to their feet and turned, eyes flashing, fists clenched to confront their antagonist. Then they saw him and melted. They embraced Max enthusiastically, carrying on in Italian, tears flowing unashamedly.

The lounge was basically deserted except for staff. Had it not been, Max figured the three of them would have been evicted for causing a disturbance. Unless a person spoke Italian, one would not be blamed for thinking this reunion was that of father and uncle greeting a long lost son or nephew. Instead it really was staff greeting employer.

"But hey," Max thought "we are a family!"

Their animated conversation continued non-stop through the lobby, into the elevator, down the hall right into Max's room. Then it became even more emotional! The two older men were obviously elated to see him again.

Max smiled patiently as he listened to them, all the while thinking "Clearly you two are intent to bring me back into the lives you have lived for six years, as if my six years did not exist. But my six years did exist for me, and before I re-enter your world, I will get the answer I seek!"

Eventually a break in their conversation came and quietly Max asked "Did Scaly give you my letter with the things I wanted you to bring?"

Lou chortled and responded, "Yeah, everything including your pet - J.D., with all of his food and essentials.. Pretty clever, Boss! Pretty clever!"

Bill, for his part, spoke with concern registered in his voice. "We did bring everything you asked for, but don't you think it unwise to pack the rod so soon? I mean you will be watched and the cops would like nothing better than to nail you! Ex cons aren't supposed to have weapons of any sort?"

"Guys, thanks for the advice, but I really have missed J.D. Don't worry. I will be wise and careful too. You did bring the two cars, like I asked, right?... With one car registered in my name, plus the cash?"

"Yeah! Yeah! We got all that, but why couldn't we all three have ridden home together?" asked Lou, his facial expression revealing a little hurt at Max's choice. He poked his index finger at Max's chest, "Max, your Mama is real anxious and excited about seeing you." He paused and scowled, "Mr. C. is too, but he just don't show it. You know how he is?"

"Do I ever really know how he is?" Max thought. *"However, if he knew what's on my mind, guaranteed, it would indeed be most displeasing to him. That's why no one but me will know. I'm no longer his or anyone's puppet!"*

Max's jaw tightened, then quickly relaxed with his next thought. *"In fact, depending on the outcome of my plan, when I do come home, it could be as the prodigal!"*

His own musings were abruptly interrupted by Bill demanding, "Boss, why did you want an empty suitcase?"

That one was easy to respond to...Max took off his jacket, spun around arms extended, and laughed. "Guys, look...my body has changed a great deal over the past six years. In prison I could work out all that I wanted. With lots of time on my hands, that's exactly what I did. So, I know the clothes I had on six years ago won't fit."

The two older men smiled approvingly. Max had filled out. He had a physique that would definitely impress the dolls.

Bill laughed and added, "I'm glad little Rosa's married up. You'll have your way with the ladies!"

Max sighed, then exclaimed, "Good heavens! Now, even you guys want me to play Casanova!"

"What's wrong with that?" Lou responded grinning. "You've got six years to catch up and a great body to attract the gals!"

Ignoring the remark, Max continued, "So, the empty suitcase is for my new wardrobe that I bought to-day. The extra car and the cash are for me to go home a different route than the two of you."

"What da ya mean?" the two men chorused. "Your Mama and Pop expect you home with us. Everyone's waiting to welcome you. If we go home without you it will not bode well for us!"

31

Max smiled warmly, totally disarming their alarm. "Guys, when in the slammer a potential business opportunity arose for me. I promised that after I was discharged, that I would go explore that potential. So tomorrow, when we leave, you will go home via the Interstate to Chicago. I, on the other hand, will head south towards Tennessee."

"Where are you going?" queried Bill.

"That's for you to know when I get home. Tell Pop and Mama I expect to be home within three months. I love you all very much, but after six years, I need a little challenge. After all, my previous occupation is no longer viable, no need to shadow Sophia." Max laughed, "...And besides, I'm in need of a little R& R. I'll be sure to phone. So, let's go get some supper. I need you to tell me about everyone, especially little Rosa! When I left she was fourteen – she had promised to wait for me! Now you tell me she's hitched." He gave Bill a playful jab.

Max had scouted out what proved to be an excellent, Italian restaurant. He had Lou chauffer them, as in the past. It allowed him to now ask the questions, whose answers he wanted to know...rather than being asked to divulge that which he wished not to share.

"Was race track Harry still hustling the bets? Rocco's kid was killed in a gang fight? Really? It's no longer just 'family' squabbles but blacks and some asian punks too? You're kidding?"

During the meal, his conversational generalities turned personal. As Max began to pepper the men with questions, he uncovered some of their real concerns.

"How's my house? Not too much for Rosa and Anna to look after as well as handling your own sections? That's good! No! I don't want you to move your families out. Keeping it as a triplex is just fine with me...Unless, of course you want to move? You don't. I'm glad. Your wives figured that maybe a family man needs more space? Sheesh! Am I a family man? No!" At this point Max started to laugh.

"I don't care if your wives figure Aunt Louisa will be gunning for me. Over the years, I've learned pretty good avoidance tactics. I know I can't use chaperoning Sophia as an escape hatch any more, but trust me I've been exploring new strategies."

It was then that Max realized Lou and Bill were genuinely concerned that he would want them to move. He chose to deliberately slow the conversation.

These two old codgers, Max knew, had a lot more going for them than what many others gave them credit for. When he bought his parents' old house he had needed help to look after his property. He was well aware that when he had selected them as 'staff' many in the Italian Community...including his own father, had figured he'd kept two 'has-beens'.

"Not revealing much leadership ingenuity, on Max's part," was how his Pop had worded it.

Chuckling to himself, Max mused, *"That's exactly why I did pick them. Everyone else would leave them alone. No threat. Furthermore I knew they would be unwaveringly loyal to me."*

As a boy, he had learned he could trust their willingness to defend him. So here he sat again with his staff. He could tell they were getting increasingly tense about his decision not to go straight home. They could read him like a book!

It came as no surprise then, when Bill asked him outright "You're not planning to look up that frigging Judge are you?"

Coyly, Max responded, "Since when was Washington considered south of Cleveland?"

"He works in Washington but lives in Pennsylvania!" blurted Lou. Bill glared at Lou who quickly added "I think maybe? Maybe not?"

"You don't say." Max jokingly feigned interest. "Well, since when is PA considered due south of Cleveland?"

The two men stared at him, reminding him of the priest who'd grilled him on his catechism.

"So then, what is your business, and with whom?" they queried.

Looking very business-like, Max leaned forward and whispered "Sorry, not at liberty to divulge just yet."

"That's no good!" whined Lou. "You know your Pop will be furious with us if we can't give him specifics."

Max propped his elbows on the tabled, folded his hands in front of him and rested his chin on his hands, directly eyeing the two men.

"Remind him," he said firmly, "that I did my time... six very long years. I'm well in my thirties and it's time I run my own show!"

His face softened as he continued, "You can then tell him that I love both, he and Mama, dearly, ...that I miss them terribly, and that I will be in touch shortly. I'll be home before they know it!"

Max left no doubt that he had closed the door on all further communication with regard this topic.

When they checked out the next morning, Max gave both men a big bear hug.

"You follow me until the Interstate south exchange. You continue west to Chicago and I'll head south to Tennessee."

He grinned and sang, "You take the high road, and I'll take the low road, and you'll be in Chicago before me!"

Lou studied him with genuine concern, "Take care, Boss. We really love ya."

"I will," Max responded softly. "Tell that sister and brother-in-law of mine, that I can't wait to see the twins and little guy they hatched in my absence!"

With that Lou and Bill got in their vehicle and Max in his. The two tailed him onto the interstate. Though they traveled that way for several miles, it seemed to Max, only minutes before his exit appeared. He waved good-bye as Bill and Lou continued westward. Then, he accelerated into the exchange lane, and as he did so his countenance darkened.

"Yeah, good bye Lou, Bill, Pop, Mama, Sophia and Tony... I hope I do see you again, but I've made my choice, and my course is set."

He checked to make sure the men had not doubled-back after him. In fact, he pulled over cautiously and waited a good half hour, while feigning sleep.

At last, satisfied he was alone, he headed for the next exit, circled back north connecting with the freeway he had just exited, only this time he was headed east, towards Pennsylvania!

.

Chapter Four

The young woman gazed pensively out the window of her father's study, absent- mindedly tugging at an earring.

"Do you think it will be the same? I mean do you think we'll still have the same attachment to each other?" She asked, turning to the man seated in the high back, leather chair.

He ran his hand through his thick, white hair, and responded with a sigh, "No, you won't! I suspect none of us will."

"But, why?" She said with start. " We all still love him. That hasn't changed has it?"

"Sophia, how can you have so much education, and in law too, but speak like a dumb blonde floozy?" he sharply retorted. "Max has endured six years in the pen, thanks to all of us!"

"But, he willingly agreed to take that fall for us. He wanted for Tony and me to get married. It was his decision," she pouted.

"His decision?" The man's eyes became slits...the sternness in his voice further accentuated by his chiseled facial features. He glared at his daughter, " Oh yeah, his decision alright... with your father-in-law, Pepi's, and my assurance...and I might add, our encouragement, that along with his clean slate - first arrest and all - he could get a maximum of a year and a half, maybe even probation. Not six years because of some pompous prick of a judge with an agenda to prove himself !"

Sophia started to challenge, her dark eyes flashed angrily, "But you – we couldn't have known."

She stopped abruptly. Her countenance softened, as the pain etched in her father's eyes finally registered. She came to his chair and gently sat on his lap, resting her head against his chest.

Her eyes met his, and she whispered, "Does Mama know that Max was our sacrificial lamb?"

He shook his head slowly, and groaned "No!"

In a fleeting glance, a mere split second she saw that look in his eyes, a window to the soul of the man only she ever saw. Don Francesco Carron, some revered him and some feared him, but she knew he was as vulnerable as anyone. He could throw up a pretty good smoke screen, appear very tough. But she could see through the charade, recognize the pain. Pain, not so much for her brother, but for the hurt this imprisonment had brought to her mother.

"So you carry that burden too." She murmured as she snuggled close to her father.

Never mind that she was almost thirty and the mother of three, she would always be "daddy's girl" and a kindred spirit with his.

He looked at her, then laid his head against hers.

Sighing deeply, he said "You know, Sophia, I promised your mother that if she married me, I'd protect her and whatever kids we had. Has Tony promised you anything?"

"Uh Huh"

"Well, I've discovered there are no guarantees in life. I've racked my brain trying to figure out a way to help Max, all to no avail."

He snapped his head back, once more his eyes hardened, and his face darkened. "Damn it, Sophia! God knows I hate that Judge, but at this point if anything happens to him, immediately suspicion would fall on us. It wouldn't matter who the real culprit was. I just can't bring anymore pain on Josie. So, I end up behaving like his frigging protector."

Instinctively, Sophia placed her hand on the nape of

his neck and began to gently massage. She'd learned this maneuver had a calming effect on her father. This day, none of them, especially him, needed to focus on that accursed Judge. Much more relevant was to prepare to deal with her brother's attitude towards herself. She was all too aware that her gain had caused his pain.

"Pop, do you think Max will hate Tony?"

"I hope not. However, you, Sophia, and all of us, will just have to wait and see. I suspect, if he hasn't changed too much, that if you're happy, he'll be happy too!' he gave her a reassuring kiss on the cheek.

"I am happy, Pop. I love Tony like Mama loves you!"

That remark produced a slight chortle from her father. "Oh, so you have a few 'disagreements' with Tony? I believe that's the word your mother uses when she does not see eye to eye with me?"

She looked up startled, surprised to see his eyes twinkling.

"So, what have you thrown?" he asked.

"I don't remember Mama throwing anything at you?"

"Your mother was always very discreet."

"So am I," Sophia replied. She laughed and then gave Frank a hug as she stood up. "Do you think Max will look the same?"

"Do you look the same?"

"No, but I do think I've matured rather nicely." She smiled as she patted her hips. "And, if I do say so myself, my figure's not too bad either, especially with having the twins and Enrico."

Frank smiled and nodded approvingly, "Well, hopefully, your brother will have matured as nicely, but not with the same curves."

His remark caused both of them to laugh heartily.

"Nonetheless, Sophia, I'm less concerned with what he looks like and more concerned with who he is on the inside. I can't imagine what he's going to do with himself. He was twenty-eight when he went to prison, and the only remotely wrong thing he ever did was to break the church window while practicing baseball. As for an occupation, sure he went to college, even began grad school but his whole life centered on baby sitting you."

"For you, I might add..." came her biting retort.

To which her father quickly replied "Not an easy task, I might add, given your impish flirting and not always with the best of characters."

"Really? I never thought you noticed." She said hotly. "You never paid any attention, even if the so-called interested party was a goon!"

"Oh, I noticed your impetuous, and at times, even impertinent attitude. But fortunately for you, and some of your suitors, there was your dutiful brother."

He laughed, "I could trust him to guarantee proper priorities were always maintained. This was to ensure that when I walked you down the aisle you could honestly wear white."

Frank gave her a sour look. "But all Max's work was for naught, because you chose to elope! Consequently, I never did have the privilege of walking you down the aisle!"

Sophia glowered indignantly, "Need I remind you that the incident that resulted in Max being sent to prison, scared the hell out of both Tony and me! We needed each other."

"Well, at least that remark is the truth," Frank replied softly.

"What remark?" she snapped.

"Scared the hell out of both of you! You both seemed to turn a corner and suddenly grow up," was her father's response.

Sophia sat down opposite her father. "Unfortunately, Pop, it all seemed at Max's expense. I often think of how I treated him. I deliberately chose rotters to date, but Max would always chase me down. No matter who they were, bad apple kids or even some of the mob, the moment he showed up they'd take off!"

Frank scowled, "Did it ever occur to you that one day he might not come to the rescue?"

Sophia eyed him smugly, "Actually, No, father dearest! Regardless how I'd try to outwit him, Max always succeeded in being there."

Frank smirked, "Which I'm sure irritated you, to no end, my darling daughter?" He rubbed his chin and continued, "Nonetheless, I suspect much of Max's clout with your perspective suitors, was me."

"Don't flatter yourself too much. The guys all knew Max was a sharpshooter, and deadly accurate."

"He never shot a living thing," Frank groused.

"He had no need, Papa dearest. They watched his target practice, and he hit the bull's eye every time!"

"That may be, Sophia, but as far as I'm concerned, if Max had not gone to jail, I'm certain he'd have ended up a priest, or in the monastery. Either of which would have pleased your mother immensely, I'm sure."

Now, it was Sophia's turn to frown. "Pop, maybe that's what could still happen? After all many guys, and even gals, get religious in jail. Maybe Max will become a priest? Hmmm...Father Massimiliano? Has a nice ring to it don't you think?"

Frank replied grinning broadly, "Well, Sophia, if that's to be, he'd better get a hustle on. Mama's cousin, Louisa, is determined to be here as an unofficial Welcome Wagon."

"Aunt Louisa? Pop, she's got to be over ninety!"

Frank grumbled, "And she is determined as ever to snare any single male Sicilian in the marriage trap. As far as Louisa is concerned it's open season on Massimiliano!"

Sophia laughed "Marriage to a nica, good, Catholic Italian girl, no matter what she looks like. Poor Max! Ugh that's horrid!"

"What's horrid?" queried a voice from the hall.

"Oh, Mama," Sophia giggled, "we were just talking about Aunt Louisa. She's not really coming here to be with us when Max arrives, is she?"

Entering Frank's study, Josephine Carron smiled at

her vivacious daughter. "Sophia, since when did any family member have any influence over Louisa, least of all me?"

Laughing, Frank quipped "Your mother's right. Louisa is God's gift to the family, she's our means of penance, if we'll but silently endure, we can suffer our way into heaven!"

For that, he received a playful cuff from his wife.

"However," Sophia said, "it seems unfair that the one called to suffer most is the one who has suffered the most, Max!"

"Why is Max suffering more?" queried a deep, baritone voice, with a distinct New York accent. His question trailed off unanswered, as three others joined the Carrons in Frank's study.

The speaker, Tony Marconi, affectionately put his arm around Sophia's shoulders. He was accompanied by his parents, Guiseppi and Michelena, known respectively in the family, as Pepi and Lena.

Sophia groaned, "Pop just informed me that Aunt Louisa will be here for Max's homecoming."

"Don't start, Pepi!" the large, buxom Lena admonished her husband.

A smile stole across Sophia's face as she recalled the first time she met Tony's parents. It was fairly obvious Tony never got his stature from his father! Lena, on the other hand was the large robust stereotypic Italian Mama.

Lena was so outgoing and friendly, Sophia had felt instantly at ease in her presence. Pepi on the other hand was another matter. Even when dripping wet, he wouldn't weigh over 145 pounds, and he was barely five and a half feet tall. Yet no one dared to cross him. Every Sicilian male Sophia knew, including her own father, treaded very carefully in the presence of Mr. Marconi Senior. You had a sense when he stared at you that he had x-ray vision. Initially Pepi had intimidated her, then Sophia noticed that it was in fact, Pepi, who treaded very carefully in the presence of his wife.

He simply was no match for her quick wit. Yet, he seemed to take delight in her sense of humor. Somehow, when he was with Lena, Pepi appeared at ease. Sophia thought perhaps it was because Lena was so gregarious while Pepi was a man of few words, and sometimes even those few words caused him grief. Thus, when he was with Lena socially, he could trust her to handle all conversational eventualities.

Tony for his part loved his parents dearly and Sophia had appreciated the deep affection they had shown her.

"Well, one thing is certain," remarked Pepi, matter-of-factly, "we can be assured that with Louisa here, Max will have multiple flowers from which to pick. That should relieve his six year celibate boredom!"

Tony grimaced, while Frank covered his eyes, both uttered in unison "Pepi!" to the accompaniment of three disapproving feminine scowls.

Looking up with the innocence of a maligned choir boy, Pepi exclaimed "Well of course, Josephine, I meant with utmost taste, prudence, and purity!"

Josephine, chose to ignore the previous comments with their not-so-pious insinuations. She was filled with joy at the prospect of being reunited with her son. This day was a good day! The best she'd had in more than six years. Today she would only entertain wholesome, positive conversation. Thus she began to gush over how well Rosa, Bill, Lou and Anna had cleaned up Max's house on Maple Grove Drive. She noted that Anna and Rosa had been busy baking and cooking to make sure Max's favorite foods were on hand for his homecoming.

It was at that point she remembered there were several things she had forgotten to ask. Suddenly, Frank was bombarded with a barrage of questions... "How long do you think it will be before Max gets here? How far is it from Cleveland anyway? What route do you think he will take? How early would he have gotten on the road?"

Frank threw up his hands in mock horror, and said, "Josephine, you've just peppered me with four questions and given no time to respond!"

Sophia walked over to her mother, took her hand in hers, and gave it a gentle squeeze.

"Mama, Max will be here when he gets here!"

Just then, Rosa and Anna entered the study. One look at their faces told everyone something was terribly wrong!

Chapter Five

Pulling into the Interstate Service Center, Max glanced at a woman heading to the restaurant. His mouth dropped.

"No! It can't be!...Mama?"

He felt as if the word strangled in his throat. Everything around him crawled to a halt; as if like time itself was frozen.

"Mildred!" a deep voice from behind called out.

The woman turned.

Max breathed again. "Definitely not Mama," he smiled. "My plan remains intact!"

He sat savoring his meal... His own meal of choice...A simple hamburger done as he wanted it!...Bacon, cheese, mustard, relish, pickles and of course jalapeño peppers... Fries loaded with gravy. Six years of no choice, but now he was back in the land of choice! And one choice he had made was to visit Jack Walters!

As he sat studying a map he was indistinguishable from any other businessman. He blended well. With his clean cut appearance and high end apparel, he was clearly the epitome of a young junior executive on the rise. Any attention drawn to him would most certainly be positive, and he knew it!

"Damn! Momentarily that woman really did unnerve me. Part of me really did want it to be Mama."

The more he thought of his mother the more he yearned to see her. As the yearning increased so did the anger that raged within him. The anger was not directed at his father, or Pepi, or Tony, or Sophia. No, it was vented against Walters and his flagrant bias against Sicilian Americans. The courtroom had been fixed against him and he would find out why!

Sitting once again in his vehicle, he began to pound the steering wheel. "Damn, damn, damn!"

He hadn't realized how bitter he was. For six years, he had worn the mask. *"Yes, Sir, No, Sir."*

His eyes began to sting. He became aware of the bitter tears trickling down his cheeks. He had stifled so many feelings.

"God," he paused "God, I've been stuffing feelings inside, most of my life!"

This sudden self-awareness caught him by surprise. As Frankie Carron's kid, expectations as to how he should behave had constantly dogged him, at home, at school... Yes, even in the pen! People always seemed to assess him, either he wasn't tough enough or he was too tough. It seemed he could never please anybody!

He shook his head, bit his lip, closed his eyes, trying to bury his angst, all to no avail! Tears were now really flowing.

"Damn, Sicilian males don't cry! Well, Damn it, I am Sicilian, and I am crying, and furthermore it feels good!"

Max threw his head back, and started to laugh. "This is insane!" But, something inside him said, *"No, it's not! It is purging."*

"Purging?" That was exactly what he sensed was happening. As if one enormous, emotional boil had been lanced and festered poison was draining out. He drew his hand across his face, wiping away the tears. Then he sniffled, just like he had done as a kid.

A faint smile appeared, *"I always seemed to time my melt downs, when no one was looking, just as now! Yeah, that is how I kept my balance, and maintained my cool so that no one could ever guess how I felt, or what I thought!"*

Instinctively, he slipped his hand beneath his jacket,

to the left, in the area of his heart, and felt "her". His hand gently caressed his one true "love".

"Yep, you are my solace, J.D." He patted the gun fondly. *"Pop slipped you to me on my 16th birthday."*

Max could see it, as if it had just happened. He could even hear his father's voice, as if he was standing beside him.

Mama had held a family sixteenth birthday party for him. Massimiliano Carron, Frankie's boy, was sixteen. Everybody was there, not his friends - their friends. Sure there were a few, young bucks, like him, but they had the gang swagger. Puberty was in overdrive within them.

He had sensed that his father had hoped to see some of that in him. Frank was a little disappointed in "his" boy, and it showed.

"Pop, never would reveal his feelings to me. It wasn't so with Sophia or Mama. Yeah, a hug now and then would have been nice. In fact, when Pop pulled me aside at the party, saying, "Max, come with me into my office, I have something for you.""

"Man, my heart swelled. At last, it seemed that Pop was prepared to acknowledge me as a man - the son of whom he was proud. I half expected him to finally comment on my grades, straight A's, Mama was always gushing over them, but not Pop. How I yearned to hear Pop praise me, maybe even laugh with me, as he did with the men."

Max let out a deep sigh and continued, "So when he called me into his office, on the q.t., I actually expected I'd come away feeling finally like one of the guys."

Like an instant T.V. replay, his father's study flashed before his eyes. It was huge! The massive cherry desk and bookcases didn't diminish the room's size one iota. The furniture was all black leather...couch, chairs, including his Pop's big swivel desk chair. Even now he could smell the leather upholstery. For Max, the office exuded masculinity!

"Inside, that day, I was so excited, filled with anticipation that at last I'd be accepted as Don Francesco

Carron's son, by him! It didn't last long."

Max grimaced as the memories began to flood his mind.

"Yeah, Pop went over to his desk, pulled out a box and handed it to me. I opened it. It was a gun. I just stared at it.'

" 'Pick it up!' he ordered, and so I did.'

" 'Look at the butt.' I did.'

" 'What's on it?' he'd demanded.'

" 'J.D.' I said.'

" 'Right, John Dillinger, know who he was?' Pop asked me.'

"My mouth had gone dry, 'Yeah', I managed to say. 'He was a notorious Chicago mobster in the 30's. The cops finally ambushed and killed him. How did you get his gun?' I stammered.'

Pop smiled slyly 'It's a collector's item. The gun got lifted from the precinct a long time ago. I have connections.' He grabbed me by both ears, pulled my face to his, and demanded that I look him in the eye."

Max closed his eyes as if hoping it would shut out this painful memory.

"Learn how to use it!'

" 'Yes, Sir.' I half whispered.'

" 'Don't let anyone know you have it.'

" 'No Sir' There it was. That 'Yes, Sir, No, Sir' I always seem to have to say to people! At the time, I simply blurted out, 'Where can I go to use it?' This was not the forceful response he had obviously wanted."

Max heaved another deep sigh. These memories were only serving to deepen the bitterness of his soul.

"Ask Lou and Bill. They'll help you' had been his response."

"Lou and Bill were two guys that were on Pop's outside list, not good enough for his cronies, but good enough for me his son!"

Unexpectedly, that memory evoked a smile.

"Surprisingly, that turned out to be for me the beginning of two really great relationships."

A sense of warmth flooded over him as he thought of the

two men. *"They encouraged me, set up areas I could target shoot. They were real creative. No Mickey Mouse ranges for them. They even secured ones with moving targets.'*

" 'Learn how to use it.' Pop had said.'

"He meant learn how to shoot it. Any ass can learn how to shoot a gun. All that makes him is a good shot, but not a gunman.'

"J.D.'s original owner was no gunman. He was a murderer. A gunman is one who chooses rightly when to fire, and rightly, when to hold fire. It's a fine line; a very fine line!" Max mused.

"It didn't take long for me to master marksmanship. And" he laughed softly, "Sophia's flirtatious ways allowed me to develop skills that propelled me to fulfilling my definition of gunman."

He started to chuckle. "Yes indeed, because of my headstrong little sister, I created my little black book, not a list of dead bodies...But a list of guys who knew that if I was the type to easily lose my cool, they would have been dead bodies. Instead, they simply were added to my 'favor owing' list."

Max was grinning now. All rancor, at least for the moment, was gone.

"I'd say to the guy 'remember when I caught you red handed with very wrong intentions towards my sister? When I rescued you from doing something that decidedly would have torqued my father and pissed me off? Well today is the day I call the favor.' So far I haven't had to use that list but one day who knows? The fact is I have the list and each one knows I have it."

Faces of some of the fellows and the situations floated across the sea of his memories. As they did, Max suddenly realized the bitterness and anger had left his spirit. Just touching J.D. had restored his equilibrium.

Swinging his car south, from Interstate 86, into Pennsylvania, he spied a Holiday Inn tucked conveniently close to a Wal-Mart Superstore. He decided to spend the night there, and go on another shopping spree. This one to create: 'Max...Your average working Joe.' He wanted to prepare himself to be able to dress for whatever the occasion demanded.

Morning arrived, and with it, April showers.

"Good for my Wal-Mart traveling salesman garb, Khaki pants, black golf shirt, loafers and the tailored raincoat."

J.D. he elected not to personally pack. Instead, he placed his trusted friend in the false bottom console beside the gear shift, just a precaution, in case he was stopped. He also had the fake ID the guys made for him in the pen, and right under the guards' noses.

"Dex was aptly named," Max thought, *"both for dexterity and detail."*

Superficially his phony driver's and owner's license's looked like the real deal. In fact those licenses did exist. He just wasn't the right guy. "So should I get pulled over, I just need to remember I'm Mat Carreli, of Brooklyn, Illinois. Personally I hope I never need to use the ID even though it is a work of art and cost me a few C's. Having them is simply good strategy to ensure my venture pans out!"

Shortly after lunch, Max arrived in his designated 'combat zone'. He knew he only had a window of one or two days before it would become public knowledge that he had not gone straight home to Chicago. So it was critical that he locate the Judge's house quickly and plan his entry approach.

Max was making mental notes of every landscape detail he passed. *"Wow, he's located near this moderately-sized airport. Why am I surprised? It's all the better for His Honor to get to his bench. He can be there to ensure schmucks, like me, don't remain on the loose to harm upright, American citizens.'*

"Damn! The moment I even think of Jack Walters the anger just eats at my guts. I didn't mind taking a fall for Pop and Pepi but I expected a fair fall, a decent sentence,

and one in keeping with all the circumstances. Instead, in addition to enduring a concussion, I had six years stolen from my life.'

"Well, I will find out who bribed that man if it's the last thing I do! Hey, there it is - his street 'Independence Drive'. Now, isn't that ironic? The one who stole my independence lives on Independence Drive. I am not amused" he groused.

The street appeared to meander upwards through forested parkland, with no house visible until it dead-ended in a cul-de-sac. He saw the number for Walters' house, but did not stop or slow down, appearing as a driver who had made a miscue. He did not speed nor did he crawl.

"Just an honest mistake...a wrong street. Wrong street, my ass!" he snorted. "Your Honor, you sir, are a sitting duck, living in an undeveloped subdivision with only two other houses remotely near you!"

Leaving Independence Drive, he searched and found another street that appeared to circle down behind the parkland forest that contained Walters' house. To both his surprise and delight he discovered a 'nature trail' on this lower level.

"Lady Luck, you're smiling on me today!" he grinned. "Good chance I'll be able to cut right across this wooded terrain and end up right behind the Judge's house."

Driving through the area he had made note of where public bus stops existed, and which bus routes he would need to deposit him at that nature trail. This had been a most productive day for Max, a day that had far exceeded his greatest expectations. He'd even been able to figure out where he could leave his car.

"Long term car parking at the airport, will not draw anyone's attention. Things are definitely unfolding just as I hoped!"

His dark blue, turtleneck pullover, jean jacket, jeans and sneakers: his "Wal-Mart specials" would definitely blend into the neighborhood. It would not be long before that nagging question, which had haunted him for six years, would at last be answered.

He furrowed his brow, "The one obstacle that might mar my search for justice could be that 100 plus acres of heavily forested escarpment. I'll have to take my chances on traversing it without getting lost. Even worse I could fall into a crevice, and if I did no one would even look for me, because no one knows I'm here."

A voice inside the car said *"Is this obsession to seek out Walters worth it?"* It startled him, and then he started to laugh. *"Idiot! That voice is you!"* Yet it caused him to pause and take stock. He'd always been extremely cautious, in control of his emotions: coldly in control, in fact. Where was this obsession to confront Walters from? He had tried to argue himself out of the "plan." Just as he thought he'd succeeded, somewhere, from deep within, again arose the passion to follow through.

"Sheesh!" he blurted out loud. "I feel like I'm talking to a daisy, picking off one petal Saying, 'No, I won't', then reaching for another while saying, 'Yes, I will'!"

He turned the car away from the town, and back the same way he'd come and pulled into the motel for the night. Although exhilarated by his sleuthing success, he found himself famished and unexpectantly fatigued. He decided to first rectify the hunger pangs. Conveniently a steak house sat adjacent to the motel, its flashing neon sign advertising an "all-you-can-eat soup and salad bar."

"Just what the doctor ordered!" He grinned.

To his delight the restaurant offered good Italian wine. He ordered a carafe. Then he turned his attention to the salad bar. Fresh salad was not a usual fare in the pen and certainly shrimp and crab never appeared. He piled his plate high and indulged. Max relished the cream of potato soup but he had to admit the T-bone was the meal's climax. Or at least it would have been, had he not ordered a slice of the home made Black Forest cake. He paid the bill, a little sheepish at all he'd devoured.

"Then again, I have no idea when I'll get the opportunity to eat tomorrow! So, Maxie, good you tanked up tonight!"

In his room, he put on his trunks, and headed to the pool and spa to relax. As he sat pool side he noticed, almost absent-mindedly, that his physique was attracting female attention. The last thing he wanted this evening was to lose focus. Deliberately he picked up "Pride and Prejudice", put on his horned rimmed glasses, as if to read this giant tome. He'd purchased the book for an occasion such as this. It would serve to cleverly divert any unwelcome social solicitation.

Hidden behind his prop, Max's mind was not engaged in reading. He was struggling with the wisdom of finally executing his plan. The one, he had so carefully crafted for six years! Tomorrow would be the day of reckoning. Should he?... Could he?... Would he? ...Follow through?

At last, he set the book down and took off his glasses. The issue had been settled! His decision brought the peace, he had both sought and longed for...picking up his book, Max headed to his room.

Chapter Six

"Well done, M.K.!" a voice boomed across the boardroom. "Well done!"

Heads around the table nodded approval. Every hand broke into applause. To a casual observer, it might appear a meeting of a United Nations caucus: Different colors; different attire; mostly male; a couple of females, and mostly forty-five or older.

The slender red head, with those piercing, green eyes and stunning features, almost looked out of place. She was young enough to be the daughter of some of them. Yet, the compliments coming her way were anything but patronizing.

In her six years, as CEO of Kayleen Enterprises, she had earned their confidence. In both good and bad markets, her ingenuity, wisdom, intuition... call it what you will... had propelled Kayleen Enterprises to the forefront of International Financial Institutions. To say she was fiscally shrewd was a mild understatement.

Her board knew she was a "no nonsense" executive, with a brilliant mind, but that wasn't her only asset. M.K. McDonald possessed a most disarming smile that, coupled with a sense of humor, could lighten even the most intense, board room situation. She seemed to have this innate ability to be as tough as steel, yet as compassionate and caring as Mother Teresa.

Graciously she closed the meeting deflecting, as she always did, personal praise, transforming it into corporate praise, team work, well done! As a result, everyone, from the most insignificant scribe to the highest Senior V.P., left the room pumped up and enthused to be part of the Kayleen team.

Kaye strode quickly back to her spacious penthouse office suite, hoping no one noticed the furrow in her brow. She closed the door then sank into the luxurious burgundy leather chair that sat behind her massive mahogany desk. Kaye shook her head, her thoughts no longer on the boardroom success, but on those late night calls.

"When they began seven months ago, I was absolutely torqued," she groaned. "The vulgarity and lewdness of them initially annoyed me. I thought it was just some punk playing a prank, who accidentally had hit on my phone number. But then, the calls became personal. Not only was he using my name, but revealing things that only someone who was observing my moves would know.'

"I tried dealing with that voice, as I would any obnoxious boardroom boar. I hung up, only to have him call back immediately. Ignoring them didn't work either. The phone just kept ringing, and when I did pick it up, the violent sexual threats began." Kaye closed her eyes, pain surged across the memories. She buried her head in her hands.

Again, she shook her head sadly. "When he would not heed my orders to stop calling, I still wasn't alarmed. I told Chief Davidson about them, and then Jack. I spoke openly about them at the boardroom, explicit about the content of the calls and the threats." She smiled wanly.

"Yeah, they all were concerned. All said, 'Don't worry! No problem! We'll take care of it. Every one took it seriously. Wire taps were set up. Right, no problem... There were no more calls... absolutely none! And that became my problem!"

She slammed shut the ledger she'd left open on her desk. "I couldn't believe it. Then the rumors began. Some said, *'I'd made it all up, that I was lonely, entombed in my business, but really seeking sexual gratification.'* " She rocked back in her chair, fighting tears that threatened to erupt.

"I was absolutely stunned and mortified when I first heard what was being said. Nothing I'd ever experienced allowed me to cope with what was happening."

Her thoughts were interrupted by a gentle knocking on her door.

"Come In."

A round, cherubic, face peaked around the door.

"Steph! Yes, what can I do for you?" M.K. queried.

The owner of the face, a young woman in her early twenties stepped into the room. She wore her brown hair curled under, just below the collar. Pleasantly plump, she would have been easy to label as plain were it not for her radiant smile and soft brown eyes.

"Ms. McDonald, I...I hope I'm not interrupting you?" She said tentatively.

"Absolutely not, Stephanie! The board meeting is all over." M.K. assured her receptionist.

"I hope it went well for you?" the young girl inquired genuinely.

"It did, Steph, and I must compliment you on your selection of note pads for the members. They were very attractive and Mr. Hassim commented that it contained the appropriate amount of paper. Not too much and not too little. As you know he likes making his own notations but he also loves the trees and doesn't want any wastage." M.K.'s acknowledgement caused the young woman to beam.

"I'm glad I could be of service, Ma'am." She hesitated for a moment and then said "Ms. McDonald, I know I'm supposed to be at the reception desk until 5 o'clock and it's only a quarter to, but I was wondering if I might leave a few minutes early tonight?"

M.K.'s eyes twinkled impishly as she responded in her feigned Irish brogue, "Ah, Steph, would ye be wantin' to leave early? There mightn't be a wee man awaitin' ye, would there?" She had hit the nail on the head.

Stephanie went all shades of pink and crimson.

"Actually, Ms. McDonald, I've been asked to the dinner theater, and he said he'd pick me up at 6:30 p.m., and the bus it takes…"

M.K. interrupted smiling, "Ah, tell me about said young man, Steph. Kayleen employees are a very prized group, you know."

Steph grinned from ear to ear at the opportunity to share her secret with her boss. She fair gushed how she'd just met this handsome man. "Oh I know I'm a plain girl but he said beauty is more than skin deep and that what attracted him to me was my warm heart."

Kaye firmly nodded in agreement, "He's right, Steph. Your young man is most perceptive! So skat and have a great evening."

"Oh, I will, Ms. McDonald." She paused and turned back, "Thank you ever so much. It's so wonderful working with you."

"Don't ye go gettin' all mushy on me now, Steph. I could change my mind."

Steph giggled and quickly left.

Kaye looked at a couple of portfolio's she wanted to peruse on the weekend and slipped them into her briefcase. She grabbed her purse and coat, shut off the lights, closed and locked her office door.

Her earlier concerns had returned and had so captured her attention that she failed to see the man standing beside her. As she turned to head toward the elevator she bumped right into him. Had he not reached out and grabbed her, she would have fallen.

"M.K., I'm so sorry!" was the apologetic response she received.

"George!" she gasped, clutching her chest, "Oh, you startled me!"

"Well, again I apologize. It certainly wasn't my intent to frighten you. I just wanted to express my thanks for all your hard work. M.K., you are Kayleen's most valuable asset."

"Ah, George, flattery will get you no where." She squinted at him in a feigned provocative manner. "You may be Italian and think you have a way with the women, but I'm Irish, and instinctively, I can smell blarney a mile away." Then she broke into that absolutely musical laughter which had endeared her to so many.

"Well, if you won't take my passes," George retorted, "at least let me be chivalrous and walk you to your car. I noticed you were parked right beside mine."

She took his arm, bantering back and forth with him. They both waved at the security guard and entered the garage.

"Are you heading back to Nevada tonight, George?"

"Yeah, I have a late night flight. Getting good connections from here to there is not the easiest thing to accomplish." George grinned and continued, "Apparently the citizens of this area have their own gambling establishments to frequent. Thus, there's not a huge demand to take a flight to Nevada's bright lights.'

"So M.K., do you have any dinner plans? Would you be willing to keep me company? Luigi's is a great Italian restaurant close to the airport and is on your route home."

Jokingly, he chided, "I understand it might even appeal to your poor, Irish, culinary tastes."

"Very well, George, I'll call your bluff. I'll go with you to Luigi's, to see if it's all you report it to be. So, do I follow you, or do you follow me?"

George cocked his head to one side, and with a smile replied smoothly, "First things first, unlock your car door, Senorina, so I can be a gentleman, and open the door for you."

As she got into the car, he said "I will follow you my fearless CEO."

She laughed and then realized, driving to the restaurant, that she was glad for his company, having dinner with him would take her mind off those vexing phone calls.

Kaye liked how he readily talked about his wife and two daughters with genuine affection.

One of his girls was already a teenager. The other would soon arrive at that milestone. Kaye often sensed that George was using her to aid his understanding of this perplexing age.

"Then again," she smiled, "George has real wisdom in the boardroom. What endears him most, to me, is his concern for others. I appreciate that trait!'

"Even better M.K., George is a truly devoted family man! At this point, the last thing I need, to further complicate my life, is a man with romantic intentions!'

"Mustn't forget, however, that George seems to sense when people have problems, he has a good listening ear. So, although I need to relax, and dinner with him will help..." Kaye paused and continued, "Be on guard! I do not intend to share with him, or any one else, that those obnoxious calls have resumed."

Luigi's was delightful. The food was exquisite! George had M.K. doubled over with laughter, as he describe with great humor, his blundering father episodes with his daughters.

With tears in his eyes, he confessed, "One afternoon, I was so tired that I fell asleep on the couch, T.V. blaring. It was an old Bill Cosby rerun. My younger daughter came in to ask me a question. She said "Dad," just when the T.V. daughter began talking to Cosby. To my daughter's shock and amusement, and to my embarrassment ...I started to converse and argue with the T.V. child."

Tears of laughter ran down Kaye's face, as she said, "George, you didn't!"

"Yep. I did!"

Then just as they were preparing to leave, George leaned across the table, put his hand on hers and looked directly into her eyes.

Kaye was shocked *"Good heavens! Is he about to make a pass at me? Have I totally misread this man?"*

But, before she could draw her hand back, George spoke firmly "M.K., have you had any more of those late night calls?"

Taken aback, Kaye blurted out, "No! No!" She hoped she was convincing. Did he detect untruth from her?

George took back his hand, sat in his chair studying her. "M.K., should they resume, whatever you do, please tell the authorities! It's nothing to fool with, don't be embarrassed. Promise me you will."

"Yes, yes, I will," she responded.

It seemed that he was satisfied with her answer. He accompanied her to her car and watched as she drove out of the parking lot.

"Don't be embarrassed!" She fumed. "Easy for you to say, George! You are a man. A married one at that and you are not CEO of Kayleen Enterprises."

Kaye knew that in addition to the crude remarks about her sexual yearnings, the other rumor surfacing was that the pressures of Kayleen's big business enterprises were too much for a "fragile" woman. "She was cracking up." Such talk could literally shake some clients' confidence in Kayleen's stability. Stability, that following her father's death, she had fought hard to maintain, striving in fact, to develop it even further.

Driving home she glanced at her watch. It would be after 2 a.m. before she got there. She exhaled slowly. Both the Walters and the Davidsons would be away this weekend. She would be the only resident at Independence Drive. She shuddered. Sometimes, she really didn't want to be so independent.

Almost imperceptibly, came that still small voice within her, *"I will never leave you, nor forsake you, nor abandon you."*

She sighed, "Thank you, Holy Spirit, I needed your prompt."

Her car pulled into the garage, the automatic door closed as she touched the little button on her car visor. The sensor light had not exposed any danger lurking inside. Still fear gripped her heart. Fear she could not explain.

She closed her eyes. Her father had taught her from the time she was a little girl to memorize scripture "to settle one's nerves", he always said. Both her parents had modeled the power combining scripture with one's prayers, had in your life. Her mother had referred to this as "praying the scriptures."

As she sat in the stillness of her garage, she could almost hear her father, *"Don't worry Kaye, about what scripture you should pray. Your role is to simply read and study your Bible so you can become familiar with God's Word. God will do the rest! The Holy Spirit will direct your steps."*

A tear trickled down her face, those words brought with them the memory of the three of them...Mummy, Daddy and her...sitting at the table, joining hands, the Bible in the center...And then they would pray together lifting up all their concerns.

Softly she said, "And you were faithful, Lord Jesus, that dreadful day I was told of their deaths. And Holy Spirit has brought to me, your specific Word for each situation all the days since then."

"Indeed Lord, Your Word is a lamp unto my feet and a light unto my path! Thank you for always being there for me, and thank you for the word that is now in my heart to pray."

The heaviness had lifted. She bowed her head and prayed:

"Psalm 17 verse 1: The Lord is my light and my salvation. Who shall I fear? The Lord is the stronghold of my life: of whom shall I be afraid? Lord Jesus, I choose to stand upon your Word! Amen."

She stepped from the car, coat, purse and briefcase, in hand. A deep peace had settled in her heart.

Chapter Seven

Max had timed it perfectly. He arrived at the airport with the other commuters. He spied the long term parking sign and had maneuvered into the correct lane.

"How long ya' be gone fer'?" drawled the attendant.

"I'm afraid May and most of June, possibly even into July. The Company's sending me to Mexico for an irrigation project, but then August's my holiday time. Don't intend to miss out on them. No, Sir!" Max smiled amiably.

"Three month ticket needs to be paid in advance. If ya' need extra time ya' pay fer' that on your return."

Max nodded and pulled out the cash, exchanging it for the ticket.

The man gestured to Max and reminded him, "Put it on your dash. The month and day of expiration is noted. The car will be checked and tagged after that date."

"Right, any place a three-month long term should park?" Max queried wanting to ensure compliance.

"Hey man, the lot's yours. Pick your spot."

Max waved and headed down one lane, then he switched to another. He didn't want the attendant noting where he parked, and he especially didn't want him to see that he exited without luggage! The lot was quite busy and that fit into his plans well.

Max smiled "No, intention my friend of being here three months, just a day will be all I need."

In the car, he slid out of his trench coat, placing it out of sight on the back seat.

"These extra-dark windows are very convenient," he mused.

J.D. was imperceptibly holstered under his left arm. Dressed in denim and cross country runners, he looked like your average, working "Joe," he grinned and said "or, someone out for a hike on this early spring morning."

Striding through the airport he headed, without hesitation to the bus stop. He took the downtown bus, which was definitely not crowded. Folks were coming to the airport to depart. Incoming flights were sparse this time of the day. That's just the way it was with these commuter airports.

"Hey, Dude, can you spare a buck?" sneered a wanna' be gang banger. Max sized him up, and knew he could take the young punk with ease. Max's brown eyes hardened as he fixed his gaze on the kid. Leaning back in his seat Max feigned co-operation "Tell you what...See that seat over there at the front of the bus?"

"What of it?" came the sullen reply.

"You sit there away from me and you can have this fiver."

The youth made a sweeping bow, "Yo', fer five, Dude ya' gotta' deal."

Max's jaw tightened, he took the bill and flipped it on the floor. The punk lunged for the money. As he did, Max's foot ensured he found the floor more rapidly than intended.

With the kid sprawled on the floor, Max leaned over, discreetly giving the young tough a peek at J.D. as he hissed, "Don't mess with me, Punk."

The fellow quickly slunk to his designated seat, his swagger gone. At the next stop, the sleaze fled the bus. Meanwhile, Max deposited the five back into his pocket.

"Amazing what the glimpse of a rod will do," he chuckled.

A few stops later, Max disembarked, transfer in hand. Methodically he weaved himself through the city. If anyone wished to trace his trail, he was determined not to make it easy. Four transfers later, he arrived within walking distance to the nature trail.

"Well, Your Honor, depositing me in the pen until late

spring wasn't too bright on your part. The leaves are now budded out, not too easy to spot a guy out for a hike."

Arriving mid-afternoon at the path, he was relieved to find no one else on the trail. The crushed-stone-dust walk way was perfect too. Not too easy to track and if a print was visible, so were many others.

Max paused to smell the air, take in the sights, it really was peaceful. "Wow! Tranquil or what! A fellow could enjoy this. Too bad I'm preoccupied," he groused.

One thing was very evident. Max had utilized all the prison's fitness and exercise programs he could, and he was indeed in good shape. Hiking briskly along the winding trails, he mentally tried to imagine at what point it came closest to Independence Drive.

As he approached the crest of a rise he was delighted to see the trail fork. One branch headed upward, bastardizing that old Scottish tune, he hummed, *"You take the low road, Buddy, but I'm going high."* It proved a great choice. Max soon realized it was leading right into the vicinity of those three houses that he'd seen on his drive.

"I bet if I stayed here long enough, His Honor, himself might take a stroll. Now, while that might be convenient it wouldn't be very sociable on my part not to pay him a home visit."

Many times in the past six years he had rehearsed this meeting.

"It will happen" he declared, spitting on the ground, "exactly as planned!"

He picked out Walters' house with ease. He started to edge toward it delighted that the new foliage offered such good camouflage. But then something strange happened. He'd had this same sensation just over six years ago.

At that time, he'd had this strong impulse that seemed to urge him not to lie down on that motel bed. A cold chill rippled through his body. He knew without a doubt that had he ignored that strange prompt, he would have been killed. Now here it was again, unmistakable, he was being drawn away from the Walters' property toward the large stone home that sat alone on this side of the street, opposite both Walters' house and the other home.

He shrugged and said ,"Maybe the Walters have recently moved? Or, maybe there's something I need to know in that house? This strange feeling I have that I should go into that stone home. It's just like that "hunch" I had in that New York State motel room. Furthermore, it's just as strong," he paused, "if not stronger. People may figure I'm crazy. Maybe I am, but of this I am certain, without that intuitive move six years ago, Maxie, you would be dead. So no more arguing with yourself, go into the stone house first! "

With his binoculars he easily detected the presence of an alarm system. He let out a low laugh.

"Bonus, Your Honor! Thank you for the education you gave me. I had first class mentors for 'Burglary 101' right through to Ph.D. training."

Memories of other convicts flooded his mind. Just listening to the one he'd nicknamed 'Old Soft Touch' always amazed Max.

"In fact, he even told me the trick of breaking through the infrared barrier."

He reached into his denim jacket pocket and his hand closed around a small rod shaped object.

"Okay, Soft Touch, today I get to experiment with your technology. Let's see? Step one discover the source of the laser beam. Figure out whether it's a door or a window you can jimmy to get in. Then give ol' laser eye your laser beam, and while the two beams cozy up as one, open up said door and go in, being careful to let it lock behind you. Wipe all fingerprints away, should you not be using gloves, which of course I am."

Max was reciting by rote all that had been taught him. "Then let your laser sweetly lead its new friend's beam back to rejoin its buddy. Voilà! I'm inside, the alarm is reactivated and no one knows the security has been breached!"

Max made mental note to bring Soft Touch a courtesy gift when he returned next year to escort Phil out of the slammer. As for the present, Max was confident he was the sole occupant of this large and rather lavishly appointed home. He'd also noted that the security system only existed on the external doors and windows. He was home free to explore. Leaving on his gloves, he carefully removed his shoes. Carrying them with him, he strode into the living room.

"Jackpot!"

There, on the mantle was a large gold framed photograph. Unmistakably, square in the center of the photo, was His Honor! There was another guy and three dolls in the picture too. Max hadn't a clue who they were, nor did he care. He was about to carefully set the photo back in the exact place he had found it, when he took a second look at the youngest doll.

He let out a low whistle and exclaimed emphatically, "You are one gorgeous doll!" He paused and chuckled, "Now if you were at Aunt Louisa's parties, I would be tempted to attend."

Picture in hand, he sat down to study it better. She was a strikingly beautiful redhead. He looked carefully at the others in the photo. None of them looked old enough to be her parents, also there seemed to be no physical resemblance.

"But hey! These days who knows," he thought.

His countenance darkened, and out loud he said, "Surely you aren't her father?", as he jabbed his finger at Walters.

So repulsive was that thought, he couldn't wait to return the photo to the mantle.

He moved cautiously exploring the first floor of the home. As he did so, he noted that the red head appeared in most of the pictures.

He grunted to himself, "Why be surprised, idiot? She's so good looking, who wouldn't want to take her photo?"

He paused to stare, at one fairly large picture. In it, the redhead appeared with an older very distinguished couple. Max actually thought she bore some resemblance to them.

"Funny" Max mused "the old guy looks familiar, like I've seen his picture before, but I can't pinpoint where."

Max continued to survey the first level of the house noting doors, windows, any escape hatch, if and when needed. The residence was a three storey structure, cathedral ceilings, open concept kitchen, dining room and living room with a large imposing fireplace. The latter was the focal point for this level. A winding oak staircase led both downstairs and up. He opted for down first, an expansive library, family/TV room with an oversized walkout to a well-manicured garden at the side. An array of spring flowers were already in bloom.

"These folks have taste big time and I suspect a wallet to match!" Max remarked, then caught himself. "Whoa, Maxie, remember why you're here old boy, to meet with one man and him alone. So let's wander back upstairs and see what we can see."

The main level was carpeted with firm plush carpets, but the color and texture was such that footprints weren't easily revealed.

"Looks nice, feels nice and I go undetected, very nice indeed!"

He cautiously approached what he expected would be the door to the garage. To his shock, no alarm system was in place.

"People, you are so trusting, must be nice, but unfortunately for you it's also foolhardy."

Unexpectedly, he thought of his father's house and his own, and a twinge of pain stabbed his chest. His eyes filled with tears catching him by surprise, then he shook his head.

"I don't allow thoughts of home to enter my reality. Then suddenly they just sneak up and ambush me."

The pain he realized immediately was not physical rather it was a longing, a deep longing to see his family again. To be able to hug Mama and just be in all their presence, including even his father's.

He closed his eyes imagining his father's presence. He so wanted his approval. Yet always he felt he came up short. He collapsed on the stairs heading to the bedrooms, sort of sprawling on the lush thick carpet. In a crazy sort of way, it seemed to him that if he could just escape into the carpet's pile, he might lose all those painful separation memories. The separation and his incarceration, had produced deep hurt, but he had not allowed anyone to see that pain. Even Phil, his cellmate, did not know his internal anguish.

His eyes burned with tears, "Damn it, Max, you want to be home yet here you sit tentatively perched at extending that separation, unless everything goes exactly as you planned. Why the hell can't I leave well enough alone and just go home trusting time to remove the pain of injustice I've experienced?"

There it was again. The more he wanted to escape, to flee home, the more urgent was the inward sense he had to remain.

"Pop would never bawl!" He was sure of that. " Yet, here I am wanting to please him, but blubbering like an idiot."

Struggling to regain his composure, he carefully smoothed out any carpet pile he inadvertently had ruffled, and headed upstairs. Once again, very large spacious rooms, elegant trappings, especially the luxurious master bedroom, extra-large walk-in closet, whirlpool bath , oversized shower, name it, this room had it all, including a king-sized bed.

Max fell backwards onto it, flailing his arms and legs like a child making snow angels. "Perfect- not too soft; not too hard," he laughed, "As if I'll ever sleep in it."

He stood up and carefully smoothed out any tell tale evidence of his presence.

Then his jaw tensed. There he was again, His Honor smiling in his judiciary robes. It was all Max could do not to pick up the photo and smash it.

"Composure, Boy!" he ordered himself.

Next to that photo were the three women he'd seen downstairs. All decked out in evening gowns. Beside them was a photo of the other guy he'd seen.

He slapped his forehead with his hand, and blurted, "Sheesh! He's a cop! This younger guy looks like him and he's a cop too!" He slouched down into a nearby chair carefully examining the picture.

He frowned and said sarcastically "It looks like it's taken outside the third house on this street. Way to go, Maxie! Way to go – how lucky can you be? Three houses, one's owned by His Honor and another has two cops connected to it. Great!"

The whole thing infuriated him. This was most definitely NOT part of his plan! He wanted to pound something, someone, anything, to scream at the top of his lungs...none of which would have been wise to do. Since discretion was the better part of his valor, he chose to be discreet. He opted to pace, yank at his hair and swear under his breath.

After a few moments had passed, he looked around the room, and declared, "Whoever you are, who lives here, I've just remade your bed and now I'm going to try out your john."

He took a whiz and somehow it felt great peeing in someone else's privy without anyone even being aware of his presence. He flushed and watched as the water swirled in the bowl and disappeared. How he wished he could flush away these past six years. For that matter flush himself out of this house, out of this city and home to Chicago!

He came out of the bathroom, held his head with both hands and as he ran them through his hair, commanded, "Think, Max! Think! Maybe that's why you sensed you had to come here first. There's no way you can get to that judge with those cops so close. Abort now! Don't panic! You got into this house without anyone knowing, and you can get out the same way. Then, be on your way home with no one being the wiser. You can tell Mama and Pop that you delayed coming home, because you needed a few days to sort out your emotions."

Max had been pacing back and forth in the room as he spoke. Suddenly he felt emotionally drained and physically exhausted. He spied the walk-in closet and stepped in to explore. It was covered in plush carpet. The owner of the house used the closet to store extra bedding and pillows.

He had an overwhelming urge to lay down and grab a little shut-eye... fifteen, thirty minutes at the most. He glanced at his watch 3:30 p.m. and bit his lip racked with indecision.

Perhaps it was the fresh air and hike, the tension of the break-in, coupled with the anticipation of his long planned meeting with Walters, who knows what clouded his reasoning. In the end, Max chose to sleep rather than escape.

He had convinced himself, that whoever the lady of this house was, her extensive wardrobe would adequately conceal him. He was also certain that he would only sleep until 4 p.m. and have ample time to leave before the owners occupied their dwelling.

Well, he slept alright, but more than a few winks. He awoke startled and a bit disoriented when he heard an automatic garage door opening.

"Good Lord, it's well past 2 a.m.! Have I slept that long?"

Fortunately for Max, the closet door had been left ajar. The light went on in the room. He saw nylon sock feet and trouser clad legs stride past the door. Their owner was humming a familiar tune.

"But what was it?"

He knew it but could not 'name that tune.' The legs moved across to the far side of the room. There Max could glimpse the whole person. It was the young red head he'd seen earlier in the photos. And then he remembered the name of the tune 'Amazing Grace'.

He sucked in his breath and whispered "Is she ever!"

Chapter Eight

Kaye took off her jacket and draped it over the chair. The big red lights of the clock on the bed side table were like a flaming arrow to her heart: 2:21! She closed her eyes, biting her lower lip.

"Dear God," she whispered quietly, "please, please don't let that phone ring again to night."

She sat down on the edge of the bed feeling totally drained. Slowly she turned and slid to her knees, with her hands clasped in front as she buried her head on the bed.

"Dear Jesus," she murmured, "You tell me to be anxious about nothing, but to give you all my concerns. I've never been so afraid before, that threatening, disturbing voice... How am I to handle it?'

"Jesus, I do believe your promise to never leave or forsake me. I do believe, Holy Spirit, that you are with me and I do pray for your wisdom to know what to do. Dearest Jesus, please rescue me from this enemy I cannot see. Lord, I feel so vulnerable. I have no idea who this assailant is or why he's doing this. I have never heard such horrid vulgar words before! I cannot fathom how one can even think those thoughts, let alone speak them."

As tears trickled down her face, sighs and sniffles intermingled, she was totally oblivious to the two eyes intrusively staring at her, from within the closet.

Reaching over to the night stand, Kaye opened the drawer taking out 'The Book,' as her father had affectionately referred to his Bible. She sat back on the bed and opened the cover. 'To R.K., with deepest gratitude to God for you, my darling husband. Love Mary'. Kaye's hand gently caressed those words as the memories of her parents flooded her mind. She remembered sitting on her father's lap, snuggling against his chest, listening to his wonderful Irish brogue as he read from the sacred Word. She could almost see Mummy sitting across from them, eyes sparkling with joy as she looked at her two prized possessions, her husband and daughter.

A smile flitted across Kaye's face. She took a deep breath. She could hear her father say, *"Kaye, never forget, they that wait upon the Lord shall renew their strength; they shall run and not be weary. Trust in the Lord; his arm is always able to save!"*

She began to turn the well worn pages, and her eyes fell on Psalm 23. Once again, she was a little girl in her mind's eye. She loved animals, loved the country, so she readily identified with the image of Jesus as the good shepherd. A smile crept across her face, she was the little lamb in his arms.

The eyes of the one in the closet widened. Absent-mindedly, he ran his tongue over his lips, mesmerized by her smile.

Ignorant of the reaction she had provoked in her concealed house guest, Kaye quietly read *"Yea, though I walk through the valley of the shadow of death, I will fear no evil for thou art with me, thy rod and thy staff will protect me."*

Max could see her lips moving but no sound seemed to spring forth. There just seemed to be a serenity shining forth from her face. Suddenly a cloud of darkness fell over his own countenance. This young woman had evoked in him the memory of his mother. It pierced his heart. How she would have suffered in his absence.

His jaw tightened, *"No mercy given to her when her son was ripped away from her! So much for a just legal system. It worked as long as you weren't Sicilian."*

71

Pain and anger swirled in his heart so consuming him that he almost missed the young woman rising, taking off her slacks and heading for the washroom.

He sat back against the wall, struggling with the emotions that raged within him. He half expected someone else to enter the room. Who he didn't know. *"His Honor? Perhaps this young woman was his mistress?"*

That last speculation was like a red hot poker setting ablaze any rational thoughts the man might have possessed. Consumed by his hatred of Walters, he rubbed his chin, pondering his next move.

Anger is a fascinating emotion, it stokes the body like gasoline fuels a fire. Suddenly, Max felt physically hot. The closet was stifling. He pulled off his turtleneck throwing it on top of his jacket, next came the socks.

"Like it or lump it, I'm stuck here for the night" he grumped. "If she closes the door, I'll roast."

He began positioning himself as best he could so as not to be detected, either now or in the morning. Thoughts began to enter his mind like flaming arrows; thoughts he'd never entertained before. He couldn't get that red head out of his mind. He ran his hand over his face and leaned back against the wall again. He heard the sound of an electric tooth brush.

"Beautiful or plain we're all the same," he grunted.

He heard the water running. She was showering.

A sliver of rationality sliced into his brain. "What are you doing, Carron?" he chided. "Now's your opportunity to escape! No one else is here but her. You're in the wrong house!"

But he didn't move. He remained stationary. For as quickly as the thought of fleeing had come, it left. In its wake, much more sinister ones began to capture his attention.

Almost mechanically he began to undo his belt and slide off his jeans, dumping them with the rest of his clothes. Those flaming darts had ignited something deep within him... Fanned into flames desires he never knew he had.

He felt like he was standing at the edge of a rushing river. The more he knew he should turn away, the more the raging torrent of passion beckoned him to enter.

He heard the shower door click open, heard a blow dryer start up. He began to imagine that red hair blowing in the wind. The dryer stopped. He heard her gently humming unaware of the stranger in her midst.

The next thought to strike him was *"She's mine for the taking!"*

His mouth went suddenly dry. He began to fantasize what she would look like, feel like. Yet, even then, when she finally did emerge from the bathroom, he was unprepared for what he saw.

Kaye carried a large white bath towel draped around her like a tantalizing fan. Her red hair fell softly around her face. A face whose features he'd only seen in porcelain statues – ivory complexion with hues of rose upon the cheeks, sparkling green eyes, rose bud lips and a pert little nose.

He was mesmerized. He'd never seen anyone so beautiful. Her pictures hadn't prepared him for what now stood innocently before him. Then, she dropped the towel!

Although the sound could not be heard by her, Max audibly gasped and stared. He'd never seen a naked woman before, even in magazines.

Intentionally, he'd made the choice to reject all forms of pornography, even the soft core ones, so easily found on the magazine racks. God knows, in his environment he'd had lots of opportunity! Whether it was his personal piety or his high regard for his mother, Max had never bothered to analyze his reasons. He had simply assessed such things as derogatory to women and chosen to abstain. Now he was confronted not by a picture but by a real woman.

He marveled at her curves. She reminded him of a magnificent Michelangelo sculpture he'd seen in Rome, only unlike the statue this one was soft and pliable. He longed to touch her, feel her warmth, but hesitated.

73

The next thought caught him off guard, from where it came he didn't care. It just snuck in, *"Better not touch her. She could be Walters' mistress."*

Its effect was instantaneous, he growled inwardly, *"Walters be damned! I will have her!"*

Stealthfully he removed his briefs, stood and grasped a nearby sash that hung beside him. Kaye had turned her back to the closet, set to retrieve her nightgown from beneath her pillow. Like a panther he moved in on the unsuspecting sacrificial lamb.

Kaye gasped as a hand clasped over her mouth, another hand went around her body embracing her breast. A strong leg entangled hers. She was held in a vice of flesh.

"Shut up. Say nothing. Co-operate and it will go well with you," snarled the voice. "Take the sash, put it over your eyes and tie it tight. Don't try looking back."

The hand, that grasped her breast, held a sash. Paralyzed by fear, at first she didn't see it.

The filthy threats of her 3 a.m. caller raced through her mind. *"He's here! He's in the room! Dear Jesus, help!"*

Her heart pounded ferociously within her chest. Her whole body trembled. What should she do? What could she do? Silently she prayed for wisdom.

The assailant's growl penetrated her thoughts. "I said take the damn sash and tie it tight over your eyes...NOW!"

It seemed the only thing she could do was obey. It was her only hope, resistance appeared futile. Limply she reached for the sash, and with shaking hands tied it around her eyes. The attacker's left hand tightened like a cobra around her body. The right hand had been removed from her mouth, but now she felt cold steel against her ribs. "Scream and it will be your last," he rasped in her ear.

From a deep place within her heart, scripture welled up again. 'The Lord is my light and my salvation. Who shall I fear? The Lord is the stronghold of my life; of whom shall I be afraid?" A calm washed over her soul.

Suddenly, she was thrust on her bed. A strong body forcefully pressed down on hers as he forced his lips onto hers. "Open your legs" came the hiss.

He had pinned her arms by her side. Terror stricken, she had no choice but to comply. She contemplated biting but to what avail? It would serve only to enrage him. She shuddered in alarm at what her late night phone caller had promised he would do. As repulsive as the thought of rape was to her, she knew her only hope of living, lay in the man's passions ebbing, after he had violated her.

As for Max, everything was happening so fast. Sensations and emotions he'd never even sought before surged through his body. His lips fastened on hers, moved down her neck, towards her firm breasts. His hands reached to clasp her buttocks. Suddenly, a jarring ring penetrated the entire room.

"Damn! Who could be calling her at this time of night? Walters?" That last thought was as effective in cooling his passion, as a bucket of ice water.

A string of profanity spewed from his lips as the full weight of his body collapsed upon hers. "Answer the damn phone but say nothing about me!" he spat. "Do you hear?"

Kaye let out a little gasp. Her mind had frozen. All she could think was "How can this be? How can that phone ring now? He's here in this room?" One thing she knew for certain, she wasn't imagining the presence of this man in her room. His weight upon her was suffocating.

He grabbed her shoulder roughly and began shaking her, "I said do you hear me? Answer the damn phone but say nothing about me!"

"Yes, yes," she finally managed to sob.

Carefully he placed the phone in her hand, slightly shifting his position so both he and she could listen.

"Hello..." she responded weakly.

"Why, my darling? What took you so long to 'expletive' answer my call?" The syrupy voice turned instantly venomous and did not wait for her reply. "What did you think, Sweetheart? That I'd miss my nightly call?"

Then came that hideous laugh that always sent chills into Kaye's heart. Next the customary deluge of names as the caller gave her every vulgar attribute in the book.

"That's right, my little sweetie...You learn quick. Don't hang up or I'll ..."

This was the point when he issued profane and violent threats, always followed by a quiet gentle voice. Everything was so predictable - a tirade, quiet words, an explosion of vulgarity and then a descriptive outline of what would befall her, when he deemed it time for him to act. All was punctuated, over and over again, by moments of silence, which she'd learned that she dare not interrupt.

Then followed his customary retort, "Ah, how sweet! I can hear your heavy breathing. Keep it up, Baby Doll."

Somehow, all this had to happen, before her tormentor would end the call. If she hung up prematurely...Or tried not to answer at all, he would let the phone ring and ring until she picked it up. Either that or he'd ring, disconnect, ring again and repeat the process until she grabbed the phone on the first ring. Then his threats would be all the more vitriolic. Only listening to his ranting, for as many moments as he, the caller chose, could end these nightly intrusions.

Tonight's call had followed the pattern of all the others. It ended with his signature sign-off..."Bye-bye, My Sweet... Pleasant dreams. Don't let the bogey man get you."... And as always, was accompanied by his piercing disturbed laughter.

Then click – the evening call was finished!

Max hung onto the phone as if in a death grip. This was a night he'd never planned! His eyes were wide in shock. The first thought to penetrate his cranium was, *"What a bizarre call! Wow! Where did that come from?"*

The annoying roar of the phone followed by that whiney voice, "Please hang up! Please hang up! Please hang up!" finally penetrated his brain. He dropped the receiver down with a thud, and tried desperately to rationalize what had happened – but reason was absent. The woman lay still beneath him. He could feel her breath upon his cheek. The passion that had seized him moments earlier had totally evaporated.

Slowly, his mind seemed to climb out of its stupor. "God! What have I done? I did nothing to deserve jail, now in hours I've committed two crimes – breaking and entering and," he silently groaned "attempted rape! How inexcusably stupid! Max, you idiot! How could you? " These thoughts began to swirl around in his mind like a whirlpool threatening to suck him into its vortex.

Simultaneously, shame and disbelief collided within him. He had always prided himself on his emotional self control. "Yet in seconds, in the presence of one naked woman, I succumbed to lust! Damn, if it weren't for her perverse phone call, I'd have violated her, and why?" His eyes narrowed to slits, "Spiteful revenge against Walters! Damn him! He's like an albatross around my neck. By imagining her to be his mistress, I attempt an act that makes me the rubbish I always protested I wasn't!" This time his groan was audible.

He had not been the only one frozen in time. His groan served to snap Kaye back to reality. It was as if, in those moments of his attack and the phone call, she had emotionally detached herself from her body. Now, she could feel his heart beating against her. He wasn't moving. Yet she could hear him breathing hard, feel his sweat against her skin. Stifling fear began to ooze back into her again. "What will he do next? Oh God, please protect me!" She bit her lip and tried hard not to let that rising fear consume her.

"This must be what it feels like to be run over by a Mack truck?" was the only sane thought that emerged in her chaotic struggle to regain a foothold on reason. A series of questions bobbed up and down in her mind, like a buoy on a rough sea.

"What is going on? I don't need to pinch myself. This is real! I just heard the phone go click. It did ring as usual. I have been assaulted violently in my own room, the lug is right beside me. But who is he? He's not my 3 a.m. tormentor, unless he's a ventriloquist; which I doubt very much! How did he get in my room, without me knowing? Where was he hiding? "

Deep disdain for her uninvited bed mate began to rise within her. He had attempted to violate her, of that she was certain. "That accursed 3 a.m. phone call actually saved me! For him to grab me so quickly, he must have hidden in my closet. Furthermore, there is a high probability that he entered that closet clothed." She frowned, "But what will happen now? At least I'm still alive, somehow I doubt this creep will kill me."

Yet, the thought that her home had been invaded by a rapist and not a murderer brought little comfort. However the next thought did. *"Good grief! This lug heard that caller! He did! He heard him!"* Immediately her fear evaporated, M.K. McDonald of the boardroom suddenly reappeared in the bedroom.

No longer was she disassociating. She was now seizing reality. At last, she had someone who could vindicate her. Someone else had heard this vulgar caller!

Despite her ordeal, she smiled inwardly in satisfaction, "Mr. Smartass caller didn't even know someone else was in my room listening to his tirade!"

By now, her eyes were wide open and for the first time she was aware of light. The blindfold somehow had slipped off. She turned her head and looked straight into the eyes of her assailant.

If she had not been through so much, she would have laughed, maybe she did. His eyes were as wide as hers. The two of them were simultaneously processing their next plan of action and neither was wasting any time in execution.

Max moved instinctively to find his comforter, J.D.,

which he had set on the side of the bed. However, the gun had tumbled onto the floor on the other side of the bed.

When Max dove for J.D., Kaye leapt from the bed, and dashed into the closet switching on the light as she did. She had surmised correctly...There were his clothes in a pile. She scooped them into her arms emerging triumphantly back into the bedroom to face a naked man pointing a gun at her, demanding "What the hell are you doing?" but not with near the authority he'd had only moments ago!

Chapter Nine

"Where the hell can he be?" Frank Carron said as he stared at his reflection in the mirror.

"It's days since his release. No contact whatsoever, absolutely nothing. Why did he want the cash that Lou and Bill said they gave him? Has he lost all feeling for his Mother?"

He peered into his own dark eyes. The anguish they had first revealed was quickly replaced by the anger that was starting to seethe within him.

"For God's sake, have respect for her Massimiliano!"

Frank grunted, "Yeah, have respect for her. A lot a good talking to myself, in the mirror, is going to have on you!" His eyes began to soften again. "Maybe it was me, Sophia, Pepi and Tony that shoulda had more consideration for her six years ago."

Every day for six years, he saw the anguish in Josephine's eyes over her separation from Massimiliano caused by his incarceration. He had kept her from visiting, aware that the visit would only intensify her anxiety over their son. For six years, he'd hated himself for thinking it expedient that his son be the sacrificial lamb to make peace between the Carron and Marconi families.

"It's a good thing I don't shave with a straight razor," he groaned. "I'd have slit my throat on numerous occasions."

Frank glowered at the mirror, "But damn it! How was I to know Judge MacElray would up and die of a massive coronary a week before he was scheduled to try him!"

Frank had begun to brush his teeth, he paused, toothpaste

ringing his lips. "With MacElray on the bench, I could guarantee, that with his clean slate, all Massimiliano woulda got was a scolding... Or at most probation!

He waved his tooth brush like a knife, jabbing at the mirror. "So what happens? My judge up and croaks and they appoint that newcomer prick, Walters, to try the case."

Frank spat angrily into the sink. "The bastard was only interested in making a name for himself. He didn't even look at Massimiliano's lack of convictions, or his excellent character references. Only thing Walters considered was his Sicilian ancestry, assessed him Mafioso and slapped him with a maximum sentence."

He grabbed the mouthwash and took a swig. As he swished it around, he glanced again at the mirror only to face the profound sadness he so successfully concealed from others.

Frank sighed deeply, " I promised Josephine, when we fled from Sicily to the States, that if she'd marry me, I'd provide for her every need." He spit the mouth wash out and gave a little grunt. "My mouth is now clean, but my heart is still full of grunge.'

His countenance darkened, "How was I to know Sophia would meet Tony Marconi, fall in love and marry him? Yeah, that meant it expedient his father and I desist our feud. Consequently, neither of us could afford the cops poking around to discover what actually did happen in that college motel room. So, it seemed reasonable to let the legal beagles follow through on what they thought had occurred...namely that Max had a drug deal go awry."

Frank leaned on the sink and glared at the mirror, "And you, Frank Carron, agreed because you had MacElray financially greased appropriately." Frank slapped his forehead in exasperation, "And the fink dies! So, we get Walters and Massimiliano gets six years.'

"Damn it! Josie's sole need was to have her children near her. So Sophia's in New York and God only knows where our son is!"

From Frank's perspective he'd failed his wife miserably, and that failure was his deep agony.

He slammed his fist against the wall, "Massimiliano, for the love of your mother, get home soon! A lota good venting your anger at a wall will do, Frankie," he groused.

A pleasant voice from the bedroom, interrupted his thoughts, "Frank, Dear, I put out your camel hair sport jacket and black slacks. I think your black stripped shirt would go nicely. What do you think?"

A wry smile crossed his face. "Show time, Frank! Better forget your son and get on with the business of the day."

He chuckled to himself, *"Dear Josie, she literally dresses me. Thank God! When it comes to clothes, I might as well be color blind."*

People saw him as powerful, some even feared him, while still others revered him. *"If they only knew the influence of Josephine on my life, she moderates everything!"*

He emerged from the ensuite bathroom dressed in his boxers, showered, shaved, teeth polished, all dark thoughts banished as he embraced his wife.

"Jo, without you I'd be hopeless, and I swear you just get more beautiful each day!" With an impish grin he reached down and gave her bottom a pinch.

"Oh, Frank!" she exclaimed in mock disapproval, swatting at his hand, while blushing like a bride.

He caught her hand, pulled her to him, and gave her a passionate hug and kiss. Then he whispered playfully, "The problem, My Dear, is that you make me attractive to all the ladies."

"Your job, Frank, is to remind them you're spoken for," was the quick retort.

As he strapped on his gun, she brought him his jacket and fussed until every tuck and crease had been erased.

"So, while I meet with some of my investors, what is the hostess with the mostest going to do? Are you taking the ladies shopping or going to the spa?"

She smiled pensively, "The game plan is for Al to take Lena, Sophia, Gina and Volante to the West Mall. Angel and I will organize lunch for us all."

In jest, he put his hand on his wife's forehead. "No shopping? You must be ill!"

She responded almost inaudibly, "There's just nothing I need."

"Nothing," her husband replied, "except a wayward son to show up."

"Oh, Frank, do you think he will soon?"

"I hope so, Jo. I sincerely hope so. You go have breakfast with the ladies. I'm going to have breakfast in the library with the men." Frank kissed her on the forehead and headed for his meeting.

When he opened the door, he smelled the excellent cuisine and soon forgot his earlier worries. The men were in good spirits and he quickly got caught up in their laughter. His son-in-law, Tony, was a natural born clown. Yet, he definitely was no one's fool. In fact, if a person chose to mess with him, they would be the fool.

Massimiliano had been right about one thing, Tony was the right match for Frank's impulsive, head strong daughter. The two made a handsome couple, and he mused quietly to himself, *"Produced handsome grand babies!"*

"Good Morning, Don Carron. You're looking rather dapper today."

Frank bowed and nodded. "Good morning to you Don Marconi, you New Yorkers benefit from the time change. For us it's 9 a.m....I haven't had my first cup of coffee yet. The cobwebs are still in my head. In contrast, your body says 10 a.m., and you're wide eyed and raring to go!"

Frank thought to himself, *"No wonder, Tony has such a good sense of humor. Musta got it all from you Pep, for you certainly have none!"*

Gus D'Amato, who many labeled as Frank's Lieutenant, started to laugh. "All I can say is thank God for our Nevada friends here." He cocked his head in the direction of two men seated to his right...one attired in a business suit, the other in a flashy orange golf t-shirt.

"Frank, while the Marconi's may benefit from a one hour time zone change, we're up two on them!

"Pardon me, gentlemen," the business suit retaliated, "you forget I didn't come from Nevada. I've been in board meetings most of the week in Pennsylvania. So the only one who could struggle, time wise that is, would be my good brother-in-law Vinnie. Problem is, Vin only sleeps four hours a night. Which means, you can't count on pulling the wool over his eyes."

Vinnie, was the obvious owner of the orange T. A portly, big jowled man, his focus for the moment was on the breakfast spread before them. He clearly was not interested in time zone trivia and its effect on business acuity.

While eating, the men continued to banter. Everything from casino intake, to the new baseball season's most likely World Series contenders, to potential Derby and Preakness candidates. It was open season for all topics, except for one. All discreetly avoided the "Where is Massimiliano?" question.

By 10 a.m. the breakfast dishes were cleared away. Those desiring a second cup had secured it. It was then that Frank's legal counsel, Carmen Scallion made his appearance.

All in attendance had the privilege of addressing him by his nickname, "Scaly". A privilege he did not readily grant to many. He greeted everyone as if all were his long lost brothers, helped himself to a coffee and sat down.

He dressed impeccably with the latest Italian, fashion designer clothes, drove a Ferrari. Everyone in Chicago knew he was Mr. Italy, or at least represented Mr. Italy...All Mr. Italy's!

Scaly himself rarely took court cases, though he had taken Massimiliano's, but usually it was others in his firm that went into court. Scaly considered himself an expert in business, real estate being a sub-specialty.

"So, my friends," he queried, "What's on your collective mind?"

Frank sat drumming his fingers on the conference table. Finally, with a short and gruff tone, he began. "I don't know what's on everyone else's mind. As for my own mind, it is filled with matters concerning Kayleen Enterprises Incorporated, and more specifically, its CEO, M.K. McDonald. I called this meeting because George here sits on Kayleen's board. Like you said earlier, George, you just finished meeting in Pennsylvania."

Turning to his new focal point, he clarified, "So, George, I figure you're the one who best can answer my queries."

George frowned. He looked at the other faces. They seemed equally surprised. The last thing George had anticipated at this "Family" gathering was to be grilled about Kayleen.

Nonetheless, he tried to respond in a positive manner.

"What specifically might you be interested in, Frank? If I can, I'll try to answer your questions."

Frank leaned forward his eyes riveted on George's. "I invest for a lotta Italians, many family members, if you get my drift. And, some of those funds are tied up in Kayleen."

"That's good!" George interjected, "Kayleen's interests are broad, diversified and global. It's a solid, financial institution, – a very sound firm!"

"That's reassuring," Frank sat back. His left pointing finger absent-mindedly continued to tap the table. "I'm relieved to hear it, but it's not so much the company but its CEO that I'm wondering about?"

"M.K.?" George smiled.

"Yeah, M.K.!" Frank's eyes had never left George's, and by now everyone else's eyes were on him too!

George chuckled and leaned forward, "Now, Frank, that wouldn't be because she's a she would it?"

Stereotypes of Italian men often classified them as M.C.P.'s, or Male Chauvinist Pigs. It was a label George thought, looking around the room, that might apply, *"especially for my friends here."*

He concluded that the only one who might be exempt would be Tony. George, however, was savvy enough not to reveal either his thoughts or his amusement, for Frank was dead serious, and so were the rest.

George sat back in his chair and looked at Frank, waiting for the older man to respond, which he did, choosing his words carefully. "Yes, because she is female, but also because she is only thirty-four years old. Am I correct?"

George shrugged his shoulders, "Yeah, Frank, you're correct, but this is no surprise to anyone. She was twenty-eight when her father, R.K., was killed. People never expected her to step in and manage Kayleen, but she did. In fact, her decisions have propelled Kayleen far ahead of any competitor."

The senior Marconi sat bolt upright, his mustache bristled. "Her decisions? What about the board. Don't they call the shots?" He demanded, his beady eyes boring into Cantaro.

George folded his hands on the table. He no longer had on his meek, 'I'm Vincente Lombardi's brother-in-law' hat. He was George Cantaro, Kayleen's board member. Their loyal board member and number one fan of M.K. McDonald.

"Pepi" George's voice was firm, "M.K. astutely and wisely uses her board members, every last one of us. There is global representation on the board, because Kayleen is an international player. M.K. values the opinions of others, delegates well, allows both staff and board members plenty of opportunity to be inventive, even imaginative.'

"She allows people to risk, and doesn't insist on success in every venture, because she firmly believes people can learn from failure. However, if and when that does occur, her modus operandi is to assume full responsibility for the ship. Nonetheless, the overall expectation is that Kayleen will make reasonable forward progress. Trust me, Kayleen's

CEO takes serious the Company's investors and safeguard's their interest!"

Now it was Scaly's turn, "Fine, George, but she is a she and she is thirty-four."

"Your point?" George replied cooly.

"His point," Frank interjected, "is that a 'she' looking like her attracts 'he's,' and depending upon the 'he,' it could change her perspective and her focus."

"And that doesn't occur with 'he's'?" George was totally taken aback with where they were going.

"Ah, come on! George, has she ever been laid?" Scaly retorted sarcastically.

Now it was the others' turn to be taken aback by George. The usually mild mannered George was visibly annoyed, no, visibly furious.

"What is this? I serve with integrity on Kayleen's board, which gives you business assurance of your investments. You all know that I am happily married. And, you bastards dare ask me about the personal sexual behavior of Kayleen's CEO?"

"Whoa, Man! George, you are pissed, and I can see how they did it. Frank what exactly are you getting at here? It can't be this broad's romantic interests?" the speaker was Tony and surprisingly he refocused the whole room.

"No, you are right, Tony." Frank spoke softly, and with intent to continue to diffuse the situation. "George, six months ago or so, Ms. McDonald reported receiving phone calls, in the middle of the night, from someone threatening her physically and sexually. I understand taps were put on the lines, but no calls were subsequently recorded."

"That's correct information and Kayleen made it fully public." George replied, tight lipped.

"At the time," Frank continued, "innuendos were made about both her sanity and her sexuality, is that not correct?"

"Yes, you are correct."

"So, I'm judging by your response to our questions to

you as a Kayleen board member, that Ms. McDonald has dispelled those rumors by her subsequent behavior these past six months? Is that correct?" Frank asked.

"Yes, again," George retorted.

"So, George, now that six months have passed, we all know that if there really was a perp, he could reappear. So, that is from where my questions arise."

George sighed, "Yes, Frank, and those are my concerns too. However," he looked intently at all of them, "I'm less concerned about your investments and much more concerned for the woman herself.'

"M.K. is a brilliant executive and fiercely committed to Kayleen. I know she would sacrifice for the company. She, more than anyone else, is aware how those innuendos about her sanity could adversely affect investors' confidence in Kayleen. Consequently, should the perp return, it's quite feasible that she might choose not to alert anyone.'

"That may be fine if the guy is merely a crackpot. All she looses is a little sleep and gets a bit unnerved...But should he be a sexual predator or worse a serial killer..."

He shook his head sadly, "the results will be devastating, not only for her personally but for the business world globally!"

George paused, "If you must know, I broached this topic with M.K. the other day. I urged her to take very serious any resumption of those phone calls."

Frank pursed his lips, looked at the others who were obviously still processing all they had heard.

"George, I thank you, both for the honesty and the candor with which you shared this morning. The meeting has been most productive. You have retained my confidence in Kayleen." He stood up and crossed the room to shake hands with Cantaro.

As he did so, there was a knock at the door and Josephine burst in "Frank, I must talk with you immediately...Please!'

It was not a demand. It was a plea from an obviously distraught woman. Frank took her arm and led her into the hall.

"Josie, what's wrong? Have you heard from Massimiliano?"

"No! Oh, Frank, it's horrible!"

"Jo," he cupped her face in his hands, "What is horrible?"

"Well, the lunch is all planned. I'm expecting the girls back shortly. Will the men join us?"

Before Frank could respond, she continued, "Frank, you must be there. I simply can not do this lunch without your presence!"

Frank could just about handle any situation except the one that now faced him. He knew his wife was about to burst into tears.

"Jo, I'll be there, all the men will be there, but what has you so upset?" He took her in his arms just as the tears began to flow.

"Louisa just called. She's fifteen minutes away. She's coming for lunch!"

"Louisa!" Frank closed his eyes and breathed a sigh of resignation as he hugged his wife.

"Josie, don't fret. I'll be there. The other men will be there." He kissed his wife and said, "Now, go finish your preparations." With a voice of authority, he stated, "I'm quite sure, the whole family will be able to cope with Louisa."

Josephine headed down the hall, and missed his additional comment. As he returned to the men, he added under his breath, "I hope..."

"Did she hear from Max? Is everything alright?" Tony asked anxiously.

"No, she did not hear from Max! And, No, everything is not alright!" Frank grumped. "Louisa will be here for lunch."

"Sheesh, she's like a shark smelling blood. Max is not even here and she's on the prowl," Vinni blurted.

George just stared wide-eyed. He'd never seen these men so animated, at least not in this way. He tried to decipher the emotion. It was not like the exhilaration they'd exhibit at a sport event, particularly if their bet was favorable. Nor was it the anger they'd manifest at unwanted competition on their perceived turfs. It wasn't even the emotion they'd express during the deliberate weighing out of risks in a business venture such as had just happened.

Yet with one word, *"Louisa,"* the whole atmosphere of the room had been transformed. It was obvious, it had rattled these macho, Italian gents, but to George's ears Louisa sure sounded female. Finally he could contain his curiosity no longer.

"Who or what is Louisa?"

"She's my departed mother's last living sister," grumbled Vinni. "She's also Josephine's departed father's second cousin, twice removed

"And," interjected Pepi, "Louisa is my eldest sister!"

George was incredulous, "How old is she?"

"Ninety-four," sighed Pepi.

George started to laugh, "Well looking at the six of you, I thought you were referring to the grim reaper."

"She is!" Tony said glumly. "Her prey is single, Italian guys."

"Her sole agenda in life appears to be matching all wanna' be Italian mamas with whomever she can shanghai," said Pepi. "It was so when I was young and it remains so to this day. The only difference is that in the old country she'd negotiate a bride price from the girl's father and then extract a fee for her services."

"Wow!" George said, "so she matched you up with Josephine, Frank?"

"No!" glowered Pepi, "We won't go there. Let's just say Josephine spurned Louisa's endeavors."

"So, that's why even now Josephine's upset by Louisa's visit?" George asked truly perplexed by the normally very composed Mrs. C.'s earlier behavior.

"No!" retorted Frank. "Josephine is upset because Massimiliano is not here," he sighed "and, we don't know where he is. As long as no one brings him up, Josephine can pretend all's okay. However, we all know that Louisa will be coming specifically for Max."

"...To notch her match making belt with one more fallen, Italian guy." Tony gave a hollow laugh.

Frank threw his hands in the air. "You see, George, aside from Josephine rejecting Louisa's services, Louisa had nothing to do with Tony and Sophia's marriage either. So, Max remains the Carron's sole opportunity for redemption with Aunt Louisa."

"View her as a merciless bounty hunter, whose coming to cash in, and you'll understand Josephine's anguish," Tony added.

"Speaking confidently," Scaly interrupted, "since Massimiliano's name has been brought up. Does anyone have an idea why he's a no show?"

"I have none," Frank replied tersely.

"Do you think maybe six years was just a bit more than he bargained for, like I mean do you think he hates our guts?" Tony asked ruefully.

"Maxie really knew how to fire a rod." Vinni reminisced, "I remember ten years ago when you visited us in Vegas. Several of us went to the shooting range. He just peppered those targets dead center, one after another."

As he glanced nervously at his brother-in-law, George thought *"Oh, no! I'm hearing more than I want,"* but he couldn't visualize a discreet retreat.

"But," Gus stated firmly, "Massimiliano never shot any living thing! My read of Max is that revenge is not even on his radar, especially planned revenge."

"Tend to agree with you there, Gus. His energy was always focused on something positive." A smile crossed Frank's face, "Only negative thing I can remember was when he smashed the cathedral window with a baseball. Knowing him, I'm sure it was accidental."

"What about the two guys who took him his stuff? He'd

asked for a fairly large sum of money, you said. Could they have rubbed him out and simply told you he went south? Maybe we need to pressure them?" Vinni offered.

"Now, that would really piss Max off!" Frank replied. "He views Bill and Lou as his men, and Max is very loyal to what he feels needs looking after."

Gus laughed, "Yes, and Bill and Lou may be seen by the cops as questionable, but trust me, neither are capable of much more than perhaps carrying a bet to a bookie. Also they are extremely loyal to Max. They took turns visiting him. They've moped about missing him, and both were extremely excited about his release - even marked the days off on their kitchen calendar. They're very distraught over his failure to return home, and trust me it's not feigned."

"Well, gentlemen, there is the door bell, which means it's to your battle stations you must go to rescue the ladies from Louisa. As for me, it's time I got back to my law practice." With that remark, Scaly bowed and exited.

"Coward!" Tony yelled after him. "Okay men, be brave! The time has come to introduce George to Aunt Louisa. George, be grateful that you're already married!"

Chapter Ten

Kaye had the weirdest thought cross her mind as she stood in her bedroom nude. Her only covering was her assailant's clothes that she now grasped in front of her. Holding the clothes of this stranger who stood before her, she remembered old Professor Dugan who had taught her "Oral Communication". It was the one point in all his lectures that she had never forgotten.

"Ladies and gentlemen," he had begun in his exaggerated speech. "REEmember when you ah..dress others in the bo..red room or aah...deetorium, YOU need to BEE in controlah. Loouk aht them intently und imagen them eitha in thara under..wara or nuu..dah!" The class had roared as Professor Dugan continued, 'La..afe if you weel but if youah do it NO aahdeeance weel ever inteeme..date youa!"

That advice had served her well. Propelled into the administrative role as a result of her father's untimely death, Kaye knew both her gender and age were handicaps. Authority in the boardroom was essential for her very survival. She had ample need and opportunity to both practice and master Dugan's words.

The still small voice within her whispered, "This is that Kaye. This is survival time! Step up to the plate."

Imagination was not necessary, her antagonist was in the buff, with a gun pointed at her heart. Cocking her head to one side, she stared at her adversary, feigning profound interest. Slowly she moved her eyes to lock onto his.

"Mmm" she smirked, "not bad."

It was working, firmness was in her voice. Control was settling in, and he broke the gaze. He was aware for the first time, it seemed of his own nakedness. Grabbing a pillow, he held it strategically in front of him.

"Oh my!" Kaye thought, *"Casanova appears a tad embarrassed. Good!"*

Emphatically she said, "You heard him!" She then raised her voice as if to overcome her own disbelief "YOU HEARD HIM!"

Max's mouth was dry, *"What on earth had he done? What had propelled him into this compromised position? This must be what a treed coon feels with hounds barking below and a hunter's flashlight in your face, a gun pointed at your head. Gun? Yes, gun! I have the gun, and she doesn't!"*

Trying to sound as fierce as he could, he demanded gruffly, "Give me my clothes."

"No!" came the authoritative voice. "You heard him!"

Max was stunned, *"Damn, I'm cold, feeling extremely stupid and this dame just keeps repeating herself. Maybe she's in shock; that must be it. Maybe she'll respond better if I tone it down a bit."*

He tried faking a laugh, "Yeah, if you mean your friend on the phone, I heard him. He didn't sound too nice, but hey, if you like his calls fine. So how about being nice and giving me my clothes and you can take your calls personally, without someone like me butting in. Trust me! I won't tell anyone!" He was trying very hard to use his most sophisticated and dignified voice.

"NO!" came the emphatic reply, "You heard him! Don't you get it idiot! I don't know that caller. He phones me at the same time, every night, with his filthy perverted talk which just keeps getting worse. Now I finally have someone else who has heard him...at last!"

Max was stunned, "You mean you figure I...um...I am your witness?"

"Absolutely!" was the affirmative reply.

"Look Lady, I am not a cop!"

"Really? I wonder why that information doesn't surprise me," said Kaye rolling her eyes.

This conversation was moving way beyond Max's comprehension level. He wished that somewhere near there would be a button marked 'eject' that he could push and escape. His mind was rushing, searching for some positive out...He tried to keep his cool, but his eyes betrayed him. Kaye saw the little furrow on his brow.

Panic, on his part, was now beginning to settle in, *"Damn, I've never bargained in my life, but if I don't start soon, I'll drown!"* In the most rational, calm voice he could muster, given his circumstances, he said, "Okay, Lady, if you don't want this guy bothering you why don't you just call the police? Now, that you know I heard him, you know for certain that he's real. Also, both of us agree he doesn't sound very nice. The cops can tap your line, trace his calls and nab him. No more worries for you, it's really quite simple," he added offering his most charming smile.

Her green eyes bored into his. He no longer felt like a treed coon, more like a deer about to be devoured by a ferocious lion.

Through clenched teeth, she said, "You really are a moron! Do you honestly believe that I couldn't think of that? Let alone try it?" Kaye was long past the intimidation point. This guy's patronizing manner was really beginning to irk her, not to mention what she had already endured physically from him.

Now it was his turn to stumble. "You did? What happened?"

"No calls, not a one! Very unflattering rumors about my sanity, even about suggested sexual neurosis, began to circulate behind my back."

"Wow! Have I ever been ticking this doll off and she is totally ignoring my requests for my clothes. Maybe it's time to get tough, end this stalemate that's going nowhere,

95

except to make us both cold."

So again, Max spoke up as gruffly as he could, "Look, Lady, perhaps you haven't noticed, I have a gun, a loaded gun," he inserted for emphasis, "You don't. So, give me my clothes NOW!"

"No!" came the firm reply, "You are my witness!"

"Well, a hell of a witness I'll be for you! You think anybody is going to listen?" Now, it was Max's turn to get angry.

Mocking a cop, he asked "Well, Sir, and where did you hear this phone call?"

"Oh, in her bedroom, Sir."

"And, what time was that?"

"About 3 a.m., Officer."

"And, what were you doing in her bedroom at 3a.m.?"

"Well you see, Officer, I broke into her house, wandered up to her closet, and fell asleep. She came in around 2:30 a.m. turned on the lights and woke me. Then she had the audacity to get ready for bed, which meant she disrobed, unaware of my leering eyes. As you can appreciate, Officer, the view was just too great for my testosterone driven body. So I attacked her, blindfolded her, and was about to ravish her when her phone rings. Well, naturally, Officer, I figure it could be a legit call and I did not want anyone to be distressed because the fair damsel did not answer her phone at this late hour. So, I made her pick it up. That is when we both heard this pervert threatening her sexually, and physically, with most gruesome details."

By now, Max was most agitated "Lady, do you not grasp what an unreliable witness you have? You call me an idiot and a moron, what do you think you are? Now I'm asking you nicely one more time, give me my clothes!"

"No!" came the reply, even more determined than ever. "Everything you said is true. But, my dear Sir, you are all I have. Your clothes are not what you need. You have three options, Sir."

The "Sir" was not very reverently spoken. She held up

her hand with the forefinger pointing upward.

"Let me lay those options out for you. First...yes, you do have the gun and you can shoot me, adding murder to your other crimes. You can hope you won't get caught. Few are so lucky. But should you do so, you've put innocent blood on your hands. Somehow, I don't think even you wish to do that.'

"Second option," up went her second finger, "you can overpower me. You did it once, but this time I will put up a fight. I remind you, the first time you caught me not only unaware, I thought you were that caller. Now, I know you aren't! Furthermore for your information I have taken martial arts training," she said, fully utilizing this opportunity to add an emphasis. "However, looking at your fitness level," Kaye simply continued, nonchalantly, "I suspect you can get your clothes by force."

Did she detect she had elicited a blush?

"But, if you don't kill me, I assure you I will report you. You will face those two charges you said earlier that you committed and you will face a long prison term."

A third finger now joined the other two. "Or, there is your third option, Sir. Even though, we have referred to each other as mentally incompetent, I suspect that your intellect and mine combined, will be sufficient to expose the asshole who is making those calls. I want him stopped! I cannot do it myself, I know that." Now Kaye's voice was softening, "I promise you, if you are willing to partner with me in this venture, what you stated you did to me will never be mentioned. In other words we both go free, me from this predator, you from any fear of criminal charges. So, Sir," the term was now being used with some air of respect, "You make the call, or come up with a forth proposal, I have not thought of, to put before me."

Max sucked in his breath, *"Wow! This dame is good,"* he admitted to himself.

Absent-mindedly, he waved his gun, "So, if I choose your 'Option 3', what happens? Do I get my clothes?"

"Is Option #3 your choice, Sir?"

"Well, I'd kind of like to know how option 3 works," was the defensive retort.

"That, Sir, is what we begin to negotiate," and with that Kaye darted out of the room.

It caught him totally off guard. "Whoa! Wait! Where the hell are you going?"

He charged into the hall after her. Seeing a light down the hall he raced to that room.

"Here put this on." She threw him his briefs and held out a luxurious men's bathrobe.

"Whose is this?"

"Given your state of undress, does it really matter?" came her sarcastic response.

Max couldn't help himself, he blushed at her retort. "Touche," he said softly.

His remark pacified Kaye. "If you must know, it's my father's."

"He lives here?" The alarm in Max's voice was obvious.

"No," Kaye said, as she bit her lip, "he is dead."

"Sorry," Max nodded as he put on the robe, hoping he'd appropriately acknowledged her sharing.

Not only was he inexperienced in relating with women, his relationship with this one had begun in the worst possible way. However, by now he had concluded that with this female, even if a guy had started off on the right foot, any relationship with her could be very rocky, to say the least. Nonetheless, he genuinely wanted to pursue her Option #3, as #1 and 2 were not particularly appealing and he couldn't think of an Option #4.

"What about my socks and shoes, or slippers, or something?"

"Good heavens," she frowned, "you are a woos! Try these on."

She tossed him a pair of handmade men's slippers her mother had knit for her father, shortly before their accident. Then she turned and started back down the hall, the remainder of his clothes in her hands.

"Lady!"

She turned around and glared at him. He was standing there staring at the ceiling.

"Now, what?" she snapped.

"Maybe, you should put on one too?" was all he said.

Kaye's mouth dropped, *"Oh, my!"* she thought, *"I actually did this dangerous negotiation with this violent man with nothing on! Not bad, M.K., not bad at all!"* A faint smile crossed her lips.

Quietly, she whispered, *"Thank you, Holy Spirit, for bringing Professor Dugan to mind."*

Turning to the stranger, she replied "Absolutely right! Pardon me a moment."

She slipped quickly back into her bedroom and grabbed her Pooh Bear pajamas and housecoat, hoping her attire would prove anything but alluring to her new house guest.

"Yep, that's definitely better" Max said raising an eyebrow as she reappeared. *"What guy wants to sleep with a dame dressed like his kid sister?"* He thought to himself.

Turning to her he queried, "So, Ms. Planner, now what?"

"You look hungry. Let's talk over the table." She headed for the kitchen, Max following like a puppy dog. As she turned on the lights, she invited, "Look in the fridge. Take what you want."

She slipped into the laundry room, as he began rummaging through the fridge.

"Man, this doll's pretty intuitive," he thought to himself. "I really am hungry and a roast beef sandwich looks rather appealing to me now." He grabbed the mustard, horseradish, snaffled the pickle jar. He was a man on a mission and he'd totally forgotten her, until he heard a machine. He whirled around almost knocking her over. "What's that?"

She smiled sweetly, "The washing machine."

"It's four in the morning! What are you washing?"

"Your clothes."

"My clothes," he yelped, "they don't need washing!"

"It won't hurt them and let's just say, it will help you to better solidify Option #3 in your mind!"

His brown eyes glared at her. In return she gave that lilting little laugh and winsome smile that melted many hearts far more rigid than his. "How about I make us a delicious cup of white hot chocolate to sweeten Option #3?"

"So, General, do you have a game plan?" Max asked munching on his sandwich.

She shook her head, "Other than us listening together to a few more of his calls, no I don't. We need to think of a way we can make you a credible witness."

Max's heart sank, he didn't have the gumption to tell her that hell would have to freeze over before that could happen, given his relationship with her neighbor Judge Walters.

"But," he thought, *"perhaps I can help her force this perp's hand. Then I wouldn't have to be anyone's witness. In fact, would it ever be justice if his Honor was the perp!"*

Now, that last thought truly warmed Max's heart. However, as a result of the sandwich, hot chocolate and his endeavors in the early morning, Max suddenly realized he was very tired. He looked at her and she appeared sleepy too. "I really need to get some sleep. I'm exhausted." He yawned.

Eyeing her carefully, he hesitated to put forth his next suggestion. Eventually, Max put his elbow on the table, and leaned forward, his chin resting on his hand. Although, dubious of the reaction his request would unleash, he decided to risk..."*After all, nothing ventured, nothing gained,"* he reasoned.

Max cleared his throat and tentatively asked, "If we're going to be Option#3 partners can I know your name?"

She glared at him and snapped, "My name is Kaye, and yours?"

"Max," he sighed.

Kaye turned out the kitchen lights and in silence started back up the stairs, Max trailing behind. When they arrived at her bedroom door, she pointed down the hall to the room where she'd retrieved the housecoat.

"You can sleep there. The bathroom's right beside it."

"NO!" was his abrupt reply.

"NO?" she said startled. She wheeled around her green eyes flashing, with the realization that this intruder actually intended to sleep in her bedroom.

"Certainly not! How dare you think you can waltz in here and sleep with me, that is not part of Option #3!" She was fuming. "You broke into my home, then attacked me, which Sir, I am willing to forgive, if you help rid me of that caller. Do you think I'm that much of an idiot that I'd let you get close to me again? I'm willing to strike a deal with you, a business deal and nothing more! Absolutely, nothing more!"

Now, it was Max' turn to be unbending. "Sweetheart, it's not romancing you I got in mind. I have chosen your Option#3, which means I need you alive not dead! It's the only way you can verify that my presence here is your idea. You have no concept who that perp is. However, he succeeded in humiliating you six months ago when you sought police help. The fact that he has resumed his calls, suggests he could be a very real threat to you."

Max now was on familiar turf and not about to back down. "If I'm down there." He said pointing to the other bedroom, "Your caller could come in here and slit your throat, just like he told you he would. I wouldn't even hear him. I'd wake up the next morning to find a bloody corpse in your bed, and guess who would be suspect #1. Me!!! No thank you!'

"You gave me Option #1, which I rejected. I'm not going to be nailed for murder. You want me to stick with your Option#3, Doll? Then I sleep here!"

With that, he brushed past her into the bedroom, and before she could respond he was standing in the middle of her king sized bed.

"Look, Honey, see this line?" With his finger, he drew an imaginary line down the middle of the bed from the head board to the foot.

Kaye just stood there, wide-eyed.

Max continued, "Which side is yours? You pick. Then you stay on that side, and I'll stay on mine. We cross once a night, when that perp phones. We listen together. Otherwise, I won't touch you. You don't touch me. Agreed?"

He hopped off the bed and stood in front of her, arms folded across his chest. "Well? Is it a deal? If so, shake on it!" He extended his hand.

Kaye couldn't believe what he had just said. He was asking her to cohabit. As if reading her mind he said gallantly, "Hey, Kaye, it's a plutonic relationship. It's temporary. We got a good reason for it, and we won't be the first or the last to live this way."

Now his face was stern. "I'm not messing here, Kaye. I'm into your Option #3, but only if I really am in a position to protect you. Otherwise, I might as well take Option #2. I'm not going to let anyone railroad me into a nasty murder rap."

Max stepped forward grabbing her by the shoulders. "Look me in the eye. I don't know if you've been with another guy or not but this was my first attempt at sex."

"Oh, how nice! I'm the first one you've tried to rape. This is going to reassure me?"

Max's jaw tensed. "Cut the smartass, Kaye! You know what I meant. I'm not blaming you. I take full responsibility for my actions. All I'm saying is I didn't expect to see you..."

"Naked" she interjected.

"Right."

"Well, I didn't know you were there."

"I realize that, but now we know we're in the same house. So, from here on, neither of us will compromise the other. Correct?" Max asked.

Kaye nodded numbly. His words far exceeded, how she had envisioned her plan unfolding.

"Well, the main thing I'm promising you is, that I won't ever take advantage of you. I'll help you nail this perp, but you need to cut me some slack to do it. Deal?"

Now, it was Kaye's turn to furrow her brow, but what popped out of her mouth caught even her off guard. "Do you snore?"

Max's jaw dropped, incredulous of what she had just said. "What? I don't know, do you?" He rolled his eyes, a smile stole fleetingly across his face. "Okay, Kaye, the one other circumstance we can touch each other is if we snore. We grant each other permission to belt the snorer. Okay?"

"Fine," she replied weakly, at last extending her hand, "Deal!"

"By the way, do you have a spare tooth brush? Necessities you know."

She gave him one, plus tooth paste, plus towel and wash cloth. She was done arguing.

Fatigue and shock had set in. She quickly readied herself for bed and fell in exhausted.

As she lay in the darkness, she silently prayed, *"Oh, Lord Jesus, please protect me. Is he your answer to my prayer for help?"* She shuddered and continued, *"Or, is he an angel of darkness masquerading as your light?"*

She ended her prayer with the Word of God that she had clung so strongly to over the past several days. *"The Lord is my light and my salvation. Who shall I fear? The Lord is the stronghold of my life? Of whom shall I be afraid."*

Max collapsed on the opposite side of the bed, totally spent. He lay still, stunned by what he would have done had that phone not rung.

"God, lust controlled me! How did that happen?" Questions paraded through his mind. *"Who is this woman? How could she excuse what I tried to do to her? How can she just forgive me? Let me go free? Given how I treated her...like an object.'*

"Can I trust her deal? Was it just a ruse to buy her time to get help? But who was on that phone? What was the guy wanting? What will the final outcome be, especially for me, as I play out this drama?" At last, sleep mercifully stilled the raging torrent of his thoughts.

Chapter 11

Jack leaned across the table and looked intently into his wife's eyes. "Hon, there's something I need to tell you."

Marnie's blue eyes twinkled as she glanced at their longtime friends and neighbors, Dave and Sue Davidson, seated with them. "Jack Walters, don't you know confessing an affair is supposed to be done privately?"

"What am I going to do with you?" Jack sighed, "I'm trying to be serious and you turn everything into a joke. Dave, tell her this is serious!"

"This is serious, Marn," Dave said using his official police voice.

"Really?" interjected Sue, "then how come you haven't told me anything, Dave?"

"That's what we're trying to do, Dear, but as so often happens, communication between Mars and Venus goes askew," he replied.

"Okay," the two women said in unison, as each leaned toward their husband, "brief us, please!"

Then they looked at each other and started to giggle. "Look guys, we have a credibility issue here. Perhaps you have forgotten but we booked this beautiful Pocono retreat weeks ago, as a romantic interlude for each couple? It's supposed to be a fresh Spring Break week. Now you two want us to 'BE SERIOUS'!" Sue used an exaggerated deep voice for the last two words.

"That's right," Marnie chimed in, "So, gentlemen, get real!"

Jack took off his glasses and rubbed the bridge of his

nose between his left thumb and forefinger. "Look, girls, I know we promised not to discuss business with you on this trip. However, Agent Epstein saw me just before I left Washington and insisted I alert you to a potential problem."

Marnie looked at her husband of nearly twenty five years and frowned. "Jack, you are serious?

"Yes."

"You make it sound so ominous," Sue replied, all laughter now totally gone.

"We're not saying that it is, Hon. It's just that an ounce of prevention is worth a pound of cure." Dave remarked as he took a folded paper out of his breast pocket, opening it in front of the two women.

A close cropped, dark haired, dark complexioned man, around thirty years of age stared back at them. Below the photo was a name, Massimiliano Carron, age 28, indicted for drug trafficking, sentenced to New York State Penitentiary. Both the date of incarceration...six years ago, and the release date were given...."

"Nearly two weeks ago," murmured Marnie, "but what does that have to do with us?"

"I sentenced him," Jack stated tersely.

"Well, Dear, that is what you do, isn't it? Yet, we've never been given an alert before and many of those you did sentence will have been released. So, why is this one different?"

"Marnie, he's of Italian origin, Sicilian actually," Dave volunteered.

"You mean he's Mafia?" exclaimed Sue, her eyes widening.

"Well, not exactly," Dave hemmed and hawed, "It's sort of yes and no."

"How can that be?" Marnie asked. "I thought you were or you weren't."

Dave sighed. "There are some grey areas, Girls, and the Carrons fit into that category. Except for this one conviction of the son, there are no other indictments of the father or any of his so called staff. Frank, this guy's father," Dave jabbed at the photo "has managed to stay squeaky clean. He's an investor, a wise investor, let's say shrewd investor and to date a legit investor. The majority of his clientele are Italian and several of those are Sicilian, some with definite Mafia connections."

"Epi told me," Jack continued, "that Carron's daughter lives in New York City. She just obtained a law degree and has begun articling with the city's Legal Aid Department. She married Antonio Marconi about the time I sent her brother to jail. They have three children, two girls, four-year-old twins and a two year old boy. The Marconis also fall into the grey area, but his father, Giuseppe is definitely a darker grey than the Carrons."

"But I don't understand," protested Marnie. "You have dealt with known Mafia cases in the past, Jack and yet we've never been given an alert before. Why now?"

"Well, Ladies," Jack smiled at his wife, "this was the first case I tried after my appointment to the bench."

Marnie had an instant flashback. "This is the one where the old judge, who was supposed to hear the case, died suddenly just before the trial?"

"That one!" Jack said, and the look on his wife's face told him she was having full recall. Did he detect anger mounting up in his sweet wife's demeanor?

"The one they all insisted you take, as the 'new kid on the block'?" Marnie's eyes were certainly not twinkling now. "Even though they had promised that if you accepted the judicial appointment it would not interfere with our family holiday?"

"Oh, yes," Jack thought, *"This memory is indeed invoking the wrath it produced six years ago."* He nodded and said, "Yes, Dear, this is that case."

As for Sue and Dave, they had ceased all participation in the current dialogue, totally amazed at the character transformation they were now witnessing in their otherwise, normally unflappable neighbor.

"The one you said you had to accept! Even though it meant breaking your promise, to me and the girls, to take the entire month off so the family could have that Mediterranean cruise and vacation we'd planned?"

"Your instant recall is 100% so far, Hon! So, I promised you that the case would not drag on. I'd be able to wrap it up in a week or less, and we'd get our time together as promised. It would just be a week or two later than we planned...And we did, didn't we?"

"Yes, that promise was kept, except I had to do everything, by myself, to have us ready while you were off hearing the case." Marnie grumped.

"Well, to keep that promise to you, I was a tad brutal to young Mr. Carron."

"What do you mean?" Marnie's expression was puzzled.

"Carron had elected trial by judge not jury. Justice Hall and old Wilkerson, in conning me into taking the case, told me these Italian Mafia type kids figured they could get away with just about anything. They said, that in those guys' world, for them a year in the pen was seen as a badge of honor.'

"So, I listened to those two seasoned justices. They told me that the ethnic lawyers, these punks' families hired, would always whine about their client's young age, no previous conviction, yada yada. As a result, the sentence was always lenient. Therefore, it was like a slap with a wet noodle. Consequently, it served little or no deterrent to criminal activity within the Italian Community."

"So, you decided, in advance, to throw the book at young Carron?" Sue interrupted.

"Yep! Wilkerson and Hall assured me that the Mafia types, of all ethnic persuasions, would realize that I was a judge who played hardball. As a result they'd try and stay clear of my court. Quite frankly, I thought that desirable. Personally, I was interested in hearing cases that truly challenged me, rather than ones where high paid lawyers tried to manipulate the intent of the law."

"As well," Dave added, "by taking their advice in Carron's case, you'd get home quicker, and would be in a position to fulfill your promise to Marnie."

"Exactly," Jack said, "so that's precisely what I did. It was obvious the prosecutor was out to get a conviction for self-advancement purpose. The defense, in my opinion, seemed a little too laid back. I figured that it was because I was a new guy on the block and he figured I'd be a push over. That thought, I'll admit, sort of torqued me a bit.'

"Carron himself seemed a little too good to be true. Dressed like a young gentleman, "No,Sir, - Yes, Sir." In my mind, he fit exactly the mould Wilkerson and Hall had described. Guilty was a no brainer verdict."

"So, what's the problem, Jack?" Marnie asked, "I don't understand."

Dave spoke up, "The problem, Marn, is that Carron was released about two weeks ago, supposedly heading to his family in Chicago. But, so far he has not arrived."

Sue sat back in the restaurant bench and scowled, concern etched across her face. She stared at her husband, hands on her hips. "What I think I hear you saying, Dave, is that Epi thinks this man," she paused to point at the mug shot, "might seek revenge against Jack?"

"That is a possibility, Sue." Jack murmured chewing on the stem of his glasses. " At this stage though Epi doesn't want us to be overly alarmed, just aware of that eventuality."

Dave leaned back, clasping his hands behind his head, "Epi's being proactive. This allows everyone in Summerside, associated with either Jack or Marnie, the opportunity to recognize the man should he arrive in our city. So, we can pick him up before anyone gets hurt, including Mr. Carron.'

"Speaking of being proactive, Marnie," Dave continued, "to be on the safe side, I'd like to speak to your teaching staff. I don't want any spiteful, wacko attack on our school kids."

"Of course, Dave, you'll have my school's full co-operation." Marnie was clearly becoming alarmed. " But what about our daughters and what about Kaye? Our neighborhood is so isolated!"

Jack reached over and put his arm around his wife drawing her close. "Remember, Hon, our small group meets at our house a few days after we return from this holiday. Kaye will be there. We will alert her then. Epi's making sure Crissy and Tiffany are informed." He gave her a gentle squeeze and kissed her cheek. "Everything will be fine, Marnie. Don't worry!"

Sue looked at her friend. "Marn, you're really troubled by all this aren't you?"

"I guess I knew that this sort of thing could happen because of Jack's work. I suspect you face the same possibility because of Dave's? It's just that while you know it could happen, you never think it will." Marnie said quietly.

"Well, Girls, if it's any consolation to you, the leading cause of death in this country is not lead poisoning but heart disease," Jack quipped.

"I know, Jack," Marnie sighed, "but still it moves us out of the illusion of being a quote 'normal upper middle class family,' doesn't it? However," she added, "there is one good thing I can see in all of this."

"What on earth can that be?" Sue inquired.

"It gives me an inkling of what Kaye must have felt, six months ago, with those terrifying anonymous phone calls. It's not really the intruder that occupies your mind is it? It really is fear itself!"

"Marnie, you're right," Dave acknowledged, "and the one thing all of us need to remember is that sometimes the M.O. of those types of perpetrators is to abruptly stop the calls for several months. Their victim reports the initial calls, but when no more are received, the victim feels foolish. Often others question the victim's sanity. All of this further humiliates the person. As a result, when the calls resume, the victim is too intimidated to notify the police."

"Dave, do you really think Kaye's calls could resume?"

"They may, Sue. Each of us needs to pay close attention to Kaye for any indication that they have."

"Surely," Jack asserted "you do expect Kaye to tell us if they do?"

"Not really, Jack." Dave said shaking his head. "Kaye, more than most people, has to publicly ensure that she is both mentally and emotionally stable. Instability in either area would have major ramifications for Kayleen."

Jack sat pensive for a few moments, finally he spoke. "Everything we've said is all very true. It seems our idyllic life at Independence Drive suddenly is starting to resemble a T.V. crime show. However," he paused and smiled confidently, "there's something we can do which they'll never show on T.V."

Dave laughed, "Right on, Jack! Let's go to our cabin and lay all this before our heavenly CEO. Afterwards, Ladies, are you interested in putting on your hiking boots and trying to make it to Bridal Falls? Just enjoying the beauty of God's creation on this sunny, spring day may help settle all our nerves."

Chapter Twelve

Max stirred and stretched, pulling the cover over his head to block out the shaft of light that threatened to prod him out of bed.

"Not yet, Ol' Buddy," he mumbled, his mind fogged by a haze of sleep. "What a dream I had!" he chuckled to himself. "Must be getting time for me to start noticing the gals? Dreamt of this gorgeous doll, actually tried to lay her."

Flipping over on his stomach, he brushed his hand against a cloth. One eye pried open and peered under the pillow – pajamas, Pooh Bear PJ's, neatly folded, lay there. Max sat bolt upright, eyes wide, mouth dry. Everything that shouldn't have been familiar was!

"What? This can't be! I have to be dreaming!"

He pinched himself and let out a yelp. "Definitely felt that!"

Max rubbed his eyes, and took a second look. "Oh God, it wasn't a dream!"

The memory of the previous night crashed upon him like a violent tsunami. He felt himself drowning in his own stupidity.

"Wait! The red head! What the heck was her name? Day? No! No! Kaye...Yes, Kaye! That was it."

Furtively his eyes searched the room, "Where the hell is she?" He let out a groan, "Idiot! While you slept, she turned you in!"

He grabbed J.D. and leapt for the bathroom door. No girl... But there, smack dab in the middle of the mirror, was a large sticky tab – "Note of instruction on top of pillow, beside yours."

He tore for the bed. "Damn! She'll have called the cops, break and entry, with weapon, attempted rape! Oh Hell, Max! You are useless!"

Then he spied the note. It had fallen to the floor.

Don't forget our late night agreement! I hid your pants and shoes in case you did. Gone to pick up some clothes for you. One set of underwear just isn't going to cut it in my house! I'm picking up deodorant, tooth paste, shaving cream, etc.,etc..

THIS IS NOT A HALF WAY HOUSE FOR BUMS!

I'll expect you to look and smell respectable. I also expect you to pull your weight. So start by cooking some pancakes for breakfast. The coffee maker is ready to be turned on.

P.S.- Left at 8 should be back by 9:30, we can eat by 10a.m. Glad you had a good sleep.

Max sat dumbfounded, staring at the note. "Who the heck does this broad think she is? 'I'll expect you to look and smell respectable.' Lady, you are really pushing the limit! No wonder you've had no boyfriends!"

He was fuming, pacing the floor, gun in hand. What he wouldn't give for a shooting range right now!

"God, this not fair! Everything bad happens to me! Always...no matter how hard I try to help others, I keep getting shat upon. Okay, yeah, last night I screwed up."

He paused a moment in his ranting to ponder what had occurred. "Yeah," he sighed, "I did screw up big time!"

He resumed his pacing, while waving his gun in the air, pointing it upwards. "Why does everything bad have to happen to me? Tell me! Isn't it time I got a break? Just one!"

The sound of his own voice, yelling at top volume, startled him. "Cripes, I'm losing it. I'm actually screaming at God and pointing a gun at God! Maybe the routine task of making pancakes might be a therapeutic thing to do? So, Step One, Max, put on the housecoat and J.D., you'll fit nicely in the pocket."

As Max headed for the kitchen, he passed the laundry room. There was his shirt, neatly folded but no pants or shoes.

"Damn, she doesn't fool around!" On the kitchen counter, he found the pancake mix, *'Note: eggs in fridge'* The bowl, measuring cup, griddle all sat there.

"Oh, this is unreal!" He rolled his eyes heavenward, "God, why does she have to be such an organizational freak?"

Nonetheless, he managed to pull it all together, got the pancakes going and turned on the coffee maker. The aroma of coffee and pancakes had a quieting effect on him. He heard the garage door open, and quickly slipped behind the laundry room door, gun in hand. The door from the garage opened and in marched the "dictator", Wal-Mart bags in tow.

"Max, grow up!" was her only retort as she passed by him.

Now, that remark was inflammatory and he let her know it! After all, for all he knew, she could have changed her mind and notified the cops.

She sat down on the swivel chair, at the kitchen island, leaned her elbow on the counter, raising her forearm she placed her chin on her hand and glared at him.

"I made a deal with you last night. I keep my word. I also told you that I'm not interested in your crime and punishment. I want," she paused, "No! Need! that annoying phone bully stopped! I will stop at nothing to do it, even if it means having to share my bed with you!"

She glowered, "I happen to be sore from last night thanks to you. I had only a few hours sleep, and I've been up for three hours without eating. I get cranky when my blood sugar levels get low. So may we eat?"

Max had many choice words with which to respond, but one look at her made him choose otherwise. Saying nothing he pulled the pancakes from the warming oven, let her serve herself and then took his share. As he reached for the maple syrup, he heard a loud "Ahem!"

"Now what?" he snapped.

"In this house, we say grace before we eat."

He had words he could have said to that too. Instead he just sat back and folded his hands on the counter. She began to pray softly, thanking God for the food and the hands that prepared it. *"Hey"* Max thought to himself, *"for once I get a favorable mention,"* and even though he'd never admit it, it actually felt good.

After they ate, he helped her clean up the dishes, all the while listening to her instructions as to 'how to'. Especially how to use the dishwasher, rinse first, prolongs the life of the appliance!

Then she took him upstairs, to reveal the purchases she'd made for him. Secretly he'd been afraid that she'd purchase clothes that would mock him, make a fool of him, but no, they were respectful. He had to admit even smart, as best one could expect from Wal-Mart. Had a pair of slippers for him too.

She turned and started to say "Now..."

"Oh boy, more instructions!" Max thought, *"She just doesn't quit!"*

But this time, he did listen. She had a plan that actually was wise. Her closet would be his closet too. They moved in a small chest of drawers from another room and put it at the very back of the closet. He could keep his things there, she would hang hers in front. A camouflage, in case anyone was in her house, which she informed him happened frequently, although she didn't elaborate further.

Over the next few days Max found himself following her around like a lost puppy. She had said she had work that she could do from her office at home. She'd spend most of the day in there at her computer. At his insistence she'd leave the door open so he could see her. For his part he busied himself making their meals and in between analyzing her security system.

He was becoming increasingly troubled by those late night calls. As she had said promptly at 3a.m. the phone rang and with it came the now predictable vulgar tirade. She, on the other hand, seemed more confident.

The reason, Max sensed, was simply because now she had another with whom she could share her burden. One who knew her problem was real. However that, he was well aware from his prison research, was no reason for confidence. It was one thing to know a problem was real, quite another to solve that problem. He had begun mentally to work on the solution.

He'd noticed no activity at her neighbors' homes and had commented on it. She simply said they were away on a joint holiday for a week to ten days, depending on the weather.

Matt was in Philly attending a three week course. She never elaborated on who Matt was and Max chose not to ask.

For the most part, Kaye acted as if he were not there. This in itself didn't bother Max. In many ways, it seemed a normal experience. In prison, you were treated as a nonentity and around his father he had never felt accepted as one of the guys. But one thing did gnaw at him and finally, one day at breakfast, he found both an opening to raise his question and the courage to do so.

"Kaye, can I ask you something?"

She nodded. "Sure, what is it?"

Max cleared his throat, "I don't understand your behavior." Before she could interrupt, he quickly continued, "rape is a serious offence, and its impact is particularly difficult for the victim."

"Your point?" she said coolly.

"Well, you said you are a virgin."

"So?"

"So, I attacked you and if your phone hadn't rung I would have raped you. Yet you act almost like what I did, how I treated you, never happened."

"And that somehow upsets your virile masculinity?" she snapped sarcastically.

Max stood up abruptly and shouted, "No, that's not it! I want to know why you treat such a crime as nothing. Yes, I said a crime."

He growled "You treat as nothing a crime against women? So much so, that you're prepared to treat me, as if it never happened."

Kaye's eyes were now steel green, her jaw firm, "Very well, Max, sit down and I'll try and answer you."

Folding her arms, across her chest, she continued, "Although, if you haven't got it now, after listening for over a week to those calls, I'm not certain you will be able to understand." He sat back down, and listened, desperate to understand.

In a firm and unwavering voice, she began , " I, like most women I suspect, would view sexual intercourse as an intimate act they would want to share lovingly with one who mutually loved them. Rape is neither loving nor mutual intimacy. Furthermore, I hold to a Biblical view of intercourse, namely that it is intended to be between one man and one woman in a committed relationship."

"In a relationship, they mutually enter into for better or for worse," Max added somberly.

She was about to snap at him for asking her to explain and then interrupting. However, one look at the man's face convinced her otherwise. Instead she simply nodded and answered, "Correct. So, a rapist steals that intimacy. The woman is not allowed to choose who she wishes to share herself with. In the case of a virgin..."

"The first time gift is forever lost." Max swallowed hard, and in a soft, sad voice said, "That's what I don't understand. If it weren't for that phone call, I'd have robbed you of your gift. Yet, you appear to dismiss that potential loss."

Kaye shuddered and took a deep breath. A tear appeared in the corner of her eye.

"Max, I need you to look me in the eye." It was not a demand. It was a very gentle request. He obliged for now he was even more desperate to understand this seeming enigma before him.

She began, "Max, there are losses and there are losses. A loss is very personal. Each person needs to weigh out both their actual loss and the potential loss. If that person on the end of the phone is not a crank, but is for real. I'd rather be in a room with you than with him. Even if he is just a crack-pot, he is violating me far worse than you. I need him stopped.'

"I can't do it alone and I know now I can not go public. So, you provide me a very viable option. Also, while I don't know why you broke in, and I can't be sure you won't do that again to some one else, my need, at the moment, outweighs any future public need.'

"Furthermore, I don't think you will attempt to rape anyone else again." Kaye sighed, "Is my explanation, as to why I was willing to offer Option #3, any assistance to you?"

"Yeah," Max nodded, "It helps a lot and I'll do my best to help you bring down that perp. But, Kaye, how were you able to do that option thing so coolly that night?"

"Agh" she retorted, "Do you think you'll get me sharing all my secrets?" She stood up, but this time he noted the green eyes were twinkling.

She cocked her head at him and laughed, "Tell you what, Max. When we actually get that perp, as you call him, I might share my secret."

She headed for the front door to retrieve the paper, calling out, "Meet me in the living room, we can share it."

Max wasn't sure exactly what had transpired, but somehow he felt better about their relationship. He sensed she did too.

Paper in hand, as they sat down, she asked if he'd like to read a section. He responded affirmatively.

"Would you like the sports page?" Kaye offered.

"Maybe later, really I'd like to read the business section first, if you don't mind." He'd figured that would be one section he wouldn't be competing with her. He missed the look on her face as he took his section.

"Do you follow the stocks?" Kaye asked inquisitively.

"I used to but I haven't been in a position to do so for a few years. I had invested fairly heavily with a company called Kayleen. You probably never heard of it?"

"Actually I have." She responded dryly.

Max was so busy getting into the paper, he was oblivious to the disbelief registering on Kaye's face. Finding Kayleen, he was pleasantly surprised to find it doing well, very well indeed. "Wow! At least I wasn't stupid there," he blurted out loud before catching himself.

"I'm sorry. I didn't hear what you said?" Kaye tried to sound ignorant.

"Oh, nothing...I was just talking to myself." Max muttered.

He looked at her and for the first time noticed that she seemed genuinely interested in what he was doing. Encouraged, he set the paper down and began to explain. "When I was younger, I read up and studied a guy by the name of R.K. McDonald, you know, his business practices, investment concepts and such. I was impressed so I invested in Kayleen stock."

"Really?" Kaye responded eyes wide open at his revelation.

"Yeah," Max went on, "couple of years later I had to put everything on hold. About that time this R.K. guy was killed in a plane crash."

Kaye was watching him intently, *"Was he trying to snow her, manipulate her, what was he up to?"*

As for Max, all that registered with him was that for the first time, in a very long while, another person was actually paying attention to what he was saying, interested in what he thought.

It felt good. He wondered if perhaps he was now starting to experience God's blessings, like she'd prayed for when she said the grace at the meals he'd prepared. Thus he continued, "Anyway, what I heard was, after R.K. McDonald died, Kayleen's board was under the directorship of his daughter. That really worried me."

"You don't say. Why?" Kaye asked, knowing full well she was not going to be amused by his response.

Now, had Max been paying close attention, he may have

detected a chill in the room.

Instead, he honestly believed her 'why' was a genuine question. Which of course he felt obliged to answer. "Why? Well, she was a doll. I mean, I like girls, you're okay, but let's face it very, very few have good business sense. This one would have been like high bred, society raised, you know parties, debutante ball stuff, not too helpful to run a global company like Kayleen."

Max had interpreted her silence as sincere interest in what he was saying. Instead, Kaye was at a total loss for words, rare indeed for her! All that came to her mind was *"He is so dumb! A complete M.C.P.! I never imagined any male, his age, would be so blatantly and naively chauvinistic!"*

"Anyway," Max continued, "it looks like what I hoped would happen did."

"And what was that?" Kaye was almost afraid to ask.

"Well, I figured the doll would probably be a figure head. I mean, if she had any looks at all, it would be good P.R. Yet the board would be the real decision makers. They'd have been handpicked guys that R.K. would have selected."

"That's a very interesting theory." Kaye managed to spit out, all the while thinking.

"Mister, it's good you have your gun, because if I had it, you don't know how tempting it would be for me to shoot you dead."

She got up to go to her computer. Then she took a second look. *"He really has no concept, how offensive what he just said is to me."* She hoped the sarcasm she felt didn't show as she tried to suggest he enjoy the rest of the paper.

Max however, was now very talkative, since she had neither shut him up nor intimidated him. "Kaye, I'd really like to know how my stocks are doing."

"Well, Max, just go online to Kayleen and ask. I'm sure you have a password."

"I have, but I can't do that, Kaye."

"Why not?" He was now stretching her patience.

"I promised to help you, Kaye. I really want to, but if I go into Kayleen, people can trace it to the computer of origin. That would compromise what you want to do. I don't want to do that. I really want to fulfill the agreement we made. Particularly after what you most recently shared, it's really important for me to help you!"

Kaye studied the man. He was as much an enigma to her as she was to him. Could it be that this guy really was a genuine, sincere schmuck?

She laughed, not in a put down way, but in a way meant to relieve him. "Max, do you really think anybody would actually take the trouble to try and chase you down?"

Max furrowed his brow, "Yeah, Kaye, they would, friend and foe alike." He just gave a sigh, "Well, I've waited six years, what's another few months?"

She looked at him, "Perhaps, I can help you?"

"How?" He got up to come to her.

"Sit down, where you are." She meant it as a command and he took it that way.

"How can you help?"

She immediately accessed her personal files, simply saying, "I do work for Kayleen"

"You do? You go into people's personal files?" Max was shocked.

"Need your last name."

"Carron"

"Spelling, Max?"

"C-a-r-r-o-n"

"Birth date"

Max began rattling off all the data she needed. He even remembered his old phone number. Then to his amazement, she gave him his address and other pertinent data.

"Okay, come here now. Enter your password." She turned her head away, saying "I'm not looking.

Then suddenly it was on the screen, for both parties to be amazed. He couldn't believe that she had actually retrieved it. She couldn't believe that this schmuck actually had more than a million and a half invested in her company.

Max was stunned. He just stood there grinning "Wow! They did okay, didn't they? I had about eight or nine-hundred thousand. Now, I got more than a million and a half! I actually did something right." He looked at Kaye, "That's what it says doesn't it?"

"That's what it says, Max."

"It is the real thing, right?"

She pursed her lips and nodded. "It is indeed," and queried, "You done looking?"

"Yeah, thanks, but how did you do that? How can you get into private files like that?"

Looking him square in the eye, holding her left hand behind her back, fingers crossed and with feet crossed, she said aloud, " Okay Max, the truth is I hacked in."

Silently she prayed, *"Jesus, forgive me for lying. I just don't think now is the time to divulge the whole truth."*

Max's mouth gaped open, "Damn, Kaye, this changes everything."

"What?" Now it was her turn to be shocked.

"I mean if you are a hacker, you could have ..." Max looked astounded, "you could have unknown enemies. God only knows who."

Kaye suddenly grasped what Max was getting at, "I see what you mean, Max. But this is true. I only did it this one time for you!"

She thought to herself, *"Somehow I'm not sure he bought that?"*

Chapter Thirteen

As Kaye came into the kitchen from her study, Max glanced up from the table where he was working. "Do you know of any good hardware and electrical stores in a neighboring town? I need to go and pick up some stuff. I've pretty much calculated what we need. Got it all sketched out," he said proudly holding up a pad of paper.

"What type of 'stuff' are we looking for?" Kaye inquired.

"Very fine electrical wire, a small transformer that will allow us to plug into an ordinary, electrical outlet and drastically reduce the voltage, batteries and both a light and pulsating sensor alarm. Kaye, it's now been over two weeks that this perp has called every night at exactly 3 a.m., with those flagrant sexual innuendos. In my opinion the vulgarity and violence is escalating. If this guy really is a sexual predator, he could move on you and we would be sitting ducks."

Kaye smiled patronizingly, "Max, what are you talking about? I've got a security alarm system in place. Surely, that will serve us better than any make shift system we'd design?"

"Have you forgotten so soon, Kaye, that I got in through your impregnable barrier?"

"Of course, I always shut it off when I come in, and then, re-arm it when I go to bed."

"Kaye, I did not come into your house after you. I was here before you arrived!"

A slight frown crossed her face, "Did I forget to arm it when I left in the morning?"

Max cocked an eye, "No, it was armed when I entered."

This information caught her totally off guard. Pulling up a chair she sat down opposite Max, obviously trying to process what he had just said. "But, if you broke in with the alarm activated, the system would have been compromised. I should have been notified of a breech."

"There was no compromise. I deceived the system." He replied matter-of-factly.

"You can do that?"

"Yes, and so can anyone familiar with alarm systems. Anyone, who is technologically savvy, is capable of breaking in, while not allowing your system to recognize that it has been compromised. Exactly as I did!"

Kaye's face registered the shock she was experiencing. "Then, what good are these alarm systems anyway?"

Max shrugged his shoulders, "They're adequate deterrents, as well as protection against common break and entry. However, if some one is a professional, with criminal intent, I'm afraid you're out of luck."

This revelation exploded like a bomb. "You're telling me you are a professional criminal?" Kaye gasped.

Max rolled his eyes. "That's not what I said. If you want me to help you, Kaye, you need to start trusting me. Let me show you what I was working on. I've diagramed all lower levels of the house thus far." He laid out his sketches for her to see. "These red lines are where I'll position the wires."

"You're putting everything on the inside of the rooms?"

"Correct."

"Why?"

"It's a double-security system. Your expensive alarm system takes care of the outer perimeter. If the guy simply cuts that system, the central security will be alerted and the response chain initiated. You'll be fine, but if he knows those systems, he will be sure to enter without compromising it."

"So that's when your secondary system will alert us?" Kaye queried.

"Right," Max grinned, "he won't suspect you have a secondary system because their use is very rare. Likewise, what I'm designing will, in essence, be hidden. I want to set it up so both a light and a vibration alerts us."

"No sound?"

"Definitely no sound, Kaye!"

"Why?"

Max looked at her in disbelief. "Kaye, we're doing this to catch the bastard, not to give him a warning so he can abort and try again?"

"Well, I suppose I could ask around to see where we could go to get what you need."

Max's jaw dropped open. "No you can't!" Before she could open her mouth he continued, "Kaye, get real! You have not a clue who this perp is. The only male you know it isn't, is me. Why? Because I can't lie next to you and speak on the phone at the same time."

He paused, "Well, I suppose it is feasible. A guy could set up a timed phone call, except your calls first began over six months ago, and I can assure you, I was not in a position to call."

"Why not?"

Max leaned back, and clasped his hands behind his head, "That I'll tell you, should our relationship become more stable. In the meantime, you'll just have to trust that I am the least likely candidate for your perp." He frowned, "But, Kaye, every other male, friend or foe, whether known well by you or on the periphery of your life, must be suspect!"

Max reached across the table and took her hand. "Don't you see? If that person got wind that you had someone working with you, they'd stop just as they did when police taps were established. Sweetheart, as much as I like your charming hospitality, I have no intention of spending more than a few weeks babysitting you."

"Babysitting me?" Kaye fairly spluttered. "Excuse me! I thought we had a business arrangement. I refuse to finger you for criminal activities, in exchange for your help in ridding me of this unwanted attention. So, Mr. Max, how many weeks would your misdemeanors bring?"

Max looked at her, cocked his head, eyes twinkling, "Ms. Kaye, you are almost attractive when you're torqued, and think you're holding the highest trump."

Not to be out done, she squinted at him, "Well, Mr. Max, it occurred to me that when you rolled your eyes under your glasses, you almost looked the part of a scholarly gentleman. Please note, the operative word is 'almost!' "

"So, now that you have had the last word, when can we go and where?" he asked.

Kaye mentally tried to remember her appointments. "How about Saturday? I could drive down to Oakton. It's about an hour and a half drive. We could check the phone book, even call ahead to save time."

"I prefer we go at night, Kaye. What about Friday?"

"No can do."

Now, it was his turn to ask, "Why not?"

"If you must know, my small group meets this Friday," she replied.

"Your what?" Max asked.

"My small group, it's my neighbors and six other long-time friends from church. We're all busy people, but once a month we meet to check in with each other and pray for one another. We share how the Holy Spirit's been working in our lives, quite often highlighting a Biblical passage that's proved meaningful to us."

Max looked like a deer caught in the headlights. "You're a religious freak?" he squeaked.

Kaye glared at him, "What? I'm a religious freak, because I believe that Jesus is alive and delights to guide and direct my life to bless others?"

Her green eyes flashed as she spoke. All his life, he had been taught that green means to 'go' and red means to 'stop'. Regardless, intuitively Max knew, *Not in this case!*

He began back peddling immediately. He put his right hand up and placed his left over top of it, hoping she'd recognize the 'time out' signal. "Look, I didn't mean to insult you. It's just, well you know, you seemed to me..." he groped for the right words both to express what he meant and to appease her. "It's just that you seemed rather intelligent and..."

Kaye was standing, hand on hips, glowering, "You think everyone who takes Jesus seriously, has to be emotionally unstable?"

"Well, no, not exactly. I guess I thought they'd be more like a hippie-type, rather than like a rational business person which you seem to be." He sincerely hoped that somehow he was diffusing the situation.

"Well, do you believe in Jesus?" she huffed

Max ran his hand through his hair perplexed at the question. "What do you mean by that?"

It was Kaye's turn to roll her eyes. "Do you believe Jesus was God's Son, who lived on earth in human form and willingly gave his life for us by dying on the cross?" She asked.

"Of course I believe that!" he exclaimed.

"Do you believe Jesus rose from the dead?"

"Yeah"

"Why?"

"Why?" he parroted.

"Yes, why do you believe all that you have just said you believe?"

Now, it was Max's turn to get a little hot under the collar. "Because I went to a good Catholic School and was taught it. I even was an altar boy and sang in the boys' choir."

"Was that when you were a kid?"

Max looked her square in the eye and started to laugh, "Kaye, do I look like an altar boy to you now?"

She didn't return his frivolity. "That's my point, Max. You are an adult. How does an adult live out the faith that you've just confessed you believe?"

"I don't know," he was trying his best to be honest. At the same time, he hoped this wouldn't be yet one more put down.

"Well, Max, for me and my friends, we enjoy reading the Bible. I try to do it daily. Can't always, but I try. I find the stories fascinating. Not just the stories themselves, but seeking how a particular story intersects with my own life. Now, I am a baptized Christian..."

Max could clearly see Kaye was passionate about this topic and for some strange reason he yearned to be included. She had just given him an opening and he leapt in, "So am I."

Kaye smiled, "Well, then you have Holy Spirit living in you."

"Holy Spirit?"

"Yes! God the Father, God the Son, God the Holy Spirit, one God relating to us as three persons."

"You mean the Holy Ghost?"

"Holy Spirit, Holy Ghost, same Dude, Max. The role of the Holy Spirit is to teach Christians about the things of Jesus." Kaye was now speaking passionately, eyes sparkling.

His forehead wrinkled, "Things of Jesus?" he queried.

"Yes, like the meaning of a particular passage of scripture and its implication to my life."

Max gave a resigned sigh. "Okay, Kaye, I confess I'm not real knowledgeable about the Christian faith. I can see that you take the things of faith quite seriously. My mother does too. I guess it's just not a guy thing."

She was set to refute his comments, but thought better of it. For the moment, it appeared more prudent to remain silent. Surely a better time would arise, to more fully share her faith?

For the first time, Kaye felt inwardly excited about having this man come into her life. *"Dear Lord, I can see how he might be an answer to my prayer, after all. Not to protect me from this annoying caller, but so I can share you with him!"*

So lost in her own thoughts, she suddenly realized that he had been talking to her about something she had failed to hear. Not wishing to reveal her inattentiveness, she opted for one of her board room tactics. Cocking her head to one side, she feigned a most pensive look, hoping he'd receive it as a positive response.

"I see," she said. "So, then how do you suggest we proceed?"

It worked. Max was delighted with her reply. *"It usually does,"* she mused to herself.

He began to pepper her with a volley of questions. "Well, assuming you do go to your meeting tomorrow night... Where is it?... When do you leave?... When do you get home?"

Max beamed triumphantly, "You see, Kaye, while you were working in your study, I've been refitting your car. I've got it pretty well set up so that I can ride in the trunk and still have a good view of you in the front seat." For clarification he added, "Just in case anyone should try and jump you."

She was about to lambaste him for tampering with her car, but felt a check on her tongue. Instead she found herself gently laughing. "Good plan, my wonderful avenger, but you need have no fear. I'm walking. We meet at my neighbors, the Walters' home, at 7 p.m.." She pointed to the large, Cape Cod house situated, to the left, on the other side of the cul-de-sac.

"Yep," Max thought *"that is indeed the Walters'. Doesn't surprise me that his wife would be in a prayer group! She'd need to be if the prick's as inconsiderate of her as he is to those he's paid to 'judge fairly', like me."* But he kept his bitterness to himself.

To Kaye, he said, "So, if you go over at 6:45 p.m., it will still be daylight. When you go, put your house lights on, and make sure, when you come home they have their lights on. I'll keep an eye on that area to ensure you get home okay."

Kaye looked at him in utter disbelief. This character was obsessing over her. She couldn't help thinking, *"Pity whoever marries him. He's bound to be a very possessive husband. The sooner we can resolve this caller thing, the sooner he can be on his way."*

She thought of her parents. *"Why even as their only and most loved child, after I entered high school they'd never require an accounting of my every whereabouts. Mummy and Daddy trusted me, and even with all their wealth, they never were paranoid about me being harmed. Instead, they always prayed for me and trusted explicitly in God's provision."*

She shook her head sadly, and mused, *"Max and I are truly from two radically different worlds. That's for sure! God, he's been here going on three weeks. Can you end it soon, please?"*

"Kaye, hello" Max was waving his hand in front of her. "Hello, have you heard anything I said?"

"Oh, no!" She grimaced, *"I've been daydreaming again! Please, Holy Spirit, help me with my answer!"*

"Yes, yes, Max, I was just considering the options." Once again, fingers were crossed behind her back.

"Yeah, well the more I think about it, going out late Saturday morning, might be best. We'd get to your Oakton around noon. Crowds usually thin out over the lunch hour. We could have our purchases made and be back here by mid to late afternoon."

"Yes, Max, I agree. I was actually thinking the very same thing. It is a good plan and leaving late morning won't rush me."

Max smiled in satisfaction, at last, it looked like something concrete was about to happen. It appeared he'd even managed to placate her, for how long he wasn't sure. *"Might as well celebrate the little victories,"* he thought.

"So" he asked, "what time would you like supper tonight, and what do you want to eat?"

"Aim for 6 p.m., I have some reports from work to complete. After supper I'll need a couple of hours to prepare for tomorrow night's study. As for food, surprise me!"

"Surprise it is!' Max laughed "Cuisine Italiano."

Kaye headed for the study. Max seemed to be enjoying his presence here. For her it was becoming more and more oppressive. She enjoyed her private time. Her work required considerable interaction with people. At times, she found that draining. In fact, the past couple of weeks were unusual. To be able to remain at home, working on these four large projects, while opportune, given the circumstances, was not normal. Next week she'd have to get back into the office.

"I wonder how that will sit with him, given his concern over tomorrow night?" She groused, "Personally, Max, I think you're going way over board. He probably has watched too many TV crime shows." She pouted. "It really was good to just come home; answer to no one. Eat when I wanted."

Half out loud she said, "You know, Lord, I've just realized I enjoy being single. Mummy always wanted me to marry, so as not to be lonely, she would say. But Holy Spirit, with you in my life, I don't feel alone, ever. Nonetheless, I thank you for this stranger. I even thank you for these horrid phone calls, because they prompted me to be open to keeping this guy around...and boy has that ever shown me how much I love my freedom!'

"Anyway, please give me Jesus' wisdom to know how to respond to these last two queries from the board. Show me how I must prepare for tomorrow night's small group meeting. And, please God, put a guard on my mouth that your will is done through me. Amen."

Before supper, Kaye pulled out her father's Bible and turned to Romans, Chapter 8, verse 28. A faint smile lighted on her face,

"I do love you Lord, and I am called according to your purpose." Her office felt bathed in peace. "So, I can trust you to work all things out for the good of your kingdom!" She sighed, "I needed to be reminded of your promise! Thank you for the prompt."

Chapter Fourteen

Jack snatched a sandwich at the delicatessen and raced for the 5:30 commuter train to Summerside. "Barely made it, Old Boy!" he gasped collapsing into his seat. "It's time you re-visited the gym." As the train lurched forward, he began collecting his thoughts.

Marnie had let him know everyone would be in attendance tonight. "Thank goodness I managed to connect with Dave," he sighed.

Knowing either Dave or Matt could pick him up at the station, reassured him that he'd get home in time and avoid the ire of his wife. That thought brought a smile to his face, as he thought of his petite and usually mild-mannered wife. "But when she's planning meals," he chuckled "she's like a Marine sergeant."

Their small group had taken a break in April. Everybody had been so busy with Easter events, family gatherings and then the four of them, he, Marnie, Dave and Sue, had taken that spring retreat in the Pocono's. Now everyone was eager to gather again and get in another few meetings before the summer.

He shook his head, "Well, Holy Spirit, as I look back on my life, I have to admit you've done a major overhaul on Jack Walters!" A wry smile appeared on his face as he said, "Truly the guys and gals in our small group really have become family, my brothers and sisters in the Lord. I miss their prayers, their God-given wisdom, and yes, their sense of humor, but most of all," he furrowed his brow, "their unconditional love."

He pulled out his pocket Bible and began to read from Psalm 133. *"How good it is when brothers and sisters live in unity ... there the Lord bestows his blessing."*

"Lord, you have indeed blessed me! Given me wisdom, insight, and down right revelation in some of the most difficult judicial decisions I've had to make. You have given me favor with so many, many people; peers, superiors, family, friends - even grudging respect from the citizens who have not benefited from my courtroom decisions."

He sat watching the countryside flash by, listening to the train clicking and clacking down the tracks. That's when his late afternoon conversation with Agent Epstein sprang to mind. It was all surreal. Epi's concern about that missing felon that he had sent to prison six years ago... seemed so Hollywood. Jokingly he had suggested to Epi that maybe he was watching too much T.V.! Still, Epi had persisted and even insisted that Jack give another mug shot to Dave.

"Sheesh! As if one photocopy wasn't sufficient, Ep gives me a dozen! Insists I show them, give them...whatever..." he shrugged his shoulders, "to my friends. He said that it would ensure Summerside kept its eyes peeled for the guy."

Jack yanked his briefcase onto his lap and opened it, glancing one more time at the photos. "Well, Mr. Carron," he snorted, "I trust you have more sense than to waste your life taking on a Supreme Court Justice? You will lose, my Dear Sir! You will lose!"

Jack grew somber, "Then again you were trafficking in drugs, so who knows? Perhaps Epi's right, we should take this seriously." Jack closed his eyes pondering the power of greed that would drive a man to care so little for others that he'd traffic in drugs. He looked again at the photo, a sense of disgust welling up inside. "What a waste, Mr. Carron! What a waste!"

He couldn't help wondering however, why there had been no appeal. He had actually believed from what Judge Wilkerson said that it would have been automatic. He vaguely recalled the man standing in court, neatly dressed, looking anything but a thug. Jack sighed and shook his head, "Outward appearances are so deceptive. The true value of a man is found in the heart, and that unfortunately, is not so easy to discern. Of one thing I am certain, if Carron is after me, obviously incarceration was of little use."

He slammed his briefcase shut as the train slowed for its next stop. "Good heavens!, This is Summerside's station!"

He grabbed his coat and briefcase in readiness to depart. Jack could see Dave waiting to pick him up. "Great! I can bounce off of him the wisdom of sharing this mug shot with our small group."

On the drive home, Jack told his friend about Epi's visit and the photograph. "I guess, Dave, if nothing else everyone could pray for the situation? That would certainly bring comfort to Marn and me. Who knows, might even help find Carron. Hopefully, he can be found alive and pursuing honest gain."

Dave grunted, "Indeed, finding him would be a relief, even if its his body. After all, that would bring closure to his family, assuming they care, and definitely relieve our concern for you!"

Two eyes stared out the upstairs' window of Kaye's house as the unmarked cruiser pulled up at the Walters. "Great!" Max grumbled, "Her two neighbors have arrived home.'

"Aren't I lucky? One's the Chief of Police and the other's His Honor! I'm so close and yet so far." He muttered. "Well, Kaye, enjoy your ladies meeting."

Kaye had entered the Walters' house just moments before the two men arrived. Max noted another car was parked at the side of the road. He hadn't seen who had been in it.

But even now, as he watched, two more vehicles pulled up. A couple got out of one car, and from the other, two men emerged. Max instantly was on the alert. "I thought this was a ladies' meeting? Could one of these guys be the phone perp harassing Kaye? Why would single men be attending a women's meeting any way?" These thoughts tumbled around inside his head.

Then, almost like he had need of a response, Max deduced that the guys must have come to hang out with the cop and judge. Their wives, for whatever reason, must have come in that other car parked by the side of the road.

Suddenly, Max became aware of a hollow deep within... He was craving male companionship. It's not that he always hung out with guys doing any particular thing. He was just used to guys being with guys! It didn't really matter whether they talked business, sports, finances, joked, told stories, played cards or chess, pool, even watched action movies together. He didn't care. He enjoyed being with guys.

He laughed softly, "Those larger, Italian gatherings, the guys just gravitated to one area. The gals headed off to another. That's why prison, over all, wasn't so trying for me. I am totally at ease with men!"

A frown flitted across his face. "What I'm not used to is being cooped up with a woman. Especially one like Kaye! The younger, unmarried ones in our Italian gatherings, would be flirting, not acting like a Marine drill sergeant!"

He drew a deep breath, as memories of his Mom and the myriad of aunts, cousins and wannabe relatives flooded his mind. "They were always talking babies, fashion, designer clothes.'

"Kaye, on the other hand, from my observation, seems uninterested in any of these women things. She hunkers down with her computer and talks on the phone, but it doesn't sound like girl chatter. She's always reading books, newspapers but not the fashion junk.'

"She grabs the stock market pages, before me. That's it!" he suddenly shouted out loud.

"That's it! That's what bugs me. She seems to do all the things I do," he furrowed his brow, "but she's not a guy."

He propped his chin on his hand as he gazed out the window. "Nope, she's definitely not a guy!" He threw himself back on the bed. "I feel like I've been sucked into the web of a Black Widow spider. I think I read once, that when the female mates with a male spider…" His eyes went wide, "Cripes! She eats him." He'd hit the nail right on the head, that was exactly what he was feeling, trapped and threatened! But how to escape?

Kaye found herself struggling emotionally, as the members of her small group gathered at the Walters. These people were like family to her. They openly confided in one another. They would encourage and correct each other with wisdom and love. However, at this moment, Kaye knew she dare not reveal the heaviness in her heart. The return of those late night calls deeply troubled her. Yet, she was painfully aware how openness on her part could generate serious misunderstanding.

Then there was the sudden arrival of this stranger. His involvement with her had been criminal. Yet somehow, she knew that not only did she need him, she trusted him. This irrational thinking only served to further unbalance her. Here was the first man she actually wanted to discuss with Marnie, Sue and the other ladies, and she simply couldn't.

She silently prayed, "Dear Lord, please don't let me do anything that gets anyone suspicious or asking questions. Help me to participate in our study even though my mind seems frozen on the quandary of those 3 a.m. calls."

The potluck meal went extremely well from Kaye's perspective. Angie and Brad were gushing about the discovery of Angie's pregnancy.

"Praise the Lord!" Kaye thought, *"all attention is on the two of you."*

Then Moiria and Todd, with a little giggle from Moiria, unveiled her new ring.

"They're like two teenagers," Kaye mused. *"Lord, you do indeed work all things to the good, just like you promise in your word!"*

She still remembered how devastated Todd had been at

the funeral of his wife of thirty years. Sharon's cancer had been one of the galloping kind. It was less than six weeks from diagnosis to death.

Everyone in both their church and the community at large were overwhelmed with grief, but none as severely as Todd. Sharon and Todd's adult children were just starting their own families and careers. For months Todd looked like a little lost kitten.

Then Moiria came to church with her cousin. She was like a crushed flower. She had worked ever so hard, on the west coast, to put her high school sweetheart through college, then med school. He finished his residency training and decided to do post-doctoral studies. All the while, promising Moiria the moment his studies were done, they'd marry and start a family. He finally graduated, ready to marry and start a family alright, but not with Moiria. Somehow, along the way he'd decided she wasn't good enough to be a medical specialist's wife, only good enough, it seemed to pay his bills.

Jack had the foresight to invite both Todd and Moiria to join his small group. Kaye smiled as she recalled how sweet it had been to watch these two wounded ones begin to heal, find laughter once more, and now this wonderful joy.

"Lord God," she thought, *"You really are the God of second chances. Indeed, true to your Word, in your time you do make all things beautiful!"* Aloud she couldn't help saying, "God is good!" The rest of the room reverberated, "All the Time!" Kaye echoed, "All the Time!" and the others chimed in, "God is good!"

Kaye glanced at Jack, he seemed unusually subdued this evening, in spite of the joy flooding into the group. He'd chosen for his discussion text 1st Thessalonians Chapter 5 verse 18: *Give thanks in all circumstances for this is God's will for you in Christ Jesus.*

"Wow, Holy Spirit," Kaye thought to herself, *"You really do inspire Jack's choices!"*

That really opened up the group's sharing. Todd began by saying that even in Sharon's sudden and shocking illness, he could thank God that she did not have to painfully linger, just wasting away.

Then Moiria responded, "When I found myself rejected, I felt so stupid for not realizing I was being used. Truthfully, at that time, had I heard the scripture Jack chose for discussion tonight, I would have believed it impossible to do. Now, however, in hindsight, I can see that I am thankful I never ended up with that jerk, nor had a child by him!"

Kaye breathed a silent sigh of relief. She knew the others would be expecting her to share something related to her parents' tragic and untimely death. So, she shared how she could give thanks; how her father had been led intuitively to prepare her to lead Kayleen Enterprises; and how his deep Christian spirituality had equipped her to know and believe she would never walk alone. Everyone nodded appreciatively.

Privately, in the depth of her own heart, she said "Thank you, Lord, that I didn't need to share the valley through which I currently walk."

When the whole group had ample opportunity to share, Jack finally spoke. "I am thankful that the Lord has given all of you as my friends. For like you, there can be ups and downs in my life. When we come to our prayer time, we'll lift all our thanksgivings to Christ, and also lay our burdens at his feet. The prayer request I have, comes as a result of a talk I've had with Special Agent Epstein this afternoon."

He then went on to share how six years ago he'd sentenced a young Sicilian American to jail for six years on drug trafficking charges. "The man," Jack continued, "was released five or six weeks ago and seems to have disappeared. Neither his family nor police seem to know where he has gone."

"Are you saying he is Mafia?" Angie said wide-eyed.

"Not per say," Dave interjected, "They are of Sicilian,

Italian descent, and while his father has never been identified as such, certainly there are extended family members who are."

"Jack, is Epi implying further that this man might be out to harm you, or our family?"

Jack intercepted the worry in his wife's voice. "Well, Marnie, that might be one possibility. Another could be that in prison he made wrong connections, who have tempted him to go further into crime. Still another is that he made enemies in prison, and they have seen fit to deal with him. Anyway, Epi gave me a mug shot, and asked that I show you his picture. Dave will also distribute it to his police force, so should any of you see this individual, you can alert the police."

Jack paused, " But I'd also like to pray for this fellow and his family. Should he be headed down a slippery slope, further into crime, that our Lord will send someone to show him God's way to live. Let's pray also that should he have run into foul play, at least his body can be found, and his family experience closure."

Everyone nodded in agreement, each adding their own "Amen."

Jack then opened his briefcase, distributing his photocopies.

Kaye froze when she saw the photo, uttering a startled gasp.

Fortunately for her Moiria was louder and much, much more vocal "Oh my, he doesn't look like Mafia. I'd never have guessed it." A sob made a surprise escape from her throat, "But then I totally missed the evil in my high school sweetheart," she sniffled.

And so the remarks went around the room until Dave began to quietly pray.

All Kaye could do was think, "Thank you, Lord, for the gift of tongues. I can appear to be reverently praying, even though you and I both know I am seething! How dare he use me to get close to Jack! Please, Jesus, don't let anyone know."

She felt like bursting into tears. Was her face flushed? Now, she had an inkling of how Moiria must have felt. She had no recall of what anyone prayed that night. The only thing on her mind was an imminent meeting and she didn't mean a 3 a.m. meeting, but one just moments away!

As the prayer time ended, Kaye pretended a yawn. Once more, she expressed her joy at both Angie and Brad's good news and Moiria and Todd's engagement. She asked Jack if she could keep a copy of the photo and then politely excused herself, murmuring that tomorrow would be a very busy day.

She wanted to sprint across the yard but willed herself to walk casually home. "I give you thanks Lord Jesus for revealing the truth to me," she managed to say through clenched teeth, hot tears flooding down her cheeks.

Max saw her leave. Carefully he studied the landscape for any sign of an intruder. He heard her open, close and lock the downstairs door. He walked to the hallway about to ask politely how the meeting went, when he saw her face. 'Rage' appeared a mild understatement.

"You! You!" words seemed to allude her. At last she spluttered, "You lied to me!" as she flung the mug shot at him.

Chapter Fifteen

Max stared at his photo. "Not particularly flattering," he ventured, "that's because they tell you not to smile."

He looked up as if he'd just offered a most profound dissertation. His intent and hope was to diffuse the situation, but one glance convinced him of his error.

Her green eyes were flashing, "You are a convicted criminal, a drug dealer, a mobster.'

"So much for 'I never did this before,'" she screamed, flinging her hand bag at him. "To think I believed you!" She turned and stormed to the kitchen.

Max's jaw tensed, his eyes darkened, as he raced after her. "I didn't!" He shouted. "For your information neither am I a drug dealer nor mobster! Just because someone gets convicted, Miss Know-It-All, doesn't necessarily mean they were guilty!"

The two squared off, one on either side of the island. She wasn't the only one furious! "Furthermore, Lady," he yelled as he pointed towards her. "May I remind you that my presence here, these past few weeks, was your idea, not mine!"

"You despicable Cad! You set me up, just to get near Jack to harm him!" Kaye shrieked as she grabbed the stainless steel salad bowl and let it fly.

Max ducked as the bowl clamored harmlessly against the floor. He felt himself go red. "You're not hearing one damn word I say! " he bellowed. "So your prick judge neighbor has you convinced that I am the worst scumbag that ever existed? Good for him! Doesn't matter what I do or say." He pounded his fist on the counter. "Your pompous ass friend never gave me a fair trial! But he's the good guy and I'm the fiend! Go ahead and believe the worst of me, every one else does!"

Max clenched his fist, stepped toward her and snarled. "Good thing you're not a guy, Doll, or I'd deck you now."

Probably, because she wasn't a guy, he missed the right hook coming his way. The slap across his face was strong and hard. His eyes watered and his jaw dropped open.

"You hit me!" he yelped.

"How dare you slander Jack!" Kaye bawled. "It's a good thing I'm not a guy or I'd pummel you. You think I'm some stupid, dumb broad that you can manipulate and do whatever you want. Playing me for a sucker, pretending to help me with that stupid caller. You most likely paid someone to make those calls? You figured correctly, that I'd be unnerved and allow you stay here so you could plan to trap Jack." She spluttered, "You are so vile!"

Max looked at her dumbfounded. "You're saying that I am behind those phone calls? Lady, this stupid sheet, tells you I was in prison when they began eight months ago." He waved his mug shot under her nose. "For your naive information, making threatening phone calls is not a privilege the slammer offers!"

"How stupid do you think I am?" She snapped, "With your Mafia connections, you could have easily set that job up."

He looked at her in disbelief, pointing his forefinger directly between her eyes, "With my Mafia connections? You, Lady, have been watching too many T.V. cop shows. Get a life!" He turned and strode upstairs to the bed room.

"Where do you think you're going?" she demanded.

"Bed!"

"What?" She flew into the room planting her self firmly in his face. "You don't actually think I'm going to keep up this charade, knowing what I know?"

"Knowing what you know?" Max glared back at her,

then scoffed, "Knowing what you don't know is more like it."

The piercing ring had Max thinking momentarily that he'd merely been in a boxing arena with Kaye. But it was not the gong ending a round that jarred them. It was the phone. He checked his watch, 3 a.m.!

"Damn! We lost track of time. It's him." He dove for the phone just as Kaye grabbed the receiver.

"You're slow tonight in picking up the phone, Slut. I don't like that!" The menacing voice yanked both back to reality. The usual barrage of filth followed as the caller provocatively began his descriptive tirade of Kaye's female anatomy.

This night, however, Kaye was having none of it. She let loose with her own tirade; the emotions pent up over the last few weeks suddenly erupted. She was so sure that she was talking to Max's accomplice, that she let this caller know in no uncertain words what she thought.

Max's eyes closed. He was straining to decipher the sounds at the other end of the line. The hair began to bristle on the back of his neck. Suddenly he heard it. His stomach turned, at last he felt certain of what they were dealing with.

There was a soft laugh at the end of the line, followed by an expletive and then.

"Damn, you're good bitch! One day, it's going to be even better in person." Click, the line went dead.

Startled, Kaye looked at the now silent receiver. Tears welled up in her eyes, as she riveted them on Max's. "You are absolutely cold-blooded. What deviant thrill did it give you to watch me listening to those perverted horrid words?" Her mouth twisted in disdain.

"You have no idea how precious Jack and his wife, Marnie, are to me. They are my family and they are good law-abiding people!" Her lip trembled, "But your Mafia family, all you know is violence. So what were you planning? To get me to trust you so unsuspectingly, I could lure them here, for you to kill them and me?"

Kaye was on a roll, she didn't pause for him to answer.

"Pretty smart, Mr. Carron, have me report threatening phone calls, then when you do kill us everyone will think it's that caller! How heartless can you be?"

Max felt like a rabbit caught in a snare. *"Lady, I have no idea what movies or sitcoms you've been watching but your reality and mine are as far apart as Venus and Mars."* Now, he thought that, but feeling discretion was the better part of valor, chose not to utter it.

Nor did he articulate his next thought. "If I was as violent as you say I am, you have provoked me enough to use my gun? A gun, you appear to have forgotten I have?"

Instead, he quietly commented, "If memory serves me correct, I wanted to leave, but somebody I know took my pants and would not give them to me so I could leave. In fact, that somebody demanded I stay, promised that if I helped her find a way of exposing this anonymous, filthy caller. She would overlook my very wrong, dare I say criminal, treatment of her.'

"So, Madam, that is why I am here and whether or not you choose to believe me is your choice. The truth, nonetheless, is that I did not need to come to your house to get to Jack Walters. As for killing him or harming him, regardless what the cops think, I've got better things to do with my life, Thank you! But I do have a question that I personally needed to ask him and that was my purpose for coming here. Furthermore, I do not know the person on the end of that phone." Max's jaw was taut as he spoke.

By now, he could care less what this woman thought of him. He noted however that her eyes had stopped flashing, in fact her gaze had seemed to drop slightly. *"What on earth was on her mind now?"* he wondered.

A chilling thought, in fact, had pierced Kaye's mind. *"What if he were telling the truth? What if he didn't know that caller? It really doesn't matter,"* she decided, *"I can't let him stay, he must go! I can't risk possible harm to either Jack or Marnie. I couldn't live with myself, if anything I did, even unwittingly, hurt them."* She bit her lip. M.K. McDonald was now back in boardroom form.

"Fine," she said, green eyes once more locking onto his, "a deal is a deal! I will consider your part fulfilled if you get out of this area. Go home! Go immediately back to Chicago. I will fulfill my part of the bargain. Namely, that I never saw you. But no games! I will make inquiries to ascertain that you indeed have arrived in Chicago."

Max shook his head. He couldn't believe what she was saying. "Kaye, I don't think you appreciate how dangerous your late night caller is to you!"

"That may or may not be so, but the one in front of me is very dangerous to my friends. I expect you to leave first thing in the morning. If you won't, Mr. Carron, then you will have a choice to make. You silence me or I turn you in, it's that simple. Now if you'll excuse me, I am very tired. I need to get ready for bed," turning abruptly she headed for the ensuite bathroom and slammed the door.

Max walked slowly down the hall to the main bathroom. Relieving himself, he turned to the washbasin, and caught his reflection in the mirror. Sadness, concern and frustration were splashed across his face. He knew what it was that he had heard tonight.

"God, why now? Why couldn't she have got that mug shot last night? Then in good conscience I could have walked away from Miss Perfect's tirade, but now? Now what?"

He began to brush - no scrub - his teeth. He glanced back in the mirror. It was hard to carry on a serious conversation with 'self' with a tooth brush and tooth paste stuck in one's mouth!

He smiled wryly and replied, "The one thing that I can agree with her 'caller' about, is that she most definitely can be a bitch! Well, Kaye, you've drawn your line; issued your ultimatum. The choice is mine you said, so I will choose!" He spit out the toothpaste, rinsed his mouth, shut off the light, and headed back down the hall.

There would be no small talk tonight. Both had said enough. He lay down on the bed and suddenly felt very, very tired. "Well, Jesus, if you are a living God, as she claims, it's time for you to show up! I lack the smarts to turn this one around," he mumbled as he drifted off to sleep.

Chapter Sixteen

George Cantaro stood gazing out the massive window that overlooked Frank Carron's prize gardens. The spring flowers were bursting forth.

"God's, amazing, technicolor, dream coat," he sighed.

The serenity of the view, however, did not match George's mental peace. His thoughts were on M.K. and try as he might, despite her assurance that *'all was well,'* intuitively he believed otherwise. "If only she would confide, I probably could help her."

"Hon," a sultry voice interrupted his musings. He smiled as he turned to find Volante standing beside him. Pecking him on the cheek, she laughingly chided, "you've got that financial wizard look about you again. Planning which new move Kayleen Enterprises should take?"

He put his arms around her, pulling her close to him. He adored his wife. His friends had freaked. In fact he had too, when he discovered the beautiful sophomore, that had stolen his heart, was the baby sister of Las Vegas' biggest casino owner. A faint smile crossed his lips, not only the biggest casino owner, but the most Italian of them all.

She'd been equally smitten by him and so had placated Mr. Italy. Over the years, the family had grudgingly come to accept him. His brother-in-law actually had applauded George's desire to become a board member of Kayleen. Vinni had promised a hands off, no interference policy and thus far had delivered. His investments in and through Kayleen were totally above board and that thought George,

"Is how it always will be!"

"Dearest," Volante's voice brought him back into the present, "today is your great opportunity to finally meet Aunt Louisa." She giggled like a school girl.

"Te," he always called her Te, right from their first meeting. "why, does everyone in your family make such a big deal over a ninety-four year old woman?"

"Oh, poor George, you're so hopelessly un-Italian! The only thing Italian is your last name."

Which happened to be very true, George's mom had hailed from Virginia, pure Anglo-Saxon stock. At twenty she'd met his Dad, a marine on his way to Nam, a whirl wind romance, quick elopement, followed by his father's deployment. Nine months later George arrived. He, along with a few faded pictures, and the medals were the lone tangible proof his mother had of that romance. His personal identity became embodied in his mother's affluent Virginian heritage. It was only as he met and married Te that he became exposed to Italian mannerisms.

"Italian in name only, you got that one right, Te!" he chuckled. "Enlighten me on Aunt Louisa so I can better grasp this missing link of my heritage."

"You poor Dear! You have no concept the power the eldest meddling sister can wield! However, the good news is that now, through me, Love, you shall indeed be informed!"

She put her arm through his and guided him into the Carron's expansive dining room. At the head of the table, did not sit Frank, but this frail-looking little white haired doll.

Apparently everyone else had genuflected before her and were now taking their seats. Josephine sat to Aunt Louisa's right with Frank next to her. On Aunt Louisa's left, sat Pepi, and beside him, Lena.

George could quickly surmise that everyone had a designated seat and that the designator, at this table, was in fact Aunt Louisa. He also noted that his brother-in-law was not his usual gregarious self. George had to admit he was a little intrigued at the power this old lady appeared to exhibit in this family. Even more so, his curiosity had been stirred to wonder why?

"So," came the shrill voice, "This is your attraction, Volante?" George suddenly felt like he was being dissected by X-ray eyes. "I understand you don't speak Italian?"

Before George could reply, Aunt Louisa had again focused on Volante.

"What ever possessed you to marry a non-Italian, Volante?" Her voice sounded incredulous and was definitely not approving.

"I'm sorry, Aunt Louisa, I didn't marry George for his pedigree," was Te's firm response.

Personally, though, George thought that she sounded a little apologetic.

"Actually, Aunt Louisa, your perception of me is not entirely correct." George surprised himself by replying so quickly on his own behalf.

"Really?" said the little old lady skeptically.

Her "really?" George laughed to himself seemed to be echoed silently by everyone else at the table.

"Volante said you were of English ancestry," blurted his sister-in-law.

George cocked an eye at his sister-in-law Gina. He could always trust her to spew out exactly what she was thinking. This time it worked to his advantage.

"Well, that's true, in part," George replied in his most officious voice. "However, I'm sure you are all aware that Emperor Vespasian in the second century had his Roman Legions well entrenched in Gaul, in the area we now know as England?" George was equally certain that none at this table either knew or cared about ancient history, unless it perchance applied to Sicily. Most likely he could even have gotten away by saying Emperor Cantaro, but he had opted to play it safe.

"So," he continued, "In Vespasian's army there was a certain General by the name of Augustus Marcus Cantaro who quite fancied a fair haired Saxon lass." George closed his eyes and shook his head sadly. "Unfortunately, Augustus Marcus never made it back to Rome. Killed in battle he was, Ma'am. But his wee son did survive. Naturally the child remained in Britain to be raised by his mother." George smiled politely, "So, as they say *"The rest is history"* or put more bluntly, my ancestral Italian heritage! That is the Cantaro side of my family." He added solemnly.

George walked over, took Aunt Louisa's hand and gallantly kissed it.

The old dowager beamed, "Well, isn't that wonderful!", as she wagged a boney finger at Volante. "I just knew you could discern Italian blood, and from a Roman General's lineage no less! Good for you, Dear, to bring this lost sheep back into the fold."

"Bull!" muttered his brother-in-law under his breath.

"Brilliant!" purred Te in his ear.

"Frank! Are you never going to give thanks to God? Otherwise, this wonderful meal your wife has prepared will go to ruin!" The tone of Aunt Louisa's voice was demanding, and clearly conveyed her disapproval of Josephine's choice of a husband.

Without a word Frank just complied. Everyone bowed their heads. Frank muttered the grace in Italian and at the mention of the Father, Son and Holy Ghost, all dutifully crossed themselves. Right on cue, Rosa and Anna appeared with the various dishes and every one began passing the platters and bowls. In typical fashion, conversation simultaneously began, across the table, down the table, animated, jovial, even combative.

George had been truly surprised at Frank's response to Aunt Louisa. He wondered how many others, if any, could force compliance on Frank Carron. Not to mention registering their disdain of him, to his face, and in his own house at that!

"A guy doesn't have to be an intellectual genius to

recognize the hierarchical authority this family allows the old girl to wield." He mused to himself... *"The big question is why?"*

All was proceeding well, when suddenly the head of the table shrilly cried, "Josephine, where is Massimiliano? I don't see him here." Her dark little eyes scrutinized the entire table.

The room went deathly silent.

"He's not here yet, Auntie." Josephine said quietly biting her lip.

"Not here? I thought he was to be released a month and a half ago?"

"He was, Auntie," Sophia leapt in to rescue her Mother, "but he sent word that he had some business to take care of before coming home."

"Business!" scoffed the old woman. "What kind of business would keep a good boy from first saying 'hello' to his family?"

"Maybe, dearest Sister," it was Pepi who now spoke, "he wanted to have a few months freedom to enjoy himself, before encountering your matrimonial web?"

George thought he detected a few little snickers. Very quiet ones, of course, so as not to be heard by those ninety-four year old ears.

However, those piercing ninety-four year old eyes were now locked fiercely on her seventy-two year old bother's eyes. "The last born is clearly the most impudent of all Mama's blessed children!"

"Not impudent," Pepi had picked up the gauntlet thrown by his sister. "Just the one most astutely aware of your need, Louisa, to ensure every male member is appropriately positioned to fulfill his God given responsibility to 'The Family'."

"Which is?" She queried.

"My dear, Louisa, procreation of course!" Pepi forced a wide benevolent smile, upon his obviously unamused sister.

George found himself totally fascinated by this family dialogue. He never, ever had experienced anything like it before. However, before he could begin to attempt to analyze the dynamics, Tony spoke up.

"Aunt Louisa," he sounded so sincere, even somber. "Rumah has it," he spoke with a deliberately exaggerated New York accent. "Rumah, has it that Massimiliano, in prison, had opportunity to considah his Deevine callin'. So before coming home to us, he needed to seek out this 'callin' monaasticahlly."

One thing became easily apparent, Tony had captured his Aunt's full attention.

"So," he continued, "when Massimiliano returns home, it will be to tell us whethah God has called him to celibacy and the Priesthood, or whetha he is in need of you're a' excellent match makin' services."

"This is true?" the old lady's eyes were open wide in joyful wonder.

As, if one, in perfect unison, the rest of the table nodded in solemn agreement. Serenity appeared to pass over Louisa's face, as if she was now part of a great Divine plan. Turning to the Carron's she sternly instructed, "Josephine! You must pray for Massimiliano's discernment in this process."

"Oh, I am, Aunt Louisa, I am!" Josephine quickly responded, as she breathed a sigh of great relief, that nothing more of Massimiliano needed now to be discussed.

For his part, Frank just looked at his son-in-law and rolled his eyes, discreetly of course so as to not be noticed by Aunt Louisa.

Chapter Seventeen

Max awoke in a sleepy stupor, *"Where the heck am I?"* Then he remembered. It was like an instant replay, the mug shot, their altercation, the bitter accusations, that accursed call with its new revelation, and her demand for him to leave. His jaw tightened, his fist clenched, did he ever remember! He rolled over and stared at Kaye, sound asleep beside him.

He couldn't help himself. Each time he looked at her she just seemed more beautiful. The more he looked, the more he wanted her. Max closed his eyes and lay on his back. He drew a deep breath.

"She doesn't even grasp how vulnerable she is to this predator. Nor can she imagine what he is capable of doing to her." He shuddered as he recalled the chilling disclosures of the men he had to interview for Professor Brown's assignment.

Anger began to ferment deep within him, *"She's prepared to throw away her security, for what? No! For Whom? Her precious neighbor, the Honorable Jack Walters. That bastard, he's like a dark omen that I can't shake, consistently making life miserable for me!"*

The anger began to swirl, like a whirlpool threatening to pull him under. It had been several weeks since he'd felt that rage. He sighed, *"I thought it had gone but now it's back with a vengeance. Oh yeah!"*

Abruptly, he remembered that he needed to escape, to get away from this place, this woman, this - this frigging Judge.

That last thought, suddenly illuminated, for him, his real need. It wasn't to find out why this guy had given him such an unjust sentence, or even who had paid him off. *"No! My real need is to put as much distance between me and that #*#*# Judge as possible!"*

He'd come quietly, stealthfully and he could leave exactly the same way. As tired as he thought he had been when he lay down after 'The Call', he'd only slept an hour. Now, he was wide awake. *"Oh boy, are those cobwebs clearing!"*

He got up tiptoed into the closet, retrieved his original clothes, picked up his shoes, secured J.D. and his car keys, exited into the hall, where he quickly dressed.

"No point worrying about finger prints or DNA, there's absolutely no way I could even begin to erase my presence here," he mumbled, as he threw his PJ's into the laundry bin.

"You can take care of my clothes, Doll, dirty and clean. This is your call!" He wanted to add "bitch", but somehow he just couldn't. Strange as it might seem, he realized that he felt no anger against her, instead an overpowering sadness blanketed him.

Max made it as far as the living room, when doubts again assailed him. He sat down to collect his thoughts, only to waken with a start, fifteen minutes later. He checked his watch, it was 5:15!

"If I don't move now, I'll lose the cover of darkness." His face flushed with anger "Well, Doll, you made the choice, your life for his Honor's. Have it your way!"

He quickly tied his runners, quietly strode to the alarm system control and disarmed it with the code she had revealed. Silently, Max slide open the patio door and vanished into the black of night. He quickly found the nature path and started gingerly down the trail.

"Whoever said that the blackest part of the night was just before dawn sure was right," he muttered. "But, I need to arrive at that street below in the dark! Stay cool, Maxie!" He admonished himself, "Don't rush, you could trip. Can't arrive at the bus stop dirty or it'll cause suspicion."

Max had dressed like a blue collar worker, planning to blend in with them when the first shifts hit the streets. "If you're lucky, Bud, cops won't have those posters yet. All I have to do is get to that long term parking, pick up my car, and..." he grinned, "Chicago, here I come!"

He paused, "Everything depends on Kaye keeping her word!" His countenance darkened, "and that I can't trust," he groused.

Then he checked himself, "I guess I have a choice in this too. I can feel sorry for myself and focus on my situation or I can try praying."

The latter seemed a more reasonable approach. Since as far as he could see, his life was figuratively and literally already on a downward trajectory. Max had watched Kaye pray and she just seemed to talk to God ordinary like. He recalled that's what some of the guys in the prison Alpha course did too. So, he took a deep breath, and began to do exactly that as he groped his way along the path.

"Please, God, let me blend in with the morning workers, so I can get across town to the airport unrecognized. Then let me get the hell away from here." A tear came to his eye as he continued, "Could you also please help Kaye escape that perp's clutches. I don't know how you can?" Max sighed, "I guess I just have to let you figure it out, because after all, you are God." He shrugged, "For once, I sure hope Kaye and Mama are right about you being real and caring about us. If they're wrong..."

He never finished that prayer. It was as if his thoughts suddenly jumped track to his mother. He tried to concentrate on his mother. He had put her out of his mind these past few weeks, past few weeks? past six years! It had been just too painful to think of her.

A smile crossed his face as he remembered the softness of her touch, her gentle smile and her feisty nature. His smile quickly faded, traded for a frown. "That was it! That is exactly what attracts me to Kaye, her feisty nature. She is exactly like Mama. Not only that Kaye talks about God and prays just like Mama."

He stopped to catch his breath, leaned against a tree for support. The wind had started to blow quite hard. He knew he only had about a hundred yards to go before the trail dropped off into the parkland. Soon he'd be on his way to the bus stop, but terrifying visions played across his mind. Memories surfaced from those prison interviews that he had been allowed to conduct. Max ran his hand through his hair. Indecision now muddled his thoughts.

An earth shattering crash and blinding light wrenched him back to reality. He saw the shadow lurching across the path, felt the wind against his face, his whole body reverberated, as less than twenty feet from him, a gigantic tree toppled to the ground. Max gasped. Had he not stopped to rest and pray, either the lightening or the fallen tree would have been his demise. He stood shaking, trying to compose himself. A large branch of the tree lay within inches of him. He was all too aware that it alone could have killed him.

At that moment, all hell seemed to break forth, lightening flashed, thunder roared and torrential rain began to pour down upon him. *"Thanks for nothing,"* he spluttered, rolling his eyes heavenward.

The tree had obliterated the nature trail. He would need to find an alternate route. Given the rugged escarpment this would be a treacherous task at the best of times, but in the dark leaving the trail could prove deadly! Regardless, Max now knew what he must do.

Kaye woke to a symphony of sound and light. She glanced at the clock. It was blinking its nonsensical message, which meant only one thing – the hydro was off.

She looked at the security alarm, "Great it's off too!"

Kaye rolled over to speak to Max and groaned. He was gone. She was alone. A shiver of fear ran through her body.

"Get a hold of yourself M.K." she chided. "After all, what is new? You were alone before he came and you are alone now." She sighed "I'm sorry, Lord. I know I'm never alone for you promise to be with me always. In fact, you call us to put our trust not in man but in you."

Kaye gave a hollow laugh, "Just when I think my relationship with you is going well, you reveal how shallow I am."

She hung her head, "It is true I was starting to rely on that Max character for security, not you. Please forgive me for taking my eyes off you, Jesus."

A rush of heat flooded through her body, tears came to her eyes. She knew exactly what the Holy Spirit was asking of her.

"Lord, You know this isn't easy! I feel betrayed. I also feel so stupid. Like I let go of my sense and actually let this criminal live in my home."

She chewed on her lip. "The truth is I actually found him charming. How dumb could I be? My selfish decision could easily have harmed Jack and Marnie" Tears now flowed down her cheeks. "I ask you to forgive me Jesus. To think I nearly betrayed my friends!"

Kaye paused, closed her eyes, her Lord was living indeed. His voice did not need to be audible. She heard it loud and clear in her heart. *"As you forgive others their trespasses against you, so too will your Father in Heaven forgive you."*

She swung her feet over the side of the bed and crumpled to the ground. "Oh Lord, how can I?" Scripture tumbled into her mind. *"What is impossible for men is possible for God."* Swallowing her hurt and pride, Kaye sighed, "I do surrender to you, your will not mine be done."

Then quietly from her lips the words formed, "Father, I forgive Max...Yes, for breaking into my house, attempting to rape me but even more so, for deceiving me, for betraying my trust. Please, will you also forgive him and bless him. I'm not asking you to bless any evil intent in him! But please, bless the good you have put in him. Please, bring someone to him, who can help him know how much you love him. Amen."

A glimmer of light was now visible as night was giving way to dawn. The storm still had the sky darker than normal, but instantaneously the hydro flashed back on.

The phone rang it was the security folk checking about her system. "Has it been turned off?"

"No, it was the storm, all is fine!" She assured them, "Thank you for calling." She hung up the receiver and headed for the shower.

The warm water she could sense was reviving her, spirit, soul and body. She began to sing, "When peace like a river attendeth my soul, when sorrows like sea billows roll.

Whatever my lot, thou hath taught me to say...It is well with my soul!"

She thought about the hymn she had just sung. Throughout the years, Christians have witnessed God's amazing grace to those around them. Yet, if they were called to be songwriters, their testimony could literally influence untold generations that followed.

Kaye marveled at the story of the man who had written those words *'When peace like a river'*. She knew he had done so in great anguish of soul. His wife and daughters had needed to sail to England ahead of him.

Their boat had sunk. His wife was one of the few survivors. All four of his daughters had perished. He'd taken the next feasible boat to England. When the Captain of his ship informed him that they were in the vicinity of his wife's sunken ship, he had gone to his room and penned the words to that inspiring hymn.

As Kaye dried herself off, a deep peace had begun to flood her own soul. "Lord Jesus," she murmured, "You are the same yesterday, today and tomorrow. If you can bring that hymn writer to the point of saying, in his circumstances, 'it is well with my soul'. Surely, I can trust that no matter what happens in my life, you will ensure that I too can say, 'It is well with my soul!' "

Returning to the bedroom, her spirit lifted, she glanced at the empty bed. She had to admit that she had been attracted to this uninvited visitor. She blushed as she sat on her bed, "For the life of me I haven't a clue why? I literally could have the pick of the cream of the crop. None ever appealed to me, until this jerk arrives."

She shook her head, "I guess, Lord, you've shown me that I'm not as self-reliant or astute as I thought. So Holy Spirit, when it comes to men, just as in everything else in my life, I really need you to guide my thoughts, feelings and desires!"

She dressed in her soft green velour track suit, looking in the mirror she smiled wryly, "after all, I am M.K. McDonald. I do not have the luxury of self indulging, do I? Every thing I do impacts Kayleen! Investors trust in the company can be influenced by their trust in me." She sighed, "My lot must always be to first consider Kayleen's well being."

Kaye proceeded down the stairs mentally planning a good healthy breakfast and strong brewed coffee. Arriving at the fridge she pulled out the eggs and fruit setting them on the counter by the stove. Reaching over she filled the coffee pot and turned to put it on. She gave a startled gasp almost dropping the pot.

Her green eyes flashed angrily. "I thought you had left!" She sputtered at the figure hunched over the breakfast island.

"I did," came a quiet retort.

"You're soaking wet! You tracked mud all over the floor!" she said, half in astonishment, half in anger.

In response, he leaned forward, folded his hands beneath his chin and simply glowered at her. That's when she saw it, in front of him. On the breakfast counter, lay his gun and strewn in front of the gun, on a tea towel were several bullets, at least that's what she thought they were.

Her mouth opened but words did not escape. She had never seen him looking so rough, wet, muddied, and unshaven. He now looked the way Kaye imagined criminals should look. The way, he stared at her, sent a chill down her spine.

"Good Lord, what is he going to do?" she thought.

He spoke firmly and deliberately, "Kaye, though it is extremely tempting, your solution to this affair, if I may use that word, is totally unacceptable. I cannot agree to it, and if your so called God is real, apparently he can't either, since he blocked my way with a very large tree."

Max sat up straight on the bar chair. Positioning his right hand on his hip, he then leaned forward propping his left elbow on the breakfast nook to rest his chin firmly in the palm of his left hand. His eyes locked on hers. Kaye was startled at the hardness she saw.

Max continued, "When I first came you wanted a credible witness to your phone calls. Now you have one."

Somehow, Kaye began to realize that he was not negotiating, rather he was being very directive. *"But to what end?"* this she could not surmise. Trying to put on her best authoritative voice she tried to interject, "I fail to see how you are any more credible today than when I first saw you over a month and a half ago?"

He cut her off, "Shut up! You know nothing about who is calling you. You are naïve, ignorant and filled with arrogant imagination." The words seemed to boil out of his mouth.

Indignation erupted within her and she rebutted, "No one speaks to me like that!" She started to move forward to challenge him but was stopped dead in her tracks by his response.

"I just did, Doll. Now you sit down and listen to what I am telling you we *will do!"*

Kaye's jaw dropped at his bluntness. No one ever had talked to her that way and perhaps that's why she did sit down as directed.

Max began to speak. The very tone of his voice sent a chill into Kaye's heart. "By his language and by what transpired last night, your caller is a dangerous, psychopathic, sexual, pervert. I suspect he has in mind for you a violent, horrific end."

"What happened last night?" Kaye stammered.

"When you spoke to him in anger, challenging him, it turned him on. He was climaxing as you talked."

"How do you know that?" she frowned.

"I listened. Now you listen! The odds are this fellow has done this before. To get a profile on him we need to get him talking about his other ventures."

"You are just stalling." Kaye snapped.

"I'm not going to be around, Doll, but the cops will be," he replied softly.

Kaye studied him carefully. *"Was he going to write a note about what had happened and kill him self? Surely not!"*

"You, Kaye, are going to call your cop neighbor over here."

"What are you going to do?" Kaye asked almost dreading the reply.

He spat out the words. "What the hell do you think I'm going to do? The gun is empty. The bullets are in front of you. I'm going to sit right here. If you want I'll put my hands on my head. Have no fear I know their drills."

"He'll arrest you," came out as a muffled whisper.

"Right, and you, Doll, can tell him whatever you damn well want to. What I will tell him is that I've been here going on six weeks, listening every night to a phone call that comes in at precisely 3 a.m. Those calls have been intensifying in vulgarity.'

"In my opinion those calls are producing sexual gratification for the caller. I will tell your cop friend that when you exploded at him, an audible excitation resulted and your caller climaxed."

Kaye's eyes were wide in disbelief. "Whatever possesses you to think he'll believe you?"

Max's eyes were now hard slits. "Two things, Doll. Number 1, you say he's your friend and a good cop. If I'm right, he'll know the gravity of the situation for you. He'll want to know the truth. Number 2, to pursue that truth he can contact Warden Blackmore at the Penitentiary where I was imprisoned. He will confirm that I was allowed to take law courses, on line, from Harvard. One of which was under Professor Brown,"

Kaye blinked in astonishment, "you were allowed to take law courses in jail?"

"Is it ever possible for you to just listen?" Max was now not only tired and exhausted, he was getting extremely irritated at being in her presence. What he was about to do, he wanted ended soon, very, very soon, before he changed his mind.

"As I said, your cop buddy will discover one of my assignments was to interview serial, sexual, psychopathic killers incarcerated there. Sorry to disappoint you, Babe, I'm not just a pretty face. I do know of what I speak." Max concluded sarcastically.

Kaye closed her eyes, and bit her lip, "But if I call Dave and he comes here, he will arrest you. He'll confiscate your gun, probably charge you with unlawful possession. Who knows what else in relation to Judge Walters."

"Don't forget attempted rape." Max added dryly.

Almost imperceptibly Kaye responded, "Not the latter. I won't corroborate your story and that surely would cast doubt on all else you say."

"Your choice, Doll, your choice!" Max murmured.

"I thought you said your gun was special to you?" Kaye asked quietly.

"It is. My father gave it to me when I turned sixteen. Told me to go learn how to use it. So, I did. I learned how to physically shoot it, yes. I also learned how psychologically to use it, or perhaps better said, how not to use it. Sure, Kaye, the gun means a lot to me."

Max shrugged, "But, the gun is no different than anything else in life. There are times to hold on to something and there are times to let go. For me, if this is what it takes to stop this guy and catch him, well, I'm willing to pay that price."

Kaye studied his face, noting it suddenly seemed softer. "You honestly believe this caller to be a serial killer and you'd give up your freedom to stop him for me?"

"No, Doll, not just for you, but for all the other dolls, even little dolls, he'll prey on until he is stopped." Tears began to well up inside, he could feel them coming.

"Damn, why now?" he sniffed, but the memories of those many victims of the men he'd interviewed flooded his mind. "You don't understand, Kaye. I don't think most people do. It's like these guys are possessed! Ever increasing violent sex becomes an obsession with them, like an addiction. They can't or won't stop until they're caught and what they do to their victims is always terrifying. They need to be stopped!" A tear trickled down his cheek.

He was speaking with a passion that even he himself didn't understand. Kaye looked at him intently. As incredulous as it seemed, this hard core criminal that she'd been told about last night, was weeping before her.

Familiar music seemed to penetrate her senses. "Oh No!" she exclaimed, "It's the doorbell." Instinctively sweeping Max's gun et al into the top drawer of the island, she moved to intercept her early morning caller.

"Coming!" she yelled.

Spying her briefcase, Kaye snatched it up. She hoped she could convey to whomever was at the door that her sense of urgency was solely business related.

Max sat frozen to his chair.

Yet both the one, on the move, and the one, who sat rigid, were caught up in mortal combat, each with their own emotions!

Chapter Eighteen

Kaye was breathless as she reached the door. To her horror it was Dave. *"How could he know? Had Max called him already? No, Max had said I was to call him. I know what Max wants, but I need more time!"*

Composing herself, she opened the door with, she hoped, a convincing grin.

"Hi, to what do I owe this early morning visit? Get kicked out of the house?" she quipped. "Would you like a good cup-a high test?"

"Please, let him say, No!" she silently pleaded.

Dave chuckled good naturedly, "No, Sue didn't boot me out. Thanks for the coffee offer but I need to decline. Reason for the visit is that last night everyone left so quickly, and we forgot to mention that Matt's away all weekend. He's umpiring at yet another Police sponsored Little League baseball tourney." Dave threw up his hand, "I know, I shouldn't complain. It's great to have a son so involved with young people's sports. However, there is the small matter of what was supposed to be his dog!'

"The four of us have tickets for the Phillies double header. We 'd like to stay over, get back for tomorrow evening's service. But..." he eyed her briefcase, "you said you had a lot of work to do today. We didn't know if you'd be working at home or if you had meetings elsewhere?"

"I'm working at home." She rolled her eyes like a martyr, "and yes I will look after Rufus, but..." she narrowed her eyes, "he be sleeping in me bed!" Even as slits those green eyes twinkled as she spoke.

Dave threw his head back in mock despair, "You always do spoil him!" He gave her a bear hug and with a laugh said "God Bless ye! You self-sacrificing Irish lass!" Then he added, "You do have the keys?"

"I have the keys," she replied. "I'll check my e-mails and be over to get the bear. Have a great and safe trip. Make sure they win!"

"Absolutely," he gave her a big salute, turned and bounded down the steps to Jack's waiting van. Kaye returned the wave and quickly closed the door.

Max had been engrossed in admonishing himself for failing to control his emotions.

"Why can't I grow up and control those damn tears? They just seem always to flow, when I least expect it. Real men don't cry! Will I ever become a real man?" he sighed.

In the midst of his struggle, he suddenly became aware of the voice conversing with Kaye.

"Damn, that's the Cop's voice!"

He heard Kaye say "Good-bye."

"Damn her, she's doing exactly what she wants again! She didn't believe one word I said!" He jumped out of his chair, sending it flying.

He yelled out "Damn it, Kaye – the cops *will be* involved!"

Cursing in Italian, he charged down the hall, screaming, "Chief Dave!"

From the intensity of his words, Kaye knew his intent was to follow through his plan to surrender.

She whirled around, "No, Max, not now, please!"

She met him in full flight as he hurtled into the foyer. More specifically, her briefcase met him full force connecting with a sickening thud into his groin.

Max gasped. Pain like he'd never experienced shot through his body. He crumpled to the floor in agony. He couldn't even groan. The shock and pain were so great!

Kaye was equally traumatized by what had occurred.

"Oh, No! Max, I'm so sorry! I never intended to hit you," she wailed.

He couldn't even reply. The pain nauseated him and with it came a sickening memory. He had just turned twelve. There was a large family gathering in Newark at the Bastaldi's. The women were off preparing the food. Sophia was playing with the younger children, babysat by the older girls. The men were discussing business ventures. At least, that's what Pop had said.

Pop told him that now that he was twelve, it was time he went with the older boys. He'd just entered the room, when this big kid about eighteen started shoving and pushing a younger skinner kid. The older guy was calling the kid names, then, the others started in on the kid.

Max had wanted to leave but didn't know how, when without provocation the bully up and kicked the kid in the balls. The kid had collapsed writhing in pain, tears started coming down his face, and the older guys began to mock and laugh at the kid. The kid threw up and they pushed him into his own vomit, yelling at him to stand. Max knew now why the kid couldn't.

For his part, Max remembered, he had cowered in the corner of the room, hoping no one would notice him. Max opened his eyes to escape that painful memory, only to find himself looking into Kaye's. There was no mocking, no harassing, only tears of concern for him.

"Tears! Damn!" He had tears again too! He tried to take deep breaths, to ease the pain he was experiencing, tried to close his eyes but when he did he saw that kid's tortured eyes.

As quick as the bullying had begun, it ended. Those older boys, that his Pop had wanted him to meet, exited the room, 'for some good stuff', Max had heard them say. He hung back. The kid was moaning. Max went to him, said he was sorry, got a towel and started to clean both the kid and the mess up. The puke had stunk real bad but he had persevered.

The boy was shaking and crying, "I didn't do anything. He just turned on me, like an animal."

Max had learned the kid's name was Mikey. Mikey had hung around Max all weekend.

"I wonder what ever happened to him?"

His own pain now seemed to be abating somewhat. He opened his eyes once more.

Kaye was now in front of him again shaking him. "Max, undo your pants."

"What?"

"Undo your pants!" She commanded, "you need to put this between your legs.

"Frozen peas?" he rasped.

"The two worst places for a man to be hit are in the Adam's apple and in his testicles," was the authoritative response. "Swelling is very serious in both places. Ice helps to keep down the swelling. Frozen peas work great because they mould to your body." She was yanking at his jeans to get them down.

"Crap!" he squeaked in disbelief. "You did this before?"

"What?" Her green eyes flashed with indignation.

His hand shot up, just in time, to block a swift slap to his face.

"For your information, Mr. Carron, I took a First Aid course. If you are well enough to be so crude, you can put this cold pack in yourself!"

"Don't," he yelled covering his crotch with both hands to deflect her throwing the large bag of peas, at his now most tender area. "I wasn't trying to be smart. It hurts like hell! How was I to know you took a First Aid course?" He struggled to get the jeans down.

The process was hampered by the fact his pants were still damp from the rain.

"Oh, no!" Kaye grimaced.

"Oh, no! What?" said Max, straining in panic to get a look at himself.

"I cut you!" she wailed.

"What?" Pain or no pain, he shot bolt upright, terror in his eyes. On the inside of his left thigh Max saw a two-inch scrape, with some fresh blood. "That's my leg!" His eyes met hers.

"What did you think I meant?" The green eyes started to twinkle and she bit her lip. "Not Laughing! Not laughing! The frozen peas go there." She pointed to his jockey briefs and gently placed them in the proper position. He winced as the cold bag touched the tender area.

"Not laughing," she repeated standing up. "Laughing," she said throwing her hand over her mouth, as she exited the room giggling. She now possessed new wisdom. In certain areas of human anatomy, a simple word like 'cut' would evoke a different understanding, depending upon one's gender.

The pain was definitely abating. With her absent, Max surveyed his wounds. Bruising was already evident on the inside of his left thigh and testicle. He reapplied the frozen peas. Once he had gotten over the initial shock, it did seem to him that the cold was easing the pain and would reduce further swelling.

"Why did that memory of Mikey come back to me? Pop said guys had to put such things out of their minds, just get on with life. Why can't I do that?"

Florence Nightingale reappeared interrupting his reflection. She was carrying a tray.

"Now, what?" he glowered.

She set the tray down between them, and then sat down cross legged in front of him. "I brought some hot chocolate and cookies, so we can discuss, in a civil manner, what has happened."

He just stared at her. "Cookies and hot chocolate? Now? For breakfast?"

"No! Cookies and milk for discussion purposes. Breakfast follows discussion. My special egg casserole is in

167

the oven as we speak."

"There is nothing to discuss. You hit me in the balls to prevent me from going to the police. So you could handle everything 'Kaye's way', full stop!" Max's jaw tensed as he spoke.

Kaye shook her head, "Wrong answer!"

"You deny you hit me?" Now it was his turn to be incredulous.

"No, I hit you but it was accidental and most certainly, I did not imagine a low blow. You, Sir, came running into the foyer, legs spread apart. When I turned abruptly with my briefcase, you and it were on a direct collision course. I had turned simply to block you getting to the door."

"Really?" he snapped. "Well, the intent was the same, to block me from involving the police."

"That, Sir, I do not deny, but your motivation I do. You accuse me of not listening to what you said, and of not taking your words seriously, of just doing my own thing. You, Sir, are wrong!"

"Really?"

"Yes, Max, really! You gave me two options. Option one was you. Option two was the police. Both plans designed to catch this person you suspect of being a serial killer. Is this not correct?"

"Apparently, you suffer from short term memory loss, Kaye? Have you forgot, that last night you rejected me, or Option One?"

Her hands were now on her hips, "That's just the point!"

Max knew where he'd been hit and it wasn't his head. "The point?" he repeated. His mind not comprehending, where on earth, this female was going with her logic?

"Excuse me, but you have just identified two options and agreed that one of those you had already rejected." He peered at her over his glasses, "You have no point, Kaye!"

"I most certainly have!" came her emphatic response. "You are correct in stating that it was last night that I had rejected Option One. Today, however, given new

information, I was reconsidering it, when the doorbell rang."
She folded her arms in front of her and added, "So there!"

"Reconsidering it?" Max stared at her in total disbelief.
"You label me a disgusting, violent criminal. Accuse me
of planning to murder your wonderful, honest, poor, dear
friend the Judge, his wife and you! Now you claim to be
reconsidering your words? Give me a break, Lady! What did
I say that convinced you that I am upstanding Joe Citizen
#1?" His tone was disdainful and he intended it to be.

Surprisingly, Kaye chose not to react, "It's not what you
said, Max. It's what you did!"

"Did?" he furrowed his brow, totally perplexed. To
himself he thought, *"What on earth could I have done to make
her reconsider working with me, trusting me, allowing me
to remain near her friends?"* He shrugged his shoulders
and looked blankly at her. "Sorry, Kaye, I give up!"

She simply said, "you cried."

"Cried?" he croaked.

"Yes, cried!"

"A guy cries and you trust him?" Max was dumbfounded.

"Yes" she said quietly.

Max snorted, "Where I come from, guys who cry aren't
real men!"

"That's most unfortunate, Max, for real men do cry.
In fact, the most real man whoever walked the face of this
earth did cry."

"And who is that?" Max asked skeptically.

"Jesus" was the simple retort.

"Jesus cried?" Max asked in astonishment.

"Yes."

"Where does it say that?"

Kaye got up slowly, retrieved her Bible from the study,
brought it to him, opened at the Gospel of John, Chapter 11,
verse 35. Max read *"Jesus wept."*

Deliberately, yet gently she continued, "As for being
a real man, Jesus did what few of us ever do. He put the

welfare of others ahead of himself. More importantly, he always put doing God's will ahead of serving his own will. Even when, to do so meant that he would die a painful and humiliating death. So whenever I see a man or a woman passionate about the well being of others weaker than them selves, I sit up and pay attention."

"So you're thinking all this when the door bell rang?" Max ventured.

"Yes."

"But you didn't have time to tell me?"

"Correct," Kaye nodded.

"So you really weren't trying to nail me?"

"Correct again," she said.

"You believed me then - what I said about the caller?"

"Yes, I do even though what you were saying was very disturbing to me. So, Mr. Carron, will you reconsider our former agreement?"

Max was quiet for a moment, everything had changed so dramatically, it had caught him totally off guard. Truthfully he was having difficulty processing it all.

"Yeah," he said at last.

"And, Mr.Carron, will you forgive my offenses to you?"

He stared at her. Her whole tone and demeanor appeared genuine. He couldn't detect any evidence of mockery. "What do you mean?" He queried.

"Will you forgive me when I said or did things that offended or hurt you?" Kaye asked.

He gave a hollow laugh, "Sure, but people do that all the time to each other."

"And," she responded, "when a person becomes aware that they have offended another, they should ask the other for forgiveness."

"You believe that?"

"Most assuredly," Kaye smiled, "for then, God will forgive them all their offences."

"What?"

"It's in the Lord's Prayer, Max. Forgive us our trespasses as we forgive those who trespass against us."

Max sat very still, his mind weighing all that she had said. At last he said softly, "When I attempted to rape you, I both hurt and offended you?"

"Yes."

"Then I should ask your forgiveness?" he queried.

"Yes, if you really want to," Kaye answered.

"I do, Kaye, I really do. Will you forgive me?"

Now, it was Kaye's turn to have tears in her eyes. "Yes, I do forgive you, Max Carron, for attempting to rape me," and she leaned forward gently kissing him on the cheek.

"Wow! That is amazing."

"The kiss?"

"Well, yeah," he smiled sheepishly, "but the forgiveness thing. It's like a great weight has been lifted off of me. A weight I didn't even know I carried."

Kaye smiled, reached out and took his hand, "We thank you, Jesus!"

"You can say that again!" He grinned.

"Max, are you able to get up now?"

He gingerly rolled over on his knees. The pain was still there, but greatly diminished.

Leaning on the hall table, he rose slowly.

"Why don't you go shower and change?" Kaye suggested, "Breakfast should be ready then. We can discuss the shopping trip you want to make and I have a surprise for you!"

Chapter Nineteen

"Do we look like New York City slickers or what? I told you we should have dressed casual," the younger man admonished his father.

"You wanna' be a pleb. You dress like a pleb. You wanna' be the Emperor, you dress like the Emperor," the older man retorted sharply.

Tony gave a soft laugh, "depends which emperor, Pop. Remember the emperor who got that new suit of clothes, the invisible suit, that fast talking tailor guy sold him?" He gave his father a sideward glance and was rewarded with a chilly scowl.

"Not so long ago," Tony mused, *"I was terrorized by that look along with anyone else, in or outside the Family, but ..."* he smiled inwardly, *"I am growing up, Pop, and you are aging! I can now joke with you whether or not it's appreciated. I think I'm beginning to master Mama's skill of cutting through your steely control with humor but..."* he chuckled *"my bravery exists, at least for now, only in my thoughts."*

Pep prided himself on being on top of anything and everything happening in the Big Apple. It was that mental aptitude which was whirling into gear right now. Pepi stood, hands in pocket, pondering his son's story. "What shyster, tailor guy are you referring to, Ton? I never saw anything in the *'Times'*, when did you read it?'

"Don't get me wrong, Ton, I don't have anything against fast talkers, as long as it's not me, on the wrong end of a deal." The elder Marconi frowned, "Nor do I like jokes played on me, so your story better be legit."

Tony looked at his father in disbelief. "You've never heard of the story of the emperor and the invisible suit, Pop? You're joking right?"

Pepi's eyes narrowed, his moustache bristled, "You think I look like a comedian?" He glowered.

Tony looked askance at his father, "Pop, The Emperor's New Clothes is a kid's fairy tale."

"Fairy tales? Don't get smart with me, Tony, what the hell have fairy tales got to do with your shyster story?"

Tony rolled his eyes, "Everything, Pop! The Emperor gets tricked because he was a very prideful person and all his advisors were filled with pride. Furthermore, they were 'yes men'. They would only tell the emperor what he wanted to hear, even if it wasn't the truth."

"Fairy tales," scoffed Pepi, "You're a grown man, Tony! Why the hell are you reading fairy tales?"

"I wonder why? Could it have anything to do with the fact that I have two lovely four year old daughters and a great toddler son?" He replied testily, "All of whom love their Papa reading them stories! It's called bonding time. Something it is obvious you neglected to do with me!"

Pepi raised his eyebrows, "Ah, come on, Son, times change, men didn't do that then!"

"Point well taken, Pop! Times do change and arriving in Vegas in a pin stripe, three piece, business suit is not something in keeping with the times!" Tony groused.

"I gather this is your way of informing me, your attire will change during our stay here?"

Tony nodded curtly, "As soon as I hit the hotel room, Pop, of comes this suit!"

Pepi held his chin, pinched his lips, making a little clicking sound, "Well, that's a relief?"

Tony wrinkled his brow, "What is?"

"You waiting to get to the hotel room to change.

Thought initially you were telling me the story of the Emperor's invisible suit because you were planning to strip here!" Without cracking a smile Pepi pointed to a News Stand, and added, "As long as it meets with your approval, I'm going to get a paper."

Tony stood there shaking his head, and grinning, "Sheesh! He got me again."

Although totally opposite his father, not only physically but also in his extraverted outgoing nature, Tony was gaining respect in the Family, particularly among the younger generation.

His marriage to Frank Carron's daughter Sophia had helped to garner that respect. This was both for the fact that it had instantly healed the long-standing rift between the Carron's and the Marconi's, and also because, in the younger men's eyes, Tony had succeeded in winning the "Prize".

Sophia Carron had been the object of many a prospective suitor. Not only was she downright beautiful, everyone knew she was the apple of her father's eye. Except for her older brother Max's presence, some less scrupulous would-be lovers believed they could easily have become the one to be Frank Carron's son-in-law. But Max was present and it appeared, commissioned by his father to ensure that his rather high spirited (some might even suggest "wild") daughter would indeed walk down the aisle able to wear white.

Tony, in spite of the Marconi-Carron feud, had succeeded in not only winning over Sophia but also gaining the confidence of Max. To every one in the Family, Tony and Sophia's relationship appeared to be a genuine love match.

As he stood waiting with his father in the Las Vegas Airport Terminal, two men, attired appropriately to the satisfaction of the elder Marconi, appeared with luggage carts. One cart held four suitcases, the other golf bags.

The older of the two men addressed Giuseppe, "Pep, Fonz has got the limo outside and we're set to go."

In the limo, the younger man sat up front with the

driver, separated by the glass divide from the trio in the back. The older man sat with the two Marconi's. Pepi pursed his lips, "has anyone, anywhere, heard from Max?" The other two shook their heads.

"Frank is going to be getting down right ugly over this, and I don't blame him."

Turning to his son he inquired, "Tony, you knew Max better than us. Is there any possibility Max is really upset at all of us? Given the fact that he didn't even do what he was sent down for?"

"What?" exclaimed their older companion in surprise.

"It's true, Manny!" Tony sighed. "I was notified that I should meet in that hotel room with four other classmates to work on our large economics project. However, I'd asked Sophia to the college prom. Max agreed to go for me. You know, get my assignment, as I told him the area I wanted to work on. He was fairly familiar with the scope of the project. Anyway my classmates weren't there when he arrived and bottom line they never did show.'

"Max was going to lie down, but said he felt prompted to sit in the chair."

"Good thing he did," his father added, "otherwise he'd be dead, and we likely would have been blamed!"

"Yeah," Tony said, "Max fell asleep in the chair. Next thing he heard a slug wiz past his ear, saw a gun butt beside him but before he could react, whoever was there saw him.'

"Max heard them say, *"Shit! It's Carron!"* and then the lights went out. When he came to, a cop was standing over him. Drug paraphernalia had been planted through out the room to suggest he'd been dealing."

Manny's eyes were wide, "Max took a fall for you? Why didn't Frank challenge it in court?"

Pep glowered at his lieutenant's apparent inability to grasp the bigger picture. "Manny, somebody was after Tony. His classmates never requested that meeting. We checked them out, clean as a whistle. Someone was intent on killing Tony. The bullet Max heard was fired at the pillows Max had set up to resemble someone sleeping in the bed.'

"From the bullet's trajectory calculated by the cops, had there been a real person in the bed, it would have been a homicide for sure!"

"Who was after you, Tony?"

"That's just it, Manny! Neither Max, nor I, nor Pop, nor Frank have a clue."

"Are you certain that Frank didn't know of Sophia and your affection for one another?"

"Absolutely, Manny!" Pep spoke deliberately, "Tony and Sophia had run off and eloped – neither Frank nor I knew of it. In fact, Sophia had smuggled Tony into her bedroom."

"In Frank's house? Where were your brains, Tony?" Manny fairly spat out the words, "that could have compromised us all!"

"Love," Tony responded icily. "She loved me and I loved her, and what my family or hers thought didn't have to involve us."

Manny was about to rebuke him but stopped short when he noticed the hardness in Tony's expression.

Pepi interrupted, "Max was charged and released pending trial. He came home, and the two star-crossed lovers revealed what they'd done and he began to fix it for them with his parents.'

"Remember, Manny, how upset Lena was when we didn't know where Tony was? And if Lena is upset, I am upset." He poked his son in the ribs, "You gave us an awful scare. We figured you were dead." Pep continued, "Needless to say Frank was genuinely shocked to find out Tony, his enemy's missing son, was actually in his household.'

"Max managed to convince Frank and Josie, especially Frank, that Tony was legit and really did love Sophia. So Josie called Lena and told her of the kids' relationship. Lena was grateful Tony was alive and also the prospect of grandbabies helped out. Let's just reiterate Lena's happiness made me happy and so all four parents gave our blessing to this matrimony."

"So, that's when you and Frank buried the hatchet?"

"Right, we decided it's foolish not to. Look what happened to Romeo and Juliet, the kids die, and you shut down the potentiality of grandkids." Pep replied.

"So neither you nor Frank wanted to pursue who tried to kill Tony?"

"Correct, we didn't know what can of worms we'd open, just stir up bad blood, after all comes a time when it's right to say *'Enough is Enough!'*, so we did."

Tony spoke up, "We all figured, if Max took the fall, he'd get maybe a year, at tops a year and a half. Max didn't seem to care. He figured, I guess, that now I had the responsibility for looking after the welfare of his baby sister. As well, Frank was sure the judge who was assigned the case would be favorably disposed to Max, since Maxie's nose was clean. Then this old guy ups and croaks and a new upstart was assigned."

"And he threw the book at Max! Oh, wow!" Manny exclaimed, "How do you think we'll find Frank?"

"Well, I know how I felt when Tony went missing and you were only gone two weeks. We're now talking a little over two months with Max! That's why I asked Tony if he figures maybe Max is just really upset with us, wants to disown us, or worse still conjuring up how to get even?"

The younger man shook his head, "that would be totally opposite Max's character, Pop. I know guys have said the pen can do strange things to you, but neither I nor Sophia believe it could crack Max."

Pepi frowned, "Well, we may be here in Nevada for our mid-year Family Business evaluation, and of course, some good gaming and golf, but mark my words our number one order of business will be Max!"

The four were now heading to their suite in Vinni Lombardi's Golden Calypso. It was Vegas' premier casino and hotel. Everybody, who was somebody wanted to be seen there. It was an undisputed fact Vinni had class. He was able to bring in the top entertainment. True his Sicilian-Italian connections had him constantly in the radar of law enforcement agencies, but like Pep and Frank, Vinni was accomplished at walking the tight rope between his legal and not so legal clientele.

When the Family gathered for supper in Vinni's penthouse suite, Pepi's earlier prediction rang true. Frank and Gus were there accompanied by Luigi and young Al. All were very grim indeed. Frank's ineptness at 'games' of any sort and his loathing of Vegas' high life, were well-known by all.

With regard the latter, both he and Pep were alike. With regard the former – well, truthfully Pepi enjoyed the thrill of gambling, nonetheless, both he and Frank calculated the maximum loss each would tolerate, and played accordingly. In a way, both saw their participation as a calculated investment in the younger generation's loyalty.

Today, however, Frank was indeed sour, and his issue was Max! It was beyond Frank how his son could just disappear and not one element of the Family's Italian connections, above ground or underground, had anything to report.

"If I find any of you are lying to me, that person or persons will wish they never were born!" Frank snarled. His controlled civility was most definitely missing as he eyed each member at the Family gathering.

Pepi was the only one who dared speak, "I imagine how you must feel, Frank and I also suspect Josie is beside herself. I know how I felt when Tony was missing six and a half years ago, and that was only for two weeks. Lena was beside herself, totally distraught."

He shook his head sadly, "Josie and you are going on over two months now, all I can wish for the both of you is that things turn out as well as it did for us. You know, it all turned out a real nice love story!"

Pep's response appeared to strike a chord with Frank. His countenance softened, he sat back and ran his hand thoughtfully across his mouth, sighed and gave a soft laugh as he looked at Tony.

"Yeah, that would be very nice if it happens to us, Pep, but your son prior to meeting Sophia, did not seem to have an aversion to dating. Max on the other hand was not noted for even remotely looking at the opposite sex."

Tony was grateful for the opening his father-in-law unwittingly had given him to lighten the atmosphere in the room.

"True, Frank, but then my sista' was olda' than me. I never had the assignment to baby sit her life, like you gave Max. Rememba' that burden was lifted just before he went to prison. Max isn't stupid. He knows how to avoid us. Maybe we need to cut him some slack and let him have a few months of fun time before he resurfaces. I mean look around this room. Your daughta' had the attention of a lotta' guys here as well as those not in our family.'

"Max was diligent in lookin' afta' Sophia. I mean she told me many times she deliberately planned to out smart him and he'd always outwit her and be there, the dedicated chaperone. He sacrificed his social life for hers."

Gus started to laugh, "That's true, Tony! That's true!" as memories of the two younger Carrons' antics, especially Sophia's, flashed through his mind. Gus' belly laughter seemed to further relax Frank.

"I suggest," Frank finally said, "that it would be most helpful to convey some of your thoughts to Josephine. She, more than anyone, has experienced pain as a result of Max's absence from our house. Devastated is a good word to describe how she felt when he did not return home immediately. Hope is something she desperately needs. Sadly my words don't seem able to give her that hope."

Chapter Twenty

For the first time in nearly seven years Max thought, *"I feel hap…, no not happy, good? Na, maybe content is the best word to describe it."* He leaned back on his chair, eyeing Kaye who was filling the dishwasher. She really was attractive, actually most attractive, no beautiful. He laughed softly, *"She's the first woman, I've ever even noticed… Interesting."* He broke the silence, "Okay, so you've apologized to me, forgiven me, agreed with me, fed me, but you haven't yet given me the surprise you promised."

She closed the dishwasher, pushed the buttons and the swish, swish sound began to fill the room. "Let's move to the den," she offered. "It's quieter there."

He was gingerly settling into the soft pillowed chair, when she said tersely, "I lied."

"What?"

"I lied."

"About what?" Max studied her totally perplexed over what she might mean.

"Remember when you wanted information on your investment portfolio with Kayleen?"

"Yeah," Max nodded.

"I gave it to you and you asked me how I got it."

"Uh-huh."

"I told you that I'd done contract work for Kayleen and knew how to hack in. Well, I didn't hack in!"

Max gave a wry smile, "You mean I don't have a million and a half? You just faked it somehow? Oh well," he shrugged, "easy come, easy go."

"No, Max, you have a million and a half in your account." Kaye said matter-of-factly.

Max frowned, "Kaye, I haven't a clue what you are trying to tell me."

"I am telling you that it was your account, but I did not hack into it. I got there legally."

"You work for Kayleen?" Max said, his voice registering surprise.

Kaye pursed her lips wondering what eruption her next words would illicit. "I guess you could say that I work for Kayleen, Max. It is, in fact, my life." Kaye sighed,

"Remember the spoiled, pampered brat who by luck inherited Kayleen? Well, I am M.K. McDonald."

"No way!"

"Yes way!"

"You can't be!" he stammered.

"Believe me, I am, Max."

"Look, Kaye, I don't mean to be insulting, but if you were M.K. McDonald, you wouldn't be living here."

"I wouldn't?" Kaye raised her eyebrows, "Why in heaven's name would you think that?"

"Well, don't get me wrong. I mean this is a really, really nice house and all that, but M.K. McDonald would live in a much bigger house, a mansion." He scratched his head, "There'd be a guarded compound, hired help. In fact I even saw a picture of the McDonald estate in one of the financial magazines, before I went to prison. It was an article on R.K."

"Dialogue is not going to win this discussion," Kaye thought to herself. "Just one minute, Mr. Carron." She went to her study, picked up her passport, took her driver's license from her purse and grabbed her company I.D. badges. Returning to the den she plunked them down in front of him.

Max carefully perused them. It was her alright. Everything had M.K. McDonald's name on it. The Passport had the address in Lakeland, which he remembered was the name given in the magazine article. But her driver's license was for here in Summerside. He finally managed to blurt "I don't understand?"

Kaye took a deep breath. Even the thought of retelling the story brought tears to her eyes. "The luck, Max, that you suggested got the pampered, spoiled brat, Kayleen Enterprises..."

Max winced and thought, *"If she really is M.K., I've screwed up again, big time!"*

"Well, Max, I don't consider that day luck, but the most tragic day of my life!" She bit her lip. "I was extremely close to both my Mother and Father. I not only had an aptitude for business. I really loved the work Kayleen Enterprises engaged in, which Daddy recognized." A tear trickled down her cheek. "I had the best corporate mentor in him!"

She smiled at Max, "When you first mentioned Kayleen, you were right in acknowledging his genius." Kaye paused, "My parents were strong believers in Christ. They intentionally lived their lives seeking to demonstrate his Lordship in all they thought, said and did. My Father had strong moral convictions which he carried into the boardroom.'

"I inherited a solid board and management staff, nationally and internationally. However, as you also recognized, I was and still am exceedingly young. I would have never succeeded in managing Kayleen if it weren't for my own living relationship with Jesus. I depend on the Holy Spirit's guidance daily. He most certainly is my friend and mentor."

Max stared at her. He suddenly grasped the weight of responsibility that she carried and glimpsed the regal, mature way she did so. Now, he began to appreciate the burden this 'perp' placed on her. Why she would overlook his crime, if in doing so she could apprehend this caller!

Kaye was too emotionally engrossed in her story to notice the shift in Max's attitude. She continued, "After I

graduated from College, Daddy told me he had bought this
property and intended to develop an estate subdivision
here. I fell in love with the area. He offered me my choice
of lots. I chose this one because the nature trail cuts down
behind it. Daddy put in the street and serviced lots." She
laughed "He named it Independence Drive, because of me.'

"Dave and Sue Davidson bought the one lot on the other
side of the cul-de-sac. Dave had just accepted the position
as Summerside's Police Chief. Daddy figured he'd make a
good neighbor for me. We both began building that year.
Six months later Jack and Marnie built. Both Mummy and
Daddy liked these two couples, and Daddy thought the real
estate a good investment for me. I liked having my own
personal space. The Walters and Davidsons became my
family, and I, theirs. I'm somewhat between a big sister and
surrogate mom with Jack and Marnie's two daughters and
Sue and Dave's daughter and son.'

"Anyway, we all love nature. The deer are wonderful
to see, as are the other wildlife. My father got caught
up in other business ventures and so put this property
development temporarily on hold. This suited all three
residences on Independence Drive.'

"I went on to get my M.B.A. and began to be involved,
under my father's tutelage, in Kayleen's affairs. Then my
life collapsed, in one split second when that jet went down
in that electrical storm. Sorry, I can't stop these tears
flowing." She paused to blow her nose. "It happens every
time I share this story!"

"Kaye, I'm so sorry I made that disparaging remark
about you, like being a figurehead CEO and all that."

Kaye smiled sadly, "Max, I do forgive you, but you're not
the first, nor will you be the last person with those thoughts.
However, I'm not living to prove myself to you or any one
else. I simply believe God placed me in leadership of this
Company for the purpose of letting Kayleen bless others as
it works corporately to make the world a better place."

She continued, "I hope through my sharing you can better grasp my intense loyalty to the Davidsons and Walters. You see when my parents were killed, they literally became my family. They were just there, ***always!*** Not in the forefront but quietly in the background, looking out for me. This is my home and until now I felt perfectly safe here. Then those calls started coming." She let out a large sigh, "I need them to stop now! For the sake of Kayleen, they can't be allowed to interfere with my mental and emotional health. Neither must I be harmed physically!"

Kaye paused to lock eyes with Max, "You see, Max, even a rumor about any aspect of my health can cause damage to Kayleen. I cannot, absolutely cannot, let that happen! Because I did not know who you were, I did not believe it wise to divulge my identity to you earlier."

Max sat silent for a few moments after Kaye finished speaking. His eyes roamed the room as if searching for the proper response, almost in the hope that the right words might appear magically on the wall.

Finally, he shook his head and returned her gaze. Giving a low whistle he said "How can you say that you have revealed your true identity to me, because you know who I am? Kaye, I am an ex-con. Those stats Walters handed out are me!"

"Those stats tell me your name, age, gender, height, weight, ethnicity and the fact that you served time. How long, and what for...That's all, Max. What I know, as of this morning, is that you did not come into my neighborhood either to get near me, use me or impress me. Yet you have succeeded in impressing me with your character."

"How?" It was a genuine question. Max could not imagine that anything he could ever do would impress this woman.

Kaye looked intently at him. "Max, I know you are Sicilian, yet if you personally were connected to the Mafia, you could easily have killed me that first night. You could have been long gone, and if ever suspected, you'd have the means to concoct a fool proof alibi.'

"However, today has been the biggest testimony of your character. Because of what you learned from the law course research that you did in prison, something you heard last night convinced you that our caller could be a psychopathic killer. Even after I insulted you, behaved like a real bitch..." a faint smile crossed her face as she observed his shock at her admission. "Yes, Max, I do have a pretty good sense of self-awareness. Bitch may even be too mild a word to describe how I treated you. I was intentional about giving you ample justification to walk away. Yet you chose to return, willing to sacrifice your own freedom to ensure this fellow is caught."

"That's what makes you trust me?"

"Yep, how a person may be classified because of what they've done, does not define who they are. One can have the title 'Doctor' and be a cad. Likewise, one can be a janitor, yet, be a prince of a person."

Max swallowed hard, "Thanks, Kaye, for believing in me and trusting me. Not too many people in my life have done that."

"So, Mr. Carron, now you know who I am, can you be as certain that this caller is a psychopath as you suspected? Or, could this be some ploy to rid Kayleen of me? Perhaps a power struggle or some deal that I might block or even a disgruntled employee or client?"

Max absent-mindedly ran his hand back and forth over the velvet fabric on the arm rest. "Kaye, if we'd had this conversation, even 24 hours ago, I would have been tempted to rethink everything. However, after last night's call I really do think the guy is using them for sexual gratification. The other question only you can answer. Do you have any evidence of such things as a power struggle or a disgruntled person?"

"To the best of my knowledge, Max, no there isn't. So Sherlock, where do we go from here?"

"Well, first we need to find an electrical store and a hardware store and make some purchases. But not in this city, for here you might be recognized." Max grinned, "I had opportunity, in the slammer, for both a formal and an informal education."

"What do you mean?"

"I had the opportunity to converse with some of this county's best burglars. I found it ingenious how they could disarm all types of alarm systems. It's how I got into your house in the first place. But if they and I can do it, there's a very good likelihood so can our perp. Like I said, this means we need a back up security system. Fortunately, my pen mates told me how to set up such systems. Even told me what materials a guy would need. It's important we do this very quickly, Kaye!"

"Why so urgent?"

"This guy seems to be escalating, both in the violence of his rhetoric and apparent sexual gratification. These psychopathic, violent, sexual offenders that I interviewed seemed to begin with fantasizing, progressing ultimately to crossing the line to do what they had verbalized."

Max's words elicited a look of horror on Kaye's face, as she recalled some of the things her caller had said.

Max continued, "Once the back up alarm system is in place, we need to set up a game plan to tease out of this character whether or not he has had other victims. If he'll talk, we'll record the specifics and send them anonymously to your FBI friend." He stopped and looked at Kaye, "You do know the agent that gave the Judge my mug shot don't you?"

Kaye nodded affirmatively.

"Good! The FBI will verify his statements for us. Assuming they're true, we'll be able to build a profile on our perp. This should help us defend against him."

Kaye frowned, "But if we contact the FBI anonymously, how can they let us know if the fellow's for real?"

Max smiled, "Newspaper adds, people pass information all the time through the classifieds."

"Well, Professor, you are the Detective. I am simply

your ignorant assistant. Yet, I too have the same passion as you to see this character apprehended! But, Max, let me ask, if anyone wanted to get rid of me, couldn't they hire someone, like this guy?"

"Kaye, if someone wanted to remove you regardless of their motivation they would hire a hit man to take you out. They wouldn't mess around with a looney like a serial killer, even if they could find one. Serial killers are secretive, one man shows. They aren't hired killers with a business card," Max responded nonchalantly.

Kaye's mouth dropped open. "Are you suggesting hired killers, assassins are normal?"

"Kaye, I'm not saying they are morally or ethically normal, but they are in it as a business, and the good ones aren't flakey. They aren't interested in notoriety. They keep a very low profile. I would think that anyone wanting to permanently remove you from Kayleen would not fool around. You'd be dead! Trust me. Those guys are professional!"

Kaye just shook her head, "I can handle business in board rooms - company analysis, growth charts, potential prospects, high risk scenarios, and that sort of stuff. But Max, in these matters you've discussed, I'm afraid it's all so far beyond me. Maybe that's why God brought you to me?"

"God?"

"Yes God! After all, don't you find it interesting that Jack sent you to prison for six years when it could easily have been one or two years maximum? It's also unusual that you would get both the formal, as you call it, and informal education critical to this case. Not to mention the fact that you felt prompted to come to my place not Jack's, even though you knew which house was his?"

Max couldn't believe what he was hearing. This normally very lucid woman was attributing his presence in her life to God. "Kaye, all of that are just circumstances or coincidence...Nothing more! Besides I'm positive God didn't have a hand in what I did!"

He gave a little laugh and added, "at least not the God I was taught about!"

"Well, Max, in my world there are no coincidences, only Godincidences! You are right that God does nothing evil, the Bible is very clear about that. However, God will use all things to work out for the good for those who love Him. No matter how bad a situation may be."

Max chuckled, "This is the Gospel according to Kaye?"

"No! This is what Paul told the Christians in Rome in the middle of the first century."

"Really?"

"Yes, really! It's in Romans, Chapter 8, verse 28, but..." Kaye paused her eyes twinkling, "perhaps we should defer our theological discussion to later. It's midmorning and if you want to shop for your materials, we should soon get started. I do believe we will find what you want in Oakton. Like I said before, it's about an hour and a half drive away, but before we can go I must make good on my promise."

"Which is?"

"Which is to take care of Rufie...That's why Dave came by this morning, he and Sue were going to Philly with the Walters and Matt is also away this weekend. So Ruff spends the weekend with me, well and you. I trust you are not allergic to dogs, Mr. Carron?"

"Actually I love dogs!" Max said obviously warming to the idea of dog sitting. "In fact other than my family, especially Mama, it was the absence of a dog I missed most in prison." Then he added almost shyly, "I think you'd like my mother, Kaye. She's a lot like you. I hope some day she can meet you. Anyway, I like all dogs, even little ones. It will be great to meet your Rufie!"

Once again, if Max had been paying attention, he may have clued into the fact that things might not be exactly as he anticipated. Kaye smiled mischievously, "That's good, Max, because Rufie is actually our Independence Drive neighborhood pet. He belongs to Dave and Sue. But with all of us working and quite busy, communal sharing of the duties is the only way any of us can have the pleasure of dog ownership."

Then she added, "Max, why don't you wear your hoodie. Remember, your photo is probably around town. So, Mr.Carron, if you are now able to walk, I thought we could take my private trail that winds behind Dave's and Jack's."

"The Sergeant Major has returned," Max muttered to himself, but secretly he was glad to finally be getting outside. Not only that, he'd get a gander at the Chief's house and the dog was an added bonus.

"I'll bet he's a cute little guy?" he ventured.

Kaye just looked at him and smiled.

Chapter Twenty-One

"This feels great!" Max exclaimed exuberantly.

Kaye laughed, "You're being facetious, right?"

"What?"

Cocking her head and raising an eyebrow, she looked at him and said, "Mr. Carron, after I accidentally hit you...you know where...and barely an hour ago, you couldn't walk or sit down. Now, you tell me, 'this feels great!', as we set out to get Rufie?"

"Oh, I get it." Max chuckled, "Well, Ms. McDonald, I wasn't referring to my body parts. I meant it really feels great to be outside. The sun's shining, the flowers are bursting forth. Spring is here, and summer's just around the corner! It's great!" He flung his arms wide and spun around.

Kaye shrugged, "If you say so."

"Come on, Kaye, I just spent six years in concrete. Time wasn't my own. You couldn't just walk out and enjoy yourself like this. When I got out, I headed down here only to end up in your house. It's great to be out doors! Don't you get it?" He looked at her almost pleadingly.

"I know the six years may not have been your choice, but two months at my house definitely was your doing Mr. Carron." Kaye scowled.

"I know that! It's also my choice to stay on, but I'm trying to share that it feels really great to have the opportunity to get outside." He threw his hands up in exasperation. "I'm trying to say 'Thank you!' Am I that bad a communicator?"

Kaye's mouth twisted into an impish grin, "You may not

be so grateful after you've met Rufie."

By this time she was at the Davidson's front door. As the latch gave way, she hollered, "Hey, Ruf! Walk time, Baby!"

Stepping inside she turned to Max, "Better stand behind me until I introduce you."

Max was about to say "Why?" when what appeared to him like a giant black bear, exuberantly hurtled down the steps. It was full of enthusiasm, that is, until it spied him. A deep throated growl rumbled from the dog's chest as Rufie attempted to lunge past Kaye at this stranger.

"Oh, Rufie!" Kaye laughed, grabbing the big dog's collar, "Quit pretending you're 'Kung Fu Rufus!' Here's a beef jerky." Ruf responded simultaneously both to the tone of her voice and to the bribe.

Much to Max's relief the dog was far more interested in the jerky than in him. "What on earth type of monster dog is he? He's huge!"

"He's a Bouvier des Flanders," Kaye responded matter-of-factly. "Originally, they were herding dogs."

"Why the heck do they call him Rufie? I expected a little sissy dog."

"Well, in part, that is one of the reasons. Dave has a quirky sense of humor. When people hear the word 'Rufie', just like you, they expect to see a little foo foo type dog. However, it was the Davidson's son Matt who named him Rufus. When he saw the pup, it reminded him of Dennis the Menace's dog. Regardless Ruf has wormed his way into all of our hearts. He really is the house pet of all three of our houses. It works out well. Even with all of our busy schedules, usually one of us is free to look after him."

She leaned down, gave the dog a big hug and whispered, "I want you to meet a new friend. Rufus, this is Max."

Turning to Max she said, "Max, this is Rufus. Now, sit Rufus, and give Max a paw." With that the big dog sat and put up his paw to give Max a high-five.

As the three began their walk, it became apparent to

...

Kaye that Max was totally enthralled with this new canine companion. *"At least it's obvious he didn't lie about his love for dogs."* She smiled to herself, *"hopefully all the rest is true too!"*

Max found a stick and Rufus and Max alternated their play between 'fetch' and 'tug-o-war'. Rufus was equally enamored with his new friend. As they headed back to Kaye's, Max was dealing with practicalities, "Shouldn't we go get his food and bowls?"

"Nope! Remember, he's a community pet. He has his belongings in each household." She giggled and added, "All are tailored to the tastes of the human residents of the respective household."

"Meaning what?" Max queried.

"Meaning in my household, you, Max, will have no need tonight of your imaginary line. Instead, we'll have Rufus as our chaperone."

Max's jaw dropped in disbelief, "You let him sleep in your bed? You've got to be kidding!"

"'Fraid not, ever since Matt brought him home, Rufus realized that at my house, my bed was his. Don't look so shocked." She admonished. "He was so cute when they got him. He looked just like a little black Teddy Bear."

"But surely you knew he'd grow up?"

"Yeah, I did, I just never imagined he'd be this big! But after all, my bed is a king size and we've bonded." Kaye looked at Max and laughed.

"So, where does he sleep at the Chief's house?"

"...In Matt's bed."

"Matt?"

"He's their son."

"The other cop is their son?"

"So where does he sleep at His Honor's?"

"In Jack's study," Kaye glanced at Max, knowing exactly what he was thinking. "You're wrong Mr. Carron. Jack is not the fastidious one. Marnie is the household organizer."

Kaye paused, "she's actually an awesome homemaker. I don't know how she does it. She's a school principal, a gourmet chef and her decorating skills are unparalleled." Just thinking of Marnie brought a smile to Kaye's face. "She's one of the most compassionate people I know. Who knows Max, maybe one day you'll get a chance to meet her. On friendly terms, I mean."

"Fat chance, Ms. McDonald! His Honor's posting of my mug shot has taken care of that, I can assure you. Our agreement is to nail the perp, and I slip out the back door. You don't mention my existence, which gets us back on topic. You agreed for us to go get the electrical gadgetry and wiring I need for our secondary alarm. What do we do with the Bear?"

"Ruf's okay on his own for five or six hours. I'll just give him his water, another jerky and my bed. Too bad my phone 'caller' couldn't come when we're gone. I think he'd rue the day!"

"So Rufus can't come with us? He doesn't like car rides?"

"By his reaction you can tell he does. But I'm assuming you do not wish to be recognized? Every police person and almost everybody in our area knows Rufus is the Chief's dog. They will all come over to pat him!"

With Rufus settled in the house, the two headed for her car. To Kaye's surprise, Max climbed into the back seat. "You expect me to chauffer you?"

"I'm not here, remember?" He settled in on the floor behind the passenger side.

Kaye looked back in amazement. "You have got to be kidding!"

"No, I'm not Kaye!" Max said sternly. "There's something else you need to be aware of Ms. McDonald. If I am right about this caller, he knows you. He could be following you. So keep a sharp eye on your rearview mirror. Always observe cars around you and let's be as evasive as we can."

An hour and a half later, when they arrived at the Mall in Oakton, Max had Kaye park in amongst all the other cars. He had her get out and pretend to stretch, while casually checking to see if anyone else was observing their vehicle. If she was sure the coast was clear, she was to rap on the window. When she had done this, he slipped out the other side of the car. The two entered the store separately.

Max went about gathering up the electronic devices and wire that he needed. For her part Kaye browsed the hardware store, checking out the many household items, finally selecting a bright red toaster. They entered different check out lines with Max exiting the store three or four minutes ahead of Kaye.

Walking briskly towards the maze of cars in the general vicinity of Kaye's dark green caddie, he headed for the pickup parked beside her vehicle. He casually strolled around the truck as if checking for something. When Kaye opened her car, he slid deftly into the back seat.

"Whew! Mr. Carron, I almost feel like I'm in a 007 movie," she laughed. To her surprise Max did not respond with the same frivolity, glancing in the rear view mirror she was shocked at the sternness in his features.

"This is not a joke, Kaye," he replied tersely. "This perp is deadly and you, Ma'am, are his prey!" The tone in his voice sent chills into her. They drove home in silence.

The moment they arrived Max set to work. Kaye went to her study, flicked on the computer and engrossed herself in the business at hand. She wanted to keep her mind off of what Max was doing and especially to erase from her memory his last disturbing words.

In spite of everything, somehow she did manage to work productively. So involved in her work, it was 8 p.m. before she stopped to check her watch. Suddenly famished, she left the study and found Max kneeling on the kitchen floor, near the patio door.

Impulsively, she grabbed her camera. "Hey, Max! Smile!"

As he looked up, the flash went off, "What are you doing?" He yelled as he leapt to his feet.

"Taking your picture! Not bad! You look very distinguished, Mr. Carron – even handsome."

His hand closed firmly over her wrist, the gruffness in his voice startled her, "Give me the camera," he demanded. "I am not here, remember!"

In defiance, she held on to the camera, her green eyes flashing, "Lighten up, it's digital. There is no film. No one else will see it, why can't I have your picture?"

His grip relaxed slightly, "Don't let that camera fall into anyone else's hands. I'm not telling you! I'm ordering you!" He let go her wrist and returned to his work on the floor.

"Who is this guy? One minute he appears as a naïve school boy. The next his manner is as cold as ice. Oh Lord God, is it right for me to trust him?" She studied him cautiously. Soon however, she was overcome with curiosity. "Whatever are you doing?"

Meticulously, he was threading the wire between the baseboard and the floor. "I'm rewiring every door and every window in this place electronically."

"But the whole house is on the alarm system, hooked to the central depot? You said you were just going to set yours up inside?"

"Right...and, I am beginning internally with each window and door. Should your perp over ride your commercial system, I'm hoping I can catch him when he enters. Remember, I over rode your system three times. When I entered the first time, when I left and when I returned. If I can do that I'm certain your evil paramour will be able to do it too."

"And he can't do that with your system?"

"Kaye, he'll be anticipating your commercial alarm system. My hope is that he won't be expecting a home made device. After I set up the doors and windows, I'll monitor all the internal doors and passage ways. The idea is to give us some advanced warning before he bursts into the bedroom. By the way, it also means when we get in the bedroom, you never leave by yourself, nor will I. If either of us can't sleep or gets hungry, we wake the other and go together. Deal?"

Kaye nodded her agreement, sighing as she did, "I just never imagined this situation would be so ominous." Before Max could reply, their conversation was abruptly halted by a wet nose stuck in his face. "Rufus appears to think we should be eating," Kaye ventured. Then she added, "...and perhaps that he should have a pee break. I'll do that while you're finishing up."

"Like hell, you will!" Max yelled once again leaping up.

Kaye froze startled both by his movements and the tone of his voice.

Max stood with his hands on his hips glaring at her. "What is it, that you don't get, Ms. McDonald, about your circumstance? It's now dark out.'

"With a dog or no dog... you live in a very isolated neighborhood. There is someone out there who wants to harm you. However, at present there are only three of us aware of that fact, you the prey, me and the predator.'

"You need to start thinking very defensively and I might add about others besides yourself. If you are so important to Kayleen, start living like it matters that this perp fail in his attempt on your life. It might also be a bit nice if you think of me. You walk into the perp's trap and where do you think that leaves me?"

He looked at her incredulously. "Kaye, you are such an easy mark, it isn't funny. You don't even know what you don't know!"

Unwanted tears began to flood from her eyes, "No!" she snapped, "I don't know a thing about this dark world, you keep talking about and quite frankly I don't want to know! I know about boardroom shenanigans and back stabbings, but not these thoughts you're putting in my head. They terrify me!"

"I am not putting these things in your path, Ms. McDonald. Your 3 a.m. caller is doing that, and while it's obvious you like to be in control, face it, Lady, you aren't! He is! You don't have any choice but to deal with it. The only choice you have is 'how to'. So far you're opting to do this quietly and discreetly utilizing me. The other option, which I was willing to do this morning, is go to the authorities like your neighbor Dave or your FBI contact.'

"Lady, it's not going to hurt my feelings if you want to take this to the cops now, or later, when we get a little more info on the perp. Kaye, if you want to live and avoid a very terrible end, you have to smarten up and start paying attention!" Max was standing about three feet from Kaye, he raised his arm gesturing to emphasize his point. Suddenly, a huge black ball of fur was between them emitting a low growl.

Max looked down and started to laugh, "Way to go, Ruf! That's showing her how to behave." He knelt down in front of the large dog and cupped the big head in his hands.

Max's demeanor had completely relaxed Rufie who now did want his walk.

"Let's both take him out, Kaye."

It was a warm spring night, and the scent of lilacs sweetened the evening. As they walked silently side by side, Kaye finally broke the silence.

"Max, I really don't mean to be difficult and I don't want to cause trouble for you. I just don't know what to do. Please, be patient with me. If you think we should go to the police, I will."

Max ran his hand through his hair, "Right at the moment, Kaye, I'm not sure either what the best route to take is. If he is a psychopathic killer as I suspect. I can tell you he will be extremely clever. It's not that the cops aren't. It's just that they have procedures to follow and these psychos seem to know how to play the system. They can get under the radar and elude the cops for quite a while, which if you happen to be a victim in this interval, that's not an overly comforting thought. Sure they'll eventually get caught. However, in the meantime you're dead and your friends and family have to deal with the horror of it, all the rest of their lives."

Kaye shuddered, "But what can we do?"

"The 'you' part of the 'we' can start taking what's going on very, very, very seriously... much, much more seriously than you have. You need to accept the fact that you are in grave danger."

"But why? What would I have done to attract this creep's attention?"

"In all probability, Kaye...nothing. Why does a hunter select a particular animal to track and bag?"

"That's this man's mentality?" Kaye gasped.

"Yes, Kaye, unfortunately it is. Why he selected you, will be known only to him, and us, if we can track him down and bag him first. That's precisely what those guys that I interviewed admitted. Every one of them said they'd select a target and begin the hunt.'

"The victim was just like an inanimate object to them. It was the prey. They never saw the person as someone's precious daughter or mother or wife. They never ever considered her age and the devastation they were bringing, not only to the victim, but to her family and to the community at large.'

"Even in the horrific acts they perpetrated upon her, her pain, her terror, her cries for mercy, her tears were only fuel for their own perverted sexual gratification. This passion – lust – rage, within them, would only subside with their own orgasm and the victim's demise.'

"Then came the thrill of hiding their tracks...eluding the one's seeking them. Again it was the thrill of the hunt only now they were the prey and..." Max concluded, "Their egos got stoked with every successful dodge. Many of them actually confessed that they'd kept a scrapbook of their endeavors containing newspaper articles, items of the victims', photos, even hair from the victim. Their "trophies" as some called them."

Kaye was now listening intently. She was sure her eyes had never been so wide. She, at one point, had wanted to joke simply to ease her own tension and to defuse his words. However, one look at Max, the pain in his voice as he reminisced about these interviews, convinced her otherwise. He was telling the truth – deadly dark truth.

"This is not a thrill for you to expose this person, is it, Max?" Kaye spoke very softly knowing, even as she asked that question, in fact the answer was no!

He shook his head sadly, "You are correct! The truth is I only chose to do the course interviews with these inmates because, I knew, there was absolutely no way that any of my 'quote' Italian family connections would be involved."

He gave a hollow laugh, "There's no money at all in serial, sex killing. It's not a remote possibility and so no incentive for anybody that I might possibly know to be involved. So I thought this would be a good safe choice for me."

Max stopped walking. Rufie was content to simply sit and bask in the moonlight. Kaye stood quietly waiting for Max to continue.

His voice was barely audible. "Kaye, I just had no idea of the depravity and sickness of the human mind." He bent over and stroked Ruf's head. When he stood up tears began to trickle down his face, and for the first time Max realized he wasn't ashamed to let them come.

"Kaye, you just can't imagine. You don't want to imagine the thinking of these men. Most of them appear like ordinary guys, even look like nice guys, but in one segment of their psyche lies this deep, deep evil. It seems to lurk there until it captivates them once again to attempt to repeat such violence.'

"At that time, Kaye, you can't even say they are like animals. Animals don't behave that way!"

Kaye and Max began walking slowly back to the house, but it was like a valve had been opened to his soul. A valve that allowed all the emotional pressure this course assignment had produced to suddenly be released.

"Kaye, it was one thing to listen to these guys, gather the data and write a term paper. It was one way to get the stuff out of me. I just never thought that I'd have to apply the knowledge, I wrote about, to catch one of these psychos."

He shook his head, "It's almost like you feel you're encountering a demonic force, if such a thing were real. Quite frankly that's a truth I'd just as soon like not to discover, much less deal with!"

"Would you like me...us to talk to Dave tomorrow? It seems that I've really asked more of you than anyone should ask of another human being."

"Yeah, Kaye, on the one hand, I personally would like to be relieved of the responsibility. On the other hand, I don't want to see you become a statistic, and the guy go free to try again. There's also another consideration."

"What's that?"

"What can you take?"

"Pardon?"

"What **can** you take? You've seen how those interviews affected me and yeah, I probably have a different world view than your Bryn Mawr world. So what can you take, Kaye?"

They now were back in the sanctuary of Kaye's kitchen. Rufie was occupied with his supper and theirs was in the oven.

Kaye sat on the kitchen stool, perplexed at Max's question. "I don't understand, it's not like I'm going to interview him. What do you mean?"

"No, Kaye, what you will have to do will be much worse. You see, in my paper I put forth the hypothesis that although these guys act independent of others, there are certain trigger points common to them all. If we're going to try and bring down this perp, we're going to have to be very intentional in each and every call."

"Meaning?"

"Meaning you are going to have to ask specific questions,

which I will frame for you. You will have to lead him into divulging if he has ever done anything to anyone before, including getting specifics."

Kaye closed her eyes, "You mean like getting the details that you got in your interviews?"

"Yes, and we'll have to trap him into identifying the victim, name, place, date, specifics that only the perp could have."

"Why?"

"Because then you and I will craft a letter to your FBI contact. Like I said before, we'll do it anonymously. We'll ask for a specific reply in the classifieds of the *'National Enquirer'*. Telling them to word it one way if our information appears to be fictitious, and another way if the info is bona fide."

"So I need to hear horrific stuff? Worse than the profanity and crude vulgarity I've been getting?"

"The answer is yes, if we go this route, Kaye. That's why I asked you, what can you take?"

She drew a deep breath, "I don't know if I could. Particularly when I see that it's so troubling to you, a man."

"A man who went to jail, a criminal." Max interjected.

Kaye flushed, "Well, yes, I guess so. If you, who would have experienced so much more than I, could be so troubled...What will it do to me?"

"That is the sacrifice, Kaye, that you would be making. The only motivation you'd have is that hopefully we could stop this guy from ever again inflicting such atrocity on anyone else."

"If we did catch him, would he ever be released?" Kaye dreaded the answer.

"Unlikely, though I can't give you an absolute. He would be classified as a dangerous offender, quite possibly criminally insane, which many are. All research thus far indicates that the likelihood of such individuals re-offending is astronomically high."

Once again, Kaye locked her eyes onto Max's but now

it was no longer as her antagonist. For the first time, she noticed how soft, brown and beautiful they really seemed. She bit her lip, "Okay, I am in! But you are going to have to coach me all the way."

"I will, I promise," he reached out, took her hand, giving it a playful squeeze, and said "Partner!" Then, almost as an after thought he added, " By the way, I've decided you can keep the picture."

"So, now that we've finally managed to agree, we face another decision." Kaye said in all seriousness.

"What now?"

"Our supper is cooked, but Rufie has long finished his... So, do we eat first and then walk the dog or do we leave our meal in the oven and walk first?"

Max laughed, "I'd vote for the former, but I think Rufie has in mind the latter and quite likely another walk before bedtime." The sharp bark affirmed that choice!

Chapter Twenty-Two

The muscular young man was perspiring heavily as he raced across the Eighth Street Bridge. He had already completed the five-mile run through the park and along the river, in two more miles he'd be back at his apartment.

He looked at his watch and grinned, "Ten minutes ahead of my best time...way to go Henry, you're getting stronger every day!"

Enthusiastically, he picked up his pace, arriving at his destination a full fifteen minutes ahead of his usual time and obviously elated at his performance.

He headed straight for the shower, "Have to smell good for my sweetie," he chortled.

Drying himself off, he stared at his physique in the full length mirror that he'd installed in his bathroom.

"Not bad, Henry Glaxton... Not bad, even if I do say so myself!"

The weight lifting in the gym combined with the distance running was producing the desired effect. Henry was also noting that admiring glances from both guys and gals were increasing in the gym. He was looking forward to this summer at the beach. Life was definitely going his way.

Pulling on his designer jeans and a smart Tommy Hilfiger navy golf shirt, he again assessed himself in the mirror. Clean shaven, blonde hair close cropped, alluring side burns, capped off with the most piercing blue eyes, he indeed cut a dashing figure.

"Move over Elvis, you are no competition for ol' Henry." Obviously satisfied he added, "Just the boy any Mama wants to see her darling daughter bring home." The mirror returned a most winsome smile, "In addition, the lad is oh so witty and clever too!"

He sauntered into the living room of his modest one bedroom apartment. "Timing is so perfect, Henry, precision is just so you! Good things always come to the one who learns to patiently wait. So since we've got a half hour before I need to catch my bus to the Baxter's, it's time for me to peruse the good things that my waiting has already secured."

From the bottom drawer of his dresser, Henry retrieved a high school year book and a large scrapbook. Opening the year book he looked sourly at the picture of a pert looking blonde.

When he had asked her to the prom, she had just looked at him and patronizingly replied, 'Oh, how sweet Henry, but I'm afraid you're just not my type!'

The next he saw of her, she was walking on the arm of the football captain. He saw her say something to the guy and then they both turned and laughed at him. He went red with embarrassment, worse still other kids were standing round and started to laugh. She'd obviously told the whole school about him. "That's when I learned you needed to be patient and not blow your cover too soon," he muttered.

He had managed to finish off the remaining weeks of school and graduate in spite of the humiliating taunts.

Henry smirked, "when the marks came out it was me, not the football jock that had the last laugh."

That summer he got a job in a supermarket but again was made fun of by the check out girls. So that job didn't last long. However, shortly after that he spied this muscle building advertisement that showed a skinny kid having sand thrown at him by this big bully.

It gave him the idea to do something about his physique. He also began to read magazines and books, even turned to videos to help him with his approach to the opposite sex. He hadn't lasted long in college, not challenging enough, he had said.

The truth was he had discovered another passion. As a result he chose to travel around the country, working odd jobs, here and there, all the while studying and fine tuning that which had become his new ambition. He'd become a computer wiz early on.

He smiled wryly, "and boy have I learned!"

Delightedly, he opened the scrapbook and began to flip randomly through it. His various 'dates', some of them seemed very plain, in fact the first few looked rather grubby. Some of the faces appeared quite young.

"Oh, My precious," he said kissing his right index finger and putting it to the lips of a young girl of about twelve. "So young, so innocent, you were special, but tonight...Tonight is the night Steph gets to take Henry to meet Mama and Papa. This is a real biggie for you Steph!" He laughed and began to hum, "Gotta' girl in every port! Babe, Babe."

He began to mimic his last date with Steph, "Shush, Darling," he had said dramatically, putting his finger to her lips, "You are not a plain Jane. You are beautiful on the inside and that's all that matters!" .

He frowned, one thing he knew all about, was how plain people felt about themselves. He'd been there and he'd hated it. He checked his watch.

"Time to go," and slammed shut the scrapbook, "reminiscing will have to wait for another time, Ladies. Won't be long, and I'll have another photo to add," he smiled, "But this one will be the best ever!"

As he walked down the street, he snatched a bouquet of mixed flowers from the corner convenience store.

"Must keep romancing my darling with tender care," he laughed.

The bus arrived at the stop just as he stepped out of the store, "There you go old boy, perfect timing once again!"

"Oh to be young and in love again," smiled an old codger as Henry got on the bus. "Must be a special date?"

"Very special indeed, Sir," replied Henry graciously. He

chuckled inside, "Oh, Henry Glaxton, you are such a nice boy, impeccable manners and all!"

As his bus arrived at Stephanie's stop, he stood up bowed to the old guy and exited saying, "Do have a good evening, Sir."

He walked down the street, crossed over at the next intersection and finally found 'Anne Street'. He glanced at the housing around him, a blue collar neighborhood for sure. Steph had said her Dad worked at a lumber yard. "Patience Henry, patience, all good things take time." That was the downside to his life. It took real talent to do what he did. The problem was no one knew just how good he was, and the lack of recognition was beginning to wear on him.

Now at her door, Henry gathered himself up preparing for a most flattering performance. His finger found the doorbell. In seconds the door flew open.

"Gad, she must have been waiting for me."

"Oh, Henry, I'm so glad you could some," Stephanie gushed.

"So am I, Darling. I've been looking forward to meeting your parents." Feigning shyness he gave her a polite buss on the cheek.

Steph turned crimson, spying the flowers her eyes sparkled, "For me?"

Just then, her mother entered the hallway. Henry could tell where Stephanie got her size, both she and her mother were stout. Neither were his type, but he was not about to reveal his dark thoughts, not at all!

He acted surprised at Steph's question. "No, Darling, these flowers aren't for you. I bought them just for your Mother."

Mrs. Baxter was clearly taken aback. "Why, Henry, how kind of you to think of me!"

"Well, Stephanie, is such a wonderful caring lady, I knew her mother would be the same. I wanted to express my thanks to you and Mr. Baxter for producing such a wonderful daughter."

Turning to Steph, and reaching into his pocket, he said,

"I picked up this little thing for you."

Stunned, Stephanie took the jewelry box from his hand.

"Open it, Dear. I do hope you like it?" Henry smiled.

She gave a squeal of delight. Her dark eyes sparkled with gratitude, as she took a little crystal cat pin out of the box. "Oh Mom, I told Henry, just the other day, how I liked cats. See how thoughtful he is! Look, it's even got a tiny black collar, just like our Tia's."

Henry pointed to the pin and remarked, "actually, Steph, what caught my attention was the emerald eyes, they shine so...Like yours do! That's what drew me to the pin, just as your eyes drew me to you." Then he added coyly, "I'm so pleased you like it!"

"Let the boy get in the door," bellowed a voice from within.

"Oh yes, do come in, Henry," Mrs. Baxter offered. "We're just overwhelmed at your kindness to Stephanie."

She ushered him into their dining room. One look at the man seated at the head of the table told Henry that it was not only the women in the Baxter household who enjoyed their food. Henry raised his eyebrows, discreetly of course. Mr. Baxter, in his opinion, bore a striking resemblance to the Daddy Warbuck character, in the 'Little Orphan Annie' comic strip. Although Steph's father was considerably shorter and stouter, than Warbuck, his head was as bald as a billiard ball, and just as round as the comic character!

"Ed, this is Stephanie's friend Henry. Look at the beautiful bouquet he brought me," Mrs. Baxter held out the flowers for her husband to see.

"Look at the gorgeous pin he gave me," Stephanie enthused.

Before Ed could respond, Henry said, "Well, Sir, I couldn't come just bringing a gift for the ladies. Stephanie told me you are a real football fan. So when I saw this issue of 'Sport's Illustrated' giving next season's most likely Super Bowl contenders, I knew you might like it." He handed Ed the magazine and reached out to firmly shake his hand.

Mrs. Baxter's meal was plain but very good. From the Baxter's perspective Henry appeared to be the best thing since sliced bread. From Henry's perspective the evening was one of his most stellar performances.

As the evening progressed, the conversation turned naturally as to how the two met. Henry shared that he had needed funds to continue his schooling. He saw Kayleen's ad requiring a clerk in the finance department and had applied for the job. Since he had the necessary computer skills, he was hired. It was in the lunch room that he first saw Stephanie.

"You reminded me very much of my mother," he lied. "Other fellows told me how caring and compassionate, your daughter is," that was the truth. "So I finally plucked up enough nerve to go to the receptionist desk and introduce myself. We began just having lunch together in the cafeteria."

"Henry may not look it but he's very shy." Stephanie volunteered. "It took him nearly two months to ask me out."

"Since then, we try to have dinner out, go to the movies or a concert about every two weeks." Henry added smiling benevolently at Steph. "I can tell how much Ms. McDonald appreciates having your daughter as an employee. It's quite a responsibility a receptionist has in a big company like Kayleen. The receptionist is the first person a potential client meets and sometimes the only one," Henry added solemnly.

Poor Stephanie, she was one of those people who blush in spite of themselves. His compliments caused her to blush even more. She murmured demurely "Oh, Henry, Ms. McDonald is such a wonderful person to work for. It makes my job very easy."

"That may be so, Steph," Henry retorted, "but not every nice boss has as dedicated an employee as you. I guess though it must be pretty cool for you, as a woman, to have a female boss as high profile as Ms. McDonald is?"

If M.K. McDonald had a fan club, Stephanie Baxter would surely have been on the club's executive. Henry was well aware of that fact. He knew once he got her on the topic of Kayleen and McDonald, she would monopolize the conversation. That suited him perfectly, for it saved him having to come up with ingenious answers to the typical parent questions. Such as, where he went to college? What was he studying to become? Where were his family? What did they do, and of course, what was his intent with their daughter?

True to form, Stephanie didn't disappoint him. She began to share that next week Ms. McDonald would be away three full days on business, in Paris!

"Imagine," Steph said to them, "being away in Paris. Wouldn't that be wonderful? M.K. says she doesn't like being away but as for me, I'd be thrilled to travel!"

By 9 p.m. Henry's patience had maxed out, yet ever so politely he excused himself, using the bus transportation and his need to get home and 'hit the books' to justify his escape.

Mr. Baxter shook his hand warmly. Mrs. Baxter gave him a hug and an open invitation to drop by anytime. Stephanie gave him a loving kiss on the cheek. He bade them farewell, stepped outside as if he were a Prince departing his loyal subjects, and faded into the night.

Henry had loathed himself when he was a plain Jane and he projected that self loathing onto all that he viewed as plain.

"Regular asses, those Baxters," he spat, "Couldn't be easier to dupe." He laughed, "If only you knew what book I'm hitting! My relationship with dearest Steph is conveniently the focus of Kayleen Enterprises attention, not my lowly clerkship in the finance department."

Henry, had he been as wise as he thought, may have paid more attention to the old saying, *"Pride comes before a fall!"* Stephanie was indeed infatuated with this gallant knight, but a lot of God given wisdom often resides with folk that Henry dismissed as plain and gullible. Had he been privy to Mr. and Mrs. Baxter's pillow talk later that night (which of course he wasn't) Henry might have been surprised to learn his performance had been received as just that - a performance.

Neither of them wanted to burst their daughter's bubble, just yet. In love they both humbly knelt by the side of their bed and prayed with tears in their eyes: *"Thank you, Lord Jesus, for giving us our precious daughter. You have given her a pure heart and great love for others. Protect and deliver her from the evil we sense is now surrounding her. Lord, we know you have some one special to be Stephanie's life companion. Please, help her meet that one. Grant her your wisdom to recognize the deceit and manipulation that is currently surrounding her."*

Then in a strong warrior voice Ed spoke up, *"In the powerful name of Jesus, I break the power of darkness that hovers over my daughter!"* and his wife gently added, *"Please, dear Jesus, keep your daughter Stephanie safe and surround her with your ministering angels to protect her."*

Then together they simply asked God to thwart all evil plans that Henry Glaxton might have, whatever they might be. They ended in a unified *"Amen!"*

Chapter Twenty-Three

"Here's some warm coco." Max pushed the cup into Kaye's hands and closed her trembling fingers around the warm brew.

Her eyes were open wide, her lips taut. "Max" she stammered, "I can't do this!"

"Yes, M.K. McDonald can do this," came a firm reply. "She has to do it!"

"No, Max, my tenacity is in the boardroom. This is not part of my world!" Tears welled up in her eyes, "How could anyone do what he said he did to another human being?"

She stopped abruptly, her green eyes began to flash, as she asked, "Do you think that monster was just making up those stories, like some teenage braggart trying to shock and impress his friends?"

Cup in hand she began to pace the kitchen, "That must be it, what a filthy mind!" Rage began to rise up within her, "I heard what you talked about." She whirled to face Max, "he is sexually, you know, doing it, isn't he?" Her face flushed red, as she spoke then her eyes met Max's.

She stopped abruptly, as pain, compassion, deep, deep sadness returned her gaze.

Gripping her cup she sat down opposite him, all rage had drained from her. A whisper was all that could escape her mouth. "Oh, Max, please tell me you don't believe what we just heard?"

The silent dropping of his eyes from hers, told her more than she wanted to know.

"Max," now it was her eyes that closed, "the things he told us, they...," It was almost too horrible to say, "they are like the things you heard when you interviewed those men in prison, aren't they?"

"Yes, I'm afraid so, Kaye," he replied softly.

"People can actually do that to other people?" She put her hand over her mouth in horror, almost as if unconsciously she was trying to rid herself of a dreadful taste.

"Kaye, I wrote down what he was saying and have summarized it. I need to read it back to you. You can affirm what we heard, or add a detail I missed, or delete something, if you can't remember that point."

"You are not serious! You can't be?" She shook her head and covered her ears.

Max gently reached across, took one of her hands and brought it down to the table. "Yes, you can; and yes, you must."

"Why?" came the feeble protest.

"For three nights now, your caller has given us grizzly details of brutal homicides that he claims to have committed. He has given us names and places of these victims, his trophies as he called them. We need to document them and send them anonymously to your FBI friend."

"Epi?"

"Yeah, that's the one." Max was speaking softly in a monotone voice.

"Dear Lord," Kaye suddenly thought, *"He sounds just like one of those old T.V. cops."* She rolled her eyes, a smile creeping across her face at the thought, *"Like Sgt. Friday of that antiquities TV show, Dragnet."*

"Why are you smiling?" Max's voice penetrated her thoughts, a look of indignation on his face, "Nothing about this is funny!"

"I'm sorry, Max, I know...It's just..."

"Just what?"

"Well, the way you were talking, you reminded me of a cop on a T.V. show."

"This, Kaye, is reality, not fiction!" was the annoyed response.

"I know so I'll try to co-operate, read me what you wrote, but, Max, can I pray first? I really need Christ to strengthen me."

Max sighed, "Yeah, sure, let's pray, but first which one?"

"Which prayer?" Kaye looked at him incredulously, "Why one from my heart."

"No, not which prayer, which cop?"

"Oh,"

"So, which one?"

"Don't laugh!"

"Do I look like this is a joke? Which cop?" he demanded.

"You really want to know?" Kaye nervously twirled her hair in her fingers. "I mean, it was just a fleeting thought. It sort of eased my tension, I mean, it really wasn't a profound thought," she added.

"Which cop?"

"Sergeant Friday," she sighed

"Who?" Max looked puzzled.

"Didn't you ever watch 'Dragnet' reruns?"

Max's mouth dropped open, "Friday? Dragnet? That was the lamest show! Why would you equate me to him?"

Kaye looked at him, with her green eyes now twinkling, "Why, Mr. Carron, you are blushing! I do declare a little ego seems to be showing."

She leaned on the table, rested her chin comfortably upon one upraised hand, and stared into his eyes.

Her banter and twinkling eyes had caught him totally off guard. They'd done to him emotionally, what her briefcase had done to him physically over a week ago. He returned her gaze speechless. She was the most beautiful woman he'd ever seen, and the most unpredictable and annoying one as well.

"So?" she said.

"What?"

"So, am I forgiven?" she asked innocently.

"Forgiven what?" came the rather bewildered reply.

"Forgiven smiling, and likening you to Sgt. Friday of Dragnet renown?"

"Yeah, of course," was his embarrassed response. Max suddenly felt like he was back in grade school. The shy little seven-year-old, trying to talk to the vivacious little Katie. He had thought she was the neatest kid in the class.

It had taken him three weeks to even say, "Hello." They'd become fast friends.

Memories suddenly bombarded his mind. He remembered her bubbly laugh. How soft her sweater was as he helped her put it on.

She never made fun of him or called him "Brownie", like the other kids did whenever he gave the teacher the correct answer. In fact, she had told him he was smart. He had told her that he loved her and when they were bigger he'd marry her. She had just giggled and then gave him a peck on the cheek. Afterwards, he didn't wash his face for two days, probably never would have, except face washing control is not in your hands when you're seven. Mothers usually frown on dirty-faced boys.

The memories flooded in like a tidal wave. He couldn't control them. The memory he'd long locked away. The memory of that day when she wasn't there...The priest had come, his teacher, the nun had gathered the children around her. The young priest looked at the kids like he didn't know what to do. In Max's mind the priest appeared to look like what Max felt when he had to go to bat, knowing his Pop and everyone else were wanting him to hit the ball and Max knew he just couldn't.

The priest talked about how Jesus loved all little boys and girls. Some he especially loved, then he mentioned Katie's name, and everything else was a blur, something about a fire. Everyone was out, but Katie had run back in and the roof collapsed.

Max saw himself, seven years old, holding Mama and Pop's hand. They went to the wake and everyone was crying. Katie, they told him, was in the closed white box. Her smiling picture sat on top that box.

On the car ride back home, Mama was crying. She said it was so sad, apparently Katie had a favorite story book. Katie's mother had told her that it was about a little blue tug boat. Her mother said Katie just loved that book. The fireman had carried Katie out of the house and set her down. The child had cried 'my book' and ran back in to get it. The fireman had tried to grab her but missed. The roof collapsed just as the child ran through the door. The fireman was devastated.

"Dear," Mama had said to him, "Your favorite book was one about a tug boat too, wasn't it?" Max recalled the horror of that truth hitting his heart and as it did he had begun to bawl. Pop said he was getting too big to cry. Mama thought it might comfort him if they read his tug boat story book, but she couldn't find the book.

Max couldn't stop crying. His parents finally gave up arguing as to the best way to stop him, cuddle or slap him, and decided to just let him cry it out.

"People do die!" his father had said "Get used to it! Men don't cry – grow up!"

He couldn't tell them or anyone else. It was his book Katie had run back for. If Pop was right that people do die, and Pop usually was right, then he would never let himself love another girl. It just hurt too much! Even now he felt the pain and tightness in his chest.

"Max, Max! What on earth is going on?" Kaye was waving her hand in front of his face.

It was like he was in a trance, tears were streaming down his face. Finally, Kaye lifted her right hand straight in front placing her left hand over top, like a referee and signaled. *"Time Out!"*

"Max" she shouted, "What are you doing?"

Max snapped back to reality, "Uh," he cleared his throat, "Nothing," he croaked hoping she'd buy that explanation. *"No, Go!"*

"No way, Hosea! You made me come clean with my thoughts. Now it's your turn. If we're to partner, Mr. Carron, we need to be totally transparent with each other."

"It's stupid! You'll just laugh!"

"That's what I told you, but if memory serves me correct, you didn't," she replied.

He glanced at her eyes. They were riveted on him.

"Fine!" he slapped the table, "Fine! You want to know what I was thinking. I'll tell you," he growled.

"Right on!" Kaye sat back, "I'm all ears!"

"Well" he cleared his throat, "I don't know why this memory just flashed back into my head now? I remembered a little friend."

"Girlfriend?"

"Yeah, girlfriend."

"I thought you didn't have any girlfriends?"

"She was seven."

Kaye raised her eyebrows, "Seven?"

"Yeah seven, it was in grade two…Her name was Katie."

"Katie, her name is pretty, similar to mine," Kaye teased. "Did she have red hair?"

Max sighed "As a matter of fact, she did."

Kaye was about to crack a joke when she took a closer look at the man in front of her. This was no joke! He had buried his head in his hands and was struggling hard to compose himself.

She leaned over touched his hand softly and gently prodded, "Please, tell me about Katie."

So he did, even the truth about the tug boat book and whose it was.

"Max, this is very important to what we're doing!"

"No, it's not!"

"Yes, Max, it is! Trust me!"

"How?"

"Don't you see? The memory reveals you made two childhood vows."

"No I didn't."

"Yes, you did! You vowed never to let yourself love another girl."

"Well I did," he snapped. "I loved Mama and Sophia... They're girls."

Kaye rolled her eyes, and exclaimed, "Max, that's your mother and your sister!"

"So what?"

"So, they are ineligible as girlfriends."

"Big deal," Max scoffed, "Kaye, this is all a smoke screen for you to avoid doing what needs to be done."

"No, Max," she persisted, "It is a big deal and relevant to what we are doing, that's why Christ is revealing it to you now. I'll explain it after we discuss the second vow. Do you know what it is?"

"Following your line of reasoning, I suppose it was a vow not to cry."

"So you could be a man." Kaye added.

"Kaye, your logic is eluding me."

"Max, Jesus said he came to give those who believe in him abundant life."

"Yeah, when we die we go to heaven. Sorry, Kaye, that has no bearing on what we're doing now."

"You're wrong, Max. The abundant life is meant to begin now, to help us live differently!" Kaye was now becoming very passionate, "That's why the Bible tells us not to make vows, simply to let our 'Yes' be 'Yes' and our 'No' be 'No'. You see the problem is we make vows with our own understanding, which when we're children is very limited.'

"Then those vows influence our behavior or trap us into doing the opposite of what we should do."

"Kaye, I need to be honest here, when you talk religion like this, you lose me."

"Max, what I'm telling you is very simple, common sense. You loved Katie and she loved you. The book you gave her was precious to her. In the panic of that night, she chose to run back for it. It was a spontaneous, childish, impulsive thing to do...a very seven-year-old thing to do... but not a wise thing to do.'

"The Bible tells us that the devil prowls around like a roaring lion seeking whom he can devour – including helpless, innocent children. He does this by putting thoughts in our mind. If we act on them it can be destructive to us and to others. It was to Katie and everyone who loved her, including you. At that time, Satan put a thought in your mind too.'

"When you were reeling in pain...to avoid future pain... You, in an equally impulsive, childish, spontaneous way responded to that thought by vowing to never love another girl. To a seven-year-old that seemed a sure way to avoid the terrible pain you were experiencing over Katie's death. Max, that vow controlled your behavior. You grew up avoiding female companionship. Such avoidance, my friend, in the end can result in more pain," she reached out touching his cheek with her hand.

"So, Kaye, if I follow your logic, you would say that my vow to not cry so I could be a man, stopped me from fully becoming a man?"

"What it did, Max, is stop you from accepting yourself fully as a man. It blocked you from appreciating the entire collection of God-given male attributes you do possess. This includes the ability to cry, so others can know when you see them hurting, that you do care."

Max frowned. "So, Dr. McDonald, based on what you've just said, I am a mess!"

Kaye laughed, "Wrong, it just means you are a card carrying member of the human race, whom Jesus came to save...To restore, along with the rest of us, to all the full humanness His heavenly Father desires we experience!"

"You are unreal! Do you preach in the board room too, Ms. McDonald?

"Sometimes, Mr. Carron, sometimes...So, can I now share the good news of Jesus?"

"Let me guess it's more than believe in him and go to heaven right?"

"Absolutely, Mr. Carron! Katie was right! You are smart, and I would add your Catholic upbringing has not gone to waste."

He looked at her dumbfounded, "I haven't a clue what you mean by that."

"Confession - we are called to confess our sins,"

"And," Max added "the Bible says, that when we do, He will forgive all our sins and cleanse us from all unrighteousness."

"Very good, Mr. Carron! So when the Holy Spirit reveals to us hidden childhood vows, we're to renounce them – in Jesus name – ask forgiveness and also ask Him to release us from all effects of those vows."

"That's it?"

"Yep," Kaye smiled.

"How do you know it takes, or that it was the Holy Spirit who revealed this in the first place?" Max queried.

It's very basic, Max. You asked Jesus to come into your life as your Savior and Lord, didn't you?

"Yeah, I did it with you."

"Well, Jesus can't be Lord, if garbage clutters our behavior. St. Paul told the Christians in Rome that they needed their minds to be renewed, so that they could trust and approve the will of God. What you're experiencing is just that happening. Christ is sweeping away from your thinking those things that would interfere with you listening to Him and following his directions." Kaye spoke ever so softly yet with absolute certainty.

Max, however, was still unsure. "Forgive my unbelief, but why would Jesus want to direct me now?"

Kaye looked intently at him, "You said we need to stop this person! An individual who is planning and has already done great evil. It appears it is not only me who he threatens: rather he has gone this route before, harming many in the process.'

"If you and I are to play a role in his apprehension, I suspect we will be unable to do so, on our own. I believe that behind this man lies a foe that is neither flesh nor blood. That is why I know that I need Jesus' help and Jesus' Name to take me through this challenge." Tears were now in her eyes, "Max, that is why I asked us to pray earlier. Your memory recall only strengthens my belief in our need to pray. Personally I have never heard a human being doing such terrible things, even to an animal, let alone another person, and doing so shamelessly and without remorse – with..." Kaye shuddered, "even joy."

She continued, "It's not that I'm that naïve. I know great evil does exist in our world. It's just that as far as I was able, I chose not to seek evil, either in reality or fiction. This evil has arrived on my doorstep unsolicited, thus avoidance is not an option in which any longer I can indulge."

Max furrowed his brow, "I don't pretend to understand all you've shared, Kaye, but I do know we need strength beyond ourselves to walk through this dark valley. So I want to do as you suggest. I may need your guidance on this prayer thing. Please, leap in when you see me floundering."

The two of them joined hands across the table and bowed their heads. Max renounced the vows in Jesus' name and asked Christ to reprogram his behavior to conform to God's way. Kaye confessed her fears of listening to the horrors revealed by this mysterious tormentor. She asked Jesus to protect her from the images she would need to hear, and to heal her mind of those memories...So, she could work with Max to check out whether or not what they heard were fantasy tales of a sadly, disillusioned, sick man or reality of a very malicious perpetrator of great evil.

After the prayer, they began to pour over the notes Max had kept on the last three calls. The victims' names:

The first was a Jane Smitherston, a nineteen-year-old college student in Houston, working in a bar, abducted, sexually assaulted, tortured not for minutes but for several days, pretending to let her go then, like a cat toying with a mouse, pouncing one more time, laughing at her screams, her pleas for mercy.

The second was a fourteen-year-old, Bessie Jackson, from Cleveland, Ohio, a promising young black student. Kaye buried her face in her hands, "How he just laughed at the fact that he'd set it up so suspicion for the girl's disappearance would fall on her twenty-year old uncle!"

"Yeah," Max added, "who is now incarcerated for her murder, although they couldn't find her body. I sure know what it feels like to be falsely accused!"

"But," Kaye interjected, "he told us that he dismembered her, and where he buried her head, beneath an old Elm tree, on Elm Street, in one of his acquaintance's backyards."

Kaye looked at Max, "If this is true, will this mean the release of an innocent man?"

"It definitely begins the process, Kaye, that's why it is so important we do what we are doing!"

The third was a Jenny Chou, from Buffalo, New York and all her specifics.

By the time they had completed their documentation, it was nearly 6 a.m., neither had slept.

"What now, Max?" Kaye asked, clearly allowing all leadership in this endeavor, to rest on his shoulders.

"Do you have a plain manila envelope? What's the name of your FBI friend and his address? We'll address it then to the Federal Bureau of Investigation, attention Special Agent Bernard Epstein. We'll put in it, what we've just documented along with these instructions:

Dear Sir:

Over the past three months I have been contacted nightly by a 3 a.m. caller. He began making lewd remarks, which soon had violent overtones. Recently I began to challenge him, taunting his validity, hoping he would reveal details of his supposed victims. This began to happen three nights ago. I have enclosed this information for you, trusting that you will be able to verify if they are fact or fiction. Please do so by placing an ad in the July 17ᵗʰ Edition of the 'National Enquirer'."

"Max, why the 'National Enquirer'? Why not the 'Washington Post' or 'New York Times'?"

Max peered over his glasses, "Do you read the 'National Enquirer', Kaye?"

"No, do you?"

"No!"

"So, Kaye, do you read either the 'Post' or the 'Times'?"

"Of course, and you?" Kaye was clearly perplexed.

Max smiled, "You know I read both the 'Post' and 'Times.' "So, here's my question to you, Kaye, at this stage of the game, do we want to draw attention to us?"

"Oh! No!" Finally the penny had dropped into Kaye's understanding.

"So," Max continued, "We'll ask them to place the ad in this manner if the information is accurate:

Dear Emily,
Everything you said is true. I'm sorry. Please forget the past. I'm anxious to hear from you again.

However, should the data we've given you not be reality, let your ad read:

Dear Emily,
**What you wrote is totally untrue. If you contact
me, I will help you.**
Love, Mother.

"They'll do that?" she asked in surprise.

"Yes!"

"How do you know?"

He reached over and playfully tapped her nose, "Trust me!"

Kaye's mind was racing, "But what do we do with their response?"

Max sighed, "We've got a week to decide, Kaye. Right now we both need to get a few hours sleep. When do you have your teleconference?"

"One o'clock."

"Everything we touch, we need to do wearing disposable gloves, the paper we use to document these cases, our instructions, the envelop, even the stamp. I can get that all ready while you have your conference call. Nothing can have our finger prints on it! After your call is finished we can drive to New Jersey to post it?"

"New Jersey?" Kaye questioned, "Why New Jersey?"

"No attention to us – remember?"

"Oh my, I really do need sleep!" she murmured.

Chapter Twenty-Four

Dave tipped the cabby, grabbed his overnight bag and started towards the steps leading up to Jack's office building. He paused to take in his surroundings. Washington in summer, provided it wasn't a scorcher, was always pleasant. For him the large imposing and impressive buildings and memorials symbolized the very character of the country he loved. Standing on these steps of Justice made him proud to be a member of his country's Law Enforcement team.

"But," he said quietly to himself, "I like the place where I work, cities of 80,000 to 100,000 provide enough challenge. It's nothing like the crime and corruption the guys in the large metropolis have to contend with. At least in my area, I have a personal working relationship with most of our citizens, or a connection to every group they potentially might be a part of."

After entering the lobby and passing security, Dave made the choice he always did.

Given the option of stairs or elevators, Dave chose the stairs. Jack's office was on the sixth floor.

For Dave it was a personal challenge to time how quickly he could go up those stairs. At forty-five he prided himself on the physical shape he had been able to maintain. At six foot and two hundred pounds he was anything but a small man, yet he could move exceedingly fast. He smiled as he eyed the stairs. He'd been a star halfback at Penn State.

He glanced at his overnight bag, "You, my friend, will have to be my ball."

He checked his watch and took off, often taking two steps at a time. He arrived on the sixth floor landing breathless,

"YES!" He lifted his bag in triumph over his head, "Thirty seconds faster than the last time! Dave, old boy, you are like vintage wine, improving with age."

He had just about managed to have his pulse rate back to normal and was ready to open the door to head toward Jack's office, when a security guard opened it.

He looked at Dave's flushed face, "You okay man?"

"Yes, I treat these stairs as a physical fitness obstacle." Dave smiled amiably at the rather pudgy young man. Perhaps that was not the wisest thing to say, he later reflected.

"You don't say," came the suspicious retort. "So what's your business on this floor?" The guard's hand had dropped automatically to his holster.

Trying to diffuse the situation, Dave extended his hand, "I'm Dave Davidson, a police officer myself from Judge Jack Walters' city. I have a meeting with the Judge in his office."

"What's in your bag?" the guard demanded, his hand still on his holster.

"My, uh clothes," Dave was taken aback by this officious young man. He added, "we're going to the ball game tonight." (He wanted to add 'to see our Phillies clobber your home town, buddy!' but didn't.)

"Show me, carefully," came the command.

Dave sighed and dutifully opened the bag revealing his casual clothes.

"That's a Phillies' cap. You're not even a Nationals' fan!" the young man scowled.

Dave wanted to say "You got that right Bud!" But he elected instead, to simply reply "The Phillies are playing your home team tonight and tomorrow." He was now more than slightly annoyed at the young man's impudence, but was trying hard not to show it.

"I don't like the Phillies," the guard grumped.

"Well, here's hoping your team can out play them."

Dave responded. "Now if you'll be so kind, I'd like to go to Judge Walters' office."

"Let's go together. One can't be too lax these days. If your story checks out fine, if not, you, Sir, will be in trouble."

Dave discreetly rolled his eyes, "Fine." He didn't divulge his next thought which was "This is absolutely ridiculous being escorted to Jack's office like a felon." Instead, he tried to focus on his run up those stairs, his personal best time, ever!

The pleasant middle aged receptionist looked up from her desk, "Why, Chief Davidson, how good it is to see you again!"

Dave beamed, "Great to see you again, Mrs. Stuart!"

"Chief?" said Dave's companion, suddenly aware that his suspicious character might have more importance than he wished.

"Oh, Jimmy, this is Chief Dave Davidson, Judge Walters' neighbor and long time best friend. He's Chief of Police at Summerside, Pennsylvania. It's good that the two of you could meet," Mrs. Stuart continued, oblivious both to Dave's delight and Jimmy's discomfort, "Jimmy has been on our security staff for three months now."

Dave noted the color was leaving the young man's face, "Well, Jimmy, I was most impressed to see how seriously you do take your work." He said graciously, "It's a pleasure to meet you. You are absolutely right; one can't be too cautious these days."

"No hard feelings?" said the young man tentatively.

"Absolutely not!" Dave said reassuringly extending his hand. Jimmy shook it staring at Dave rather awkwardly then asked, "You really did run up those stairs like a physical fitness obstacle course?"

"Yes," Dave nodded.

"Sheesh!" Jimmy scratched his head.

"However, Jimmy, my advice to anyone planning to learn how to use them, would be to start with only one flight at a time."

"Right, of course!"

Just then Jack arrived, warmly greeting Dave and allowing Jimmy the chance to quietly retreat.

"I'm afraid I disappointed Jimmy," Dave laughed after the two men were alone in Jack's office.

"How so?" Jack looked surprised.

"Well, first, I wasn't a dangerous suspect fearlessly nabbed by this clever fledgling security officer. Then when he made me open my night bag, he discovered I was a Phillies' fan!"

Jack grinned, "The latter would be a great disappointment for any Nationals' fan, I'm sure. But seriously, Dave, Security has been put on alert because of this Carron thing. Personally I don't understand why. I checked with Warden Blackmore and he indicated Carron was a model prisoner. Even said that he was allowed to take several university courses and did quite well."

"So, what's all the concern for your safety? Is it just because he is a Sicilian American?"

"With supposed connections to the mob, and one who apparently has literally just disappeared."

Dave frowned, "His parents are in Chicago aren't they?"

"Yeah," Jack said, "and evidently just as upset with their son's no show."

Dave scratched his head, "Why would or even how, could a guy just disappear?"

"That is the big question. Epi is concerned that Carron has a vendetta in mind, simply biding his time. Epi even considered Carron might be trying to provoke his father into taking action against me."

"The other possibility is," Dave mused, "what we said before. Namely, maybe there was more than meets the eye in what you sent him down for. Perhaps somebody had unfinished business with young Mr. Carron?"

"Possibly? Anyway I figure Epi had ulterior motives in getting us tickets for the ball games. My suspicions heightened when he asked us to meet him in his office, before we go to dinner. Normally Epi does everything possible to avoid meeting me in his office."

"Why do you say that?" Dave queried.

"That, Chief Davidson, you will soon discover for yourself."

The two men had been conversing as they traversed the one block that separated Jack's building from Epi's.

Now they stood before a door whose simple brass plate identified the room's occupant as "B. Epstein". Jack grinned and looked at Dave as he turned the door knob.

Dave broke into an amused smile, "Yes, Your Honor, I can understand why Agent Epstein might avoid inviting you to his office."

It wasn't because the furnishings or trappings were shabby. The carpet, the desk, the bookshelves, filing cabinet were all of good quality. That is, what one could see of them. Books, papers, files were cluttered everywhere.

Not that they were strewn helter-skelter, all were neatly arranged. Even the two leather chairs for visitors were occupied by stacks of files. In fact, only Epi's own leather bound chair could be called a "productive" chair, that is one useful for sitting down. A Pizza box perched on a file cabinet beside the computer screen. The keyboard was tucked safely out of harm's way...away from errant crumbs or soda pop spills. The waste bucket clearly spelled out Epi's preference for Pepsi.

Dave's mind flashed back to Jack's office where everything had a place and was in place!

"Hi guys, glad you could come early." Epi had arrived! "Just a moment, let me move these files, have a seat."

"Why don't we just head out for dinner? You might misplace something by moving it." Jack ventured good naturedly, his attempt at humor lost on his host.

"No, seriously guys, we need to talk!" Epi sounded grave.

Jack and Dave exchanged quizzical glances.

"I've asked Agent Berkhof, my new trainee, to join us." Epi's face darkened as he sat down behind the computer desk, gesturing for Dave and Jack to sit in the now vacant chairs.

Jack pursed his lips, and queried, "why the thunder brow, Ep? Have you found Massimiliano Carron?"

"Carron? Sheesh, no Jack! I'm sorry he totally slipped my mind." Epi replied apologetically.

"Then, what on earth, do you want to discuss with the two of us?" Jack asked furrowing his brow.

Neither he nor Dave were prepared for Epi's reply!

"Kaye!"

"Kaye?" the two men spoke in unison, "What's wrong with Kaye?" Their faces mirrored deep concern.

Before Epi could respond, his door flew open. The culprit appeared to be a huge filing box. But no, the box was simply preceding its bearer, a short man, about five foot five.

Epi nodded his head and said, "Gentlemen, Agent Berkhof." Then, as if clarification was needed, he added, " I mean the guy, not the box."

"Very funny, Sir!" the man glowered.

As he struggled with the box, his eyes darted furtively around the room. "Where am I supposed to put it?"

"Here's fine," Epi pointed to a bare space on a small cabinet. He had dispatched the pizza box to beside the waste basket.

Dave put his hand over his mouth to conceal a smile. With the guy's horned rim glasses and bald head all that popped into his head was the kids' T.V. cartoon character "Arthur the aardvark."

He thought *"If Epi says this guy's name is Arthur, I'll lose it for sure!"*

Fortunately for Dave, when the young agent had deposited his box and could at last focus on them, Epi commented, "As I said earlier, this is Agent Berkhof. Brian, this is Chief Dave Davidson and Judge Jack Walters."

Jack rose and shook the agent's hand. "Please, call me Jack."

"Likewise, Brian, call me Dave." He had inserted "Brian" to re-emphasize the man's name in his brain, to ensure that he'd never refer to him as "Arthur."

Epi then stated the obvious, "Sorry, Brian, I've only three chairs. You'll have to stand," adding absent-mindedly, "that's just the lot of a junior agent, I'm afraid."

He massaged his forehead. "Now, what were we discussing when Brian came in? Oh yeah, Kaye!"

Epi leaned across his desk. The sternness in his face had returned and startled both men. "Guys, remember about eight or nine months ago, Kaye reported some perp calling her late at night with sexual innuendos?"

Dave nodded, "We tapped the wires for over a month, absolutely no calls. Furthermore, Kaye was mortified and deeply hurt, when it got back to her that some people thought she was making it up."

"Did either of you?"

"Of course not!" Dave replied indignantly.

Jack echoed his sentiments and added, "Kaye's as solid as a rock. We never did doubt she got some calls. Whoever it was, probably some prankster, realized she was serious and just backed off."

"Any indication, from Kaye's behavior, that the calls may have begun again?"

"Epi, you personally asked her that a few months ago and she said 'no', don't you remember?" Jack frowned.

"Nor do we have any indication," Dave inserted, "Why the questions?"

"Last week I got this letter," Epi shoved the document at Dave.

Berkhof's eyes widened, "Sir, that's classified!" he objected.

Epi peered at his junior agent in disbelief, "Brian, Jack is a Supreme Court Justice, Dave is Police Chief in Summerside, where the lady that I'm questioning them about lives!"

"So who is Kaye?" Berkhof queried?

"Our neighbor," Dave and Jack sighed in unison.

"M.K. McDonald," Epi said slowly and deliberately.

"The M.K. McDonald, of Kayleen Enterprises?" Berkhof said incredulously.

"The same," was the trio's response.

"Whatever would make you think Kaye wrote this?" Jack demanded.

Epi coughed and said, "Gut instinct, guys. It was addressed to me personally. Kaye knows I'm an agent. She knows where I work. Furthermore, Kaye is the only one I know who had a questionable caller about nine months ago. If the perp had laid off for about six months, it would fit the timing in this letter. In addition, as you both know this is not my current sphere of activity in the bureau."

"But you don't know if any of these things mentioned in the letter, are fact or fiction," Dave interrupted.

"Oh, but we do!" Epi responded curtly. "Gentlemen, these are real cases and whoever wrote this letter either is the killer or someone talking to the killer."

Jack was dumbfounded, "You found the body part mentioned?"

"Absolutely – exact location described," Berkhof added.

Dave shook his head, "Kaye doesn't read the *'National Enquirer'*, if it had said *'Washington Post'* or *'New York Times'* maybe?"

"Whoever wrote this does not yet want to be identified. They'll neither mail from their location, nor use a paper known to be read by them," Epi replied bluntly. "So try and think fellas, is there anything that Kaye's doing differently that might indicate something's going on?"

Both shook their heads. "The only thing, I'd say, is that she seems to be working more at home these past few weeks...But then again from time to time she does that, particularly if she's got heavy projects on the go," Dave offered.

"She also does that to recharge her own batteries," Jack added, "in summer it's really nice where we live."

"Yeah and quite honestly both of us have been away a

lot. We had holidays and our son, Matt, is up to his eyebrows with little league activities. All this means is that Rufus, our neighborhood dog, has needed a sitter. So Kaye's been pitching in, but once again this is seasonal," Dave replied.

"Dave and I know Kaye well enough that we'd have no hesitation in asking her directly, would we Dave?" Jack turned to Dave, who was indicating his willingness with an affirmative nod.

"Thanks, but no thanks! What I really want is permission to tap her line without her knowledge – to simply listen in, hoping that she is the one receiving those calls."

Jack recoiled in disgust, "You don't know what you're asking. Kaye is like family to us. As much as I want to help, I just couldn't go behind her back and do that!"

Epi sighed, "Jack, I know it is remote that it's Kaye, but the caller this letter identifies is a serial killer. These three cases, that this letter details, no law enforcement agency had ever linked together. Even worse this perp is a serial, sexual predator. He tortures his victims before he kills them.'

"Brian, pull out the first files in that box. Let them read about those victims, their families' statements and the coroners' reports."

As they read the countenance of both men turned ashen. "But why can't Kaye know about a phone tap?" Jack asked.

Epi ran his hand through his hair and stated, "Jack, if it is Kaye that he is talking to, she's obviously got him opening up. Any change in her voice, the creep might detect and we could lose him. Two or three calls are all we would need to pin point and nab him."

Epi played his ace, "Look, guys, both of you have daughters, would you not do anything you could to protect them, including wire tapping if it could catch someone bent on harming them?"

"The other reason, Sir," now it was Berkhof's turn to speak, "These perps usually don't open up until they're ready to make a strike! It's like they're pumping themselves up, playing cat and mouse for a few weeks, then boom they hit."

"Look, guys, Brian's right! I'm not saying it is Kaye, but if it is, trust me, she is in real danger. Why I'm asking the two of you is that I'd like not to let anyone local, except you, in on the tap. If possible, I'd like to set up in your house, Dave. Jack, you have federal jurisdiction.'

"You can see from these cases, the perp has crossed state lines. This gives the Bureau authority to act." Epi leaned back in his chair and studied the two.

Jack returned his gaze, "And if it's not Kaye, Epi?"

"If it's not Kaye we'll destroy all tapes in your presence. We only need two or three bites at tops. Once it's done, you can tell Kaye everything. I'll even let her read the cases, you have just read, if she wants. This will show her why we acted the way we did."

"Are you answering this letter as they've asked?" Dave questioned.

"Chief," Epi stated, "by tomorrow whoever sent this letter will know the Bureau has authenticated the validity of these crimes."

"So, if we agree, when would you want to tap?" Jack queried.

Berkhof looked at Epi, "Next week if possible, don't you think, Sir ?"

Dave stroked his chin, "Toward the middle of next week, my wife Sue is away at a Nurse Practitioner Symposium in Boston."

"Isn't Matt away at a Law Enforcement workshop in Pittsburgh?" Jack commented.

"Yep, Jack, you are right. I will have the house all to myself for about four or five days." Dave eyed Epi, "But, if there's no bites, after three nights, it stops – correct?"

"Deal!" Epi leapt up from his chair, "So, will you please authorize it, Jack?"

Jack took a deep breath, "Yes, if it protects Kaye, I'll do it."

"Great!" Berkhof slapped his leg, "Let's go eat and help the Phillies win."

"Personally, Epi," Jack shook his head sadly, "this is

one meal I don't even feel like eating and one Phillies game I don't have any enthusiasm for. Kaye is like a kid sister to me...The thought of going behind her back sickens me."

"Jack, one thing I'll be glad to promise. Not that we will discover anything about Kaye we wouldn't want to know...But should we...You can word the wire tap order to be specific for detecting whether or not this serial killer is making contact with her.'

"Anything else, absolutely anything else will not be covered. Okay?"

"Fine," Jack sighed, "I'll issue the order on that condition. I certainly do not want to do anything that would compromise Kaye's trust in either Dave or me!"

Epi stood and reached for his windbreaker, "That's great, Jack! Here's my hand, Sir, on our deal."

As the four men headed down the corridor, Epstein chuckled, "I'll even treat the three of you to supper. It is the least I can do for you Phillies' fans, because the rest of the evening is going to be all downhill. Washington is bound to skunk you tonight, I can feel it in me bones."

Chapter Twenty-Five

"Pull over to the rest area coming up and we'll change seats there. I'll go to the John and you'll climb into the back seat like you're going to rest."

"You know something, Max?"

"I know a lot of 'somethings', Kaye but I'm not sure any of them are your something."

"Very clever, Mr. Smarty Pants! Well my something is you've finally got me interested in all this clandestine stuff."

"What?"

"Oh, we're here. Okay, Sir, bathroom break for you, rest time for me." Before he could reply she had swung her long legs out of the car and was stretching. She spied a near by park bench and jogged over to it. Extending her left leg out on the bench, Kaye bent over and touched her toes with the right hand. She repeated the procedure with her right leg.

As Max climbed out of the back seat, there she was in the cross hairs of his vision - stretching. He ran his tongue over his lower lip. It was impossible not to notice her lithe body, slender, yet strong legs. She reminded him of a graceful ballerina. Kaye had chosen to wear a baggy T-shirt and her exercise shorts, in keeping with her pact with Max, to avoid sensuous clothing.

"Lady," he thought, "You could dress in a burlap bag and still be alluring!" He groaned inwardly, "Eyes off! Don't lose focus, Maxie, the stakes are too high!"

He turned and sauntered nonchalantly to the rest room, carefully scrutinizing the parking lot for any suspicious vehicles. Just a van with a couple and four children. All the kids looked to be under eight.

"Bet they have their hands full," he mused. Then his mind flipped to Sophia, a smile creased his face, "Bet you have your hands full, little sister, with twins and a toddler?"

A wistful longing tugged at his heart. It not only caught him unaware, he wasn't sure of it's source. Was it a desire to see his sister? Her children? A quiet thought slid into his mind, *"A family wouldn't be all bad!"*

That threw him totally off balance. If he had his druthers, he'd have remained in the washroom, suppressing his hormones and sorting his emotions. Unfortunately, a camper had drawn up just as he entered the men's room. He thought the driver looked like a senior, but under the present circumstances, Max knew he couldn't let down his guard.

He set out for the car and soon was in the driver's seat. He remarked, "Won't be long now and we'll know for certain whether my fears are real or unfounded."

As he backed the car out, her hand tapped him on the shoulder. He turned and found himself being sucked into her twinkling green eyes. Increasingly, he found this woman drawing him like a magnet. Emotions he never knew he had, seemed to rage within him.

But unlike that first night, Max refused to let his feelings dominate. In fact he'd even opted for her strategy – prayer! Continually he thanked Jesus for not letting temptation over take him thus far, and asked God to empower him that he might fulfill the mission he'd agreed to.

"Max, are you tuning me out?"

"No, I am trying to listen and back out at the same time, but I'm having trouble concentrating."

"Well back out, then I'll tell you my important pronouncement."

"Okay, I'm out, speak!"

"Very well, now I must confess," she giggled like a school girl, "dying your hair blonde with this teen drugstore product was fun but..." she leaned close to his ear, "while you're not bad looking as a blonde... I really think, Partner, that your black hair is far more stunning with those little streaks of distinguishing grey, in just the most appropriate places!"

"That's your pronouncement?" He stared in the rearview mirror, dumbfounded, "you are comparing what I look like with my hair dyed blonde to my natural color?"

"Precisely, Sir! Why should that surprise you?"

"It surprises me because you're normally so astute, so factual, no nonsense and what you've just said is so trivial."

"That's what you think! I believe, Mr. Carron, what you are trying to say is you have related to me like a male and this is comfortable for you. My color comparison forces you to communicate with the female segment of humanity and that makes you uncomfortable.'

"Newsflash, I really am female!"

She was now sitting in the back seat, leaning forward, her head on the back of his seat beside his shoulder. "So there!" and she gave him a playful poke.

"I had noticed you were female, Ms. McDonald, remember our first meeting?"

"Yes I do. However, I haven't seen any recent evidence to suggest that is anything but a dim, distant, faded memory, in the recesses of your mind, Mr. Carron."

His jaw tightened as he said, "We have a deal, Ms. McDonald."

"Indeed, we do! However, I had no idea it would allow me the pleasure of turning you into a blonde, even for a day. It was fun, that's what I was trying to say. Why, you are blushing, Mr. Carron!" She laughed softly.

"Am not! Which exit do I want."

"Number 23, it should be your next turn."

"Anyway," she flopped back in the seat, "I also wanted to tell you I had absolutely no idea this cloak and dagger thing could be so..." She rolled her eyes searching for the right word, "Maybe for now, I'll just settle for interesting! I'm actually starting to enjoy it. I wanted to thank you, for bringing this excitement into my life."

Had she looked in the rearview mirror, she may have seen the total disbelief in his eyes. Instead, she simply continued, "All this clandestine stuff, I have to admit is exciting. Certainly makes life more exhilarating!"

By now, the car was parked in the large Shopping Mall lot. Max tried to look casual, as he opened the door, but he struggled with Kaye's words. It was like they were traversing a mine field and she viewed it as a joy ride. How could he get through to her the danger she faced? Would he, could he ever succeed in getting this woman to realize the peril she was in? Why could this otherwise normally super-intelligent woman not grasp the gravity of what they were doing?

"Kaye, I'm going to get the paper. Make sure you keep the car doors locked! By the way, is there anything else we need, that I could pick up?"

"Cashews"

"Cashews? We need cashews?"

"No, Max, I like cashews. They're normally where the newspapers are. I haven't indulged for a long while, so cashews would be good. What do you like?"

"What?"

"What do you like to eat, that you haven't had, for a long time? Something you enjoy that relaxes you. Why don't you get that?"

Max stared blankly. "What do I like?" It had been a very long time, since he'd been asked that question. He stood thinking, finally he said, "I like chocolate-covered almonds."

"Well get some. What kind of soda pop do you like?"

"Diet Coke."

"Me too. Get some!"

Max frowned as he repeated the list, "Paper, cashews, chocolate-covered almonds, Diet Coke."

"Want to write it down?"

"I can remember that!" he snapped, as he slammed the door. *"Did I imagine it, or did she laugh?"*

Kaye opened the door a crack as he started to walk away, "Max!"

"What?"

"I like carnations."

"Carnations?"

"They're flowers."

"I know that!...What color?"

"Good question...Surprise me!" She closed the door.

He did hear her laugh. What the heck was she doing? She was right about one thing! Whatever she was doing, she was succeeding in making him uncomfortable.

Inside the Mall, he decided that, given his list, the Supermarket might be his best bet for one-stop shopping. He'd show her. He could remember! *"Chocolate-covered almonds – found and into the cart; cashews found and secured in the cart; Diet Coke found – secured; ahha , one 'National Enquirer'...into the cart.'*

"Flowers? Carnations? What the heck did they look like?" He spied a clerk in the flower section. "Did she have any carnations?"

She looked at him like he'd asked her where the United States was. She pointed to the one large cabinet and said, "They're all carnations!"

"Everyone?"

"Everyone, Sir, what color did you want?"

Max began to frown "Kaye knew this all along. You pick she said. I haven't bought flowers for...I can't even remember ever buying flowers!" He felt a sense of panic rising within him.

The clerk must have sensed it, for her voice now sounded compassionate, "What colors does she like?"

"She never said."

"But what colors does she have in her home, like the living room, the bedroom?"

Max was now desperate. Then he looked at the flowers and he pointed to a burgundy, pink bouquet, "those colors."

"Excellent choice, Sir! Your lady friend obviously has class." The clerk gave him an encouraging smile, "I'll wrap them for you. If you want you can take one of those cards."

She pointed to a rack containing small, miniature post-card shaped cards. "They are free, help yourself. Then, put on it, what you want to say. Be sure and take the envelop that goes with it."

"Card? What I want to say?" Max felt his heart palpitating inside, no wonder he'd never done this before. It was sheer anguish! He found a card. It looked like his bouquet, taking out his pen, the words seemed to pop into his head. So he wrote, "To Kaye, Thanks for trusting in me! Max."

"Here you go, Sir. Here's your flowers, and here's a bit of scotch tape."

"Scotch tape?"

"To tape your card onto the flowers."

"Oh, Yeah," he smiled sheepishly, "Thanks!"

As he stood in the quick service line, he looked at the other customers. He realized that he looked just like them. They all had "Mickey Mouse" stuff just like he did. He even spied a young guy, in the next line, who had flowers and looked as self-conscious as Max felt.

"Wow," he thought, *"Kaye's not stupid, she's brilliant! I look just like everyone else. Security camera check it out, I'm just your average Joe shopper!"*

He paid the cashier and walked back to the car decidedly pleased with himself. "That was brilliant strategy, Kaye!" he said setting his parcels in the front on the passenger side.

"What was?"

"Giving me that list of stuff to get."

"Cashews and chocolate-covered almonds are strategy?" Now it was her turn to look bewildered. "Did you check the paper?"

"No, of course not! We don't want to draw attention to ourselves. We can read it together, when we get home –

eating our cashews, chocolate almonds and drinking our Diet Coke."

"Smelling my flowers?"

"What? Yeah, and smelling your flowers!" It was Max's turn to laugh and inside he felt very warm.

"Can I peek now?"

"What?"

"Can I peek at my flowers now?"

"Yeah, if you want," he handed the wrapped bouquet back to her.

She noticed the note immediately, "Max, that's very sweet, Thank you!"

"What? The flowers smell sweet?"

"No, Dummy, your note!"

His note, he'd forgotten all about it.

"I really appreciate what you said, Max. Thank you." She leaned forward as she spoke and gave him a gentle peck on the neck. Then she settled back in her seat to peek at her flowers. She gasped, "Max, they're absolutely beautiful! I love this color, how did you do it?"

"Well the sales girl asked what color furniture, rugs etc. you had and I thought it was those colors."

"You were right on, Max, Thanks again."

He turned into the rest area, so they could switch seats. Only this time, he didn't bother going to the washroom. They both were anxious to get home and read the paper.

But on the way, he did confess, that it had been a long time since he'd bought flowers for a lady. In fact, he couldn't remember when. Kaye had laughed her perky little laugh and had suggested that since he made such a good start, he ought to keep up the practice. He wondered exactly what she meant but didn't want to ask.

Getting home, Max was set to tear into the paper but Kaye had insisted they wait. He could pour their drinks. She'd put her flowers into a vase and set out the chocolate almonds and cashews. That proved to be a good idea, Max later thought, for somehow the message encoded in the 'National Enquirer' didn't cut so deep.

'*Dear Emily, everything you said is true - very true* (They had added those words) *–I'm sorry, please forget the past, I'm anxious to hear from you again – soon* (They had added that word too!) For what seemed like an eternity, neither spoke.

Finally, Kaye broke the silence, "It means this person really is a horrid murderer, doesn't it?" Her voice was barely audible.

"Yes," Max sucked in his breath, "It does! We've got to get the other information we've gathered to them this week. We'll mail it first thing tomorrow."

"We could send it by Fed Ex," she offered.

Max peered over his glasses, "No, Kaye, we can't! It would be traced."

"Oh, right, I forgot," she murmured.

"So what is on your agenda for tomorrow?"

"I have to be in Kayleen's office by 2 p.m."

"If we get up and leave by 8 a.m., we should be in Oakton by 9:30. We could head up to your office from there. Maybe stop and catch an early lunch? Get you to your office before 1 p.m., what do you think?"

She looked at him, "But we have to get you back here first."

"No, Kaye, from now on I'm with you. I've been thinking. Is it feasible I could go into your office as a repair man? You know like a computer specialist to put in some soft ware or something? I actually want to install an alarm system, maybe even a 'bug'...So, if I'm in your car, and you need help you can signal me. Then, I can get there to help you or at least call the cops."

Max was on a roll, "Let's see, today's the 17th so if we mail this tomorrow, hopefully the Bureau will have it by the 22nd..." he stopped abruptly his face turning pale, "Shit!"

"What's wrong, Max?"

"Oh crap, No!" he exclaimed slapping his forehead.

"What a scholar! You bedazzle me, with two slang words, for fecal matter. I'm impressed, Max!" Kaye quipped, in an attempt, to lighten the tenseness that suddenly had crept into the room.

"It's no joke, Kaye! I parked my car in long term parking. I never dreamt I'd be so long. I chose a date that I thought would not attract attention, yet give me ample time to meet and confront Walters."

"And?"

"It expires tonight!"

"So you'll just pay more, what's the panic?" She was a little annoyed that he had sounded so alarmed.

"No, Kaye, you don't understand! If I don't get it tonight, it will be flagged tomorrow. Kaye, not only are the cops looking for me, so will be my father. The car is registered in my name, when it is found they will know I'm in the area. More specifically they will know why I'm here, and it all points to Independence Drive.'

"Kaye, I believe we're very close to hauling in this perp. We both know what this man has done and we both agreed he must be stopped. Unless we get my car, the whole project is in danger of being torpedoed!"

Max was pacing the floor now, clearly perturbed, "We need to get my car tonight. Your neighbors are both away aren't they?"

"Yes, but I expect both could return late tonight."

"Fine, as soon as it gets dark, we'll leave! Kaye, will you pray that we can get my car without a hitch? We should also ask, that what we're mailing to the FBI, can get into the hands of your agent friend, very quickly."

Max smiled lamely, "I guess, I need to give thanks that God reminded me about my car!"

243

Chapter Twenty-Six

Josephine Carron hated to see Frank go to these "Family Gatherings", as he called them. Most of the men she trusted, but some she knew were both vile and vicious. She longed for him to disassociate, but the answer was always the same, "If I'm present, I'm alive – disassociate and I'm dead."

Personally, she doubted that very much, at least literally. However, figuratively she realized it was probably true, since Frank's investment clientele included all members of 'The Family' and their many associates.

The perk for her was that during his absence, she was free to visit her daughter and grandchildren. Sometimes Sophia did bring the children to Chicago, but as the twins began school and as Sophia herself progressed further in her legal studies, it made sense for Josephine to visit them.

She would never fly alone. "Oh, the airports are just too big, far too confusing," she would say. So, her friend Angel D'Amato always accompanied her. In New York, Angel would visit her cousin and her family, while Josephine spent time with Sophia. The two women would reconnect to fly back home.

With her friends and family, rarely was she called Josephine. "That's far too formal!" she would scoff, insisting it be "Josie or just plain Jo." Then she would add the proviso, in case any should choose to write her, "That is 'Jo', without the 'e'!"

Even though she had lived two thirds of her life in America, old world ways dictated her manners. Anyone,

who had the audacity to ask what difference a little 'e'
meant, received a firm and stern reprimand. "Why, no lady
would ever allow herself to be known by a 'man's name'!"
So, "Jo" without the "e" it would be, if the individual wished
to remain in her circle of acquaintances. Since her circle
included her husband, the "e" was avoided by all, like a plague.

It wasn't hard to treat Josephine as a lady. She carried
herself regally. Even relaxing in her daughter's living room, she
sat posture perfect, legs crossed appropriately, hands folded
in her lap. She was as well poised as either Jacqueline Kennedy
or Queen Elizabeth would have been for a formal portrait.
But there was no pretense on her part, it was just her way.

In fact, at this moment, Josephine was in her glory!
After her husband, Josephine's passion lay with children.
She was in her element, as she sat surrounded by her three
little grandchildren.

"I suggest, Mama, that you put the handsome prince to
bed while I escort the princesses to their chamber." Sophia
tousled the hair of her toddler, giving him a goodnight kiss
and hug.

"Now off you go to bed with Grandma, Rici. Make sure
you sit on the potty. You've been almost one whole week
without a diaper or a wet bed! If you get another gold star
tonight, tomorrow you'll have a big Winnie The Pooh sticker!"

Josie watched her little grandson puff with pride as his
mother praised his potty success.

She couldn't help smiling as she thought, *"Sophia you
are such a motivational person! Your presence in a room
always did set it on fire. You possess that same magical
touch even with your little son."*

Sophia glanced over at her mother, conveying with her
eyes, "It's show time, Mama!"

Turning to her son, she said, "Come along now, Rici,
Grandma has a really great story about a little dog who had
a very loving family, but he wasn't satisfied, so he ran away
from home."

Josie stood and took Rici's chubby little hand. The tot's eyes grew wide as he asked his Grandmother, "What happened, Gama? Was there more fun away from home?"

"Oh, Rici, that is a really good question! I can't wait to answer it. However, you need to go potty first, and then show me how good you are at brushing those teeth."

As Rici headed to the bathroom, Josie turned to her little twin granddaughters, "Good night, Micki and Jo. Come, give me a big hug and kiss. I look forward to going to the park with you tomorrow!"

The twins rushed over to hug Josephine. They loved it when Grandma visited. There was always so much to do! After the hugs, the girls ran off to their room giggling – each declaring that they would be first in bed and so the one to pick tonight's story.

"Gama, look how clean my teeth are and don't I smell good?" little Rici huffed into Josie's face a minty breath.

"Why, Rici, your teeth are the shiniest I've seen and your breath smells so good I could eat you!" She grabbed the two-year-old smothering his neck with kisses pretending to gobble him up.

Amidst giggles, he managed to gasp, "Please, Gama! Tell me about the little dog!"

So, Josephine began to spin the tale of the little white dog with a few black spots, named "Spot". Josie knew the story off by heart. It had been one of Max's favorite books. He had demanded to read it over and over. His favorite book had been the "Little Tug Boat", but then one day he just stopped bringing it out.

Instead, he brought out the story of "Spot." Rici snuggled in close to his grandmother as she told Spot's story – a little white dog with black spots.

"He was loved very much by his family. They kept him very clean and smelling nice. Every week he got a bath," Josie said, "but Spot didn't like baths. One day, somebody accidentally left the gate open and Spot saw his chance to run away."

She glanced at her grandson with his big, brown eyes. "You look tired, Rici," she teased, "maybe we should finish the story tomorrow?"

"No, no, Gama, I need to know what happens to Spot. I won't sleep if I don't!" he replied ever so serious.

Josie laughed softly. Children never change. She had elicited the same reaction in Max, night after night – even when he was eight. Tears came to her eyes as she remembered her son, but she willed herself not to go there. She chose rather to focus on the little boy currently cuddling up against her. So once again, she recounted all Spot's antics as he strove to be the dirtiest dog ever.

Rici listened intently to this story of the little dog who chose to run away from the people who loved him. Tears came to his eyes when he heard how sad Spot's little boy and girl were at the loss of their pet.

"I'd cry, Gama, if I was them," he said solemnly.

However, as Grandma continued her story Rici began to realize what a dangerous thing the little dog had done. He had got so dirty and smelled so bad that everyone chased him away. He had become a black dog with one or two white spots. No one wanted him near them. He had no place warm and safe to sleep and of course he had nobody to feed him.

"Pretty soon," Josie continued, "Spot became very, very hungry and began to miss his home, so he decided to run back home. What do you think happened then, Rici?"

She paused to get his response.

"Oh, Gama, I bet his little boy and girl were very happy," he said clapping his chubby hands together.

But Josie eyes got very big as she looked at her grandson, "Well, that's what we'd want to happen, for everyone to be happy again, wouldn't we, Rici?"

He nodded his head then looking at Gama's face realized maybe that's not what happened. "Something bad happened?" his voice quivered.

"Well, yes!" Josie said, "Most definitely! Remember, Rici, the children had a white dog with black spots who smelled real nice. This was a black dog with only one or two white patches, and he smelled very bad!" Josie stuck up her nose pinching it dramatically for effect. Rici's eyes were so big at this sudden turn for the worse, it was all Josie could do not to laugh. "So," she said "they chased him away!"

"Gama, doesn't Spot ever get loved again?" he said tearfully. "Oh Rici, that's the good news I want you to remember," Josie said earnestly, "When we make mistakes and finally realize we were wrong, just like Spot did, God always helps us find our way back home. So, if one door closes, God opens another for us and that's what happened for Spot.'

"His little boy and girl had a wading pool in their yard and their daddy was filling it with water from the hose. Spot ran for the pool and jumped in and splashed around in the water. The parents joined their children to chase this dog away, because they all knew their pet hated baths. However, Spot jumped out of the pool and began to roll on the grass. Can you guess what happened next?"

By now, Rici was afraid to hope any good could come to Spot, so, he quietly shook his head "no."

"Well, Rici," Josie smiled broadly, "most of Spot's dirt washed off in the pool. The family suddenly realized the little black dog with white spots really was their little white dog with black spots."

Rici jumped up and hugged his Grandmother, "So they let Spot live with them again?" he yelled.

"They did, indeed," Josie laughed, "and never again did Spot hate his bath."

"I also bet that puppy never ran away from home again!" her grandson retorted.

"What a smart little boy you are! Spot had learned to be happy just as he was. He now knew the most important thing is simply to love and be loved."

"That's a real good story, Gama!" the little boy yawned sleepily, "I love my family. I don't ever want to run away!"

"Oh, I'm so glad, Rici, for we love you so very, very much too. Plus, we'd be so sad if you weren't here." She bent over and kissed him gently on the forehead. Even before she turned out the light, he was sound asleep.

Josie tiptoed past the girls' room, as she heard Sophia finishing up her story time and begin listening to the twins' prayers. She headed down to her daughter's sunken living room and collapsed into the overstuffed, wing back chair. She just wanted to disappear.

Her 'Spot' had run away from home. "Lord, only you know where he is!" Her heart was breaking being near Rici. It had only served to bring back memories of those special moments all mothers cherish with their children.

The pain of Max's absence had seemed to intensify, "Son, wherever you are – please be careful and please, please come home to me! Oh Lord, please send your angels to protect him. Please, Jesus, let me see him again!" she silently pleaded, warm tears flowing gently down her face.

So lost in her world of grief, Josie had missed her daughter entering the room and coming up behind her chair.

Seeing her mother's tears, guilt stabbed Sophia's heart. She threw her arms around her mother, and pressed her cheek against hers. "Oh, Mama...I'm so sorry! It's all my fault."

"Sophia, whatever do you mean?" came the sharp retort. Jolted out of her pain, Josie turned to cup her daughter's face in her hands. "That's pure foolishness!"

"No, it's not, Mama, if I had never gone to that dance with Tony, Max would never have gone to that rotten motel room."

"And," her mother paused to let her word's sink deep into her daughter's heart, "if he had not, your Tony would be dead. You not only would not have the man you love, but neither would you have those three precious children you adore!" Her mother's piercing grey eyes studied her daughter, "Sophia, shit happens!"

Sophia's eyes flew wide open, "Mother!" Her very refined, gentle and yes, cultured mother never swore, never used any vulgar expressions, even mild ones, never ever!

Josie looked at the shock in her daughter's face, "My Dear, you may think that I was born yesterday. However, it is I, who made the choice as to how I would express myself. I found crude language generally unnecessary to get one's point across. Occasionally though, there are rare times when no other expression really adequately conveys the truth and this, my daughter, is one such time!"

Sophia couldn't help herself, she just burst out laughing. Josie smiled at her and the next thing her grown daughter was in her arms – the two simultaneously laughing and crying.

"Mama, I know you miss him so and I know Pop does too! I just want you to know so do I."

She stood up and retrieved the tufted velvet parlor chair from the other side of the room, placed the chair in front of her mother and sat down.

Sophia leaned forward, took her mother's hands in hers, and gently rubbed them. The two women sat silently gazing at the pain in the other's eyes.

At last, Josie began to share the secret fear that tormented her. "Sophia, as time passes I become more and more certain something terrible has happened to your brother."

"Mama, Tony keeps saying that Max is almost thirty five years old. He hasn't had a girlfriend. For six years, sex has been denied him. So, we should leave him alone, and let him have a fling or find romance or whatever."

Josie closed her eyes, "Sophia, with all due respect, that sounds very plausible, if Max were Tony, but do you honestly think that sounds like your brother?"

The younger woman sadly shook her head, "No, I don't," she murmured.

"Let's face it, Sophia, our Sicilian heritage is tainted with blood and violence."

"Other cultures have blood heritages too!" Sophia frowned.

"But," sighed Josie reaching out to caress her daughter's cheek, "You and I aren't other cultures. Sophia, do you know how, or more bluntly, why your father and I came to America?"

"No," Sophia replied softly, wondering what her mother was about to divulge.

"My father was very influential in our town, and I, like you, was considered a good catch. In part for who I was, but in a large part, for whose I was. Let's face it, Dear, as you had males after you for sex, you also had ones desirous of linking up with your father's influence. So it was with me."

Sophia looked at her mother quizzically.

Josie continued, "and then there was Aunt Louisa."

"But she wasn't either of your parent's sister!" Sophia protested.

"Of course not, she would have been like a second, or third cousin, to my father. However, then as now, everyone referred to her as Aunt Louisa."

Josie bit her lip, and shuddered, "Only then she was not ninety-four and feeble. She was really in her power and believe you me, she wielded it. Her mission was to match make, and in doing so, to amass wealth for herself. I think personally that even with her money, power and yes sex, Louisa was unhappy in love. Thus, by orchestrating arranged marriages for others, she strove to make them as unhappy as she was!"

"But you're not unhappy with Pop, are you?"

"No, Dear, I love your father as you love Tony. Louisa, however had no intention of matching me with your father. He was not at all on her radar screen. He was simply a strong, hardworking young boy trying to eke out a living to support his widowed mother."

Josie grimaced at the bitter memories that flooded her mind. "Oh yes, Frank was way too poor. Definitely not a candidate for my father's daughter...for in Louisa's game plan...I was indeed a very rich asset, not to be ignored!"

"So, who did Louisa have in mind for you?"

"A lecherous old goat, about forty years older than I. The man was financially loaded and violent. He would have added much to my father's influence, for I commanded a high 'bride price,' so my father said."

"Oh, no!' said Sophia totally repulsed.

"Oh, yes," Josie nodded sadly, "when my father told me, he was definitely delighted with the arrangement. I was horrified! I was strong willed," Josie's countenance softened. She reached out, stroked her daughter's black hair, and added, "a little like yourself, Dear. So I refused." She closed her eyes. Even the thought of the next memory chilled her heart.

"So, what happened?"

Tears came to Josie's eyes, "My father slapped my face with such a force, I was black and blue for a week!"

"Mama, No!" Sophia looked at her mother in disbelief.

Josie sniffled, "I pleaded. I begged. I reminded him of the man's age and mine, of his known violence."

"Fine," was his reply, "That's just the point my sweet. In ten years or less, he'll likely be dead and all his money will be yours. At the most you'll be thirty five. Then marry for love." He strode out of the room. It was the last I ever saw him."

"Thankfully, I had hidden some money away, simply to one day indulge myself. I never envisioned such a need as I now faced. I grabbed it and some of my expensive jewelry and ran out of the house.'

"Like the little dog, 'Spot,' in the story I told Rici tonight." Josie smiled, "You know that story, Sophia, both you and Max loved it.'

"Only unlike that dog, I had not planned to leave home. I had no idea where I could go or what I should do. All I knew, is that I was terrified of even being touched by that old man, never mind becoming his wife. For me, nothing could be worse. I had no plan, absolutely none!'

"Fortunately, it was early morning, and still dark. No one saw me leave the house. I just ran and ran. I finally collapsed down by the docks behind a shed. I was sobbing uncontrollably. Your father had gone down to the area to pick something up. He found me." Josie paused, recalling that bitter sweet moment, brought a smile to her face.

Looking at her mother's countenance...the smile in the midst of tears...Sophia couldn't help think of those rare days when the sun shines even when it's raining. "Please go on mother," she urged, anxious to know more about her parents' relationship. A relationship, that up to now she had merely taken for granted, never imagining they had to overcome any difficulties.

"Years later, your father confessed to me that he'd fallen in love with me the first time he saw me. He said that he knew that I had never seen him or even given him a glance. He had figured, given my social status, that I was out of his reach.'

"...But, when he saw me crying, my face bruised and bloodied, he was filled with rage. After I told him what had happened, he asked me if I was really serious about escaping. When I assured him I was, he promised to help me."

"Mama, he could have been killed, even tortured if you'd been caught!" Sophia exclaimed horrified.

"Oh, most definitely, Sophia, but I am ashamed to say I never thought of the consequences to Francesco. All I thought of, selfishly, was the consequence to me if I remained! So the plan was hatched. He purchased two tickets on a boat that was departing immediately for New York."

"Must have been romantic?" Sophia gave her mother's hands a gentle squeeze. "Never thought of you and Pop as Romeo and Juliet."

"Sophia, your father was the epitome of a gentleman. He said we'd wait until we got to America. And if I felt like he was good enough for me, he would be delighted to be my husband."

"So, obviously at some point you agreed!"

"I did indeed, and sometime I will share more of our relationship," Josie smiled mischievously, but then her voice turned grave. "Suffice to say, we were pursued. My father believed himself dishonored, betrayed. The lecherous suitor was furious. The money he'd given to Louisa had not bought the plum he'd wanted. Louisa physically paid the price."

"He beat her?"

"Yes and more"

"Rape?" Sophia was incredulous.

"Yes, so Louisa, in her fury, charged her youngest sibling to dispose of Frank and bring me back to appease both my father and my supposed suitor. Needless to say, Pepi had a much bigger bank roll than we did. He almost succeeded in New York, which is why we fled to Chicago.'

"Fortunately for us, the connections your father secured in Chicago were ones who hated those with whom Pepi had aligned himself. Your father had made himself most useful to his protectors. Frank had an instinct for business, legitimate business. The mob wanted and needed a solid trustworthy investor."

"Mutual admiration society?" Sophia interjected.

Her mother smiled, "Perhaps, it is better to say 'mutual need society,' Dear! As for your father, he saw me as a princess...His radiant princess."

Sophia laughed, "And, he was your knight in shining armor!"

"Yes, and I have been proud to be his lady!"

"Well, you've indeed acted that part, Mama!"

"That has not been hard, Sophia. I was raised privileged. But with regards to your Papa, he strove to succeed and did for me. So, I strove to live for him. I learned English and tried to fit usefully into Chicago life.'

"One thing your father promised me is that he would live legitimately and avoid violence and bloodshed. This way I would not be widowed in a foreign country and our children, especially any son, drug into the mob violence that both of us knew swirled around us. He vowed that neither he nor his sons would ever disgrace me with jail."

"Oh, Mama," Sophia whispered, "I'm so sorry!"

"Sophia, the vow your father made, he could never keep. It was beyond his control. It was foolish, just as your feeling sorry for something over which you had no control, is! Neither you, nor your father, nor Max, nor I are God.'

"Bad things happen to all people, along with the good that each of us experiences. The thing that defines every human being is how we respond to the trials that we face. The simple prayer that I say each day for you and your family, is the same I pray for your father, Max and myself – that God will help us to choose His way."

Sophia looked lovingly at her mother, "Lead us not into temptation and deliver us from evil."

Josie sighed, "Yes, Jesus' prayer is the very best one we all can pray...One that brings me great comfort, Sophia, especially at this time."

Josie stood and beckoned to her daughter, "Please, Sophia, come...Give me a hug and pray with me for your brother's safety, that God, in his mercy will allow us to be a family again."

Chapter Twenty-Seven

Kaye, where did we put those walkie-talkies we bought?
"Why?"

"You need to drive me to the airport. We'll synchronize the walkie-talkies. When we get to the airport, you park your car and go inside. I'll slip out and get into mine. You come back out and head down the exit ramp. There's a service center just outside the airport, I'll wait for you there.'

"When you get there park in front of me, appear to be calling some one on your cell. In fact what you will be doing is calling me on the walkie-talkie. After we've made contact, then drive off, but try and stay within about 500 yards of me. I think that's the range we have with these ones. You have to lead me back to your place. This is pretty unfamiliar territory for me, even more so since we're driving at night!"

"I'll draw you a map," Kaye volunteered.

"That's fine, Kaye but, it's better if you lead me. Then you are not out of my sight. Don't forget why I'm here!"

"True," she said, "but should you get lost you can call. Here's my phone number."

Max just looked at her, "Kaye, we don't know who we are dealing with, or even if anyone could be listening. It's best to take no chances that anyone might discover I'm here with you." He got up and started for the stairs.

"Where are you going?"

"To get dressed, in the darkest clothes I have. Good idea for you to do the same."

"It's probably wise for me to tidy up my flowers, and

our drinks and comfort food, just in case any of my 'loving' family decides to spontaneously pop over!"

Max turned and said "And your 'Max card' better not be evident either, Kaye!"

"Don't worry, Mr. Carron, I'm wearing that card next to my heart," Kaye laughed.

A sense of foreboding began to flood over Kaye as she pulled on her jeans, put on her black sneakers and began to button up her dark jacket. "It is all happening too fast," she groaned. "Why all of a sudden is his car an issue? Is there something else he's just remembered he has to do?" She closed her eyes, "Please Lord, don't let him abandon me now! Help me to continue to trust that you have sent him to help me. I need your peace to trust enough, so that I follow Max in what he is now asking of me."

As she got in the car, Kaye saw the *'National Enquirer'* lying on the passenger seat. Before she could question him, Max directed "when we get to the airport put the paper in your bag. After you get inside the Terminal sit down, take out the paper and appear to be reading it. Five minutes later get up, look at the arrival screen, shake your head as if you've just noted a delay. Check your watch and head back to your car, dumping the paper in the garbage bin."

"Why?" she asked.

"Why? We don't need it anymore, and Kaye, you don't read the *'Enquirer'*, remember? So, you don't want it found on your property, that's why!"

Everything went according to his plan. Max directed her to his car. Fortunately there were several cars in the vicinity. Kaye stopped nearby, while he slipped quickly out into the shadows.

She pulled ahead and parked in an empty space, following his instructions to a tee. It was all she could do to control the mounting panic she felt in his absence. She looked around furtively, "It's so dark in this garage. If Max is right that someone could be watching me, this would be the perfect place to grab me."

The bright lights inside the terminal helped cast aside some of her fear. There were few people around at this time in the evening. "I'm not sure if that's a good or bad thing!" She thought, as she sat down on an empty bench.

Kaye pulled out the *'Enquirer'* and couldn't help returning to the classifieds. "God, this person calling me, actually murdered those women!" She closed her eyes, "I can't comprehend his pleasure. It has to be more than lust, even more than sexual? I've never hunted anything, even Easter eggs. I can't imagine that whatever is motivating this man can even be close to that which drives an ordinary hunter?"

She drew a deep breath, her hands trembled as she carefully closed the paper, folding it for disposal in the nearby trash can. Kaye murmured, "Of one thing I am certain! I'm more observant, than I used to be, of people around me. I hate to think of leaving this bright terminal to go back into that dimly lit parking garage." Nonetheless, she stood, and dutifully studied the arrival monitor, as directed. "Lucky me, there's two flights with big delays! So, I can conclude my performance by checking my watch, frowning, and tossing this paper..."

Once more she checked her surroundings, "Can't see any threatening person. So, here I go." Her stomach knotted, as she turned towards the garage. It took all her resolve to walk at a normal pace back to her car.

Tonight, she even checked the back seat before climbing into the caddie. "Apparently old dogs can learn new tricks," she groused. As she started the motor, fear sliced into her heart, "What if Max had left her...Gone back to Chicago? Please, No!" was all she could cry.

It was less than a three minute drive to the Service Center, but to Kaye it seemed an eternity before she finally spied his vehicle. "Thank you, Thank you, Jesus," was all she could breathe as she pulled up a couple of cars in front of his. Her heart pounded, as she grabbed the walkie-talkie. "Max?"

she spoke softly trying to quell the fear rising within her.

"Good girl, Kaye! Did you get rid of the paper?" She nodded yes.

"Kaye, Kaye can you hear me?"

She started to laugh at herself, "Yes, Max, I hear you perfectly. I can't believe what I just did though."

"What did you do?"

"Well instead of answering you verbally, I just nodded." She paused , "Max, I'm so nervous and afraid."

"That's okay, Kaye – you've every right to be. This is a serious situation!"

A police cruiser suddenly stopped beside Kaye's car.

Now, it was Max's turn to be alarmed. His knuckles went white, as he held the steering wheel in a death grip. "Damn, the perp could be a cop! Shit, yes! They knew about the wire tapping. "

He saw Kaye roll down her window say something, and as she rolled up her window the cruiser speed off.

"What was that, Kaye?" he crackled over the walkie-talkie.

"Oh, it was just Sergeant Tom, I know him very well. I told him, I was on my way home, after rendezvousing with a Kayleen staff person at the airport. It's something I often do, Max. Are you okay?"

"Yeah, I'm fine." He heaved a sigh of relief, then added, "let's head out, try and keep close to my vehicle so I don't lose you."

Once or twice, the two did lose contact. Each time fear gripped Kaye's heart like a vice. Over and over, she repeated Psalm 27, verse 1 to herself.

"The Lord is my light and my salvation: whom shall I fear?... The Lord is the stronghold of my life: of whom shall I be afraid?"

And like a broken record, one prayer ricocheted continually through her mind, "Please, Dear Jesus...Please don't let him abandon me now!"

As they neared Independence Drive, Max barked, "Kaye,

I want you to go home but keep your car doors locked. Then, open the garage door with the remote in your car. Go into the garage, shut your car lights off, and wait in your car for me.'

"I've turned off your garage sensor lights, so you'll be in darkness. No matter what, do not open your door for anyone, until I get there! I'm driving down a few more subdivision streets. I'll circle back to Independence Drive and then I'm going to cut my lights.'

"When I come into your drive, I'll be entering the garage on the right-hand side of your vehicle. When I shut off my motor, close the garage door. You got all that?"

"Yes," Kaye said weakly, "What is going on Lord? I do trust you and I believe you are asking me to trust Max...But why, oh why, am I so afraid?"

As she sat in the darkness alone, she realized to her horror that Max's car had been all black, even the windows were heavily tinted. She covered her mouth with her hand as if to stifle a scream and began to shake. "I don't even know whether he was alone in the car?" Arrows of doubt fired into her brain. She fumbled for the walkie-talkie desperate to hear his voice. Apparently he'd turned his off. "Why would he do that? He told me it was important that I always be in contact with him!'

"I've never known fear like this! God, what that caller said he'd do to me," she whimpered. "What if I was wrong about Max? He said these killers seem like nice people." She pounded her head against the steering wheel and cried, "McDonald, get control of yourself! He was beside you listening to that call. It can't be him!" But somehow that thought didn't bring relief. It was all she could do to remain locked in the car. Her whole being seemed to scream... Run!...Flee!...Hide!

Although it was not longer than five minutes, it seemed to Kaye like a thousand lifetimes, before she was aware of a car entering the driveway behind her. Kaye's heart was pounding so hard she thought her chest would burst.

The vehicle pulled over and began entering the garage beside her. By now her eyes had become accustomed to the dark. "It looks like Max's but with the heavy tint on the glass I can't even see the driver," she moaned. The car's motor died.

Obediently she closed the garage door as he had directed. Suddenly, sheer terror overcame her... "Who is in the garage with me? Is it Max? Is it the killer? What if the killer overpowered Max?" Fear paralyzed her mind!

The car door opened slowly. Cupping her head in her hands she silently pleaded, "Please God, let me know who this person is?" The dark figure that had stepped out, held a flashlight in his hand.

Kaye held her breath, "What was he doing?" He went to the light switch and flicked it on. It was Max. Kaye began to breathe again. Somehow, the light had chased the darkness away not only in the garage but in her heart.

She was about to open her car door when Max headed back to his car. "What's in his hand? It's long and sharp... A knife?" Once more Kaye was seized with awful dread.

Max had bent down low between the two vehicles Kaye couldn't see where he went or what he was doing?

At last, he emerged in the line of her vision holding a long flat package. He proceeded to a storage box at the front of the garage, opened it and deposited whatever he had held underneath the other items that were in the box.

That's when she noted he was wearing gloves. "Why?" Once more fear stabbed her heart. Max moved to the front of the garage and that's when she realized the long sharp object had been a screwdriver, which he was returning to its place on the tool rack.

The tool rack! Memories flooded her mind. When she first moved here, her father had set up that rack for her, plus all the tools he felt she would need. From R.K.'s perspective, a girl needed to learn how to use them as much as a guy. She sighed, "Daddy you promised to teach me! But the plane crash meant your lessons on how to use those

261

tools was never given. They've sat in that rack unused by me." The next thought caused her to bury her head in her hands, "Surely your gift of love, won't be used to harm me?"

Overwhelmed by fear and grief M.K. McDonald's shoulders began to heave. A torrent of tears erupted from the very depths of her being with the force of a flash flood.

Eventually she became aware of a pounding on her car window. She looked up...It was Max He was shouting, "Kaye, it's okay, open up! It worked, we did it!"

Max was exuberant! Triumphantly he declared, "I took the plates off, even the front decorative one. The only way to trace it is with the car's I.D. number. Someone really needs to want to do that. In the meantime you can just say that you've bought a new car for Kayleen purposes."

For her part, nothing Max was saying registered. "Come on!" he urged, "open up, get out, let's celebrate with some cashews and chocolate almonds!"

Somehow, she found the lock and managed to unlock the car. Max flung the door open and immediately froze unprepared for the scene that greeted his eyes. Kaye's face, hands, and clothes were drenched with tears. It was as if all resilience had drained from her, and still she sobbed.

This was beyond any of his experiences. After what seemed to him like an eternity, Kaye began to finally sob not just tears but words. He leaned closer straining to hear what she was saying.

She wiped her face with her sleeve, and sniffled, "I didn't know who was in the garage! I was so afraid...And I thought you were leaving me!" she gasped.

"Leaving you? Is that what you wanted, and I didn't do it? Is that why you're crying? Kaye, if you want me to go, I will. Just stop crying – please!" Max was almost pleading.

"No!" Kaye was shocked at the force of her voice, "No! I don't want you to go. I want you to stay! I want you, I love you!" she choked. She grabbed onto him, holding tightly to him, her lips found his.

Instinctively he grasped her, drawing her into his embrace. The inhibitions of both seemed to collapse – the passions each had held at bay erupted like a volcano. Suddenly Kaye was aware of Max pushing away.

"No!" she heaved, "Please, no!" More tears cascaded down her face. "Max, No! I love you! I want you! I need you! She opened her eyes and it was then that she noted tears flowing down his face.

He was trembling as he pushed away from her, "Kaye, I want you more than anything, but please help me! I can't!"

Now, emotionally and mentally bankrupt, Kaye struggled like a drowning person to grab hold of reason. *"What's going on? What's wrong? He wants me, I know he does! I've never felt like this with any man before. I want him, desire him! Why's he struggling so? He's drawing away but why?"*

Max was now backed against the garage wall, his face buried in his hands, gulping for breath, striving to push that passion for her away, attempting to bury it somewhere deep inside.

Kaye collapsed against the side of her car. "Max, I don't understand," she finally managed to softly say, "Please help here." By now she figured that the only thing allowing him to stand was the wall. He looked at her weakly, as if all the strength he ever possessed had just been sucked right out of him.

"Kaye, please help me. I want you so badly...I love you... I never had these feelings ever before but I can't – we can't!"

"But you were going to Max ...The night you first saw me. Why can't you now?" Her response drew a weak laugh from him, which only perplexed Kaye even more.

"Kaye," he finally was able to say, "It's not because I physically can't make love to you. It's because of what we're involved in that I must not! Believe me, Hon, there's nothing I'd rather do. Trust me!"

Kaye put her hand over her mouth, "trust me?" Of course, the card... 'Kaye, Thanks for trusting me. – Max'.

263

"Okay, Max, I do trust you, but you will need to explain, I don't understand what happened here."

"Can we go inside and sit down?" Max said limply, "maybe even tackle some cashews and chocolate-covered almonds?"

They sat looking at each other across the table, both emotionally drained.

"Kaye," Max began, "remember what that perp shared about that couple in Arkansas?"

"You mean how he boasted he had raped and tortured the woman in front of the man. Then murdered her in front of him?"

"Yeah, and then how he killed the guy making it look like suicide?"

Kaye's eyes were wide, "and how he boasted 'the stupid cops actually believed it to be a murder/suicide'?"

"Right," Max shook his head sadly. "They got that idea, because there was semen from two different DNA sources in her vagina."

"So," Kaye said, "they theorized that the guy had caught her fooling around. In a jealous rage he bashed her up, to teach her a lesson, killed her and then himself."

Kaye felt the blood draining from her face, "That could happen here is what you're saying...Right, Max?"

"Right on, Babe, that's exactly what I'm saying. He's done it once and it worked."

Now it was Kaye's turn to shake her head, "So why mess with success," she said sadly.

"Exactly, Kaye, and with me it would be so much easier for the cops to lay it on my doorstep. I came for Jack, got the wrong address, saw you, ravished you, murdered you." New tears trickled down his cheeks, but not tears of sadness. These were tears of anger.

"I'm angry, Kaye," he said, "because in Joe Q Public's eyes that's what Sicilian trash are all about: violence and ruthlessness...morally depraved bastards!"

Max paused, "Kaye, I don't know if I'll be able to help you take this guy down or not. But, one thing I don't want to do is give him any chance to slur my family."

Max was now up pacing the floor, "I care about my father and mother and I don't care what your friends think or say about me. It's easy to slam people you don't know."

Kaye sat silent listening to Max, with a dawning awareness of the precarious position she had placed him in.

"Max," Kaye paused and drew a deep breath, "I won't lie to you, I have been attracted to you. However, I realize that trying to share my affection with you was most unfair. I need to tell you that you are the most principled man I have ever met, and I have met many very, very good men. Tonight, however, is the first that I've really appreciated the dangerous position that I have created for you."

She smiled sadly, "I promise that I won't compromise you again. I will also follow your directions, and if you wish me to call Agent Epstein, I will."

Max rubbed the back of his neck pensively, "The thing is, Kaye, I think we've got this guy on the line. These perps can sense, and sometimes even monitor, their intended victim's voice to detect any wavering that might indicate that they're being set up. It's really a "Catch 22" situation that we're in right now. Maybe we simply need to risk and reel this fish in, otherwise we might lose him?"

"Then, Max, will you do something for me?"

"If I can, what is it?"

Kaye swallowed hard, *"I'm not sure how well, Max will receive my suggestion. But, I can't risk having something happen to us like that couple in Arkansas had done to them, without at least attempting to set the record straight with the Walters and Davidsons. So, here goes!"*

She cleared her throat,. "I'd like us both to sit down and write a letter of explanation. You will write yours to your parents, and I will write mine to the Walters and Davidsons. I'd like us to write it as if it would be the last word we could share with them. It will be up to you, if you wish, to share the content of your letter with me. However, I would like to read mine to you. The letters need to be hand written. So it can be verified that we did write them. I will place both of them in my safe at work.'

"No one else can retrieve them unless I am dead. On the envelope we will instruct that the letters be given to your family and mine. If you'd like we could make a copy, take a chance and hide them in the house, but only if you felt that to be wise," she added.

Max sat back, "I like that idea very much. I'd be glad to share what I wrote but, Kaye, I'd like to write my parents in Italian. Would you trust me to translate what I said?" he queried tentatively.

"Of course," she laughed softly, "I trust you... remember?"

So, for the next two hours, they sat across from one another, a new passion consuming them. A righteous, self-giving passion, flooded through the room as they wrote to those they loved. It totally displaced any self-serving passion that either had exhibited earlier in the evening.

They described how their own relationship of mutual respect had developed, and how their choice to co-operate was unmasking a confirmed, serial, psychopathic killer. Both stated that through this choice, it was their hope the individual might be apprehended.

They acknowledged their choice was not without risk. Their fervent prayer was that both would survive. If not, both hoped that through their respective letters their loved ones would know the truth, and the love each held for their family. As well, if they couldn't stop this killer, perhaps the letter might provide the authorities clues as to the individual's identity, so that he soon would be caught.

Kaye began to focus on Max's parents, and wrote, *"Your son is the finest man, I have ever met. He was willing to risk both his life and his reputation to help me, a virtual stranger."*

She chewed her pen momentarily, and then continued,

"I have never experienced fear like I did this evening. When we went to retrieve Max's car, there were moments when I was left alone. By now, I knew that my 3 a.m. caller was a serial killer. I imagined Max was leaving me alone to the mercy of this vicious man. Terror literally paralyzed me. Fortunately he stayed.'

"That decision while blessing me, left you to worry about him and miss his wonderful presence. I do apologize for the pain, his remaining with me has caused you, From the bottom of my heart I thank you for the gift of your son."

Tears began falling once more as she concentrated on the Walters and Davidsons. But no longer, were they tears of fear or grief. These were tears of joy! *"I can't thank you enough,"* she wrote, *"for welcoming me in, as a bona fide member of each of your families, after the death of my parents. Your love sustained me, in all my trials!'*

"Please, please, forgive me for not being upfront about the resumption of those threatening phone calls. As I'm sure you've surmised, I could not risk the potential damage to Kayleen should those calls not be authenticated a second time. That is why I chose to reject seeking traditional protection.'

"I also need to apologize for not being truthful about Max's presence in my house. I came to know he would not harm you, Jack. He did come wanting to meet you, to learn, from you, what lay behind your unusually harsh sentence.'

"All of you need to know that Max knew which house was yours, Jack, but he felt prompted to come to mine.'

"I came to believe that his presence with me, at this time, was Holy Spirit answering my prayer for help. His arrival was timely, occurring just as the 'call' came in. So, Max became my first witness as to the reality of those calls. Unfortunately his criminal conviction cast a shadow over his reliability. So, we formed an alliance to unmask this caller.'

She concluded her letter by writing, "I pray we can survive the attack of this assailant, but if we don't, I trust that Jesus will work our alliance out for the good."

As for Max, with tears falling on his paper, he wrote, *"Mama and Pop, I needed to let you know how proud I always was to be your son. I wanted to come home right away after my release, but I felt I had to see Jack Walters. Have him tell me to my face why he gave me that severe sentence. As a result, I ended up on his street, but even though I knew which house was his, I felt prompted to go to another house. It turned out to be Kaye's and I arrived just when the perp placed his nightly call."*

Max set his pen down, got up and stretched. When he returned his face was stern, *"In prison, they allowed me to take some law courses. In one of those courses, I had to interview serial, sexual murderers. So to help Kaye, I put into practice some of the things I theorized about in the course paper that I wrote.'*

"By the way Pop, thanks for giving me J.D. and pushing me to learn how to shoot." He grinned as he wrote, *"theory on these perps is fine but not much help when push comes to shove. J.D. on the other hand, at least gives us a fighting chance.'*

"Mama, you always wanted me to find a nice girl to settle down with. Kaye sure is all that, so if we do survive this attacker, she's the one I'd want to marry." (This latter statement was the one thing he didn't translate, when he read his letter to Kaye. It just seemed too bold!)

"Please let Sophia know how much I love her. Especially tell Tony and his parents I never regretted for one minute going to bat for Tony. I sure hope we survive this attack. I want so badly to see their little kids. That would be my only regret, that I might not see them. Please tell them Uncle Max loves them...And give them a hug and kiss from me." (He paused to think about that last phrase... Uncle Max...WOW!)

He sat real still for a moment. Nodded to himself, "Yep, I have to save the best for the last. Now, it's time to tell about how God blessed me!"

Picking up the pen for the last time he continued, *"Got something real special to tell you, Mama. In prison, I started to read the Bible. I had lots of discussions with the Chaplain and prison Priest. Then I took the prison Alpha course. Pretty cool! It helped me begin to talk about my faith. By the way, guys, Alpha's offered outside prison too!'*

"Kaye's got a strong faith, she prays like you, Mama. I'm sure you'll like her, and of course she reads her Bible. You may think this different, at least you might, Pop. Mama, I think it'll sit okay with you...But I have to credit God both for bringing me into Kaye's situation and for not being seriously hurt, even killed, in that college motel room. Anyway I do want you to know that I invited Jesus into my heart. Yep, I'm a card carrying member of the Christian faith!"

He signed it: *"Love Ya, forever – Max!"*

The letter writing completed and shared, the chocolate almonds devoured, cashews half gone and the large bottle of Diet Ccke empty, the two signed, copied and sealed their letters. Max placed the copied letters in that large tool box in the garage. Kaye put the originals in her briefcase to take to her office.

Max looked at Kaye impishly, "So, Ms. McDonald...may I move in?"

Kaye eyed him quizzically as he went to the garage. There he opened the trunk of his vehicle taking out both a garment bag and suitcase.

"Where did you get them?" she queried.

"I went on a shopping spree before I came here."

"So do I get to see your true tastes, now that I've already written my impressions of your genuine humble nature?"

"You do indeed!" he laughed.

She curled up in her easy chair waiting for him to display the wares from his garment bag. "Ooh, impressive suit, Mr. Carron! When the blonde dye is washed out of your hair, those Italian designer clothes will compliment

269

your distinguished, dark hair wonderfully!"

"Glad you approve, Kaye!" With that he spun around to face her and asked, "Can I tell you something?"

"Why not?...After all I've been through in the last twelve hours, nothing will surprise me!"

"Good! Then the truth is, I've never really dated before."

Kaye raised an eyebrow, "I believe at one point awhile back, you did confess that."

"Well, I was wondering, can I start dating you?"

Kaye sat bolt upright and stared at him, "You're joking right?" She covered her mouth with her hand to hide her smile, all the while thinking. *"This is insane, we can't even be seen together!"*

"No, I'm serious...Really, I am!" Max stood grinning, *"Gotcha that time, Ms. McDonald!"*

"Well, Mr. Carron, I would be delighted to date you, but since you can't be seen around here, just how do you propose to do so?"

"That's easy! You can rent some videos. We make popcorn and voilà we have a night at the movies!" he exclaimed. "Furthermore, now that I have a suit we can dress up. You got some cool dance albums, your family room floor makes a neat ballroom and even better there's no windows in that room."

He laid his suit on the bed, went over, bowed gallantly before her and extended his hand. "May I have the pleasure of this dance, Miss McDonald?" He laughed, "So is that proper Bryn Mawr etiquette?"

By now Kaye was laughing, " Yes, Mr. Carron, it is! Your movie nights and dance nights sounds doable to me."

"So you accept then?"

"Yes, Max, I do," she curtsied and extended her hand to him.

"Thanks, Kaye. All joking aside, this means a lot to me. I really appreciate it!" and he looked at her with those big, brown, beautiful eyes. Those eyes which she now realized were responsible for stealing her heart.

Their idyllic thoughts were suddenly shattered, once more, by the jarring ring of the phone. It was 3 a.m.. Her hideous suitor was, if nothing else, obsessively punctual!

Tonight, Kaye knew unequivocally, this one was no boastful prankster. She was speaking to the killer of each woman he had victimized. *"But I shall be oh so careful not to let you know what I know, perp! I shall continue my ruse of unbelief at your disclosures!"*

He went on again – another name – another dreadful story. It seemed the man reveled in providing details of, as he termed them, his former lovers.

At one point all she could do was gasp, "You horrid fiend!"

The response by now was equally predictable, "Well, thank you, my Dear, for your compliment. It will be such a wonderful night when we meet face to face. I have such great expectations but as for now just the sound of your despising voice fuels my passion, my lovely."

Kaye's stomach turned to know this man used these calls to sexually climax. How sick he had to be! How absolutely dangerous he had to be! "Repulsive" was the only adjective that sprung to mind to describe him!

"Yet, something changed in me today," she mused. "It's like that dreadful fear, I experienced earlier this evening, has evaporated. In it's place is a steel reserve to do all I can, to bring this one to justice."

A still small voice within seemed to whisper, *"Earlier you were unsure, if you would face this foe alone. Now, you know, for certain that Max is with you...And I...I am with you both. A cord of three strands, is not easily broken!"*

So strong was that last impression, she barely noticed the perp's usual 'oh, oh, oh's' which always terminated his evening call.

Max had written furiously the new name, the details. Now he clarified them with Kaye. "He did say, Kaye, this was another teen?"

"Yes, Max, he did," she sighed, tears stinging her eyes,

"a street kid from Indianapolis. This guy really moves about! What a despicable predator...Shirley Tatters he said was her name."

"Tatters, the name appealed to him he said, what a deceitful bastard!" Max literally spat out the word. "I'll add all that he's given us tonight, to this morning's FBI mailing.

Kaye was drained, "This has been a trying twenty-four hours for me. First, facing the truth that my caller is a brutal murderer, not a boastful prankster, was not easy. Then as we went to get your car, I felt bombarded by all sorts of fears, that seemed so real? I've never experienced such sheer terror in my life. But, you didn't leave me for Chicago and I realized I wasn't going to face this foe alone." She paused and lifted her eyes to his. "Then, just now, as the perp was speaking, I sensed something had changed within me. Fear seems to have given way to a steel resolve to bring this fiend to justice regardless of any personal cost."

Tears were forming in the corner of her eyes. But now, they were tears of joyful peace as she shared with him the verse from Ecclesiastes, she felt the Lord had spoken to her.

"Even so, before we sleep, will you pray with me, for Jesus to heal us of the horrid memories of those murders? And to ask, that in God's mercy and grace, he heal and comfort the families of those women?"

So they bowed their heads and prayed.

As they prepared for bed, Max commented, "Hopefully, Kaye, apprehending this guy can give some closure to these families. That's all we can strive to do for them," he sighed. Then, he added "Do you think we can sleep till nine and still make Oakton to mail the letter and get you to your office? I'm wiped," with that Max was sound asleep.

Kaye glanced at him. He'd been through so much. He was strong psychologically, as well as physically. Yet sleeping, he looked like a little boy, an angelic little boy at that!

"*Not!*" Kaye laughed softly to herself, "*Lord, if Max is going to my office disguised as a computer geek, what should he wear?... Please, let no one who sees him either recognize him or associate him with me. Yes, Jesus, do heal me please, of the memories of these many crimes that my 3 a.m. caller has revealed. May you bring comfort and closure to the many family members of this man's victims. May he soon be caught! Amen.*"

Chapter Twenty-Eight

Leaving Oakton, Kaye turned onto the freeway heading north towards her office, "Max, what do you think Epi will think when he gets the latest list, especially the dreadful details of that Indianapolis teenager's demise?"

"He will think that he's either dealing with the killer or someone talking to the killer," was the matter-of-fact response.

"He could think we were the killers?" Kaye was aghast!

"Fortunately for me, Kaye, I have an iron clad alibi for at least six of those crimes!" He started to grin, "all courtesy of your friend Jack. Never thought I could be grateful for those six years spent behind bars."

Max sat deep in thought. Those two little words, 'iron clad', that he'd uttered in jest as a pun, had yanked him back into his past. He exhaled slowly, *"Yeah, it was iron clad alright! Bit of a shock to the system, Maxie, hearing the automatic closure of all those cell doors locking."* His jaw tensed, as he recalled his decision. *"Yep, at that moment on that very first day, I made up my mind, that I'd be damned if I'd let anyone see the horror I felt. Nonetheless, inside me, there was sheer panic at the thought of confinement."*

What surprised him now, however, was the absence of anger. In the past, whenever he thought of his incarceration, anger always seemed to shoot through him like a white hot firebrand. In fact, he had used humor to mask his feelings, whenever he talked about prison.

"But today," he mused, *"although I joked about my*

imprisonment, I didn't use it as a mask to hide either my anger or my pain." A smile stole across his face, *"I really did intend it as a pun! Which reminds me..."*

Leaning forward between the two front seats he put his head close to her ear, "So, Ms. McDonald, what's your alibi?"

"What? You're joking of course?" Kaye snapped.

He tried to put on his best poker face, "No!"

"Idiot, I'm a fcmale!" she snorted.

"So?"

"What do you mean, "so?" Females were the ones who were sexually assaulted and murdered."

"You could be his accomplice, Luv."

She was about to react to this insinuation, when she checked the rearview mirror and caught the twinkle in his eye. "I don't think it's funny to joke about those people, Max!"

"Nor do I, Kaye, but teasing you is not making fun of his victims. Besides, what I said is true. The way that the Bureau responded to the information we gave them, is significant. It tells us that what we gave was knowledge that only the killer would know. The FBI's role now is to ferret out if we are the hunter or the hunted."

"Somehow, I don't find that thought particularly comforting. I just wish it were all over!"

"So do I, Kaye."

"Really?"

"Well, yes and no, I suppose."

"What's that answer supposed to mean?" she questioned.

"Yes, that the perp is apprehended. Yes, that my parents, especially my Mother would no longer have to worry about me. Yes, that Pop wouldn't do anything foolish..."

Kaye furrowed her brow, "I don't understand that last one."

"The two old guys that look after my place, I really care about them. Unfortunately by not getting home quickly, I've put them in a very vulnerable position. They brought me the money I asked for and they were the last ones to see me.'

"The more you've taught me about prayer, Kaye, the more I pray for the two of them. I ask Jesus to protect them. As for the 'no', when this is over, you've got no reason to see me." Max smiled lamely. "We're from two different worlds, Kaye."

"You are an Italian, pardon me, Sicilian, American, Catholic male. I am an Irish, American, protestant female." She frowned and stated, "Max, news flash, we are living in the U.S. of A.! Where is the exclusion? Religion and ethnicity don't count!"

Max sighed and remarked, "You, Ms. McDonald, are also wealthy, established in business, with a great reputation. I, on the other hand, am an ex-con, with no trade and only in a select segment of society remotely viewed as having a useful reputation."

"Max," she countered, "Maybe there are external differences but it's not the outside that counts. It's what is on the inside that matters. When I look at you I see integrity, faithfulness, trustworthiness, dependability and I see love. So, Mr. Carron, be forewarned, when this is over do not think I will let go so easily!"

In the rearview mirror, she saw his face soften, creases forming at the corners of his eyes. Kaye felt his hand reach forward and touch her arm giving it a gentle squeeze.

"Thanks," he murmured.

"But!", she added.

"Oh, oh, beware the 'but'...one of my English Prof's used to say that when a 'but' appears ignore everything that preceded it." Max rolled his eyes and grimaced. "The truth always follows the 'but'!"

"What I was going to say Max, is that my father, on one of the rare occasions when he offered matrimonial advice, warned me never to enter into a relationship believing that I could change something that I didn't like in a prospective mate. He said if you see something you don't like in another, simply decide whether or not you can live with it. If you can't live with it, end the relationship immediately."

"You see something you don't like?" his question was barely audible.

"Yep!"

"What is it?" gone was all bravado, as he pondered what his offence could be.

"Max, I cannot stand you blond, you look like a geek!" She burst out laughing.

He sat back heaving a sigh of relief, "If that's your concern, Ms. McDonald, have no fear, it was you who made me blond and I don't like it either. Also, in case you forgot, I'm supposed to be a geek, a computer geek. Speaking of which, maybe you should pull over and stop for lunch, so I can ride in the front?"

During lunch the two went over their routine but nothing Kaye could have said would have prepared him for the security at Kayleen's headquarters.

"Sheesh," Max thought, "it's like Fort Knox! Everywhere there are armed guards, security cameras, coded doors. I'm glad to finally make it to her office. The contrast between Kaye's home and this place is startling. If this perp is going to nab her, I think Summerside would be the place to do it, certainly not here!"

What overwhelmed him, even more than the security system, was the esteem in which she was held by everyone. It wasn't simply employee / employer respect. It was genuine affection and it was clear that she reciprocated those feelings to them.

His heart sank, "What an ass I am to think I'm in her class." He wanted to run. The panic he'd felt that first night in prison flooded over him. He was as trapped now as he was then, only now there were no visible bars or guards restraining him.

She had introduced him as Mr. Watson from Compu-Tech Industries, and stated that he'd be there all afternoon to work on her computer, upgrading its hard drive and installing a new software program. The moment the door closed, Max set about wiring her office with an alarm system he could link back to her car. From now until all this ended, he would remain in her car, every time she came to work.

Secretly, Kaye had managed to enter him into Kayleen's security data base. He would have instant access to her office, should he ever have need to respond to her alarm.

Afterwards, they were even able to map out the fastest and most direct route from the parking garage to her office.

It was well after five o'clock when Kaye finally returned to her office. Max had just completed the final check points. Several people had corralled her outside the open door.

"Ms. McDonald can you please sign this?"..."M.K. here is the draft of the Hasinko proposal." On and on it seemed to go.

"Good Lord how does she remain sane?" Max thought. *"No wonder she just flops when she gets home!"*

The last minute, end of day, employee demands finally seemed to abate. Kaye was just about to step into the office, when Max heard her receptionist hesitantly address her, "Pardon me, Ms. McDonald, but I'd like you to meet my fiancé Henry Glaxton."

Kaye turned to see Steph, shyly blushing and behind her stood a very handsome young man. Kaye guessed him to be in his mid to late twenties. She admitted to herself later, that she had been taken aback. Steph was a wonderful young woman but a little on the plump side. She dressed very plainly.

In contrast Henry looked like he could compete for the sexiest M.V.P. of whatever.

Steph was gushing about all Henry's attributes as she introduced him to Kaye. Apparently Henry was working in the finance department as a junior clerk, so he could help finance further studies.

Kaye just smiled at her receptionist. She was very fond of Stephanie, who was a most competent young woman. What Kaye appreciated most about her was Steph's compassionate heart. She was always so considerate of everybody.

Furthermore, Steph's kind and gentle voice created an excellent first impression for anyone contacting Kayleen either by phone or personally.

Tonight however, Stephanie was like a giddy teenager on her first date. "Ms. McDonald, look at my ring, isn't it pretty?" she enthused with a little giggle. "Henry, thinks that it is too small. He said that when he's further along in his career he will get me a bigger diamond." She turned, smiled sweetly at her young man, and said, "But I told him that no matter what he gives me, this will always remain my treasured engagement ring! "

Kaye stepped forward to examine the ring, and gave Stephanie a big hug. "Fiancé? Stephanie, I'm thrilled for you and so pleased for both of you. Except," she paused and looked at Henry, "Does this mean you'll be whisking Steph away from my office?"

"Not at all, Ma'am," was the very polished reply, "at least, not immediately. I've got another twelve more months of study. We've set our date for next September following my degree. I'm going for an MBA, also." He added, "Soon I will need to take a temporary leave of absence from my job, to go finish up my degree. I hope Steph will wait for me?" He looked at her anxiously.

Stephanie beamed, "I told him he never needed to worry about me fooling around, Ms. McDonald, he's won my heart!"

In all this conversation Max had opportunity to get a good look at this couple through the open door. In his mind they certainly looked like a mismatch and something inside him made him feel uneasy, something about the man. But, the sensation was gone as quickly as it came. If he could look out the door, they could look in, and his focus was now on maintaining his own charade.

Stephanie and Henry were anxious to get on their way. They had a dinner date planned followed by a movie, then

Henry had said he'd have to get home to 'hit the books'. As they were leaving, Henry reached out and firmly shook Kaye's hand. He smiled warmly and said, "Stephanie enjoys working for you very much! I am most grateful for my clerk's position, especially my pay check! It pays for my schooling."

Putting his arm around Stephanie's waist Henry said, "We must be going now, Dear." Then to Kaye he added, "I look forward to meeting you again, Ms. McDonald," with that the love birds turned and were off down the hall.

As she watched the couple leave, all Kaye could think of was her small group friend Moiria. "I pray Steph, this Henry's love for you is genuine and he doesn't use you, like Moiria's schmuck fiancé did...to finance his education." She shrugged her shoulders, "But hey, who am I to judge? Beauty is more than skin deep and one thing is certain, you Steph, do possess the most beautiful, caring heart!"

At last, Kaye was free to retreat to her office. Closing the door behind her, she slumped into her plush leather chair. "Welcome to Kaye's World, Mr. Car...I mean, Mr. Watson."

Sitting opposite him now, she looked like any ordinary, albeit beautiful ordinary woman. Not the dynamic executive that had periodically flitted in and out of this office throughout the afternoon. The woman now in the room, he felt comfortable with, but the other seemed so far out of his league, never mind reach.

"In truth," he thought to himself, *"two good words to describe that other woman would be formidable and intimidating."*

He was glad to get away from her office, but as they entered the car park Max found himself studying the security cameras. "Kaye, look that camera is a dud!" He exclaimed, turning and pointing to the one over the door through which they had just come.

"How do you know?" was her indifferent reply.

"How do I know? It hasn't been properly installed. Look for yourself! See the cap has not been removed."

Kaye rolled her eyes, a little smile appeared. "This means we're not seen?"

"Unless there's another camera somewhere, that I can't see, but I can't find it." Max said as he scrutinized the garage in their vicinity.

"Does this mean you could sneak a kiss?" she said playfully.

"Definitely not!" Max scowled. He grabbed her shoulders and spun her around. "Look!" he demanded, once again, pointing to the deficient camera, "that camera is the only one covering your parking space, Ms. McDonald! It's not functioning and given your circumstances that should cause you great concern!"

Kaye turned suddenly pale and murmured, "Oh, no! I'm sorry, I totally lost focus. "

Max nodded and simply said, "get in the car, as we planned, only I'm going in the back, in fact I'm riding in the trunk." He closed the rear door after him, and pulled on the strap of one of the seats. As it folded down, he slipped into the trunk compartment. Tugging on the strap he soon had the seat back in its upright position.

Kaye threw her jacket over the back seat, and was about to protest that his latest precaution wasn't necessary, when a voice from behind startled her, "M.K. I'm glad I didn't miss you!"

"George!' Kaye gasped, "Oh, you surprised me! I'm sorry I jumped so."

"No need to apologize, I shouldn't have come up behind you so quickly. I wanted to catch you before you left. There are some aspects of the Saudi venture I'd like to run by you. Could you give me a lift to the airport and we could talk on the way?"

"Now?" It almost squeaked out of her, but she quickly regained her composure. "George, you amaze me! You are one of Kayleen's most productive directors." She laughed, "even when you're resting, you find ways to work. Sure hop in."

Laying in the trunk, Max was grateful that he'd had

the foresight to set up this hidden outlook. He had a clear view of the front passenger seat. *"So, go ahead and try something, Buddy. Make my day!"* Max frowned, "That darn camera was out and I suspect not coincidently. No one has seen this guy enter Kaye's car." He decided to pull J.D. out, just in case.

Whatever business the guy wanted to discuss, as far as Max could tell, it seemed pretty routine, which only further sent alarm bells ringing inside him.

He heard Kaye switch to the guy's family and the conversation again became routine. Yet, something about the guy's family, he just couldn't pinpoint what it was, made Max's hair stand on end. "Something's familiar, but what the heck is it?" he muttered to himself.

Then just as they neared the airport, out of the blue, at least that's how it seemed to Max, the guy asked, "M.K., remember our conversation a couple of months ago?"

"George, you and I have had many conversations. How on earth am I supposed to pick out the one you are alluding to?" Though if the truth be known, she already knew the conversation he meant. Her mind was racing, *"Oh God, Max said it could be someone I know. Jesus, how could it be George? He's always so caring, but never in any sexual way. Lord, those terrible calls...horrid words. Please, not George!"*

Beside her George sighed.

In the trunk, Max's hand closed tighter around the butt of J.D.

"M.K., I can't get out of my mind those calls you reported some eight or nine months ago. I asked you a few weeks past, if they had begun again and you said 'no'. Lately I just keep thinking of you. Have those calls begun again? If they have please tell me, I think I could help."

The man in the front seat turned towards Kaye, resting his left hand over the back of the seat.

Max's heart sank. This he never anticipated! He almost swore out loud. The man wore a ring, Max could see it clearly. It was unmistakable...The ring was his 'Family' ring!

Chapter Twenty-Nine

"Alice, did you go over the French itinerary with M.K. today?" the demanding voice on the other end of the phone was unmistakably Philippe's.

"Philippe, do I sound like I spoke to anyone today?" rasped Alice. "I'm running a fever, and can hardly talk, my throat's so sore. All I saw today was the Doctor who thinks I have Strep throat. I've just taken my first antibiotics. Thank you so much for inquiring though!"

She was about to slam down the receiver but before she could, Philippe's high pitched voice intervened. "Alice, you weren't at work today?" Alarm was now evident in his tone and Alice was certain the cause would be that Philippe's well manicured organizational plans had been screwed.

"I sent you an e-mail at 8 a.m., Philippe, that stated I would not be in," Alice snapped.

Of M.K.'s two aides, Alice was the calm, cool, collected one. Philippe was her exquisite, detail assistant and I do mean, exquisite. Philippe's tastes were impeccable. It mattered not whether he was organizing banquets, board meetings, travel or heads of state events...Philippe did it with flare and class!

Early on M.K. had recognized their collective creative and organizational skill and gave them free reign to operate. Together they planned her travel schedules. Both were faithful long-term employees of Kayleen.

R.K. had brought them into his office staff, but it was under M.K. that the two had blossomed. Alice was of similar build to M.K. and so was useful to Kaye as a decoy. Wigs had been fashioned for both. Thus, from a distance, it could look like M.K. was boarding a plane to fly to another destination, when in fact Kaye had remained behind. As for Alice, she enjoyed both the intrigue and the drama. She was fiercely loyal to M.K. but not tonight. Tonight she was one sick puppy...going no where!

"Alice, I'm so sorry, really I am," much to Alice's surprise her co-worker's voice was registering genuine concern. "Are you going to be alright alone, Dear?"

"Yep" Alice thought, "This is our Philippe, at times he can be a real prick, but underneath is real compassion. I guess that's why we make such a good team for M.K.? If we need real hard-nosed stuff, I'm the gal. Philippe covers the sensitivity aspects."

By now, it was obvious to her that Philippe was almost in tears that he had not known how sick she was. As she listened to him speak, she could even envision him pacing and gesturing as he spoke.

"Oh, my dear, dear, Alice! Had I known how sick you were, I would never have called. I'll arrange for Stephanie to call you tomorrow, first thing, to make sure those antibiotics are working!"

Alice couldn't help chuckling to her self, "Now he is organizing my health."

"Listen, Philippe," she managed to croak, "I will be okay. You need to focus on M.K., and getting her to Paris."

"Hardnosed, Alice, that's exactly who I am!" She mused to herself, "and you, old girl, know exactly what priorities we need to deal with now."

She was soon dictating those priorities to Philippe... "Phone M.K. with the details...Yes, tell her I'm sick, but on the mend, no need to worry!...Very important have Lewis pick up M.K., 8 a.m. *sharp*...That should get her to the International Airport by 11 a.m...Then, all things being equal M.K. should be in Paris by 10 p.m. their time. One more thing, make sure that there is a very light meal ready for her and everyone else when they arrive, and encourage everybody to then get to bed."

"Yes," Philippe assured her, "I have the itinerary for the meetings. Yes, I have all the briefs for each meeting. Yes, I have already planned for our team to go over most of them on the flight over. Yes, I've scheduled three hours in between meetings to ensure M.K. can review the material alone, and then have time to discuss it with the rest of the team."

Philippe was now becoming a little exasperated. His priority at this moment was Alice. He finally managed to butt into the one-sided conversation, "Alice, the real issue right now is you! Are you going to be okay?"

He went on to tell her that he had read all about Strep throat. "Alice, it really is very, very dangerous! Besides the antibiotics, I read that gargling with aspirin can help, even wrapping your neck and keeping it warm could be useful."

"Philippe," Alice interjected, "I'm doing all those things and more. I will be okay. You take care of M.K. and Kayleen. Use your French ancestry to help us win that French contract, okay Bubba!"

She giggled to herself, *"If there was anything Philippe wasn't, it was a Bubba. He was no redneck, much, much too sophisticated, at least in his eyes anyway...But that term, I've learned, always seems sufficient to ground him emotionally, to the task at hand, while terminating any conversation with me."*

True to form her strategy worked once again, "Very well," sniffed Philippe, "M.K. and Kayleen will be fine. You see to it you are when we return!" Klunk went the phone.

Alice lay back wearily on her bed, all would take place as planned, she could now be sure of that!

Philippe, on the other hand, was moving at a furious pace, setting up all the things he had believed Alice would have already arranged. "Thank God, I had the foresight to call her!" he muttered to himself. He wanted to continue to worry about Alice and her health, but there was just too much to do.

"I'll be exhausted when I hit that airplane. I'd better put my sleep mask in my pocket to ensure I get some rest."

He called M.K., "It's 8 p.m., she should be home by now, where can she be?" The answering machine came on and he left the message concerning Kayleen's Paris trip.

Then, he decided it might be wise to call the Walters and the Davidsons, just in case she was there. Fortunately, he got a live voice at the Walters. It was Marnie who answered, so Philippe explained his dilemma and received her promise to go to M.K.'s house and leave a note for M.K. to check her phone messages.

Unfortunately, for Marnie, she made the mistake of asking Philippe how he was. Half an hour later, Marnie hung up. She was indeed a truly gifted and compassionate listener. Consequently, Philippe's whole demeanor had changed from the start of the call to its conclusion. He had been able to share all his burdens, for Alice, for M.K., for Kayleen.

He smiled as he set down the phone, a small tear forming in the corner of his eye. "I always feel so good talking to Mrs. Walters. She's promised to pray for Alice, for me, for us, that all would go well. A lot of people say that," he mused, "but then forget. She never does! M.K. is smart to live beside them."

Several phone calls later, everything was arranged. He had crossed all the T's and dotted all the I's. Philippe put on his favorite classical CD, poured a glass of his favorite sherry and sat back to relax.

It would have worked too, except suddenly, he remembered that Lewis was picking him up first! And at 6 a.m.!

Both hands flew up to his face, in horror. *"6 a.m.! Whatever am I doing relaxing? I could fall asleep, perhaps miss my alarm wake-up!"* He stood and declared, "Far better, Philippe, that you shower now, get dressed, pack your clothes, and have those Kayleen briefs at the door!"

He smiled, "that way, I will be sure to be ready for Lewis' knock."

So he did and he was!

Chapter Thirty

"M.K., the departure lane is coming up on your right. You'll need to get over," George directed.

"Sorry, George," Kaye replied as she deftly eased her car into the correct lane. "With everything we were discussing, time seemed to fly. We were here before I realized it."

"You never answered my question."

"Which one did I fail to answer?" Kaye coyly acted confused.

"Those calls...have they returned?"

George was staring at her intently, fortunately for Kaye, before she had time to reply an airport security guard rapped on her window. "Passenger drop-off only, no waiting, Lady!"

"That's what I'm doing, Officer. He's just gathering his bag." So with her head conveniently facing the window, Kaye responded emphatically to George, "No, George, not yet!"

Then she turned to face him, "But I am so glad you do care and have asked. I will let you know if they do."

She waved as George headed into the terminal. As she pulled out into the traffic, she suddenly remembered that she had another passenger.

"Max, do you think I sounded convincing? Do you think he believed me?"

"Yes, to the first, I don't know to the second," was the muffled reply.

"Why don't you come out now?"

"I like riding in the trunk."

"You're kidding, right?"

"Not! It allows me to break the law."

"Whatever do you mean?"

"No seat belts here!"

"You're impossible!" Kaye responded.

"Told you that all along," to himself he softly added, *"Actually, Babe, I need to be alone to get my bearings. Who the hell is George? Why did he have that ring? Oh God, don't let her be on the wrong side of them! George? George? Why won't that name surface in my memory?"*

"Kaye"

"Yes"

"Who is George?"

She bantered, "You jealous?"

"Terribly, who is he? Where's he from?"

"He's a director on Kayleen's board. He's been with us about two years now. I find him to be extremely astute with the markets and very much a gentleman. He's fun to work with, and he's got a terrific sense of humor. He appears to be a pretty devoted husband and father of two teenage girls.'

"George seems very sensitive, better put I guess, would be to say that he reads people very well. That's why I asked you if you thought I was convincing. I'm really glad that guard knocked on the window, so my face was away from George when I replied. Is your jealousy abating?"

"A little, so how do you get on Kayleen's board?"

"Why, you interested?"

"Might be," the banter was good. It suited Max's purpose to hide his alarm.

So far, Kaye appeared oblivious to his growing anxiety. "Investors can put forth names of potential board members to be considered at Kayleen's annual general meeting. George's name was put forth along with one or two others. Their credentials are given and a vote is taken. George was elected to fill a vacancy...One of my father's long time advisor's had passed away."

"What did he die from?"

"Pardon?"

"Your father's advisor, how did he die?"

"He was eighty-four. He'd been in failing health for awhile, prostate cancer, I believe. He actually had resigned about nine months before he died."

"Eighty-four! How long are you on your board?"

"No term, you can be asked to resign, though that's not usual. Of course individuals do resign, health, retirement, other interests, personal, ordinary things you know.'

"Kayleen's directors are all productive. In the older ones, there's great wisdom."

"So this George, where does he come from? Or where does he live?"

"Nevada."

"Nevada? Shit that's it!" Max slapped his leg, "He's Volante's husband!"

"What did you say? I'm sorry, I couldn't hear you."

"Nothing....Just mumbling, in jealousy."

"Why don't you come out? We're almost home. I'm turning onto Independence Drive now."

Max had started to push down the seat when Kaye shouted, "Max, quick put the seat back, stay in the trunk!"

"What? Make up your mind," he grumbled.

"Marnie's on the road waving for me to stop." Kaye rolled down the window, "Hi, Marnie, is anything wrong?"

"Everything's fine with me, Kaye but not with you I'm afraid." Marnie replied.

"What do you mean?" Kaye asked, as her mind raced. *"Could they have found out about Max?"*

"Philippe phoned to ask me to make sure you listened to your phone messages. I left a note on your kitchen counter. Apparently Alice has Strep throat but..." Marnie put up her hand to silence the questions she knew would be erupting from Kaye. "But she's okay. She's seen a doctor and is on antibiotics, but..."

"Another but?" groaned Kaye.

"Another 'but' indeed!" Marnie laughed, "It was Philippe who called me. He had failed to get Alice's message in the morning. When he found out after supper, he had a lot of scrambling to do."

"Scrambling?"

"Yes, to pull together your Paris trip tomorrow." Marnie looked at Kaye incredulously, "Kaye, don't tell me you forgot all about it?"

Kaye slapped her hand to her forehead, "Oh, yes! Oh, no!"

A whispered *"Oh, no!"* echoed in the trunk.

Regaining her composure, Kaye tried to appear as unflustered as possible. "That's what it's like being a busy corporate executive," she quipped, "Oh, what we have to endure?...Another trip to Paris?"

"I'll make sure Dave and Jack check your place daily. Well, maybe not tomorrow, because you'll be leaving that day. They can check it the next two days and then, of course, you'll be home."

Marnie reached through the window and gave Kaye a hug and kiss. "Be careful now and don't let one of those suave Frenchmen sweep you off your feet. We don't want you traipsing off to France!"

Kaye laughed, "Yes, thanks for the romantic admonition, Marnie. Do you want to come in for a drink?" Silently she screamed, *"Please say no!"*

"Thanks for the invite, Kaye, but I was in the midst of finalizing my staffing requirements for this fall, and doing an inventory of next year's curriculum needs when Philippe called. I must get back at it, but I am glad I caught you coming home. Otherwise, I would have worried that you might not have seen my note. God bless, Love, and have a safe trip!" with that Marnie turned and sprinted home.

Kaye was numb. She hit the garage operator, drove in as the door opened and then shut the door. "You can come out now. I'm going to check my phone messages."

Receiver in one hand, the other hand on her hip, M.K.

paced back and forth listening to Philippe. *"How could I have erased this French meeting from my mind? It took us nearly a year to set it up with their board! Kaye, how could you let yourself be so distracted?"* She moaned, "Good heavens! I have to leave for Paris at 8 a.m. and I am so unprepared!" She set the receiver down and slumped over the kitchen counter.

Forgotten was what had been going on for nearly three months, forgotten even was what they'd done today and almost forgotten was the fact that she was not alone in the house...Until his firm hand clasped her shoulder, "Kaye, not now! You can't go to Paris!"

She wheeled startled, the strain of the past three months written all over her face. "Max, I have to go! It is not optional! You don't understand."

"No, you don't understand the danger you are in! You cannot afford to go anywhere unescorted! Kaye, do you remember seeing a ring on George's hand?"

She nodded and furrowed her brow.

"Does it look like this?" He held up his right hand to her face inches from her nose.

She blinked, "It looks like the same ring. Do you know George?"

"Yes and no...I believe he's married to a distant cousin of mine. If so, I was at their wedding about sixteen years ago. I'd have been about eighteen to twenty years old at the time.'

"Truthfully, I was most uninterested in weddings and quite stressed out at having a precocious sister who fancied herself much older than she was. She flaunted that fact to any male in eyesight."

His jaw tensed as he remembered the antics Sophia performed. He grumped to himself, *"Perhaps more aptly worded, the antics that I had to perform, to try and ensure she fulfilled Pop's desire that she walk down the aisle in white."*

"So you and George are like family? That's wonderful!" Kaye's facial features seemed to relax.

"No, that's not wonderful!"

"What?"

"His wife's brother, another distant cousin, owns the biggest Casino in Nevada. Being in that business and being Italian, he's…"

"Mafia" Kaye interrupted, eyes wide in disbelief.

"Not necessarily, but he would have acquaintances who are, just like I would have."

"Are you suggesting that the Mafia is behind those calls?…That George might be?"

Max stood hands on hips, shaking his head, "Kaye, initially I would have said no. I do believe your late night caller is a sexual predator, a sexual psychopath, and quite frankly, as I said before, there's no money in that business. No money usually translates into no mob interest. But…"

"Damn, 'buts'! Why are there always 'buts'?"

"Ms. McDonald, I don't believe it, you just swore."

"Max, I haven't time to banter. What is your 'but'?" she snapped impatiently.

"Kaye, I don't know why, George would ask you, about those calls."

"Possibly because he cares, and he's kind and compassionate, and if he has connections like you, he'd be aware of that six month thingme that you were aware of?" Kaye stood there, her hands now on her hips, green eyes flashing.

"Quite likely, but because of his connections, we can't rule out a set up."

"But the FBI has verified that all those sadistic sex killings are real. You've just said that the mob wouldn't do that." Kaye was clearly fatigued and irritated.

"That's the point, Kaye, like I said before, if the Mob wanted you killed, there are many guns for hire. They would nail you without even getting close. But sometimes they don't want to kill someone, just mess with them. That's what those first calls could have been."

"But our present caller claims he made them," Kaye protested.

"True, but that doesn't mean he did. Maybe the guy

is an opportunist? It was public knowledge that you had received those first calls. Maybe your current caller saw you and decided you would be his new prey to fill his current fantasies?

"Max, are you telling me there could be two groups or people out to ruin me or kill me?"

"It's feasible. I just don't know, Kaye." He ran his hand through his hair, "Think, is there anything you could have done? I mean, anything Kayleen might have done that would torque the mob?"

"Absolutely not!" She growled, "Kayleen is 100% legitimate. I have never slurred any race, any person. We have a Sheik, a Jew, Christians, all ethnic diversities, white, black, brown, Asian, Native American on staff or on our board."

At this point Kaye collapsed onto the sofa, the past three months had obviously taken their toll. She grabbed at the decorative pillow and clung to it like a drowning person would cling to a life preserver. Burying her face in the pillow, she began to rock slowly back and forth.

"I can't go on like this any longer. I can't! I can't! I totally forgot about my important business meeting! What am I to do? What am I to do? A dreadful sadistic murderer is calling and threatening me. They aren't idle threats! What he's telling me he'll do to me. He will! He has done this to others. The FBI confirmed it! Now I'm told one of my directors could be connected to the Mafia. Was George really being caring or was he sent to further unbalance me? God, help me please!"

Her lips moved but no audible sounds came forth. Max stood quietly by watching.

"Shit! She's at the breaking point! It's a wonder she's held together this long." His hand cradled his chin, as he tried to think, *"Lord, how can I help? I have no productive ideas in my head. At this point even the right words spoken at the wrong time or in a wrong tone could prove disastrous."*

He slide quietly onto the floor beside her. It was as if she was oblivious to his presence.

At last Kaye lifted her tear stained face from the pillow and began to speak in a whisper, "Dear Jesus," she murmured, "I don't understand all this. I feel like curling up in a ball. I can't go on like this anymore. To you, and you alone, do I come. Teach me to stand on your Word. To trust your Word, and to believe you will fulfill your Word and work all things to the good. Only you can bring order out of the chaos I am experiencing. Only you can calm this violent storm I'm in!"

The more Kaye prayed the more the tension in her seemed to be swept away. She continued, "Jesus, I need your help simply to get through the next few days. You promise to right all injustices, so, Jesus, if I have erred in some way, let Holy Spirit reveal to me that error. I want to confess it to you and make amends as you direct."

Kaye again buried her head in the pillow and concluded, "Please, Jesus, teach me to walk by faith, and not by sight, or by how I feel. Help me to always trust you and not lean to my own understanding. Amen!"

She paused. It seemed to Max, as if she noticed, for the first time, that he was there.

"Max, aren't you going to say Amen?" she queried.

It wasn't a demand. It really was a plea. It caught him off balance.

"You were praying?" he stammered.

"Of course, what else can I do?"

"For starters, stay home from Paris."

Sadness crossed her countenance, "Unfortunately, that is not an option."

Max stood up and glared at her, "You are so stubborn! I've never met anyone like you. Either that, or you are very courageous," he said grudgingly.

"I'm neither, Max. However, God commands us not to be discouraged but to be strong and courageous, because he is with us." She smiled weakly, "Really, he does give me strength to do what he wants, even if it is difficult." She sighed, "I believe he is directing me to go to Paris and, Max, that means I must trust him with you."

"What? Whatever are you talking about?"

"You said once that I didn't trust you and I didn't. I was afraid you'd hurt Jack, but as you know, now I know you won't. I do trust you." Her hand reached out and caressed his cheek.

Her action flooded him with those crazy turbulent emotions he couldn't fathom or seemingly control. On the one hand he longed for her touch, on the other hand he dreaded it.

"You heard Marnie...Jack, Dave, Matt, either one, or all three together, will be here to inspect my house...Not tomorrow but the two days following."

"When?"

"That's the problem. You won't know when they will come. It can be any time, day or night. They'll just do it when it's convenient."

"For them?"

"Of course for them, they don't even know you are here, silly."

"Silly, is not a nice adjective," he glowered.

"I wasn't meaning it in any derogative way, Max. I think you are anything but silly! I'm sorry," she said, "I just am rather overwhelmed."

"Kaye, maybe it is time to tell the authorities everything."

"Can we wait until I get back?"

"What if, you don't get back?"

"I'll get back!" she said biting her lip.

"Okay, when you get back, but then we do report!"

"But, what if he gets away? You said that awful person might catch on that he's being monitored and run, only to find another victim somewhere else."

Max looked into her eyes, he felt swallowed up in a sea of beautiful green. She was indeed, one remarkable lady. *"One remarkable lady, who has captured my heart!"* He reached out and took her hands in his. "So, when do you leave?"

"8 a.m."

"Well, you'd better pack, and at least we'll learn one thing, Kaye."

"What's that?"

"If there's no call when you're away, you'll know our perp has an inside track to your agenda."

"If that's so, we'll also know it isn't George."

"How can you say that?" Max asked.

"He doesn't know I'm away for three days."

Max smiled at her, "Kaye, you think of everything. There is one more thing though. When you are away, do not call home here to leave a message for me."

"Why not?"

"Just in case it's tapped."

"You think?"

"Kaye, right now I haven't a clue what to think. However, for the moment, let's set out to do what we can control. Which for you, means pack your bag." He reached out and tweaked her nose. "Hopefully we can get a few hours sleep before our 3 a.m. call comes in, because afterwards you'll be on your way to good old Paris."

"Ever been there?" Kaye asked.

"Never!"

"Someday," she grinned.

"Someday, maybe," he gave her a playful poke.

Chapter Thirty-One

Kaye woke early, her garment bag and briefcase she had already set at the door the night before. Hours earlier there had been yet another dreadful phone call. It seemed to her that the caller's threats to her were escalating in both vulgarity and viciousness. Even Max had said so.

She swung her feet out of bed and headed for the bathroom. "Time to shake a booty, girl...Forget about what was... Concentrate on the now, Kaye!"

As the warm water from the shower flowed over her body, Kaye slowly began to relax. "If only water could wash away those horrid things this man both confesses and threatens," she sighed. "Try as I might, nor can I fathom how I personally or Kayleen corporately, could have done anything to provoke organized crime into treating me as their public enemy Number One? It just makes no sense!"

She pursed her lips and a frown crept over her countenance. "Dear Jesus," she began to pray, "Please look after Max in my absence. Give him your wisdom to hide his presence from detection. Blind anyone who might check my house from realizing he has been living here," Kaye paused, "I'm no longer worried about him hurting the Davidsons and Walters. Now I'm concerned about what they might do to him, should they discover him."

Wrapping herself in her towel, she found herself eyeball to eyeball with her own reflection in the bathroom's expansive mirror. "It's amazing, only a few weeks ago I never knew the man existed. Now I find myself thinking of him all the time!'

"Funny, I never minded any business trip before, no matter how disruptive it was. Yet, for the first time I can remember, I find I really don't want to go on this one." She wrinkled her nose, "even though this happens to be an important business venture, with promising benefits not only for Kayleen but for both America and Europe!"

Kaye closed her eyes, "Lord, I need to trust you to look after me! Like the words of that scripture song say - 'some trust in chariots and some in horses but I trust in the Name of the Lord my God'- I guess, Jesus, that pretty well sums up how I believe I must act right now!"

With that she donned her white sleeveless pullover and the chic flowing emerald green pant suit that she had selected to wear on the flight. She glanced at her watch and was shocked to discover it was only 6 a.m..

She laughed and chided herself, "Kaye, you're all dressed up with no where to go for two hours!"

She quietly opened the door to the bedroom so as not to wake Max. To her amazement the light was on and he was not there. As she opened the door to the hallway, it soon became obvious where he had gone. The scent of fresh brewed coffee wafted up the stairs. She smiled to herself and hurried downstairs.

Bouncing into the kitchen she queried, "Is this part of your dating concept? Gourmet dining at 6 a.m. with..." she peeked over his shoulder, "steak, eggs benedict, hollandaise sauce, and asparagus. Wow! Mr. Carron, I am impressed! You definitely have outdone yourself. If I knew you did breakfast like this, I would go on business trips more often, but..."

"I thought you didn't like 'buts'?"

Kaye laughed, "I don't when others use them, but when I do its okay."

"Really? So what is your 'but' Ms. McDonald?"

"Well if this was a real date, a genuine dinner date, I would have anticipated the gentleman to have shaved." She squinted at him, "and maybe to have worn something other than PJ's."

Max chuckled, "Ms. McDonald, you need to get with the times, all the fashion magazines and celebrity newspapers declare 'stubble' to be fashionably sexy! As for the PJ's, the lady was occupying the shower."

Kaye made a mock curtsey, "Apology accepted, Mr. Carron, I receive this breakfast as a real date."

"All joking aside, Kaye, you be careful. At all times, be very aware of your surroundings," Max instructed sternly.

"I will," she promised, "and so should you!"

"When are you back? On Friday?"

"No, Max, I'll be in later Thursday night, possibly even by 8 p.m. and please, don't forget Jack or Dave, even Matt will check the house."

"I won't and remember, Kaye, do not call here. We have no idea who this perp is and whether or not he's monitoring your phone."

It seemed like their breakfast date had just begun, when the doorbell rang. "8 a.m. already?" Kaye moaned.

She quickly blew Max a kiss, mouthed "Bye Max," and to avoid Lewis coming into the house hurried to the door.

Max heard her informing her chauffeur, "Lewis, my garment bag is right by the door. Go ahead and put it in the trunk, but please, be careful not to crush it.'

"Right! It is a lovely summer morning, and I agree it could be very hot by this afternoon, if it doesn't rain.'

"No, it's okay, I can manage my briefcase. I'm just going to lock the door and arm the security system and I'll be there."

The door clicked shut, and with that she was gone.

Left alone with his thoughts, Max mused, *"It's good that it's summer. I can clean up with out any lights on. I suspect her neighbors might consider it a tad peculiar if the lights went on and off when the lady of the house was absent."*

He set about going carefully through the house to remove any evidence of his presence. He had organized a hiding place for himself on each level of the house, so her 'neighborhood inspectors' wouldn't catch him off guard.

Later hidden in the upstairs window, two eyes solemnly watched the Independence Drive neighborhood depopulate. He noted the departure of the Judge and his wife. Then the young cop left with the older cop. Out went Rufus and in went Rufus, followed shortly thereafter with nurse practitioner backing her car out the driveway and heading down the street.

Max sat silently at his post for another twenty minutes just in case some one returned. At last he stood up and stretched, "so, Max, for a few hours, you are free to exercise, sleep, read and snack unobserved. However, old boy, now that it has started to rain, better stay inside, no footprints that way!"

He was really grateful for the gym Kaye had set up in the basement. "One thing about prison," he reflected, "a guy could elect physical exercise and keep in shape." He smiled at the memory of how some of the inmates and the guards too, had admired his abs and the muscle tone in his arms and legs - not a 'gay' thing but a 'guy' thing.

"I am in shape and I want to stay that way! The other thing, Maxie, since you were allowed to take those law courses, you were able to remain in shape intellectually. Come to think of it, I also grew spiritually because I could interact with both the Catholic and Protestant Chaplains. They had some pretty cool stuff!"

It wasn't long before he had worked up a good sweat. In fact, the harder he worked out the more various prison memories flooded his mind. Like the 'The Alpha Course' the Chaplains introduced. "They had said no question was considered dumb. Consequently, we were all encouraged to open up and ask what really was on our minds.'

"I guess it was through that course I met Mr. Lobsinger and some of the other guards. Kinda neat how just talking about Jesus seemed to help everybody see the other 'guy' as a person... Whether they were a guard or an inmate."

Max smiled wryly, "You know, old man, Walters'

sentence really wasn't all bad. Sure, it wasn't fair whether you did, or didn't do, what you were accused of, but..."
he grinned, "there's that 'but' again! The truth is, if Jack Walters hadn't made the sentence six years, and if Pop and Pepi hadn't agreed on the 'Pax Roma' thing...Which meant we wouldn't push to see who tried to kill Tony, but just let bygones be bygones..."

Max wiped the sweat from his face, "Wow! The truth is even my anger at Walters has been used constructively. It made me determined to find out why he ignored everything and just threw the book at me." Max wiped his brow again, threw the towel around his neck and sat still on the exercise bike. "Yeah, the truth is that all that stuff, absolutely everything, seems to have coalesced to bring me here, just when Kaye needed help."

Max had now exercised on the bike, the tread mill and rowing machine each for a half hour. The cardio work out had been good. Not only was he dripping wet, he'd left little rivulets on and around the equipment. He carefully mopped up and deposited the towels neatly in the laundry bin then headed for the upstairs shower.

His mind continued to regurgitate on those prison memories. Professor Brown's course that he'd taken set him up to interview and study those serial sexual offenders. The more Max thought, the more he sensed an inner presence reminding him of that verse Kaye always quoted from the book of Romans. Out loud he suddenly said, "You have used every thing I experienced for good, just like the Bible says you promise to do!"

Standing in the shower, Max became very still, aware that he was not alone, aware that he was being washed not only with physical water but with The Spirit.

"By the way," he said quietly, "since you and I are now talking, I want to thank you for Kaye. She's a pretty good mentor. She just goes about talking to you normal like and says she feels you near her. It feels like that's what's happening to me now? If it is, and you do the same thing with guys, I'll sign up." He raised his right hand upward, as he used to do as a boy, when he pledged allegiance to the flag

Max paused unsure how to continue, then the words just seemed to flow, "Actually what I'd really like is to meet some guys who know you, who could teach me more about you. Kaye's great but she's not a guy."

Max gave a low whistle, "One more thing, if it's not too much to ask, I'd kinda like to do the guy thing outside prison." He bit his lip, "Don't get me wrong. I'm grateful for all I learned in prison about you. It's just that you must have some guys outside, don't you?"

By now, he was drying himself off. Wrapped in the towel, he sat on the side of the tub and lowered his head, his voice barely audible, "I think an awful lot about Pop and Mama. I ask you to look after them. Please, help Mama cope with me not coming home right away."

Max drew a deep breath, "Jesus, I don't know if you can do this. I read in the Bible all things are possible with you. I don't even know if it's right to ask this, but one thing prison didn't develop in me was the ability to properly express my emotions, especially the ones with women. Being with Kaye is really stretching me in this regard. Forgive me if this isn't the right thing to pray about, but if it is okay, well I kinda would like to marry Kaye."

There, he finally had said it. It felt like a great weight had been lifted off. Max paused feeling as if he should add something else, "I mean if that's what you and of course Kaye want. Whew! I never knew praying was so intense!" He murmured.

Then he had an additional thought, "But if it is okay with you and her, my next request would be that she'd like Mama and Pop, and they'd like her."

Max stood up, carefully took his towel and face cloth and dropped them into the laundry chute. Everything was dead still, all he could hear was his own breathing. Yet, in this stillness, he suddenly realized that deep within him now resided a profound peace.

Equally eerie, he now knew for certain that he was not alone. Another presence was with him. He didn't understand what he was experiencing, nor could he explain it. All he knew was this was real! *"Wow!"* was all he could say, *"Wow! Oh, Wow! You are real!"*

He didn't know how long he stood there before he dressed. Needless to say his morning encounter, of the very best kind, remained foremost in his thoughts, as he went throughout the day. He'd done up his supper dishes, checked and rechecked, the downstairs gym and family room, on the lower level. Then on the main floor he scrutinized every area, even Kaye's study to ensure there was no trace of himself.

Upstairs he'd smoothed out the bed, cleaned the bath room and was just thinking he'd slip downstairs for a late night snack, when he heard the latch on the front door click. Instinctively he glanced at the alarm system. It had been turned off. He knew Kaye had armed it in the morning.

Then he heard the sound of male voices. Max had already grabbed JD,. but soon realized the men were too noisy for burglars, even if they thought they were in an empty house.

Suddenly it hit him, *"No! It's Jack and Dave!"*

Carefully arranging Kaye's clothes to serve as his camouflage, he dove for the closet moving the false wall he'd made to hide behind. It may have been a few minutes, but to Max it seemed mere seconds before the light was switched on in the bedroom.

He sat motionless behind his wall of refuge. Max's mind raced, *"Was it Jack and Dave? Kaye had said they wouldn't be here until tomorrow."*

He strained to hear what they were saying. Then one opened the door to the walk in closet. Max held his breath as the man rummaged through the clothes. "Boy, does she ever have a lot of clothes!"

"She has to, Dave," was the muffled retort from the bedroom, "She's constantly in meetings, even dinner engagements for her are work, I would not want her life!"

"Me either!" the voice nearest Max replied. "She was just so young when R.K. and Mary were killed. So much responsibility got dumped on her. She really has no social life at all. Our small group is her only outlet for friends apart from her work colleagues. Are you sure Marnie said that Kaye would be gone for three days?"

The voice was now almost over top off Max, who felt as if simple breathing would give him away. *"Dear God, what do I do? What do I say if they find me?"*

"That's what Marn said, Dave." The voice in the bedroom was now speaking and it continued, "You know I don't feel right about giving permission to tap Kaye's phone."

"Jack, for crying out loud," the person turned away from Max, back towards the bedroom."

"Thank you, Lord!" Max mouthed, *"Wow! That just popped out, without me even thinking about it. Kaye must be rubbing off on me,"* Max thought, *"because that's exactly what she would have said!"* However, he quickly subdued his own thoughts to concentrate on the conversation taking place between the two men.

"Jack, you heard Epi," the man exiting the closet retorted. "Two or three nights of no calls and he removes the wire taps. Furthermore, it's us who will be with Ep and a couple of his agents. It's not like we're spying on Kaye. If she is the one getting those calls, she is talking to a dangerous serial killer and I suspect he has earmarked her as his next victim."

The speaker left the closet and grabbed Kaye's cane rocker. He pulled the chair adjacent to the man sitting on the bed. Max peeped through the crack that he'd had the foresight to make in his false wall. Fortunately the man had not closed the closet door and so Max found himself staring directly at the two men. He sucked in his breath, *"unmistakable, His Honor looks just like I remembered him. There he is square in my sights."* His hand instinctively closed over JD's butt.

Almost immediately Max recalled the Bible story that he'd read last week. King Saul was chasing David seeking to kill him. David had done nothing to deserve the King's wrath. He and his men had retreated deep into a cave to avoid detection. Saul unaware of David's presence had gone into the cave to relieve himself. David's men urged David to kill Saul, but David refused because Saul was God's anointed King. Later, David had the opportunity to show Saul that he could easily have killed him but did not do so. Thus, Saul realized that his pursuit of David was unjust.

"Sheesh! Why that story now?" Max looked at the man sitting on the bed. This was the one whose sentence had ripped him away from his family, unfairly, unjustly! Then inside himself, he began to experience a warmth that seemed to ooze through his entire being. *"Whoa! It's all gone, no anger, no bitterness, no revenge, nothing! Jesus, you took it all! I'm looking at this guy like he is a total stranger, or even someone I actually care about."* Max's hand slipped silently away from JD as he continued to stare at the two men. *"God, it's true! You really can make a new person out of someone and you've done it for me!"* Profound gratitude flowed from Max. He became aware that Walters was now speaking and strained forward to hear the conversation.

"What you say may be true, Dave, but you know Kaye is like a kid sister to us. She trusts us and somehow I feel like I'm betraying her confidence."

"Would you rather do nothing and find her murdered?" Dave responded bluntly.

Max saw Walters draw his hand over his face and then look up sadly as he shook his head. "No! Of course not, so when is Epi doing this and what exactly is he going to do? He isn't going to plant 'bugs' in Kaye's house is he?"

"No need, all he is interested in is the phone, if Kaye is the person sending him the information on those victims, Epi is assuming the communication is occurring between her and the killer through the phone."

"What if it's by e-mail?"

"Epi's got her e-mail address and checked her most recent messages. He reported that nothing was there. Don't forget that the letters he's received specify the messages are being received by phone. In fact they designate the time of the call to be 3 a.m.."

"So, Dave, The Bureau just taps in through the street box beside your house?"

"Right on!"

"When?"

"Tomorrow, Epi's going to set up surveillance in our house. Sue's away at her conference until Sunday. By the way, is Marnie home?"

"Tonight, but not tomorrow during the day. In fact I'm working at home the next two days. I have to leave Thursday night for Washington. I've appointments there Friday but expect to get home late Friday night." Jack chuckled, "Marnie can't get enough of kids at school, so she's going to the Paynter's Friday night to baby sit their two little ones. We had tickets for the theatre in Philly which we weren't going to be able to use. Marn figured the Paynter's could use a date night. She insisted they take the tickets and she'd baby sit. She even secured a free night at the theatre hotel and meals for them."

Dave laughed, "That's Marnie, for you, always looking out for others. I don't know how you managed to convince that warm heart to marry you."

"She saw my deep need." Jack retorted, "and I truly believe the Paynter's need this little holiday too."

"Fortunately, for our plans it couldn't come at a better time," Dave added. "It means you can join us Friday night, when you get in. After all, if I have to stay up so can you."

Forgiven

"What are you going to tell Sue about the guys in your basement?"

"Hopefully nothing!"

"Nothing?"

"Yeah, Kaye's supposed to be home Thursday night. We'll be listening Wednesday but if Kaye is the one that killer is contacting, chances are he'll know she won't be home until Thursday. Therefore, no phone call Wednesday...no big deal. Even if there's none Thursday, the perp could assume she's not home yet. But no phone call Friday or Saturday, I suspect Epi's barking up the wrong tree with Kaye. So, if Sue gets in Sunday, even late Saturday, I'll just say I had Epi and the guys over for some cards. They were traveling through to New York State for an investigation Monday."

"You think it will go that quick?"

"Yep!"

"Dave, do you really think that Kaye's involved with these tips to The Bureau?"

"No, Do you?"

"I don't know. But why don't you, Dave?"

"Kaye is an open person. She's always been honest with us. I don't see drastic changes in her behavior. Yet, if she was listening to what was sent Epi about those murders, I think she would be losing it. Now let me ask you, Jack, why would you consider she might be involved?"

Jack frowned, "It's just that she was devastated by the innuendos that were made when she confronted those earlier calls. I think she realized the negative impact they could have on Kayleen. Personally, I believe that Kaye would sacrifice herself, if it would save Kayleen. In Kaye's eyes, Kayleen represents everything R.K. stood for, so in a sense it is a way that she can continue to relate with him and honor his memory."

"R.K. was a very principled man, I must say. Our world needs more like him," Dave smiled sadly, "and you're right,

308

he seems to have instilled those traits in Kaye. You my friend, could be more right than I, unfortunately."

"So, are we going to check her place tomorrow?"

"No need, the wire tap will be in place."

"But a guy could hide here, waiting for her," Jack argued.

"True, so Thursday we'll give the place a thorough going over. When do you leave for Washington?"

"I plan to take the evening commuter train."

"Kaye thought she'd be back around 8 p.m.. Can you plan to meet me about 4 p.m. so we can give the house a once over? It'll be daylight, when she's dropped off. I can post a man to watch the back for a couple of hours, and we'll keep an eye on the front. And, of course, the house's alarm system will be armed. So, once she's safely inside our wire tap should be all we need."

Jack stood up and saluted, "You're on el Capitan! But you know, Dave, I'll be glad when this is all over."

"Me too, Buddy, me too. Let's not forget to put on the alarm as we leave."

Max listened as their footsteps receded. He heard the door click shut and then the beep, beep of the security alarm being armed.

He sat back and shuddered a sigh of relief, only then did he realize how heavily he'd perspired. "Well, one thing, I can agree with them on, is that I too will be glad when this is all over. In a way, I'm happy that the feds will be listening in on those calls. So, my not so friendly perp," he smiled slyly, "I think we'll up the ante for you, and see if we can flush you out. Tomorrow, I'll write a new script for Kaye."

Chapter Thirty-Two

Max squinted as a beam of light streaked across his face. He opened one eye to check the time, 6 a.m.! It was daylight. He sat bolt upright, grabbed for the phone and lifted the receiver. The dial tone was strong. It took a moment for the truth to hit home. No call had come through the night!

"Whoever it is knows she's away," he groaned as he flopped back on his pillow. He shook his head, "please, Jesus, don't let it be them!"

He scowled, "Crap! George could know she was away, even though Kaye thought he wouldn't. If he was tracking her, all he'd need to do is call one of her assistants. At least it can't be Dave or Jack for they're set to tap the phone." He paused as he turned on the shower, "Not so fast, Maxie, can't rule either out, just yet. One could be faking it.'

"Well, if it is one of them, I'd lay odds it's the cop." He chuckled, "Sure why not? In the 'who dun it murder mysteries,' it's just as likely to be a crooked cop, as it is the butler."

The warm shower felt good. It seemed to revive him. "A lot more appealing, I must say than those darn cold showers I take every night, before I hop into bed beside Kaye. But, at least they curb my testosterone urges," he sighed, "and enable me to stay on my side of the invisible line. Maybe I should fill the bathtub with ice water and dunk Kaye's perp in it when I finally get my hands on him? Nope, Max, not a good plan, too tempting, I'd drown him for sure!"

As he shaved and dressed, it all seemed so unreal, the very moment Kaye leaves town, the calls stop. "Maybe the guy just fell asleep himself, or maybe he stepped in front of a Mack truck," Max mused. As comforting as that last thought was, he knew it was merely instant gratification and escapism mentality.

"In fact what would we do if they just stopped? There would be no closure for any one. Nope, definitely not desirable to have these calls just stop. This guy needs to be exposed and nailed but good!"

Max's mind flashed back to the men he'd interviewed in prison. They were a scary bunch, maximum security indeed was needed. They'd all had agreed to him interviewing them.

Max smiled. "I'm certain Lobsinger secured their agreement by telling them that I was Sicilian, son of a Mafia Godfather. It was the one time the negative association of my ancestral identification actually proved beneficial to me. In their eyes, I was the 'oddity', the 'curiosity' and it worked. They opened up to me."

His countenance darkened as the memories of those interviews returned. "Their propensity for violence was no joke! Each interview, I had to enter dressed only in a prison T-shirt, pants with no belt, and shoes with no laces. Armed guards watched the whole time through one way glass. One guy actually had restraints on for my whole visit."

Max flopped back on the bed and lay there, hands behind his head, staring at the ceiling. "The thing that struck me the most was that except for the guy in restraints and maybe one other one...They all looked like your average Joe. Nobody would ever suspect the dark, deviant behavior that lurked within them."

A couple of the fellows, even looked downright handsome. A lot like the Bundy guy he'd seen in the article that Professor Brown had suggested he use to research his paper.

"I wonder," he said aloud, "What Kaye's perp will look like, a freak or the guy next door?"

One common denominator, in all the ones he interviewed, was that they were fans of hard core violent pornography.

In fact a couple of them had actually videotaped their actions.

"Why? Who knows?" He shook his head, "Some admitted viewing them re-stoked "their furnaces", as one guy put it. A couple thought they could sell them on the porn market and some deluded themselves into thinking the videos would make them porn stars."

Max frowned, "Another common trait was that rarely was any remorse shown. Most seemed incapable of acknowledging their victim as a person, unwilling to identify with the horror and pain they had inflicted on the victim or the victim's family and friends. It was all about their gratification!"

Two or three had appeared to show remorse, but whether it was genuine or simply put on, Max felt uncomfortable in assessing. Every one of them had been skilled in deception. He sat on the side of the bed, his thoughts continuing to pound relentlessly like a stormy surf. After all, their ability to manipulate and deceive is what had allowed them to have their crimes go undetected for so long.

"The one fellow, whose remorse, I felt might be genuine, was the one who consistently used alcohol to inhibit his conscience and drugs to fuel his passion before an attack. Now free from the influence of both drugs and alcohol the guy had to deal with what he had done."

One thing Max did know was that these convicted serial killers were all over the board as to the number of their victims and as to their own upbringing. Some appeared to come from good homes, others from abusive homes. One guy was himself victimized and brutalized as a young teen. Yet all shared how they used hard core porn to climax.

Each had moved from magazine to video, to eventually believing that satisfaction would only come as they themselves crossed the line and did it. "So," he grumped, "the only consistent profile of our 3 a.m. caller that my research offers is that in all probability he will be a porn addict. A lotta help that is in identifying the perp!"

Max sat down in the cane rocker, closed his eyes, and as he rocked back and forth a sly smile began to emerge. "But, what I did learn through those interviews can help me draw Kaye's perp over that line with her! And when he crosses it, we have the chance to snag and reel him in!"

He recalled the police profiles on these killers. Whether they subconsciously wanted to be caught or not was debatable. However, one thing was constant, as they acquired multiple victims they began to have a high, sometimes very high, opinion of themselves and their abilities. In fact, it almost got to the point where they saw themselves as invincible, and that's when they would error.

"At least one thing we have going for us, in that regard," Max murmured, "is this fellow is no novice. Perhaps it's time for us to play to his ego?"

He took out pen and paper and began to script a dialogue for Kaye. "Actually, it's more of a monologue," he mused. Finished, he scratched his head and perused what he had written.

"Definitely not the language of a Bryn Mawr graduate. I'll have some convincing to do to get her to spit out most of these words! Unfortunately for Kaye, from my interviews I learned that these guys got riled up over coarse vulgar language, when that language challenged their abilities and virility." He snorted, "they could dish it out but not receive it. Well, perp, what's good for the goose is good for the gander!"

He was glad to get the writing over with and headed off to make himself a good breakfast. "More like brunch," he grumbled checking his watch. Crafting the script had taken him much longer than he had anticipated or for that matter wanted.

He had just finished cleaning up after his meal, when he remembered that there was a big piece of Marnie's chocolate cake left in the fridge. Kaye had actually walked off with a huge piece, "just to snack on" she had begged. Marnie had been delighted to get it out of her house. "Neither Jack nor I need it," she'd said.

"Neither do I" Max chuckled, "but it sure is good! Chocolate is comfort food and right now, I need comfort."

He had to admit that although Kaye had been gone only a day and a half, already he was missing her terribly. In fact, he had never missed anyone like this before!

Max had just got himself settled in the upstairs bedroom, cake, soft drink and Bible in hand, when a utility van pulled up across the street.

He smiled, "There's the Bureau masquerading as phone repair men." It didn't take ten minutes and the van was gone.

Within an hour he was treated to more action. A white SUV pulled into Dave's driveway. The Chief's cruiser was right behind. Two men got out of the SUV and with Dave, began carrying equipment into the house.

"Real glad you and Jack dropped by for a visit the other night," Max grinned in amusement. "Now I don't have to wonder what's going on."

He had to admit that knowing they were eavesdropping actually brought comfort not annoyance. It also evoked another memory, as he recalled a visit his family had made years ago to the Bastaldi's in Newark. Old man Bastaldi was going on about "those damn coppers invading his privacy."

Max could see Uncle Tommy and his gold capped grin as he said, "so, I gave them an earful. On purpose, I forgot to put the receiver back on the hook. Instead, I just set it down while Leo practiced the trumpet for his grade five concert." The whole room had erupted in great glee.

"Well family dearest, while none of you might approve, I have to say that I'm relieved this line is tapped." Max paused then continued, rolling his eyes heavenward, "Just don't let Kaye call, please!"

Other than that, the day and evening went fairly fast. Max watched the White Sox clobber the Yankees. "Man what I'd give to see Tony's face, or for that matter Pepi's!" That was one aspect of the Chicago – New York rivalry that their Pax Roma had not dispensed with.

Max already knew what the inhabitants in the Davidson's house did not. There would be no late night call this evening. Sure enough, he had another night of uninterrupted sleep.

Waking up, Max had a chilling thought, "Family, I sincerely hope you have no connection to what is happening to Kaye." His jaw clenched, "However, if you do, my loyalty no longer lies with you. It is with Kaye!" The ferocity with which he spat out those words shocked him, but one thing he was certain of, he meant it!

"Better do my housekeeping, so everything is ship shape for my four o'clock inspectors," he chuckled. Once again he checked and rechecked the family room, gym, main floor, especially the kitchen and the upstairs. Confident all was well, he retired to his own retreat cubby hole in the closet.

One thing about Jack and Dave, they sure were punctual. Max could see through his peep hole the alarm being disengaged. He heard the men enter and their conversation as they began their upstairs inspection. They were affirming that the monitoring of Kaye's phone calls had begun.

"Yeah," he heard Dave say, "As I suspected no call, nothing on Kaye's line."

"Yes," Jack retorted, "But don't forget that Kaye's not here."

"That would mean the perp had fairly accurate info on her whereabouts," Dave replied.

"I thought they said that in most cases the victim knows the perp?" Jack asked

"Not sure that holds in serial killers," commented Dave.

"Yes, it does," whispered Max quietly, "that is the victim may not know the predator but the predator knows the prey. Usually he's had his prey under surveillance for awhile."

His own thoughts were interrupted by Dave coming out of the bathroom. "There's a tooth brush here that I don't remember seeing on Tuesday."

"Damn! How did I miss it?" Max choked in horror.

Jack responded, "Dave, you were in and out so quick, you probably missed it. Don't forget, it was here that I preoccupied you with my angst over the wire tapping."

Dave chortled, "Well, do I remember that! So, Your Honor, from now on, you are hereby banned from any stake outs that I might be on."

Unknown to them, from deep within the closet a solitary figure began to once again breathe!

"You're leaving for Washington tonight but will be back late tomorrow?"

"Yes, Chief Davidson, I will report back to you at twenty two hours Friday," Jack intoned somberly.

"If we get a hit tonight, want me to call you?"

"Yeah, Dave, that would be great, call the apartment, I'll be the only one there. Let me know whenever you hear. I intend to be up at six and in the office by seven. Friday is a full day and I want to finish my reports before heading home."

With that the two men exited the bedroom and any other conversation they may have had was lost to Max.

He was still chastising himself about the tooth brush an hour later. Slowly, however, his annoyance at himself was giving way to thoughts of Kaye's eminent arrival. Just like a watched pot seems to take forever to boil, so time crawled for Max as he waited for her chauffeur to arrive.

Initially, he had planned to hide and surprise her, but quickly revised his thinking. Had the circumstances been different he would have enjoyed teasing her, but not now. An unnecessary scare was something she definitely didn't need. He saw her disarm the alarm, heard the lock open, and her thanking Lewis for bringing in her bag.

"No, I won't need you to pick me up Monday. I plan to drive myself, thanks and be sure and have a great weekend, Lewis!"

The door closed. Both watched as Lewis got in the car and drove away. Then she was running up the stairs calling his name. They met in the hall and embraced. This time Kaye noted, he didn't pull away.

She cocked her head to one side, green eyes twinkling and quipped, "Not bad, Mr. Carron, for a first date kiss."

He exhaled deeply, and gave a hollow laugh, "Well said, Ms. McDonald, and given our current situation, timely. I'll step back and let my passions retreat to first date level. But, Kaye," he cupped her head in his hands, "I missed you terribly."

"And I you, Max," she murmured. Then she asked that question, whose answer she had been dreading. "Were there any calls?"

"No," was the quiet reply.

For a moment, she fell silent. Finally she said, "he knows my schedule then, doesn't he?"

"Yes" Max nodded sadly.

"Oh, Dear God, please help us expose him soon," tears welled up in her eyes. "I don't know how much longer I can carry on like this."

"I know, Kaye," he said softly. "I've thought a lot about it in your absence. I tried to recall my interviews for Dr. Brown's paper. I've written some things down which I'd like you to start using beginning tonight."

"*If*, he calls!"

"If he knows your schedule, he will call at 3 a.m. Kaye." Max looked at her sternly, "I forewarn you, Kaye, what I've written for you to say won't be easy for you. You will not like it."

"Why?"

"Because they are vulgar and filled with profanity. You don't talk that way, but you need to do so. We need to challenge his virility and his ability."

Kaye's eyes widened in disbelief, "Whatever for?"

"All the guys I interviewed had a huge ego problem… Prick it and they lose control."

"Meaning?"

"They get angry…It incites them to rage and hopefully carelessness."

Max was correct. When Kaye read what he had written

for her to say, she was horrified at the language and repulsed by the concepts the words painted. He spent the good part of three hours coaching her on the inflections and voice tone. The bottom line was that Kaye was to present herself as the boss, the bitch, the one in control, conveying in no unmistakable fashion that this perp was simply a bluffer, the fool, the sexless buffoon, the coward.

As anticipated, once more, the call came, precisely at 3 a.m.!

"Nooo," moaned Kaye, "he does know me." She looked pleadingly at Max who quietly picked up the receiver and handed it to her. Kaye's "Hello," was barely audible.

"My, Dear Ms. McDonald, how I so missed hearing your..." the now accustomed profanity then spewed forth, followed by the solicitous voice "Did you enjoy those two nights of unbroken rest in Paris, my dear?" At this point her caller broke into a snicker.

Max nodded and mouthed "Now, as practiced!"

Kaye exploded into the phone. "You are a pathetic wimp of a man!" In no unmistakable vulgar terms and with many expletives she continued, "The way you fantasize, I suspect you've already been castrated. You can't even manage an erection let alone carry out your ### threats to me, any more than you can fly #### to the moon!" She concluded her tirade with a disdainful laugh.

The response was instantaneous. "Stupid Bitch! You think because you're a high and mighty business woman you control the whole damn world? Two days away, Slut, have softened your brain. I'll call tomorrow, Sweetie, and you'd better coat your "Sugar Daddy," or you'll discover what I can do!" With that he slammed the receiver down.

Kaye was stunned. Max gently pried the receiver from her hand and placed it back on the phone rack, before he erupted with a triumphant "Oh, yes! Bingo, Baby, we did it!"

Kaye just stared at him. "I'd say we got him furious, but is that wise?" she asked, worriedly.

"Absolutely, Honey," Max assured, obviously as pumped

as any star athlete who just scored the game winning point. "Kaye, you said that you didn't know how much longer you could hold out. Well, you cast your line and the fish took the bait. You were terrific!"

He leaned over and gave her an exuberant kiss. "We'll practice Friday night's monologue, in the morning."

Barely two-hundred yards away, three other pairs of eyes registered equal shock at what had just occurred.

"Dave, have you ever heard M.K. speak like that?" Epi was finally able to croak.

"Never!" was the emphatic reply.

"Well, Sir, at least you know this lady is the one getting those calls," offered a third voice.

"Dave, surely she would have gotten the messages we inserted in the tabloid according to her directive?" Epi's voice clearly registered concern.

"I would hope so."

"Chief, this guy she's dealing with is a serial killer," Epi interjected. "What the hell is she doing messing around with him? This is no joke!"

"Sometimes, Sir, people get cranked up by the cops and robbers thing," offered Epi's assistant. "You know, gets their adrenalin going. Perhaps, that's where this lady is coming from?"

"Never!" Dave interrupted, "Never, that just isn't M.K. she...she..." He groped for the right words. "...she is just always in control. Yes, she takes risks but they are always very carefully, calculated risks."

"Maybe tomorrow night we can get a better fix on what she's doing but at least we know this perp is the one who connected with her last fall. And," Epi paused, "we know something else, Dave..."

"What's that?" was the puzzled retort.

"He knows her schedule, which means he knows her."

All Dave could do was sadly shake his head in agreement.

"Brian, can you check if the call was long enough to grab a trace?"

"Already on that, Sir, and unfortunately the answer is no. We were about fifteen seconds too short."

"Can I use our phone now?" Dave asked wearily.

"Sure, why?"

"I promised to let Jack know if or when we had a hit."

A sleepy "Yes" responded to Dave's call.

"Jack," he was interrupted before he could say more.

"It was Kaye, Dave?"

"Yes."

"Something's wrong?"

"Yes"

"What?"

"Kaye spoke like I've never heard her speak before."

"What do you mean?"

"Vulgar – profane"

"This is a joke, right?"

"Sorry, no! I don't know what to make of it...Just totally out of character for her. Jack, have you ever heard Kaye swear or be vulgar?"

"Never! You don't think she's losing it, do you?" Jack queried?

"Jack, Epi here. The phone is on the speaker setting. You and Dave know Kaye better than I do. I'm assuming in Paris that she had two nights uninterrupted sleep, then coming home jet lagged and all, maybe Kaye just thought...*"This bastard's really pissing me off! I've had it! I can threaten too...I'll call your bluff, you S.O.B.?"* Unfortunately, Kaye's response has created a huge problem for her!" Epi had been pacing as he spoke. He stopped abruptly and heaved a deep sigh, before he continued...

"Jack, I have no doubts now that Kaye is the one who mailed those letters to me. This means the guy calling her is the perp who fed her the facts she wrote about. Make no mistake, her caller is a vicious, psychopathic, serial killer. M.K's playing with a live grenade!'

"We'll monitor again tomorrow night. Hopefully the conversation will last a little longer so we can get a trace.

Regardless, we'll watch the situation closely, and intercede if needed. No doubt about it, M.K. is in need of protection big time!'

"As for now, we're heading off to bed. Have a good day, Your Honor."

"Thanks," was the muffled reply as the phone line went dead.

"Sir?"

"What, Brian?"

"You don't think it could be him?"

"Who?" Epi asked, puzzled as to what his young assistant meant.

"Him," Brian nodded toward the phone.

"What?" said Dave angrily, "You are suggesting this perp could be Jack?"

"Well, we all know it isn't one of us," Brian replied testily. Epi laughed, "Brian, Jack knows we're tapping the line. He is the one who gave us permission."

"Maybe, but he knows her schedule, and he was by himself," Brian persisted.

Dave closed his eyes, "Sorry fellows, this is way too bizarre. We need to get some sleep. Good night, Gentlemen, I am off to bed!"

Chapter Thirty-Three

Jack stared at the clock – 3:45 a.m..

"Try and get some sleep, Buddy," he tried to encourage himself, "There's a good two and a half hours before you need to get up. Remember you've got a full slate ahead of you!"

He checked the alarm. It was set. He flopped back on the bed, burying his head in the pillow and closed his eyes. Seconds later, his eyes opened wide.

"Quit kidding yourself, Jack, you are not going back to sleep." He reached out and turned on the light.

Sitting on the edge of his bed he bowed his head. "Lord, I don't understand. What Dave shared is just not Kaye. She's always polite; proper, but not stuffy. Kaye is a lady in every sense of the word. Even if she was stressed out, I can't see her speaking like they said. What is going on?"

He sighed and continued, "Whatever it is, Dear Jesus, please protect your servant Kaye. Amen"

He stood up, "It seems I have two choices, Lord. I can tackle the memos on my laptop or I can turn and read your word." A strong urge came over him to pick up his Bible and read. It actually opened at First Samuel, Chapter 21, beginning at verse 10.

David was running from King Saul who simply wanted to kill David out of jealousy. Saul's motives were insane, his passion fueled by a raging inferno of spiteful hate. In this particular story, David had actually fled to an enemy king's territory to escape Saul. Unfortunately, this King was equally suspicious of David, so David feigned insanity and slipped away unscathed.

Jack sat back and frowned, "Lord, why this story? How does it apply to Kaye's situation? She's trying to deceive... but whom? Pretending...but why?" The only thing that Jack knew for certain was that he was now wide awake. It was 4:30 a.m..

"Might as well forget sleep, Jack." So he headed for the shower and by the time he had shaved, dressed and eaten it was 5:30 a.m.

Packing his overnight bag and snatching his briefcase, he headed for the street, hailed a cab and at 6 a.m. was in his office. By the time Mrs. Stuart arrived he had managed to clear off his e-mails and was starting to work on the Pender Appeal.

"Well, Judge Walters, if the early bird gets the worm, you have sure aced this day," quipped Mrs. Stuart. "Can I interest you in a coffee? I have some fresh baked muffins to accompany the brew."

"Mrs. Stuart, I do declare you're an angel in disguise," Jack laughed as he sat munching on her banana-nut muffins. "Even whiffing the aroma from my coffee mug has restored sanity to my day. Thank You! By the way, when Professor Brown arrives, please notify me immediately."

When she did buzz him, he had just finished his Pender dissertation. Jack checked his watch - 11:30a.m., he had actually accomplished what he'd thought would take a day to complete! He smiled, "That's what occurs, Lord, every time we put you first and give you our day. Thank you!"

Mrs. Stuart ushered a large, impeccably dressed, bespectacled man into the Judge's chambers. "Professor Brown...Judge Walters" she announced politely. She closed the door and retreated to her desk.

Jack stood up and strode over to the man, hand extended, "Brownie, great to see you again!"

"Haven't lost your grip, Jack," retorted the man as they exchanged a very firm handshake, followed by a sincere embrace. "But, like me, our svelte gridiron figures are becoming a little more bulky."

Jack gave him a playful jab, "So, Roomie, how is the famous Harvard Law Professor doing? Good night! It seems like only yesterday that we were sweating out those exams, worrying about where we'd practice, who we'd marry and most importantly concentrating on beating Yale."

"Also chasing the girls," Brownie added laughingly, "and here we are respectable members of society, solid family men, now with daughters who are being pursued by frat boys we totally distrust. So how long you got for me today, Jack?"

"I'm not timing this lunch, Brownie. Let's just enjoy the time we got. I'm glad you called to let me know you'd be in Washington. By the way, what does bring you here?"

"You!"

"Me?" Jack eyed him quizzically.

"Yep, let's head for lunch. I want a nice fancy restaurant, where you can treat your old roomie well."

A pleasant July day encouraged them to walk the several blocks to Jasmine's, a favorite Steakhouse of the Washington crowd. They filled each other in on their wives' careers and health.

"Had a big scare a couple of years ago, Mary discovered a lump in her breast." Brownie stopped walking, looked at the sky, rubbed the back of his neck as he struggled to compose himself. "You know, Jack, that was a defining moment in my life. I realized just how important Mary was to me. It was with a great deal of chagrin that I remembered the locker room banter we all used to engage in concerning women's breasts. Like they existed simply to turn on our libido." He ran his hand through his hair and gave a slight cough. "I looked in the mirror and said what a callous, immature ass, you were then, Brownie."

Jack grunted and put his hand on his friend's shoulder, "We were exactly that! All the hype over our Intervarsity letter blinded us to what those wiser than ourselves knew."

He gave a little laugh, "The truth is, Roomie, both Mary and Marnie, knew exactly what ignorant conceited oafs we were, but for reasons known only to them they stuck with us."

Jack's expression registered genuine concern. "So tell me, is everything okay with Mary, now?"

Brownie's famous grin returned, "Yeah, Jack, fortunately for us, the lump turned out to be only a cyst. Thank God! But..." he added. "that lump caused me to do a major overhaul in what I thought I valued in life. It caused me to appreciate how quickly our perfect manicured lives can spiral out of control." He sighed and continued "Remember our frat days, when having fun, getting ahead... gaining that reputation...being financially well-off seemed to be what life was meant to be. Well it's not, is it?"

Jack gave a hollow laugh, "Sure isn't! You know what turned me around, Brownie? I took our youngest daughter, Tiffany to a youth group meeting at the church. They invited me to stay and watch the teaching video they were showing. It turned out to be a "Focus on the Family" video about "Knowing God's Will for your Life".

James Dobson told the kids to give themselves an end of life quiz to see what really mattered. He said that at that moment, money, fame, prestige becomes immaterial. Instead, what becomes important as you lie on your death bed is, 'who you loved and who loved you.' I guess it was at that point that I really began to rethink my relationship with Christ, with Marnie, my daughters, my friends, my Church family, and my work."

That's pretty much how their luncheon conversation went, as within an hour these two close college friends found themselves once more honestly sharing their personal struggles and joys, not their professional accolades.

Rather than remaining mere legal colleagues, the transparency, the two had held in their youth, once again weaved them back together as friends. It also allowed them to kibitz over the merits of their favorite baseball teams.

Jack staunchly defending the Phillies, while Brownie extolled the merits of the Red Sox's.

They were well into their dinner, when Brownie, with an impish grin on his face, said, "Since we're being so open with one another, like when we were college roommates, I'd better come clean as to why I actually wanted to talk with you."

"I know," Jack jested, "You've finally admitted to yourself that being an Ivy league Professor at Harvard isn't where the action is. You want me to forward your name as a candidate for The Supreme Court."

"Hmm...I actually hadn't thought of that, Jack, but now that you mention it, I would be an excellent candidate. But no, that is not it."

"So?"

"So, about six or seven years ago, you sentenced a young man by the name of Massimiliano Carron, from Chicago, to six years in the New York State Pen for a drug trafficking offense."

"Yes, so?"

"So, Carron was released about three months ago."

"And?"

"And no one's heard from him since. A friendly guard dropped him off at the bus depot, which apparently took him as far as Cleveland. Near as my informants could tell me, he met two of his men who brought him his car. He sent them back to Chicago while he supposedly went South on some business deal, only to totally disappear off anybody's radar screen, including his own family."

"Your information jives with mine, Brownie. Epi, a friend of mine at the Bureau, was concerned that Carron might be labeling me for retaliation."

Brownie smiled wryly, "My information also, and that's why I'm here. To tell you I have a vested interest in Massimiliano, who incidentally does not like that moniker. Since it is Italian for Maximilian, Mr. Carron's choice is simply Max."

Jack sat back and studied his friend, "I can't believe,

Brownie, that you traveled all the way down here, simply to inform me that if my antagonist shows up to shoot me, all will go well with me if I simply call him Max."

Brownie let out a low chuckle, "You are correct, Jack, that is not it either."

"Why on earth, Brownie, would you be interested in a young Mafia punk?"

Brownie leaned forward, "Because, Roomie, I don't think he's a punk nor do I think he's Mafia material."

Jack's jaw tensed. "Do tell, so far I'm not on your wavelength."

"Jack, in all my years at the law school, Max Carron has one of the most brilliant legal minds that I've ever encountered. Believe me, in my tenure at Harvard, I have met many very sharp cookies. I genuinely desire to see that mind on our side of the law! That's one of the main reasons I want to track him down."

"Forgive me, Brownie, but how on earth did you manage to have anything to do with a convict? Now you have me very intrigued."

Professor Brown began to describe how Carron had applied to take a law course that he offered by correspondence. "I think initially Warden Blackmore allowed Carron to pursue it more out of amusement than anything else. He was also curious to see if I would allow it?"

Jack raised his eyebrows, "Carron actually had the credentials to take the course?" he asked, "What was it, an undergraduate course in law?"

"Yes to your first question, and no to your second. The course was a first-year law correspondence class on jurisprudence. Carron had an honors B.A. from Chicago. So I allowed him to take the course. Max aced it with brilliant perception. One thing led to another and with both the prison administration and Harvard in agreement, Max was granted permission to enroll in all our Bachelor of Law courses."

Jack was dumbfounded, "They let him out to go to class?"

"No, of course not! He did it all by correspondence.

From time to time, I and one or two other Professors would go to the prison to personally interact with Carron. In fact I was designated by our Law School to be Max's personal mentor. A task I might add I found most rewarding. His insights were fresh and nothing short of astounding. Had he been in class and eligible for the Bar, Max would have won the Gold Medal for academic achievement, hands down, no contest!"

"But he wasn't and he can't, so what's the point," said Jack frowning.

Now, it was Brownie's turn to sit back and look his friend in the eye. He smiled and gently replied, "Jack, I'm aware of your theological bent, and I would have thought that you would have grasped the point immediately. I'm certain you must believe in redemption?"

"Redemption? Of course, but you're talking about someone who is Sicilian...Mafia related or at least with possible Family connections. Don't forget, Brownie, to be redeemed one needs first to desire it."

"True, there is a role for the individual to play. You are right. An individual must recognize their personal need for redemption and reach out to receive it. However, before an individual can do that, the process whereby redemption can be obtained must first be established. That responsibility does not rest with the individual. After all, from a theological perspective, God set up the process whereby we humans could be redeemed apart from our works. Our role is to respond to God's plan. Therefore, Jack, I believe that there is a need in our penal system to establish avenues where qualified and deserving inmates can have real educational opportunities to better their lives."

"So, you see Carron's experience as a model for this type of program?"

"Exactly!"

"So it's in the best interest of this program that Mass..., I mean Max Carron not fail?"

"Precisely!"

"Why, at this time, do you tell me this?"

"Well, truthfully, Jack, I thought he might seek to contact you. I didn't let him know that I knew you."

"That's charitable, Thank you!"

"But," Brownie pursed his lips in an attempt to camouflage the smile that threatened to break forth, "I actually encouraged him to do so."

"You are joking?" Jack's eyes were now blazing fire.

"No!"

Jack spluttered "I love you too, Brownie!"

Before he could protest further, Brownie interjected, "Jack, I'm very suspicious Max took a rap."

"Brownie, have you gone soft in the head?"

"Please, Jack, hear me out. I thought I could trust you to respect my ability to judge character."

"I did up, until now," groused Jack.

"Max is a fascinating person. He's quiet and quite brilliant."

"Obviously, he's bedazzled you!"

"Cut it out, Jack, quit being defensive! I'm not questioning your judgment in his trial. I'm simply trying to tell you about this guy and the penal educational model we were working on."

"But why?"

"In the hopes that if he does show up on your doorstep, and you have this information, you won't simply refuse to see him or sic the cops on him. Instead, you'll take a moment to engage him, even challenge and encourage him to use his talent and ability positively for society. He doesn't have to have a degree, or be able to go to the Bar, to be of use to our legal system. Jack, this guy is really top notch. I'd rather have him on our side of the law than on the other side...especially when the other side is the Sicilian Mob." Brownie's voice now took on real passion, "I believe Max, not only to be salvageable, but worthy of salvaging."

Jack stared at Brownie sternly, "Why would Carron

want to see me, except for revenge?"

"Like I said, for whatever reason, I believe he willingly took a fall."

"For someone else?"

"Yes, but what was gnawing him, was why you chose to hit him with a maximum sentence? Particularly, when he had no record of anything, even a parking ticket."

"You want to know?"

"Only, if you care to share, Jack. What I want you to know, is that Max figured you must have taken a bribe, and he wanted to know who."

"A bribe? You must be kidding? That really offends me, Brownie!"

"I'm not kidding and yes, without revealing our personal relationship, I firmly tried to assure him that no one could bribe or threaten you, to cause you to forfeit your personal integrity."

"So that's all Carron knows of our relationship?"

"Yes!"

Jack sighed, "Well, his case was my first on the bench."

"Yes, I knew that."

"Brownie, the original trial judge died suddenly before Carron's case was heard. I was pressured into taking the case. This brought me into conflict with my family...Marnie in particular. We were scheduled, about that time, to take a major family trip. Two of the more senior Justices convinced me that it was a cut and dried case and should be over quickly. Told me it was a good opportunity for me to send a message to the mob not to mess with me. They inferred that regardless of what I did, it was sure to be appealed and the guy would end up getting only a few months anyway.'

"So," Jack said, "I went in and threw the book at him. Quite frankly, Brownie, I was shocked to discover that he actually served the full term."

"Sheesh, I wonder why they didn't appeal?"

"For that, Brownie, you'll have to ask his lawyer, if he's still alive. Personally I take full responsibility for my action.

The advice of the older Justices was bad, no way around that, but I chose to accept it.'

"If what you say is true about this guy's character, I would have to admit I made a wrong judgment call, but that doesn't really help him now does it? Given the above, I fail to see how I can have any positive influence on your Mr. Carron." Jack grinned, "However, the one thing I can do for you, today, Roomie, is ask if you'd like desert?"

"Yes but no," Brownie sighed, "we're both in danger of losing our superb football physiques! Best we pass, Jack."

"Well, let me pay our bill, and then please come back to my office. My instinct tells me you have more to say about your marvelous Mr. Carron. It may help me to convince him of his potentiality before he shoots me," Jack said wryly.

On the way back Brownie started to describe one particular project Carron had undertaken for one of his courses. "Carron had secured permission to interview a selected group of convicted criminals. Max set up and designed the protocol. He even wrote his observations and conclusions in a format suitable for publication in the prestigious Criminal Law Journal. So I submitted it, because the paper was truly brilliant, far above any student paper I'd ever received. That's another reason I want to contact Max. His paper has been accepted. He needs to sign the release for it to happen."

Both men, arriving at Jack's office, cheerfully greeted Mrs. Stuart. Their conversation continued as they entered Jack's private chambers.

"Aha!" Jack teased, "So the real reason for our meeting finally comes out. The eminent Professor Brown wishes to have his name on yet another published paper. It probably would be, as you implied, an exceptional paper. Your Mr. Carron would have had an inside track on interviewing some of these convicts, presumably some Family connections?"

"Jack, I see that you haven't lost your unique ability to handle sarcasm," Brownie replied good naturedly.

"However, I'm afraid you have misjudged again. For this particular project, I gave the students different crime categories from which they could choose.'

"Interestingly, this paper was the one subject I actually sat down with Max to discuss the rationale for his choice. It happened to be a category that no student had ever chose before."

Jack now found himself quite intrigued, "So what was it?...His rationale that is?"

Brownie started to chuckle, "I can still see him sitting there in all earnestness saying, *'Professor Brown, I'd like to do my paper on this topic'* as he pointed to the one he'd selected. *So I asked 'Why that one, Max?'* For the first time, I was beginning to wonder about his stability. Anyway he said, *'Professor'* as he looked me in the eye..."

By now, Brownie was laughing so heartily, Jack had to strain to hear what he was saying.

Between gales of laughter, Brownie continued... Max said, *"Well, you see Professor, there's no money involved in that crime category."*

"What?"

"That's exactly what I said, Jack. I think I must have looked like a high school kid trying to understand Einstein's theory of relativity. Anyway Max went on to seriously remind me of his Sicilian ancestry. He then said prostitution, drug trafficking, racketeering, gambling, even robbery...big money could be made in them. He struggled visibly to find the right words to express what he meant. Simply stated it was that he wanted to avoid researching any topic that would put him in a position to run across Family members who he might offend." Brownie was laughing so hard tears were coming down his cheeks.

Jack looked at his friend in utter disbelief, "So what crime could he possibly choose to ensure that the mob would not be involved?"

"Serial sex killers," Brownie said matter-of-factly, "and you know Jack, I'm not laughing because of the topic. I'm just laughing because of Max's rationale." Brownie was now very serious as he spoke. He later admitted, however, that he was totally unprepared for Jack's reaction. Because when he looked up Jack was just standing there, jaw gaping and eyes wide like saucers.

"What did you say?" Jack finally managed to croak.

Brownie paused, "Serial sex killers."

Jack's fist came down hard on his desk. He began pacing around his office while repeatedly hitting his forehead with his hand.

"Shit!!!"

"What's wrong Jack?" Brownie was now very much alarmed at his friend's behavior.

Jack wheeled around to face him "Did you drive down here?"

"Yes, you told me to park in your spot."

Jack grabbed his briefcase and overnight bag, "Come on!"

He turned to Mrs. Stuart, and snapped, " I'm leaving for the day."

"Should anyone call, Judge, is there...?"

"No, I cannot be reached today...at all!" He slammed his office door shut.

Both Professor Brown and Mrs. Stuart exchanged bewildered glances at Jack's uncharacteristic and very volatile out burst.

"Jack, please you're obviously distraught what...." Brownie started to say.

"I'll tell you in the car and you, Mrs. Stuart, I'll see on Monday. In fact, why don't you close the office and take the rest of the day off." With that he was gone, striding for the parking garage, Brownie jogging to keep up

When they reached Brownie's car, Jack barked, "Brownie, you drive. I'll talk and soon my friend you will have the one you seek!"

Chapter Thirty Four

The sound of running water roused Kaye from her sleep. Peeking out from under the covers, she groaned, "9a.m! He's up showering! He's been laying around by himself for three days. All while I jet hopped the Atlantic, and sat through intense business meetings, only to arrive back and have to deal with that heinous caller. I even had to use words I loath." She pounded her pillow, grabbed the sham, slammed it over her head and disappeared further beneath the covers.

Moments later, she felt a pressure beside her. *"He is on my side of the bed! As if it's not enough to wake me,"* she fumed to herself, *"now he dares cross the line!"*

"Has he ever raised my Irish dander!" She heaved the covers back, sent the pillows flying and in one apparently seamless motion went from the belly down prone position to kneeling on the bed, fists clenched, jaw thrust forward, eyes blazing fire.

"What do you mean crossing the..." she stopped mid-sentence. Max sat beside her on the bed, dressed in his best suit, looking like she'd dreamt he might, but never dreamed he would.

"Ms. McDonald, cat seems to have got your tongue? I never thought I'd see the day when you were at a loss for words." He grinned impishly, "Were you trying to say 'What are you doing, meaning me of course, crossing the imaginary line?'"

He noted that the green eyes had stopped flashing and

now seemed to have a distinctly glazed look. "I was sitting down to extend this to you."

"It's a blank piece of paper!" She blurted.

"Mais Non, Ma'mselle, and that, Kaye, is the extent of my French," he laughed. "This is not just a blank piece of paper. This is your dance card!"

"A dance card?"

"Yes, a dance card...If you'll get up out of bed and get dressed I'm offering you an unlimited dance date."

"What? Are you crazy?"

"Absolutely not! His Honor is in Washington, getting home late tonight. The Chief has left at least for the morning. The wives are elsewhere. So, here's our opportunity to dance away the morning!"

"You can dance?"

"I can dance!"

"What?"

"What do you want?" he grinned.

"Waltz?"

"Waltz it is."

"Fox Trot?"

"Fox trot."

"Rumba?"

"Then, Rumba you shall have, Senorita."

"Tango?"

"Tango...Olay!" he said, clicking his heels together, then sitting back down beside her.

Green slits sternly eyed him, "Something, Mr. Carron, is not adding up. You claimed you never dated before prison."

"I didn't."

"So, you learned to dance with guys in prison?" she fairly squeeked.

He grinned at her mischievously, "I'd love to say yes to that question, but that wouldn't be the truth, Ms. McDonald, and we agreed to be honest."

As he sat on the bed, she perched on her knees, in front

of him, and stared eyeball to eyeball. "So, how did you learn to dance all those dances?" she asked skeptically.

"Had a sister remember? A kid sister...A fiery, spoiled brat, kid sister, who was awful cute though...and funny!"

Kaye watched his eyes soften, noticed them crinkling at the corners, as if sharing the memory suddenly reconnected him to his family. It was the opening that allowed her a window to enter into his intimate moment, and enter in she did!

"You're on, Mr. Carron," she laughed as she leapt forward. Her hands pushed him off balance, so that he fell backwards onto the bed. She was on the floor in a bound, swirling around in her baggy PJ track suit.

She feigned a glamorous pose, "I shall shower and dress for the ball. You select the music. I shall meet you, Sir, in the family room in half an hour!"

As she dressed, she began to berate herself, "McDonald, you are behaving like a giddy teenager!"

Glancing in the mirror, she continued her conversation with self, "and guess what, Kaye...It's about time!"

She bit her lip, tears coming to her eyes as the truth slapped her in the face. This joy she felt welling up inside her had not been free to flow for nearly seven years.

Her mind flashed back to that last evening with her parents. She had forgotten the playful banter she had shared that night with them. R.K. was encouraging her to become more deeply involved in all aspects of Kayleen, while her Mother gently chided him that, just in case he'd overlooked the fact he had a daughter, and not a son.

"Funny, I can almost hear you word for word, Mummy.'

"Now Mary Kathleen, you are not getting any younger. You are nearly twenty-eight years old. You've had date after date...prospect after prospect. You mesmerize every one of them but when is that special 'one' going to appear?"

Kaye's eyes moistened, "and I can remember my reply to your question too."

She recalled everything about that moment. She had

giggled and snuggled up next to her Mother. She knew her green eyes were twinkling as she engaged her Mother.

With as stern and serious a look that she could muster she had said, *"When you, Mummy Dearest, spot him coming through the door and say 'M.K. this IS the one!' then I'll know."*

"Oh, Kaye, you are impossible!" had been her Mother's exasperated reply, as she gave her daughter what turned out to be her last embrace.

Kaye sat on the edge of the bed, "Yeah, you left Independence Drive forever, that evening. Yes, you telephoned the next night to say good-bye."

She closed her eyes straining to remember the sound of their laughter. "You were so excited about that trip, called it your 12th Honeymoon. And..." she sighed, "How could I ever forget your last words, Mummy?...*"Perhaps M.K. you should consider looking into your first?"*...Well, you never did get your 12th one in," Kaye said wryly, "Nor have I had my first!"

She stood up and looked wistfully into the mirror. The plane crash...She had for so long buried those memories, refused to let them gain access to her conscious mind...The identification of her parents by dental remains. Only photo's, responsibilities and duties remained for their daughter.

"Lord, you left intact my smile, my laughter, my ability to care for others, my business sense and wisdom." She moved slowly to the window gazing out at the roses.

Kaye tugged pensively on her hair. It was, as if today, for the first time, she could define what she had lost. "The joy that for twenty-eight years had flowed so freely within and through me, was stolen that night. It felt like a giant boulder had been placed over my well of joy – totally stopping it up!'

"But you, Jesus, promised the woman at the well that the water you give would never dry up. It would flow forever. You were referring to the presence of Holy Spirit within us and one of The Spirit's fruits is joy! Somehow, I sense you are reopening that well!'

"But, Lord Jesus, I must confess, I am afraid to let that joy flow. Please help me to risk loving again. Help me not to shut down. Let me live once more! Jesus, I give my heart to you anew.'

"Only now do I realize how badly my heart was traumatized by that plane crash. Heal me, I pray."

Her silent reverie was shattered by a booming voice, "Hey, McDonald, are you chickening out on our date? You said a half hour. It has now been forty-five minutes. The morning is escaping."

"McDonald? What do you mean addressing me as McDonald?" Eyes flashing, she flew out the bedroom door. "It is either Ms. McDonald, or M.K.!"

"Or Kaye," came the playful banter.

"Whoa!" He sucked in his breath, a soft whistle escaping, "And Kaye, you are..."

"What?" she frowned.

"Absolutely gorgeous!"

"Pardon?"

Max watched in total disbelief as the most beautiful woman he'd ever seen floated down the stairs in a shimmering gold gown. How could he have not recognized it before? His mind flashed back to the high school prom as the girls, those ordinary gals, who went about in school uniforms, suddenly appeared as young women in wonderful tantalizing grown-up dresses. They had hips, soft skin and yes... chests, or boobs, or breasts.

Then he remembered his reaction. FEAR! He just stepped back, not one dance in the whole evening. Oh yeah, he also remembered the ride home. His father berating him *"The best looking guy there. The dolls all wanting you and you don't ask one to dance!"*

Even his Mother had chided him, *"Massimiliano, poor Rosa, you could have been nice to her. The poor dear needed someone to ask her to dance."*

"If you didn't know how to dance, Sophia could have taught you!" they both had uttered in unison.

How, could he tell them, either of them, that he had taught Sophia. But dancing with your kid sister was just enjoying dancing. Dancing with a girl, any girl, well, more was expected, and it was the more that terrified him. Now, as Kaye stood before him that same fear tried to encircle him. But somehow, this time, he wanted to break free to at least explore the more.

He tentatively took her hand. Both he and she sensed it. She, not he, was leading.

"How come you took so long? I thought maybe you changed your mind?" he said hesitantly.

"So, I take a long time to make me look good. Want to make something of it?" she quipped.

Her teasing brought forth laughter from both. As they walked into the 'ballroom' his tension lessened.

"Do you wish a minuet, or a waltz, Ma'mselle?"

"A waltz, I don't believe you can do a minuet."

So, the dance began. Max had cleared the gym equipment to the side which created a substantial dance floor. The music of the Blue Danube enfolded the room as the two glided effortlessly. The foxtrot, jive, the Charleston, rock n' roll, the Tango. On and on they danced. Joy permeated through both their souls.

Responsibilities, threats, danger, fear, injustices, grief, loneliness, inadequacies, rejections, inferiorities faded in this magical moment. Everything negative seemed sucked right out of them as the music swirled and reverberated throughout the room. In their place...love, peace, joy, gentleness, kindness, faithfulness, patience and yes, even self control streamed into their being. At last, the music stopped. Breathless, they collapsed on to the sofa.

"Now that was exercise!" Max exclaimed as he mopped his brow.

"How could you have learned all that with your sister?" Kaye asked suspiciously.

Max laughed, "Sophia wanted dance classes, so I agreed to take her. This really pissed her off. At least, it did until she realized all the other thirteen year olds were most impressed that she had an older man."

"They didn't know you were her brother?"

"Nope, that was her terms."

"But don't you look alike?"

"Not too much. She looks like Mama, and I look more like Pop. I mean if you know the family, I guess you could figure we were related, but nobody did. Not only that when I was in high school I was kind of scrawny, sort of the 'before' Charles Atlas character.'

"In twelfth grade, I looked more like a sophomore kid, maybe even a freshman. Anyway, they had competitions in these dance schools and we won them all. Sophia was and I suspect still is very competitive. She may look like Mama but she sure acts like Pop. We soon became our dance instructor's favorites. She even entered us in competitions with adults. We placed well there too."

"I bet your parents were proud of you?"

Max looked at her shocked, "Are you kidding? They didn't even know!"

Now, it was Kaye's turn to register surprise, "What? Why not?"

"Don't forget Kaye, both my parents are from the old country. I'd have gotten 'you- know-what' for taking Sophia, 'a mere child,' to a grown-up event and exposing her to 'heaven knows what'. Pop probably would have cuffed me for 'dating my sister.' Anyway, fortunately for us we managed to keep it secret. Italians weren't really into dance competitions at that time."

"But, Max, those competitions would be a lot more like an athletic event. You know, like figure skating?" Kaye said smiling. "I know there can be the romantic, sexual innuendos when people date and go dancing, but it's too bad your parents didn't see how good you were in those competitions."

Max chuckled, "Maybe, but in the end, I'm glad they didn't. Cause there was the Grand Championship event for greater Chicago and we were eligible contenders. However..."

By now Kaye was thoroughly enjoying his sharing, "However what? Did you win?"

"We would have, except just before the final competition, Sophia got braces. I don't think there was anything wrong with her teeth, but the dentist convinced Mama that Sophia should have them. Personally, I think it was because he knew Pop could pay. Anyway, every time Sophia opened her mouth, all you saw was metal. To me, I thought she kinda' looked like what I envisioned Frankenstein might look if he smiled."

"Let me guess. You were dancing and Sophia smiled and you lost it! Oh Max, that's way too funny!" Kaye was now laughing so hard the tears were flowing down her cheeks.

"Yeah, but definitely not funny to Sophia!" He started to laugh, "We actually were winning, and the last dance was the Tango. I mean, after all, we're Latin. Sophia had it in the bag. I could do all the sexy moves and so could she. We just flowed together but just at the grand finale..."

"Oh, No!" Kaye brought her hands to her face, in feigned horror.

"Oh, Yes! She opened her mouth."

"And you burst out laughing."

"Right on! So we placed second, Sophia was furious. If she had a gun, I would have been dead! As it was, she pouted for a week. My parents kept asking *"What's wrong darling?"* She'd just snap *"Nothing!"* and go to her room slamming the door behind her.'

"After one such episode I innocently suggested that maybe she had her period?" Max grinned, "For that I got a wop over the head from Mama, who considered such discussion most improper."

By now, Kaye's imagination was running wild. She could 'see' the whole scene and she erupted with great belly laughter. The mirth spread to Max.

When the two finally collected their breath he concluded, "But perhaps for the first time, I actually connected, as a male, with my father. When Mama was out of earshot, he looked at me and nodded, adding, *"you're probably right."* Anyway, his response finished the issue."

"How so?" Kaye looked perplexed.

Max was now serious, "Well, I think Pop had his explanation, so he just ignored Sophia. As long as his precious Princess couldn't push his buttons, the household had peace.'

"For her part it was the first time Sophia couldn't tattle on me. After all it was her that didn't want the parents to know that she'd learned to dance. So she had to face her disappointment herself and deal with her own anger, alone. She's pretty resilient, and by nature, cheery, so after ten days she was back to herself relating with everyone, including me...as always."

"Did she forgive you?"

Max chuckled, "Only as a Sicilian's capable of forgiving."

"Which is?"

"You owe me!" he laughed.

"Max,"

"Yeah?"

"Thank you for a most wonderful date, the best I ever had, and the therapy I really needed!"

"You mean all that?" he asked rather dubiously.

"Oh yes, most definitely!" She reached over and kissed him on the cheek. "I'd give you more but we did agree."

"Yes, a bargain is a bargain," he sighed. "Better restore the gym though."

"And I had better change. People would really question me working in a formal evening gown!"

"I need to shower," Max said, "that was a real workout!"

"Me too! Rock, Paper, Scissors will determine who goes first." To Kaye's amazement, not only did Max know that little game, he beat her. "Okay, Mr. Carron, you win! The shower is yours!"

Chapter Thirty-Five

The drive from Washington to Summerside took the usual time, give or take fifteen or twenty minutes. Traffic was light on the thruway and Brownie made good time. However, the atmosphere in the vehicle was anything but usual.

The two roommates / classmates and gridiron compatriots were used to disagreements but this one was unprecedented. Both men usually argued persuasively intellectually. Now, however the emotions of each intertwined, and sorting out emotional stuff was the forte of neither. It took nearly a three-hour drive before each could even grasp the emotional drive within themselves, never mind the other.

After a forced fifteen-minute silence between the two, Jack began to speak ever so slowly and deliberately. "Brownie, you and I have been close friends and colleagues for nearly thirty years. So, what exactly is going on here?"

"Well, Jack, let's try and sort it out together. Why don't we begin with our professional roles? You are?"

"A Supreme Court Justice."

"And I am?"

"A very esteemed professor of law."

"So," Brownie said, "your passion is to...?"

"See that justice is delivered fairly."

"Right! And mine?"

"To mentor and coach potential lawyers and legal experts to be able to deliver justice fairly."

"And?"

"We are arguing over the character of a man I sentenced to prison and you coached as a student," Jack paused, "Ah hah, so that's it!"

"What?"

"Carron isn't the real issue. The real issue is that our passions are colliding over him."

"You mean," Brownie said, "that if I'm right, you have not fairly delivered justice?"

"Correct, and if I'm right, you mentored in error." Jack added.

"So how do we resolve our differences, my friend?" Brownie asked.

"It would appear, Brownie, that you and I need to step back from our initial assessments of Massimiliano Carron and re-evaluate him. Because if memory serves me right, both you and I have been wrong in the past?"

Brownie started to laugh, "Now, you wouldn't be thinking of when you were supposed to call a 'Quarterback Sneak,' but you elected to pass, so our opponent intercepted and romped for a touch down?"

Jack grinned and rolled his eyes, "Yeah, that one had crossed my mind, but so did the one where you were so certain the quarterback was going to pass that you blitzed him. And, the fullback barged right up the middle to score."

The two men looked at each other. Brownie spoke first, "Remember what the coach told us in both those situations, Jack?"

"I do, indeed, and that's what I'm getting at, Brownie. He told us to get that play out of our heads and focus on what lay ahead of us."

"Right, and we did and our team won both those games despite our blunders. So, Roomie," Brownie said, "let's shake and move on!" and he extended his right hand to Jack who grasped it firmly.

"So, before we get to my place, let's lay out the things each of us knows about Carron."

"And," interjected Brownie, "why don't we begin by you telling me why you bolted for home so quickly?"

Jack sighed, "I'll give you the Reader's Digest condensed version. "About nine months ago, Kaye, our neighbor, who just happens to be M.K. McDonald."

"The CEO of Kayleen Enterprises?"

"The same."

"She's your neighbor?"

"Neighbor...like a very loved family member to Marnie, the girls and myself. Remember, Brownie, I'm trying to give you a thumbnail sketch as to why I rushed off. Anyway, Kaye started getting these suggestive, vulgar middle of the night phone calls. She confronted them head on...Notified police...Wiretaps went in... NOTHING!'

"Innuendos began to surface about Kaye being a woman with deep seated sexual needs that had been thwarted by her forced ascendancy as the head of Kayleen Enterprises"

"Ouch!"

"Ouch, indeed! Kaye was devastated. Our neighbor Dave, is Police Chief, and as six months approached Dave asked Kaye several times to tell him if those calls resumed. She promised to do so. However, nothing was said so we presumed the original caller was just a prankster.'

"About a week or so ago, our friend, FBI Special Agent Bernard Epstein, asked us about Kaye. It seems the Bureau had received anonymous letters directed to Epi, that detailed several unsolved murders. In fact, for one of those murders a person was convicted and jailed, even though the victim's body hadn't been found. However with the info contained in the letter the body or at least part of it was recovered."

Brownie glanced at his friend, "You're telling me the Bureau is trailing a serial killer? But how does this connect to Max?"

"The Bureau knew that the info in the letters were details that only the murderer or someone communicating with the killer, would know. As a result Epi asked me to authorize tapping Kaye's phone line. Truthfully, I found it repugnant to even consider doing so.'

"I did agree because as Dave and Epi convinced me, if it was Kaye to whom this killer was talking, she would be in eminent danger. Kaye left for Paris early Tuesday morning. The wires were tapped Wednesday, but no calls then.'

"Last night, or Thursday night, Kaye had returned home. The call came in at three in the morning. Dave let me know shortly thereafter."

"Oh, wow!"

"But Brownie, that's not all. In the call, Dave said that Kaye used vulgar, violent, profane language. She never ever speaks like that."

"And you think Max was coaching her?"

"Well, yes. I know nothing about him before prison but I'm certain in prison he would have heard the gutter language Dave said that Kaye used. Epi told me no one knows Carron's whereabouts, even his father.'

"A few weeks after Carron's release, Epi contacted me, I'd forgotten all about him. I even figured that he'd be long out of prison. I was certain they'd appeal his sentence get it reduced. Then today, you arrive telling me that Carron took law courses from Harvard, and did assignments for you. One involved studying serial sex offenders... No, I mean serial killers. Why wouldn't I deduce that Carron could be involved?"

Brownie chewed on his lip and commented, "It's plausible, Jack, wild but plausible. Perhaps he is there but your neighbor Kaye doesn't know who he is?"

Jack grunted, "No! Go! Epi gave me Carron's mug shot to give to Dave to distribute in our area. Figured if he came after me, someone would likely spot him, and he could be intercepted. Brownie, Kaye saw those pictures. In fact, I think she took one with her."

"So, Jack, in that case she is voluntarily co-operating with him, or he with her?"

Jack frowned and questioned, "Well, yes, but what

about those hostage identification cases? Couldn't something like that be going on?"

"Remote chance, Jack, I mean she was just in Paris for three days. Max couldn't have accompanied her. She would have had ample opportunity to divulge his presence, if she wished."

"True," Jack nodded. "It's just that Kaye is like a sister or daughter to us. I can't believe that she'd co-operate with someone who would harm either Marnie or me."

"Maybe she was convinced that he wouldn't."

"Like you," Jack said ruefully.

"All I'm saying, Jack, is that if we are stepping back, forgetting what was behind and looking forward to what lies ahead, that has to be one option. Isn't this your exit coming up? You need to direct me to your house."

Soon the two were pulling into Dave's driveway. Brownie looked at his watch 3 p.m.

Twelve hours away from another call.

He eyed Jack and asked, "So what does the quarterback call?"

"I'm not the quarterback. Epi is. Let's go in and you tell them all you know. We'll see how he assesses it."

The two walked into Dave's house startling both Dave and the two agents. They were even more surprised with Professor Brown's startling revelations about Massimiliano Carron.

"At least, Jack," chortled Dave, "it seems one thing is for certain. If a call does come in, we can rule out one potential suspect. Don't you think, Agent?" he said nodding in Brian's direction.

"Who?" queried Jack, oblivious to the reddening in Brian's face.

"You, if you stay and listen to the call."

"Me!"

"You weren't here when the call came in," Dave tried to sound oh so serious.

"I was asleep in Washington!"

"Jack, you could have phoned from Washington just as easy as from here."

"See my good Judge," interrupted Brownie, "circumstantial evidence can be very damaging."

"So, Jack, if you stay here and the call comes in, we'll know for certain that it isn't you," laughed Epi. "One thing we do know...the perp is someone who does know her schedule."

"What do you think about Professor Brown's information?" asked Brain. "Do you think Carron could be there? Should we get a warrant, surround Ms. McDonald's house and flush him out?"

"Whatever for, Brian?" Epi retorted. "Everyone may want to know where Carron is, but he is a free citizen entitled to go wherever he wishes."

"Even next door to me?" snapped Jack.

"Normally, no, but for the moment yes."

"What?" Jack scowled.

"Jack, as far as I know there's been no restraining order given him. So, let's think this through rationally. If he is with Kaye and I suspect we'll know tonight, particularly if her aggression to the caller intensifies. If he is there, from what the Professor has said, I suspect that Carron is attempting to flush our killer into the open. Second, if he is there, he's there with Ms. McDonald's permission and likely invitation. She is the victim in this case, not the perpetrator, let's not lose sight of that!"

Epi continued, "Furthermore, based on what we know of Carron, and given what you've told us, Professor, I believe he can provide Ms. McDonald the best personal protection that anyone could. Rumor has it, he is a crack shot."

"Really, well that's good, as an ex con he shouldn't have a gun!" Jack grumbled.

Epi peered over his glasses and said. "Jack, up until now I thought you were a very astute man. Do you really think if Carron wanted to carry a gun that he's going to say *'Oh dear me, I can't, I'm an ex con!'?*"

349

"Furthermore, if he's done the research Professor Brown says he has, and he's got verification from us that the guy on the other end of the phone is a serial killer, and he knows how to use a gun, do you honestly think that the man is there without one?"

"Given the manner in which you have so succinctly put it, I would have to say, no," Jack concluded. "So, what do you propose Epi?"

"Let me lay out my plan, I'd like for all of your input. But first, let's begin with you, Professor. You, have read Carron's paper. Based on his findings, if we are dealing with a psycho, is there something in that paper that can give us insight into what could transpire next?'

"For as of right now, this would be my strategy. Tonight, try as best you can Brian, to fix that call. My suspicion is that Carron will continue to force the guy to play his hand... to set him off and force him to act. From Carron's perspective and ours, the sooner the better."

"Not necessarily, Sir," Brian piped up. The others just stared at him.

"I mean, look at Ms. McDonald, he might enjoy being penned up with her. I would..."

He was about to say more when he glanced at Dave and Jack. Both were glaring at him with the intensity of a father whose daughter's reputation had been questioned.

In an attempt to disarm the mounting tension, Brownie cleared his throat and with his deepest professorial voice intoned, "Brian's comment is relevant. It could be a possibility. However, personally from what you told me of last night's conversation, I would suspect the truth lies closer to Agent Epstein's assessment.'

"I found Max to possess a brilliant legal mind and so I would speculate that our predator-killer is now himself being stalked. Can I ask this question, though? Do you think Max is aware of the tap?"

Epi simultaneously shook his head while emphatically

saying "No!"

In sharp contrast, Dave and Jack stared at each other and in unison said, "Oh, Yes!"

Brownie raised an eyebrow, and commented "Now, isn't this interesting? Can you explain this discrepancy, gentlemen, please?"

"How could he know?" Epi questioned.

"Well, if he is in the house as you suspect, Jack and I told him." Dave said as he slumped down in the nearest chair. "We were in Kaye's house checking it out. We routinely check each other's house when any of us are away for an extended period of time."

Jack leaned against a wall, "My wife, Marnie, told Kaye we'd do it. The two of us were actually in Kaye's bedroom and I was still struggling whether I'd done the right thing in authorizing you to tap her line. Dave was convincing me I had. We said precisely when the tap would go in.'

"Oh Crap!" Jack slammed the wall, "The tooth brush!" He looked at Dave and said, "You were right, it wasn't there the first time we checked! He is there!"

Dave put his hands behind his head and said, "That answers another question?"

"What?" was chorused in four part harmony.

"Carron is not in that house to get at Jack, and harm him. If he were he had ample opportunity that day."

Epi stood, "Gentlemen, your information solidifies my belief that Carron is both present in that house and is attempting to raise the ante to flush out our perp. Brian, it's key that we get a fix on the call. To that end, I'm personally comfortable holding our surveillance tonight and Saturday. But, if we don't have a fix by Sunday, we need to alert Kaye and Carron that we are aware of his presence with her.'

"Professor, would you be willing to remain with us until Sunday. Your relationship with Carron could prove very beneficial to everyone. I believe we will need everyone on board and working as a team to lure the fly into our trap, before he harms another individual."

"How do you know this creep won't attack tonight or tomorrow," Jack questioned anxiously. "My real concern is for Kaye."

"We don't, Jack." Epi turned to Dave, "I share Jack's concern for Kaye's safety. In addition it is imperative our perp not evade the trap that is being set for him. Dave, is there any way that you could discreetly bring in three or four more officers from now until Sunday?"

"Certainly," was the quick reply.

"They need to be seasoned and trusted. Those whose absence isn't going to be questioned or noticed. What I'd like, just in case our perp enters the house, is to cover it both front and back. Especially the back, for that is where the ravine is. We don't want this perp having easy access to the ravine so that he can get away. On the other hand, the ravine must serve as a red carpet for our perp, offering him access into the house. Thus we can't post cops there prematurely to scare this guy off."

Dave picked up the phone and soon had it all arranged. Matt's course had concluded earlier than expected. He had returned to Summerside and was filling in for another officer at the station. Dave asked him to drive the other three men home in the station wagon. The tinted windows would hide their presence from prying eyes. Matt could bring the wagon into the garage and there the officers could disembark unnoticed.

Dave had grinned "Then, my son can be our gopher. I'll send him out later for Pizza."

And so the game of wait began.

3 a.m. arrived once more. Only now eleven pairs of ears listened to the dialogue with the caller. Six pair registered a seismic shock wave of at least 7.1 on the Richter scale when they heard Ms. McDonald's language.

Professor Brown just nodded grimly, while Jack sighed silently all the while thinking, *"I now have my alibi."*

Brian was acting like a midwife in an attempt to fix the call. "That's right...." He muttered, to no one but himself. "Keep him on the line...Don't stop...Push him further...Keep him talking...Please, don't let him quit!"

The perp suddenly erupted in a violent explosion of vulgar profanity. The phone slammed down and the line went dead. The ante had definitely been raised tonight!

Eight pairs of eyes riveted expectantly on Brian. " I couldn't get a precise hit but the net is narrowing. I can tell you the call is originating from the Morristown area, a borough of Centerville."

Epi looked up "Centerville, that's where Kayleen's head office is located, isn't it?"

"That would explain how our perp knows her schedule," Dave chimed in, "On the positive side it might even mean that while he's got her phone number, he doesn't know where she actually lives."

"That would be most advantageous if it proves true, Dave." Epi commented. "However, I'm not that optimistic. Our perp is no novice and in my experience it would be most unusual for him to have the intensity level we have experienced tonight without him having a physical fix on the location of his prey."

Epi spoke firmly, "Gentlemen, in the next forty eight hours, we need to exercise extreme caution and observe due diligence."

The Davidson's household was not the only dwelling on Independence Drive where due diligence was being exercised.

Following the phone call, Kaye slumped exhausted against Max. "I'm sorry, really sorry," she sighed, "I don't think I can do this much longer, Max. I can't talk like that and I'm afraid that I'll never be able to forget the images those words convey."

"Yes, you will," was the soft reply as he gently kissed her forehead. "They will disappear forever, I promise. How about we sneak downstairs and I make us a cup of your gourmet hot mint chocolate?"

"Sneak? Why did you say sneak?"

He took the flashlight, "come with me Ma'mselle and I will let you in on a secret."

Once in the kitchen, he turned the light on over the stove.

"We don't appear to be 'sneaking' here" she said puzzled.

"It's at the back of your house, Kaye," he replied quietly.

It wasn't long before the hot chocolate was steaming in their mugs. "Max, something's going on, isn't it? What is it? Please tell me."

"Nothing is wrong, Kaye. It's just that when you were away, Dave and Jack came over to check out everything, like you said they would. I managed to overhear their conversation.'

"Epi knew of your previous calls. He also knew that you knew him. He added 1 plus 1, and came up with two. He wanted Jack to authorize a wiretap of your phone."

Kaye's eyes grew wide with horror, her face blanched, "No! Max, you had me say those awful words knowing others would be listening. How could you?" She began to cry, "How can I ever live that down!"

"Kaye," the sternness in his voice shocked her. He cupped her head in his hands, drawing her face upward so that her eyes made contact with his. "Listen to me, Kaye, the people who are listening are FBI agents and some cops. Trust me, Kaye, they've heard much worse, much, much worse. They aren't stupid, they know what you are trying to do."

"Me trying to do?" She whimpered plaintively, "What am I trying to do?"

Max couldn't help but smile. Every ounce of Miss Independence had vanished. "Right, Kaye, it's not what you are trying to do. It's what I am trying to do through you. For the moment, I don't think that the cops know I'm here, but eventually they will. Believe me when they do, they will link those words to me, never fear!"

"But what are you trying to do?"

Max looked at her and for the first time it dawned on

him that what was so logical, so apparent to him, was totally hidden to her.

He put his cup down, looked her square in the eye, "Kaye, these past two nights we have been casting the bait." He motioned with his arm, as if he were a fisherman casting his reel.

"I know that," she protested, "but what does it mean – getting him to bite?"

"To lure him here, Kaye, to lure him here," he said softly.

"Here?" her mouth suddenly went dry. "Max, I don't want him here!"

"Yes, you do, Kaye."

"No," she shook her head vigorously, "I want him caught!"

"Yes, Kaye, and you are the bait!"

"No," all color had drained from her face.

"Yes, there is no other way to flush this guy out. He has to move on his next prey...You are that prey!"

She threw her hands over her mouth in horror. "No, no" were the only words uttered.

Once again, he cupped her face in his hands. Once more, he spoke sharply, "Kaye, this is what we talked about, the plan I laid out for you to escape. Tomorrow we will go over that plan, over and over and over again. So, if you need to flee, every move will be instinctive. Do you hear me?"

She closed her eyes and nodded, "Max, I'm so afraid! I'm so cold! I'm really, really afraid!" She leaned into his chest.

He held her tight and whispered, "Tonight, Kaye, what say we remove the invisible line? Let's go to sleep dressed like we are, in our baggy PJ's and I'll hold you in my arms. Okay?"

Like a small child, she curled up against him and fell asleep exhausted.

Chapter Thirty-Six

As she awoke, one thought kept racing through her mind. *"The Lord is my light and my salvation. Of whom shall I be afraid? The Lord is the stronghold of my life. Who shall I fear?"*

"Psalm 27, verse 1," she murmured sleepily to herself. "It is indeed one of my life verses – a Biblical verse that has the power to sustain me whenever I am troubled."

She felt instantly comforted but as the light of dawn crept into the room, she suddenly recalled the early morning events precipitating her need. "Oh Lord, please deliver us and grant us success," she sighed.

She leaned her head back on the pillow and listened to the soft rhythmic breathing of the one beside her. "Please Jesus, protect us both from the perils of this day and night," she whispered quietly. Stronger than her desire to rise, was her desire to burrow her head against his chest.

"If only I'd met you under ordinary circumstances," she paused, "if only I'd met you under ordinary circumstances? If the truth were known, McDonald, you'd have passed him right by...Too good looking would have been your judgment, Italian, likely a womanizer. Yep, Max, I would have been so judgmental! I never would have taken time to know your name. Well, Mr. Carron, you are anything but a womanizer."

She smiled to herself, "As for you, Max, you would have distanced yourself so far from me! You would have fled like a scared rabbit. So I guess, Lord, sometimes you do need unusual circumstances to move your children onto the path you desire them to take?"

Laying there resting beside Max, she began to reflect how he had stuck around for her instead of bailing out. Emotionally she became aware of her own growing affection for this man. "I wonder, my 'knight in shinning armor,' if you are aware that you've stolen my heart?" she thought ruefully.

Max raised an eyebrow and found himself gazing into a beautiful pool of green, "How long you been awake?" he mumbled.

"Not long, only a few moments," she rose up on one elbow, kissed her finger and touched it to his lips. "Good morning, Mr. Carron."

"Good morning, Ms. McDonald. Are you prepared for this Commando Training Day?"

"I don't think I could ever be prepared, Max. I keep praying it will go away."

"You don't like being bait?"

"Decidedly Not!" was the emphatic response.

Max reached over to the night table and grabbed her Bible. "Here is something we both need to consider," and he began reading from Philippians, Chapter 2 verses 5-8.

"Your attitude should be the same as that of Christ Jesus, who being in very nature God, did not consider equality with God, something to be grasped. But made himself nothing, taking on the very nature of a servant, being made in human likeness. And being found in appearance as a man, he humbled himself and became obedient to death – even death on a cross!'

"When I read that the other day, Kaye, those words spoke to me. This guy has killed several innocent people just to satisfy his own whim. He'll continue to do that until someone stops him. Maybe you and I can't stop him but God put you and me together to at least try."

Max set the Bible down and continued, "Jesus calls us to follow him. He cared about people and so even though I don't have the guts or courage to take on this task, I know he gave me his Holy Spirit to help me try. I believe the promise in the Bible which says that I can do things that I normally couldn't because Jesus is there to strengthen me."

Kaye looked at him and smiled, "Max, you should be a preacher. Mr. Graham had better move over."

"Kaye, I'm not joking! I'm serious."

"Neither am I joking, Max. You are letting his Word live through you, even when to do so is anything but easy."

"It really upsets me, Kaye, to think about the people whose loved ones he has killed. I can't even begin to imagine what it must feel like to lose a mother, or sister, or little daughter and not even have the closure of knowing that the one who did it was caught."

"Or, where he got away with it altogether, with another person falsely accused and convicted of the crime!" Kaye added.

They sat on the side of the bed, holding each other's hand, resolved to persevere, as best they could, to see this man apprehended regardless of any personal consequence.

"Max, know what I was thinking when I woke up?"

"How could I? I was asleep," was the logical retort.

She gave him a playful cuff, "You are so practical and unromantic!" One look, at his hurt expression, told her that he'd taken her remark as personal criticism. She laughed and leaned against him, "I was not criticizing you, Sir."

"Sure sounded like it," he groused.

"Believe me, that's not what I intended. I was trying to tell you, Mr. Carron, that you have committed thievery."

"Whatever do you mean?" he asked, with a clearly defensive tone.

She giggled, "You, Sir, have stolen my heart!"

Her words stunned him, "Really? This is another one of your jokes, right?"

"Most definitely not! You have captured my heart."

"Well, for what it's worth, you stole mine a long time ago."

Kaye leaned her head against his shoulder and

murmured, "thank you for sharing."

"Wow! I don't believe it! She said she actually loves me! I feel like bouncing up and down on the bed, like I did as a kid." Max now had a grin like the Cheshire cat.

However, a polite, "You are welcome," were the only three words his brain seemed capable of processing, as he turned to embrace her.

"Not so fast, Mr. Carron. I want to tell you what I was thinking!"

"Fire away, Ms. McDonald."

"It occurred to me, that while I may not like the circumstances in which I find myself, I've come to realize that without them, I would never have met you. So, I thank God not for the circumstances but for bringing you into my life, Max."

She noted his eyes moistening as he drew her tight. "I really love you, Kaye," he whispered, "and I thank God for you!"

"So, El Capitan, now what?"

"Now, Kaye, we shower, dress, eat and begin our escape maneuver drills.

"That's it?"

"Until this is over, Kaye, that has to be it. Our feelings for each other don't negate the fact that we are in a very precarious situation. We sit in the cross hairs of a very formidable predator, and to escape his snare we need to be well prepared. You go shower and dress and I'll make breakfast. While I dress, you can clean up." Max stood and headed for the door. As if in response, Kaye leapt across the bed and beat him to the door. Planting herself in front of him, brow furrowed, green eyes squinting she demanded, "Un moment, Monsieur, I have an important family of origin question to ask."

"What?" came the startled response.

"This bossy ordering around, Mr. Carron, is that modeled after your Sicilian Father?"

Max burst out laughing, "Most definitely! It's the Godfather thing – get used to it, Ms. McDonald," and he gave her a playful swat on the rear as he went by.

That was the way the rest of the day went for both of them, each feeling, as if they were on an emotional roller coaster. One moment, they were rehearsing in detail their method of escape, believing they were up to the task of challenging a very evil adversary. The next moment saw them plummet to the reality that these hours ahead might prove to be their last in this world. Even worse was the unspoken dread that they might fall prey to this perp's fiendish threats.

At one point, after they'd discussed the escape scenario for what seemed to be the umpteenth time, Max faced Kaye and held her shoulders firmly. "You must promise me that no matter what, you will get out of this house. You will not return under any circumstance. Instead you will go directly to Walters' and dial 911. Please promise me that, Kaye!"

He had mapped out various get-a-way routes, depending where and when their assailant should find them. Tied around Kaye's wrist was the front door key to Jack's house. His phone was on the hall table, just inside the door. She rehearsed the information she'd give, - name, address, armed intruder threatening murder, send police and ambulance quick.

For his part, Max checked his home made battery operated alarm system, if the perp did cut the hydro, all still functioned!

At 10 p.m. the two decided to retire early; no TV, no radio. Their ears needed to be tuned to any foreign sound. Whether the perp would show tonight, they did not know. What they did know was they were as prepared as they could be. They had spent over a half hour in prayer and had just turned out the lights when the phone rang.

Kaye's heart pounded as she answered the call, "Hello."

"M.K.?"

"George?"

"You sound out of breath. Is something wrong?"

"No, no, not at all! I was just doing my exercises before retiring."

"Sorry, M.K. I forgot the time change. It's not quite 10 o'clock here. I apologize for calling so late."

"Oh, it's no problem, George. I'm wide awake. But what is the reason for your call? Is it something to do with the MacGregor merger that you're overseeing? If it is, I'll need to get back to you to-morrow. I don't have my files handy."

"No, M.K. It's nothing to do with Kayleen. It's you, I'm calling about. To be honest, I just can't get you out of my mind."

"Who is this George?" muttered a voice audible only to those in Dave's rec rom.

"One of her board members," Jack replied.

"He's hitting on her?" Brian queried.

Dave glowered, "He better not be...He's married!"

"Shut-up, Brian, and get a fix on him."

"M.K." her caller continued, "I know you told me a couple of times that those calls had never resumed. You know? The ones you received about nine months ago."

"That' right, George...Still none." Kaye had her fingers crossed as she mouthed, "Please, forgive me, Lord."

Her caller left no doubt as to his seriousness, his tone resonated over the line. "Kaye, I hope that you are telling the truth. I know how you give your all to Kayleen. I don't want you to fail to report those calls, because of the insinuations that occurred last time, when the calls ceased the moment the line was tapped. I realize you were humiliated, but worse you felt they could impact negatively on Kayleen's perceived stability."

"Oh, George," Kaye thought to herself, *"if only I could tell you how perceptive you are, and that is precisely why I value your presence on the Board!"* Audibly however, she simply said, "George, it is so sweet of you to be concerned about me, but really I am okay."

"M.K., I just need to reiterate again to you. I know I've said it before, but sometimes these callers can be very dangerous! It's not board room stuff. I'm not sure you are really prepared for that type of thing."

"Got that right too, George," Kaye silently mused.

"Well, M.K., there is another option, if you don't want to go to the police. I have contacts that could check it out quietly for you, if you need it."

"I know, George. You mentioned that before. I appreciate both your offer and your concern, but really I am fine! I'll see you next week in New York at our special board meeting."

Kaye bit her lip as she asked, "You are planning to come, aren't you?" Under her breath she said, *"At least, I hope that I will be there!"*

Her caller sighed, "Yes, M.K., I expect to be there. I'm relieved you are okay. Please, continue to take care of yourself. Good-bye."

"Good night, George," Kaye replied demurely, all the while thinking, *"not one thing I said, have you believed, George Cantaro!"*

"Why the hell would George choose to call to-night?" Max snapped.

"I don't know, Max, I honestly don't."

Max worriedly scratched his head, "Kaye, if this is a real set up and I've misjudged, our game plan won't work. My strategy hinges on our perp being a single psycho. Perhaps, it's time to call this off. If organized crime is behind this, we can't handle it on our own. Maybe we need to call Dave?"

"Max, we've come this far. Let's wait at least two more nights and re-evaluate. I can't believe George would be behind anything to harm me. It's just that he's very perceptive in the board room, and I suspect it's the same perception kicking in here." She added, "Besides, you said he's connected to your family. If someone comes to hurt me, couldn't you find out why they are upset? Maybe I could correct any misperception?"

Max shook his head sadly, "You are forgetting, Kaye, that no one in my family knows I am here. If it is organized crime behind this, they will shoot first, without caring to pre-identify the target."

In a barely audible tone, Kaye responded "Oh."

Softly, she continued, "Max, we're less than four hours away from our nightly call, and within seven from daylight. Why don't we continue with your plan for tonight, then if nothing untoward happens, we can call Dave in the morning?"

Max squeezed her hand, "If that's what you want fine, we'll follow our game plan one more night. But tomorrow we call your friend Epi and come clean." He didn't have the heart to tell her that George's call might simply have been to ascertain that she was home. Nonetheless, of one thing he could be certain, the cops would have monitored that call.

"Well, Family Dearest," he mused silently, *"if this is any of your doings, you deserve to be taken down, and no one will be happier than I to see it!"* He pursed his lips, *"the bonus will be if both she and I survive to see it. I only hope J.D. that you get to be part of the action!"*

"Max, can we go over everything one more time, before we go to sleep?"

"Okay. You have your shoes by the bed, ready to slip on?"

"Yes."

"Jack's house key is on your wrist?"

"Yes."

"Good! Let's turn out the lights and get some sleep."

Laying beside him in the dark, Kaye reached out and gently touched him, "Max, can we say one more prayer... Please?"

"Oh yeah, Kaye, we are indeed in need of all the help we can get."

As the lights went out in one Independence Drive household, they went on with intensity in another. "Did you track the call, Brian?"

"Oh yeah, we got a good fix on this one! Mr. George Cantaro used his calling card, but the residence from which he called is just coming up now." Brian's face suddenly went ashen.

"What is it?" Epi demanded.

All Brian could do was point. "Francesco Carron" was the name on the screen.

Epi immediately secured a search on Cantaro. As it came through, he read aloud, "He is a Kayleen Board member like you said, Jack. He is squeaky clean with regard any of his activities."

He paused and rubbed the back of his neck. "Oh my, his wife Volante Lombardi, is the younger sister of Vincente Lombardi, who owns the largest Casino in Las Vegas. And guess what? Francesco Carron is related somehow to the Lombardi's through his wife's family."

"Can this get any murkier?" moaned Jack.

"Is there any possibility that Max was sent as a hit man to Kaye?" Dave queried.

"Gentlemen, please," Professor Brown interjected, "Mafia hit men are not known to sequester themselves with their intended victims for weeks...even months, as Max appears to have done with Ms. McDonald."

"But, what if this George character's call was to signal Junior that Papa wants action now?" Brian asked.

"And what if those letters were just smoke screens to point us to a serial killer?" Jack questioned.

"I suggest for Ms. McDonald's sake we get Carron tonight," spoke up one of Dave's men.

"No!" was the emphatic response. "Absolutely not!" It was Epi who now spoke, "I'm sorry but I am in charge! The buck stops with me. I am not deviating from our original plan! Brian, this will be our last night to get a fix on our 3 a.m. caller. I remind you all, our caller is real and the letters documented details that only the killer or someone talking to the killer could know. Carron was incarcerated for most of those homicides.'

"I don't want that killer slithering past our net! We are three and a half hours from his call and less than seven from daylight. It is I, and I alone, who will take responsibility, for better or for worse, regarding Ms.

McDonald's life and safety.'

"Jack, I suggest this might be a very good time for you to offer up a prayer that daylight will reveal that good has triumphed over evil."

"Lord," Jack prayed, "May we be successful in exposing the identity of this serial killer. Please, protect Kaye, and keep all who seek justice safe this night. In your Name I ask it."

Audible "Amens" were murmured throughout the room.

Stillness settled in the room, no one spoke. After several minutes had past, Jack broke the silence. "I think that I should head home, Marnie, is there tonight. I hesitate to leave her alone." Then he added, " especially when we're not sure what could be a foot in our neighborhood."

"How about I go with you, Jack?" Brownie offered and the two men headed off to the Walters'.

One of the officers chose Matt's room to rest; while Dave suggested the other two sleep in the upstairs guest room, since both rooms boasted twin beds. By midnight the surveillance room inhabitants were down to three: Brian, Epi and Dave. The latter two each flopped on a couch leaving Brian to man the monitor. The waiting game had commenced for yet another night.

Chapter Thirty-Seven

Max had J.D. oiled, loaded and strapped to his body. Somehow sleep was eluding him.

He lay watching the clock – those bright red lights staring him in the face. Midnight came and went, then 1 a.m., next came 2 a.m.. He had just started to doze off when he felt the vibration in his pocket.

It took a few seconds for its significance to register. His alarm had been set off! He looked quickly at the clock. Its numbers now flashed like a neon sign.

His stomach turned. His mouth went dry. He placed his hand over Kaye's mouth and gently shook her, whispering softly in her ear, "He's here!"

"Whaa ..?" she sleepily mumbled.

"Shush! Remember our drill? No talking, shoes on, hide by the door, don't move until he gets past the door then run. I'll slam the door so he can't follow. Whatever happens do not come back!"

Max used the pillows to feign a person sleeping in the bed. Then quickly positioned himself on the other side of the door poised to pounce when it opened.

Kaye chewed nervously on her lip, silently pleading, "Please, Dear Jesus! Please help!"

It was only minutes but it seemed an eternity as they waited. Kaye's heart was pounding so hard, she was sure the intruder would hear it.

By now both of their eyes had become accustomed to the dark. The one advantage both had over their adversary, was familiarity to their surroundings.

"Provided," Max had cautioned her, "that he has not placed obstacles in your path. So be very aware of your footing. Don't assume a clear path!"

She had just begun to think maybe it was a false alarm when both saw the door knob begin to turn, ever so slowly, and ever so quietly the door opened. A dark imposing figure began to creep stealthily forward. She couldn't mistake it, belted to his side was a large dagger.

Max silently prayed, "God, please hold Kaye to our plan. Don't let her bolt prematurely, give her grace to wait."

The man appeared tall and powerful, a balaclava covered his face. Both heard him whisper, "Well, my darling rich bitch, tonight you'll learn who is strong and who the real whimp is!"

The figure inched closer to the bed. Kaye started to tremble. Her whole body broke out in a cold sweat. "Lord," she sobbed inwardly, "my legs are like rubber. They won't work!"

It took only seconds. But to Kaye, it seemed hours before the intruder was at the point where Max could easily close the door. Deep within her, a voice commanded, "Go, now!"

Obediently, she slipped silently into the hall. That's when she saw it. Her tall ornate vase had been strategically placed at the head of the stairs. She put her hand over her mouth to stifle a cry. *"Fiend! Had I run, I would have pitched down the stairs! I would have been a broken china doll, at his whim to twist and torture."*

Gingerly, she stepped over it. *"Without Max's insight, I would have been doomed!"*

She shuddered, in horror at her next thought. *"We could have ended up like that poor couple, he massacred in Arkansas."* A tears trickled down her cheek, *"Lord, he really has done this before!"*

Cautiously she inched her way down the stairs. *"I can't see any more traps. The path looks clear?"* With that, Kaye sped for the front door.

The killer was just reaching for the bed covers when the click of the front door lock echoed in the silence. Pulling the covers back, the man recognized he had been outwitted.

He spun around, profanity filling the air. He lunged for the door intent on retrieving his escaping prey. As he did, Max slammed the door shut.

Kaye ran as hard as she could. She fumbled with the key to Jack's house, *"Oh God, please don't let there be a double lock!"* She realized she hadn't paid attention to that detail.

Jack was always so cautious, he could have doubled his security after Epi's warning about Max. She glanced over her shoulder...no pursuer yet. The lock finally gave way and the door opened. She slammed it shut locking it behind her, simultaneously turning on the light, grabbing for the phone and dialing 911.

"Hello. What is the emergency?"

"Oh Dear God, where is my voice?"

Her mouth opened but nothing came out. *"Please, God help!"*

"Name please," she heard the Dispatcher request.

She managed to blurt out her name, address then gasped, "Please, please send police and an ambulance, there's a murderer in my house!"

"Ms. McDonald, is that you?" the Dispatcher's voice registered concern.

"Yes! Yes! Oh please hurry!" by now Kaye was crying and shaking. The Walters' house suddenly lit up as Jack, Marnie and another man came bounding down the stairs.

"Kaye, what is wrong?" Marnie stared wide-eyed at her trembling neighbor.

In her excitement, Kaye inadvertently hung up the phone and collapsed into Marnie's arms weeping uncontrollably. Jack grabbed the phone and punched in Dave's number.

"Dave, it's Jack," he barked, "Kaye's here. The killer is in her house now!" He slammed down the receiver. "Where in the house, Kaye?"

"My bedroom," she stammered. "He cut the power, Jack. I heard a shot as I ran!"

Jack strode to his office, unlocked his desk drawer and pulled out a revolver, snatching a flashlight from the adjoining drawer. "Brownie, we can't let the bastard, escape!"

In the next instance, he was bounding to Kaye's house with the other man at his heels. Jack heard the men coming out of Dave's house running. Each was being deployed to the area their plan had dictated.

The sound of breaking glass, followed by a sickening crash greeted Jack's ears as he entered Kaye's house. The sound came from the vicinity of her bedroom. He raced up the stairs only to stumble over an object laying across the top of the stairs.

"Damn!" he gasped struggling to regain his balance. He grabbed for the door handle and twisted. As he did so, he heard a dull pop followed by a thud. Jack turned on his flashlight and flung the door wide open.

Max Carron lay sprawled on the floor. Blood oozed through his upper left pant leg. The leg spread at an awkward angle to his body. The flashlight beam caught his gun. It lay a foot from his hand. Max screamed in pain and lunged for the gun.

With his attention focused on Max, Jack had failed to notice the shadow behind him that was struggling to stand. Unwittingly Jack Walters had positioned himself between the two combatants. All that registered with Jack was the fact that he was now staring at the muzzle of Carron's gun pointed directly at him.

Brownie had seen Jack fall over the vase. He had stopped to push it aside to ensure it tripped no one else. Arriving at the bedroom door, he had an unobstructed view of Carron's intended target and the real danger to his friend.

"*Jack...duck!*" he shrieked, as simultaneously Max screamed "Down!".

Instinctively, Walters dropped to the ground. A bullet

whizzed by, as out of the corner of his eye, he glimpsed its intended target. The shadowy figure that lurched toward Jack's back, his dagger poised to strike.

The light from Jack's flashlight caught the assailant just as the bullet exploded into his neck, tearing upwards into the killer's skull driving him backwards and away from Walters. Blood splattered everywhere.

Epi and Dave had joined Brownie in the doorway, in time to witness the hit and see the dagger intended for Jack, drop out of harm's way.

Epi's flashlight caught Max and his bloodstained pants. He quickly handed the light to Brownie ordering him to keep the light on Max's leg. Epi snatched a small pillow and stuffed it into Max's mouth.

"Keep it there Dave," he commanded while he pulled Max's pants down. "Jack, gimme your housecoat sash, quick!"

He encircled Max's leg with the sash. "This is gonna' hurt big time, Buddy...Sorry!" as he quickly tightened the sash.

Max writhed in agony, sweat beading on his brow.

When Jack had left his house heading for hers, Kaye was torn with indecision as she recalled his animosity toward Max. "Lord, I promised Max I wouldn't return under any circumstance."

However, when several men ran from Dave's house towards hers, she knew they would be police officers. "What if they assume Max is the culprit? I can't let that mistake be made! I must return!"

Kaye arrived just as Epi stuffed the pillow into Max's mouth and applied the sash to his leg.

"No! No!" she yelled, "You don't understand, he's not the bad one, he's been helping me!" She collapsed at Max's side, horrified at the paleness of his face, and beside herself at his pain.

Epi spoke quietly but firmly. "It's alright, Kaye. We're not deliberately hurting him.

He's bleeding. We have to stop it. I put the pillow in his

mouth, so he wouldn't bite his tongue while we applied the tourniquet. You can take it out."

Max opened his eyes, as he heard the sirens. Murmuring, he said, "Kaye…You got through okay." A faint smile crossed his lips in spite of the pain that racked his body.

Jack was demanding a towel and some light. "It's his femoral vein that's torn. It's still oozing. I think I can grab it with my fingers. Good got it!" He dabbed again with the towel. No more oozing.

Max was moaning softly as Kaye leaned over him weeping. "Max, open your eyes, listen to me. Please fight to live. Please don't die," she pleaded, "I love you!" She was kissing him, stroking his head, wiping away the beads of perspiration, shocked at how clammy he felt.

"Max, don't die! I can't take it. My heart won't take it. Please, Jesus, help him!" she prayed with desperation.

"Kaye," he whispered faintly into her ear.

She leaned forward, "Yes?"

"If I live, will you marry me?"

"Yes, oh yes! I would be honored to do so." She bent down and kissed him firmly on his lips. Sudden dread stabbed her heart. They were so cold!

At that moment, the paramedics arrived. Dave pointed to Max, "Save him!"

"Good guy?" one murmured.

"Yes!" Dave said tersely.

One of the paramedics bent over Max, "Any chance you know your blood type, Sir?"

Max nodded. Kaye handed them the card from his wallet. The paramedic smiled, "We happen to have a bag with your type, we'll set up the drip before moving you."

"It won't be easy," stated his partner, "He's in shock and his veins are collapsing."

"I can see the femoral vein above the tourniquet. It's right there." Jack said pointing to the vessel dangerously close to a jagged piece of bone. "I'm holding the distal side closed. Do you have a hemostat?"

"Wow, Judge, you've even clamped the vein on the right side," chimed the young medic in admiration.

"My father was a veterinarian in Idaho. I'd go out on calls with him. Figured one day that experience might come in handy," Jack responded.

"Probably kept him alive, this far, along with whoever applied the tourniquet," commented the other medic, matter-of-factly.

Epi spoke up, "Yeah, I was a military medic, and that training has indeed proved beneficial on several occasions."

"We've just about stabilized his leg as best we can. Ma'm, we need to get your friend on the stretcher now. Judge can you ride with us in the ambulance? Your hand is already in the wound. Can you keep it there, and help steady this I.V?"

Jack nodded in the affirmative.

"Kaye," Dave said gently, "They need to move him now. We have to stand back." He helped her to her feet. She felt as limp as a little rag doll in his arms.

"Can't I go with him?" she pleaded.

Epi stuck the pillow back in Max's mouth as they moved Max onto the stretcher. Once more, the pain overwhelmed him.

"Can't you give him anything for the pain?" Kaye begged.

"Unfortunately, not until he's more stable, Ma'm, that's why we need to get him quickly to the hospital."

With that, Max was transferred to the ambulance. Its siren pierced the night air as it raced to save the life of its critically-injured patient.

Kaye collapsed in Dave's arms. The police had managed to restore the hydro to the house.

Dave held Kaye in his embrace whispering softly in her ear, "Kaye, we need your help here. We need you to look at this man's face to see if you recognize him. Tom has turned his head, so you'll not see the fatal wound."

Kaye shook her head, "Dave, please I don't want to see

his face. The horrible things he said and did. The thought of putting a human face to it is unbearable!"

Dave gave her a hug, "I know, Kaye, but this guy had access to your schedules, we need to know how. We need to act quickly in case he has an accomplice."

Now it was Dave's turn to beg, "Please, Kaye, help us!? We don't want to prolong this case."

Kaye nodded wearily, "No, we don't!"

"That's my girl!" Dave kissed her on the forehead.

It was as she raised her head to his that she caught a glimpse of herself in the closet mirror doors. "Oh no! There's blood all over me!" she wailed, horrified. "Look my hands, my pant leg...Dave, my face, it's all over!"

"Kaye, Max lost a lot of blood." Dave said gently, "You were beside him, comforting him. This is what we'll do. You point out some clean clothes and Professor Brown can carry them for you. His hands are clean. Matt and he will take you back to Jack's. You can shower and clean up. Marnie, I'm sure, will be happy to go with you to the hospital. Matt will drive you."

Sergeant Tom had been kneeling on the floor, on the other side of the bed, out of Kaye's vision. Abruptly he stood. "The perp's ready for Kaye, Chief," nodding as he knelt back down.

The body lay grotesquely on the floor. In the exact spot where it had fallen after Max's fatal shot. Dressed in black, a balaclava had covered the head."

Kaye shook just looking at the still form. Her mind was bombarded by all the dreadful things that he'd said he do to her. All the vicious things he had admitted doing to others.

Epi and Dave both had to support Kaye as they escorted her to the body. Tom had cut away the balaclava, and turned the head slightly so as not to expose Kaye to the gaping wound on the other side of the man's face.

The bullet had severed the aorta, shattered the jaw and penetrated the brain. Death had been instantaneous. A towel had been discreetly positioned to cover any unsightly areas. The men were sensitive to the trauma Kaye had already endured. Their desire was to do all they could to minimize further suffering. But neither they nor Kaye were prepared for what followed.

Kaye's eyes grew wide as the assailant's identity struck home.

"Oh, Dear God, No! No! Oh, NO! Oh, poor, poor Stephanie!" Her hands flew up to her face as if to cradle it in disbelief.

EPi leaned close to Kaye, "You recognize him then?"

"He's my receptionist's boyfriend!"

Dave threw his head back and grimaced, "No wonder he knew your schedule!"

Kaye was overwhelmed with grief for Stephanie. Forgotten, for the moment, was her own grief. For a split second, the resilience of M.K. McDonald surged forth when it was suggested that Stephanie might be an accomplice.

"No! Absolutely not! She is too sweet...too loyal. Never would she do anything knowingly to hurt me!"

Epi's eyes met Dave's, and without uttering a word each knew the thought of the other. *"How often have I heard that one!"*

Turning to Dave, Kaye's eyes brimmed with tears, "Dave, this is dreadful! Stephanie is such a compassionate person, with a wonderful, wonderful heart. Her beauty is on the inside – this person, if I can call him that, pretended to love her. He said he wanted to marry her. Stephanie will be horridly devastated. Epi, when you break this news to Stephanie, her parents and I must be there, with her, to protect her!"

The two men exchanged glances, this was the M.K. McDonald they both knew. Epi smiled to himself, *"No point in debating that issue with her right now. Very soon we should know if Kaye's right. For her sake, I hope this perp really did dupe her receptionist."*

Dave too was wrestling with his thoughts. *"With all I've witnessed this evening, something more than a business relationship is brewing between Carron and Kaye. I don't think she's gotten over her parents' death?"* He shook his head, *"And then enduring this attack...not sure she's up to much more!"* Thus he silently prayed, *"Dear Lord, please, let this Max guy live, for this one's sake!"*

Chapter Thirty-Eight

The ambulance tore to the hospital sirens blazing, as the medics worked feverishly to stabilize Max. Jack assisted by firmly holding the femoral I.V. in place for them. His free hand, he rested on the gurney. The vehicle made a sudden lurch, Max groaned and in pain clutched at Jack's hand. The two men locked eyes for the first time. The one was struggling desperately to hang onto life. The other struggled to bring reason out of the internal chaos he was experiencing.

Jack broke the gaze when into his mind popped the movie, *"Guess Who Is Coming To Dinner."*

"Lord, that is exactly what I feel like," Jack thought. "Kaye is family to us and her behavior moments ago, leaves me no doubt about her heart's affection for Carron. Yet he is a convicted felon. Also, I have no doubt that he was in our neighborhood for me. Still, back there, he could have killed me, and not only that when he shot that perp, if it didn't save my life, it at least kept me from serious injury."

He looked again at Max whose eyes were now closed. Perspiration beaded his forehead and soaked his clothes. The man was in great agony. It appeared to Jack that Carron's left femur had to have been shattered by a bullet. " I figure that must have been the shot Kaye heard as she fled. It's amazing, wounded as he was, that Carron could have held off his assailant as long as he did."

A quiet voice within him said, *"Love bears all things."* It took Jack aback, ordinarily he would have acknowledged the speaker, but now? He turned again to the man on the stretcher and heard the same voice say *"Bless those who curse you."*

The ambulance pulled into the Emergency bay. Jack comforted himself with the thought that soon he would be relieved of his duties. It was obvious everyone had been alerted to the serious needs of this patient. The Emergency ward became a beehive of activity. Surgeons barked orders here and there, but instead of being dismissed, Jack found himself commissioned. A hand fell upon his shoulder, it was Ralph, the anesthetist, a fellow elder in his Church. "Jack, the medics said your dad was a veterinarian. You are used to blood and stuff. We can use your help with your friend."

"Friend?" Jack wanted to scream, *"He's not my friend! Darn it, I sent him to jail. He's a convicted felon, who has no business being here!"* But before he could utter a peep, Ralph had disappeared to scrub up.

Jack felt his hand being squeezed. He looked down. Carron was hanging onto him like a man hanging over a precipice. One glance at the man and Jack realized that perhaps he was.

The O.R. team had moved in an operating gurney. Ralph had reappeared in his scrubs. He bent over Max, yet motioned to Jack, "His name?"

"Max," Jack heard himself reply.

"Max, my name is Ralph. I'm a friend of Jack's."

"Wow! That is certain to reassure him," Jack thought to himself.

Max's eyes were now opened and fixed on Ralph. He was trying to grasp what the man was saying, but the pain was like a searing, hot branding iron. He just wanted it to end. *"Why couldn't they give him something?"*

"Pain is real bad, isn't it, Bud?" Ralph spoke soothingly as if reading Max's thoughts.

"You are not stabilized enough that we can give you pain medication. It could tip you over, Bud, which neither you nor we want. So, this is what I'm going to do. We're taking you to surgery. Like I said, we can't risk a general anesthetic with you. I'm giving you an epidural." Ralph laughed.

"It's sort of like what we do with the ladies to allow childbirth to be pain-free. You'll get the same relief. Plus, when the ordeal's over, you'll be one of the few men that can identify with their wife's birthing experience."

Ralph continued, "In all seriousness, Max, you will remain conscious during the surgery but you won't feel a thing. This way you can work with us on your recovery."

All Max could comprehend was that something was going to be done to ease his pain. He wanted it to happen soon for he was beginning to doubt he could hang on much longer. Unfortunately Ralph's next words didn't bring the comfort he sought.

"I'm afraid, soldier, that before it gets better, it will get worse. To give you the epidural, I need you on your side. We've stabilized your broken leg and we're going to turn you on your good leg. I warn you the pain will be excruciating. I'm putting this gauze in your mouth. It will ensure that you don't bite your tongue. As soon as we do, I'll be inserting the needle into your spine, the anesthesia will flow and your pain will ease."

Ralph focused his attention off of Max and onto the O.R. team that stood ready to move at his command.

"Once the epidural kicks in, we'll move him onto the stretcher and be off to the O.R.!"

"Jack, you're still in the right place for the moment. Our nurses are stabilizing the leg ensuring none of those bone fragments touch the femoral artery. If you can just continue to hold the I.V. in place for us, we want no interruption in the blood transfusion. Nurse, is the epidural kit ready to go?"

Ralph received an affirmative reply both to that question and to the one that ascertained the gauze was in Max's mouth.

"Okay then, on the count of three, we turn him. One... Two...Three..."

Max was on his side. Even with the gauze in his mouth, Max let out a gut wrenching moan. Jack's stomach twisted.

"Got it!" Ralph said triumphantly.

Literally, within seconds, everyone could see Max relaxing. His breathing and heart rate started to return to normal.

"Pain easing, Bud?" Ralph said gently.

Max nodded.

The nurse began washing his face. The cool water felt good. Slowly they began to cut away his pants and top. Jack was impressed at how physically-fit Carron looked.

Apparently so were the others, for Ralph said, "Max, you obviously exercise – you look in pretty good shape, that will stand in your favor right now. Did you ever smoke?"

Max managed a firm "No!"

"So, you got the odds in your favor, friend. Can you feel any pain?...No, well that's the way we're going to keep it! How many units of blood has he had?"

From the back of the room someone answered, "We're just beginning the fifth unit."

To which, Ralph grunted, "Good," adding, "with his pain controlled and his blood pressure stabilized, it's time we get the I.V. into his left arm."

Max blinked, licked his lip and for the first time thought, *"Maybe, there is hope for me? I got to try for Kaye's sake! Please, Lord, help me!"*

Ralph continued, "Okay, remove the I.V. now from his femoral vein. No offense, Jack," he chuckled, "but we have to get the antibiotics started to control any infection those unsterile hands of yours may have brought to the wound."

"Thank you, Lord!" Jack breathed a silent sigh of relief, *"Now, I will be out of here!"*

"Jack," Ralph now directed his orders to Walters, "What I want you to do is go scrub up quickly, the nurse will show you how. Then you can join us in the O.R.. Max, Jack will be your coach." Ralph laughed good naturedly, "You'll be just like a husband and wife team in the delivery room."

Before either could protest, Jack was whisked away by the male nurse to strip off his blood soaked PJ's, shower, put on scrubs, mask and scrub up ready to head for the O.R.

By the time, Jack arrived, Max was already positioned on the operating table. The nurse stationed Jack on an O.R. stool beside Max's head. She explained reassuringly, "a large drape will be placed over where you two are. This way neither of you will see the surgery area," with that she scurried off.

The two were left by themselves, surrounded by a bee-hive of activity, as the O.R. team prepared to save not only Max's life, but also his badly damaged leg.

Any animosity that Max could ever have imagined against Jack was gone. One thought and one thought only occupied his entire being.

"I could die!" For all of us, life gets pretty basic when that reality hits. It has been said that there are no atheists in Intensive Care. So pain removed, Max was now free to began an internal dialogue.

"I do believe in you, Jesus, as my Savior and Lord. I do believe you died for my sins. I do believe your Word that all who trust in you…You will give eternal life, and you won't condemn them, but…" he paused and frowned, "Kaye's right, I don't like buts either!"

He knew what the thought was that he didn't want to acknowledge. He tried to dismiss it but it was like a Pit Bull. The thought had hold of him and wouldn't let go.

"Okay," he finally muttered.

"Okay what?" Jack said, "Are you talking to me?"

"Yes, Kaye said you're like a priest in your church."

Jack nodded, "Well, yes we have lay pastors in our denomination and I am one." All the while Jack's mind was whirling trying to imagine what on earth prompted Max's query. It didn't take long for his answer to come.

"I could die!"

"I suppose," Jack shrugged, "But everyone here is doing all they can to ensure you don't."

"But still, I could?"

"Your point?"

"Well, if someone thinks they could die, aren't they supposed to confess everything they know they did wrong to the priest? Then, he can tell them they're forgiven."

Jack hung his head a little ashamed of himself. Of course, Carron was Italian and a Catholic. Naturally, he'd be thinking of Confession at a time like this. "Yes, you are right."

"So you can do that?"

"You mean substitute as a priest for you?"

"Yeah."

"Yes. I can do that for you, Mr. Carron."

Max's eyes squinted, "So, are you like the Father? He can't use a confession against a guy?"

"Crap!" Jack thought to himself, *"What am I getting myself into?'*

"Yes, Mr. Carron, you are right." He gave a little cough, and added, "It is like that."

Jack closed his eyes, "Well?" he said tersely.

Max furrowed his brow, "I'm not telling the whole room," he whispered. "You have to come closer."

By now everyone else in the O.R. was focused solely on Max's leg, and were totally oblivious to the conversation of the two men.

As far as Jack was aware, the priest's role was not to debate a person in the Confessional booth but to listen. So he sighed and complied with Max's wish. He bent his ear down to the man's mouth. "Okay, Mr. Carron, you can begin."

"Actually, Your Honor, it's okay you can call me, Max."

Jack rolled his eyes, *"How could this guy be for real?"*

Out loud he responded, "Fine, Max. You can call me Jack."

"You sure? It's not Pastor Jack? I'm serious, I want to do this right."

"It's fine, Max. We are more informal in our church."

Jack hoped he sounded convincing. He wanted this confession thing to soon begin and soon end. Never before had he felt so conflicted about being both Pastor and Judge. He found himself uttering the most frequently used prayer in all of Christendom: *"Help!"*

As the O.R. team worked on his leg, and Dr. Ralph monitored his epidural, Max began his confession.

"I lied."

"When?"

"It was in grade school."

"I don't believe this!" was all Jack could think, but then he looked at Max.

The guy's eyes were closed. He was indeed trying to recount all his sins. *"I do believe this!"*

Jack tried desperately to remember what his friend, Father Pat, had told him about their Rite of Confession.

"You never confessed this before?"

"No, I didn't think I should. When I tell you, you'll understand."

"Okay, so how, and why did you lie?"

"Well, a bunch of the boys, a few years older than me, were playing baseball in the yard between the cathedral and the school. I was just sitting there, watching them. I mean, I wasn't very good at sports. I wanted to be, but I was kinda small..."

"And?"

"And the head boy for Grade 10. Rob was his name. He walloped the ball a good one and it sailed over to where I was sitting and it broke one of the cathedral's stained glass windows."

By now, Jack was really intrigued. "So how on earth did that involve you?"

"Well I mean they shouldn't have played ball there. You could get expelled for breaking the window."

"So?"

"So, Rob came running over, bat in hand. I picked up the ball to give it to him. I could see he was really scared and I saw all the other kids taking a hike. So I grabbed the bat and told him to run."

"You what?" Jack's voice sounded incredulous.

"I took the bat and told him to run."

"That's the lie?"

"No, the lie came next. Father Angelo came running out, saw me with the bat and ball and hauled me down to the Bishop's office. They asked me what I was doing. I told them I was practicing hitting the ball, and accidentally hit it into the window."

"What happened?"

"They called Pop. I got expelled for two days. Pop had to pay for the window. Mama said she was mortified, but loved me anyway. Pop gave me a few swats, secretly though I think he was pleased."

"Because you broke the window?"

"No, because he thought I finally hit the ball. I just wasn't any good at baseball."

"So you took the fall for this Rob. Why?"

"Well, he got into the school cause he was smart. His parents couldn't afford it. He was a nice guy, popular with everybody. If he was expelled he coulda' lost his scholarship. My Pop was able to pay for the window. Plus, he was a significant contributor to the school and church; and Mama was an active volunteer. So, I knew they wouldn't kick me out. But hey, a lie is a lie, right?"

Jack could not believe what he was hearing, but he managed to squeak out an affirmative "right." He was beginning to wonder if Max was getting more than an epidural.

"By the way," Max continued, "Rob went on to become a Chicago cop. I think he's even a captain now, but guess what?"

What?" Jack sighed.

"When I was in prison, Rob took the time to visit me about three times a year. He's a born-again Christian now. He told me a lot about Jesus. Stuff I never knew. It was him that got me to attend the Prison Alpha course. That was the best thing that ever happened to me. Kaye's right."

"About what?"

"That Romans, Chapter 8 something?"

"Verse twenty eight?"

"Yeah, it says God works all things to the good." Max wrinkled his brow and said, "I never thought about this before. I wanted to help Rob, but to do so I had to tell a lie. A lie is bad right? But then, years later, God used that person to help me get to know Jesus better...and that's a good thing."

Jack had an expression on his face akin to the coyote in the road runner cartoon. He managed to sputter, "Right!" The added, "So, Max, Jesus does forgive that lie."

Max actually smiled, "Confession is good for people isn't it?"

"Yes, Max, it is." Jack studied the man, and thought to himself *"What on earth did they use in that epidural? I can't remember Marnie talking like this."*

He cleared his throat, "So anything else?"

Max sighed. He was obviously trying to be truthful. "Well, Holy Spirit's reminding me of when I really did break the prison rules and managed to get away with it."

"What rules?"

"The no violence stuff."

Now, it was Jack's turn to close his eyes, *"God, I do not want to hear this!"*

However, turning to Max he tried to speak like he thought a concerned priest might sound. "So, what exactly are you confessing?"

"Well, in prison there's okay guys, and not okay guys... guards and inmates alike. You know what I mean?"

Jack didn't have a clue what *"okay"* and *"not okay"* could possibly mean to Max, but he wasn't about to acknowledge that fact. "Uh-huh" was all he said.

So Max continued, "Some are really rotten apples. A couple of years after I was there, this hulking big guy is brought in. He is rotten to the core. He gets a following and starts terrorizing...pushing into others' space...especially weaker guys, even guards."

Max's face was now registering total disgust. "Like they'd rape a guy not for sex, just to humiliate him. One fellow they did that to, killed himself."

Jack was being educated far beyond his desires and way beyond his comfort zone. He knew this was a dumb question but asked it anyway. "Why wouldn't people report that to the prison authorities?"

Now it was Max's turn to look at Jack in disbelief. "You have to be kidding. Do that and you are as good as dead, or worse. I mean some of this intimidation stuff is bound to go on but this character...'Vich' they called him. I think his real name was Oskovich. He carried it way beyond reasonable. Know what I mean?"

Again, Jack had no idea what Max meant so he resorted to his standard, "Uh-huh," reply.

"Continue."

"The guards were even getting nervous. This is a guy over which riots could start.'

"Anyway, Phil was my cellmate. We'd been together about six months.'

"Phil was an okay guy. He'd been a good accountant. Problem was he had a gambling addiction. He embezzled some funds. Got caught and that's how he ended up my cellmate.'

"Phil isn't a big guy. Like most white collar crime guys, he wasn't street tough." Max gave a little shrug and continued, "Just the type of guy Vich liked to bully.'

"Vich tried on a couple of occasions to isolate Phil, which wasn't hard cause I was preoccupied with my studies or working out in the gym. However, by this time Phil was accepted by a lotta' guys so they watched out for him too."

Max frowned and added, "Come to think of it, Jack, I kinda' wonder now if Vich went for Phil to get me."

Jack was now beginning to wonder, *"How on earth do priests manage to survive Confession?"*

Jack decided that perhaps a little refocusing was

needed. "Max, remember this is Confession. What did you do that you need to confess?"

Max looked at Jack like he had forgotten what he was doing, probably he had. He cleared his throat and said, "Well, yeah, I knew I'd have to stop Vich. But I couldn't figure out how without starting a riot...which I didn't want to do." He added.

"Very good, Max!" Jack caught himself.

"Yegads, now I sound like his shrink!" Jack thought.

"See, when you sent me to prison..."

"Didn't forget that detail," Jack mused silently.

"Certainly, lets me know that he's rational, if nothing else."

"Tony's father, Pepi."

"Who is Tony?" Jack interrupted.

"My brother-in-law,"

"Oh."

"Well, Tony's Pop and mine wanted to make sure no one messed with me. Pepi knew a couple of lifers so he employed them as sorta like my baby sitters."

"Your baby sitters?"

This time, Jack could not camouflage his ignorance.

"Yeah...Like they ensure nobody messes with you."

"Oh?"

"Anyway, that became more problematic for me than helpful."

"How so?" was Jack's dumbfounded response.

Max looked at Jack like he was from another planet, "How could you get to be a Judge and not know things like that?"

Jack gritted his teeth and forced a smile. "I'm not a Judge now. I'm a Pastor hearing your confession, remember?"

"Jack?"

"What?"

"I can't move my hands..."

"They are tied down."

"Yeah I know that but my nose is itchy, would you scratch it for me, please?"

"That it?"

"Yeah, thanks. Now, see if I got these baby sitters and I want to send a message to Vich, but I don't want a riot, I got a problem. Like I have to settle with Vich when my sitters are so far away that they can't react."

Jack surprised himself, at last he finally understood what Max was talking about. He wanted to settle with this character in such a way that it would minimize involvement with anyone else. "So what did you do?" Jack was now expressing genuine interest.

"Well," Max took a long deep breath, "I realized I had to do something quick to Vich before he hurt Phil. I couldn't let him go any further. Also you could start feeling the tension creeping into the joint. It wasn't good."

"And?"

"I figured the only safe place to make a move was in the middle of the dining hall."

"Don't they have cameras?"

"Of course!"

"Then how could that be safe for you?"

"No, not for me – safest for everyone else. I knew that I could nail Vich good. Bullies are a bunch of sissy pants, especially big bullies like Vich. So, if I caught him by surprise, he'd be down whining before anyone else could move."

"And you?"

"Oh, I'd get caught red-handed, but at least the tyrant's reign would end. I'd have a few black marks on my record, but for most in the joint, I'd still have my respect. So I did it!'

"Phil and I were eating together. I told him to follow me close as we went to put our trays away. Vich was seated in the center of the hall with his cronies. My baby sitters were far away at either end of the hall. I timed it so we arrived just as Vich stood up.'

"I handed my tray to Phil, and called Vich's name. He turned to look at me, and I pasted his nose but good. Blood spurted every where. He let out a squeal like a stuck pig.

Then, with my other fist I pounded his Adam's apple. He went down like a ton of bricks, and laid there whimpering like a baby. I took my tray from Phil, poured a glass of water over him and said, *'Quit messing with Phil and everyone else! Leave everyone in peace!'* and I walked away to put my tray in the rack."

Jack's mouth was wide open, "So what happened - to you, I mean?"

"Nothing."

"Nothing?"

"Yeah nothing, that was the big surprise. Everyone just remained in their places like they were frozen. Guards and inmates, everybody looked the other way. After a minute or so a couple of guards made their way over to Vich.'

"Over the loud speaker someone said, 'somebody has slipped on some water. The medics are coming. Every one remain where they are.' So, Phil and I stood at the trays. I stood a little apart from Phil so as not to involve him. I expected it would only be minutes before I'd get hauled on the carpet."

"What about the cameras?"

"That was the funny thing. The guards said they saw me getting up and walking with my tray. But, as I got near Vich, the tapes all went blank. The next thing the tapes show is Vich laying on the ground whining. Since the guards saw the water, they figured he slipped. Anyway, after that Vich and his cronies minded their manners with everybody!"

"So nothing happened to you?"

"Right and that's why I'm confessing I hit him."

Jack bit his lip. He wasn't sure if it was to hide indecision or to ensure he didn't laugh. Nonetheless, he heard himself say, in all seriousness, "Well, Jesus died that our sins could be forgiven. What you've confessed is under his blood!"

As near as Jack could recall, it was at that point the Doctors announced that after five hours of surgery they were about to close up the wound. They were infusing it with an antibiotic wash and packing it with antibiotics hoping to avoid infection. After all, they pointed out that Jack's bare hand had been in the wound, as well as unsterile towels and the makeshift tourniquet.

Ralph reassured Max that all was well with the epidural. Max had asked if they thought he'd live. Ralph laughed and said that with all the work they'd put into him they sure hoped so. However, Ralph had then stopped laughing and somberly told Max that his recovery time would be long.

As for Jack, he was rather glad he had been asked to stick around. He could see why Brownie was intrigued by this character. He was about to lean back over Max and say a little prayer, when he observed Max's countenance.

He bent over and asked, "Is there something else that you feel the Holy Spirit is asking you to share, Max?"

Max nodded and Jack saw tears in his eyes. "Jack, you need to come real close for this one." Jack positioned his ear close to Max's mouth. This time there was no descriptive narrative, Max simply turned and stammered softly, "I ...I...I tried to rape her."

Jack recoiled at this pronouncement. However, one glance at Max convinced him the man was not jesting. Remorse was written all over his face. Jack whispered gently into Max's ear, *"Who?"*

In an almost inaudible tone, Max replied, "Kaye."

Chapter Thirty-Nine

Dave and Epi arrived at the Walters' before Kaye and Marnie were ready to leave for the hospital. Their expressions said it all. Kaye had never seen either looking so grave. Her first thought was that they had come to tell her Max had died. It was as if Epi had read her mind, reaching out he clasped her hand, "Kaye, I know Max's well being is foremost in your thoughts. I have no news of his condition. I'm here because I need your help. Will you delay your trip to the hospital and hear what I have to say?"

Marnie smiled sympathetically and put her arm around Kaye, "Hon, let's listen to Epi. I'll put the coffee on. We can talk in the kitchen." Kaye nodded numbly. Marnie called for Matt and Brownie to join them.

Marnie set the fresh brewed coffee on the table along with her famous, baked scones... warm out of the oven. Their delicious aroma would normally brighten the face of even the most dour soul. But, not now! All sat grim faced, as Epi brought them up to speed.

"Brian has notified the local FBI Agency and Centerville Police of the circumstances surrounding Glaxton's demise. He's requested that they immediately locate and search Glaxton's Morristown apartment, which they are doing now, as I speak."

Epi unconsciously massaged his temples and sighed, "It didn't take very long to realize Glaxton was indeed our killer." He tensed his jaw. "The man kept scrapbooks along with other memorabilia that detail all his exploits...listing names, places and dates. Naturally our agents are going to need many more hours to sift through all our perp has left behind. Their suspicion is there could be several unsolved slayings solved tonight! They've already begun feeding data into our Washington Bureau.'

"Even from what they have now though, they wanted to let me know that the guy coming after you, Kaye, really was one nasty dude! Also, I thought I should let you know that the evidence, at least initially, supports your belief that your receptionist is innocent of any wrong doing."

"And that's why we're here, Kaye," Dave interjected, "A little while ago you indicated that you wanted to be with Stephanie and her parents when she was told the truth about her boyfriend's real motivation for his relationship with her."

Epi continued, "Kaye, it appears that Glaxton's modus operandi was to befriend someone close to his intended victim. Of course, he would have very little or no contact with his prey. Then, just before he carried out his attack, he'd offer a plausible reason why he would have to leave the area. So, his absence, after the crime, would not be thought unusual."

Dave reached over and took Kaye's hand, "Kaye, I know you want to be at the hospital with Max, but the reality is that he will be in surgery for several hours. You are not going to be able to see him until at least noon."

"But what if he..." she hesitated and then softly uttered the word she dreaded, "dies?"

"Kaye," Dave replied, "I pray with you, that he doesn't, but should he, the reality is that his body will remain there for you. Furthermore, I know for certain, that if he dies in the operating room, you would not be allowed to see him until they had removed the body to another room."

Kaye's normally vivacious eyes now looked like two sunken tombs. "What is it you want me to do?" she whispered resignedly.

"Several things," Epi said, "I'd like to outline a strategy and the rationale for each move."

Turning to the others in the room he invited them to give input when and where ever they felt. "First, I suggest we, meaning the Bureau, announce with you, what has happened this night. Namely that a serial killer has secretly stalked you these past nine months and this evening tried to attack you.'

"Because you are M.K. McDonald, CEO of Kayleen Enterprises, the media will initially focus on you. You, Ma'm, are exhausted, and do not need the attention. If we are present with you in a joint press announcement, we can begin giving info on the man's other victims. This will allow you to fade into the background, Kaye.'

"For example, we are pretty certain that in one case, a person is in jail, serving a sentence, for a crime he didn't commit. The media gets excited about stuff like that. In all probability, that case will refocus their attention away from you and onto details concerning Glaxton. The second thing we need to decide is what information we are going to release and how?"

"Whatever do you mean?" Marnie queried.

"Well," Dave said, "for starters one of Kaye's board members called earlier this evening asking if she was receiving any calls and offering to help if she was. He had done that before, as did we, Marnie. Kaye denied there was a problem, told him there were no calls, as she did us. Our thought was that maybe, Kaye, you should call him before the press conference. Thank him. Apologize for not telling the truth. Tell him you were working with a private investigator to trap this caller, whom the FBI had already verified was a serial killer. Together all of you were attempting to lure this sexual predator into the open."

"Oh yes! Thank you," Kaye responded, "I really do need to apologize to George. In fact, we need to notify all my board members before the media gets hold of this."

Marnie suddenly realized that Professor Brown had been a guest in her house and she hadn't even known he was there. "Brownie, you are here, why?"

"I had a meeting in Washington with Jack on Friday. We realized that Ms. McDonald's private investigator was likely a former student of mine who had done an excellent research paper on serial sex killers. I wanted to contact him so I came home with Jack."

"So, Kaye," Epi quickly interrupted, "Since Max's injury is very severe..."

"We were wondering," said Dave, "If we should tell the media that your private investigator is ...."

"From Indiana," added Epi.

"His full name, of course, is Maxwell Kerr," Brownie retorted.

"We also felt it important not to divulge where he is being treated ," suggested Dave.

Marnie had a puzzled look on her face, "Why would you do that?"

"Two reasons, Marn," Dave grinned, "One, we don't want to let everyone know Kaye's primary residence is in Summerside. Secondly, we've come to assume that Kaye, and her private investigator, have developed a little affection for one another beyond the professional level. Given the very intense and stressful circumstances of their working relationship, particularly over the last several days, and now his injuries...we felt that these two could use a little private, personal time to regroup."

"Maybe, see if their relationship is a little more than professional?" smiled Brownie.

Kaye blushed and said, "Yes, that's probably a good idea. We could begin on the premise you've proposed and when Max is able to respond check to see it meets with his approval."

Marnie turned and studied her neighbor, a smile slowly crossed her face, "I don't believe it! Some guy has finally succeeded in penetrating your heart, Ms. Mc Donald. I can't wait to meet him!" and she gave Kaye a big hug.

Epi, Dave and Brownie eyed one another, Dave cleared his throat, "That being the case, Matt, you can drive Brian and Professor Brown to Glaxton's place in Morristown. Brownie, the information you have from Max's paper might be of assistance to the investigation. When you're no longer needed, Matt can bring you back here.'

"I will drive Epi, Marnie and Kaye to her official residence in Lakeland. Kaye, I suggest that you contact Philippe and Alice. They are the ones, aren't they, that you often use as your media spokesperson?"

Epi inserted, "Your Lakeland estate is where I would suggest we meet the press. It will divert attention from Summerside. Hopefully, it will be assumed the attack on your life occurred at your estate in Lakeland or at corporate headquarters in Centerville." Epi smiled grimly, "I will be the spokesperson at the press conference, and I assure you, I will be most discreet in describing the attack."

"However, if you could Kaye," Dave interrupted, "it would be very good if you'd make a brief appearance – a very brief appearance!"

"Looking like this?"

"Looking exactly like that, Kaye!" Epi counseled, "You have been through a horrendous ordeal. You allowed yourself to be bait to lure a dangerous serial killer. This wasn't a publicity stunt or a fashion parade. This was real, terrifying! That individual brought untold suffering to many. You and your private investigator broke this man's power to victimize by being willing to sacrifice yourselves.'

"People need to see you to realize there is no glamour in what you did. They also need to realize there was a distinct plan you followed. I think you owe it to the public to let them see that the choice you made took its toll. Even though you, personally, came through physically unscathed, that choice critically injured your coworker."

Kaye took a deep breath, "You are right there! I am very worried about both Stephanie and Max."

"That's the concern people need to see. They need to see it from you, especially your concern and support for Stephanie. She is as much a victim as you are," Epi reiterated.

Dave reassured Kaye and Marnie, "My officers are securing our neighborhood and particularly your place, Kaye. It soon is going to be 5 a.m., if we leave now we can be in Lakeland, by 6 a.m..".

On the drive to her Lakeland residence, Kaye had Dave call Philippe and Alice asking them to meet her there, ASAP, and to notify the household staff of her imminent arrival. Epi had requested the Centerville Police to transport Stephanie and her parents to Lakeland by 6:45 a.m. He asked them not to alarm the Baxters, or reveal anything about Glaxton. He had also requested that both the Centerville Police and FBI agency have someone from the investigative team present to answer media questions about their preliminary finds.

On the way, an exhausted Kaye leaned against Marnie and fell asleep. Dave drove to the gated compound. He showed the guard his badge and rolled down the rear window to reveal the sleeping M.K. Once inside they could see that the lights were on in the mansion. Everyone was up and anxiously awaiting the mistress of the house. All equally perturbed at what could have prompted such an urgent visit. When M.K. did step into the foyer there was a spontaneous gasp. Their mistress was visibly shaken. Her color was ashen. None could recall ever seeing her so devastated...even at the death of her parents.

Jackson the butler ushered her party into the living room. Epi quickly determined that this would be where they would meet the press. Kaye closed her eyes and a tear trickled down her face, "this is the same room where I met the media to announce that my parents had been killed in the plane crash. This is not a happy room."

Marnie gave her a reassuring hug, "It looks as if this occasion will be better though, Love!"

As Kaye slumped beside Marnie on the couch, Epi quickly briefed the household staff on what had transpired and what was soon to take place.

Dave came and knelt before Kaye, "As soon as you've addressed the media, Kaye, Epi will jump in with details. You will retire and Epi will divert the attention to Glaxton and his many victims. We'll wait an hour and then I'll quietly whisk you and Marnie back to Max and Jack. Okay?"

"Ms. McDonald," it was Flora her housekeeper who gently spoke. "I've set up some tea, coffee and hot chocolate for you and your guests in your den."

A smile flitted across Kaye's face at the thoughtfulness of her housekeeper. "Oh thank you, Flora, we'll come right away. Epi, you arrange this room however you like for the press conference. Philippe can be a big help in that regard."

Alice and Philippe were both speechless as they observed Kaye. Then the normally unflappable Alice burst into tears, "Oh, M.K., you look dreadful, why would any one want to harm you?" Kaye looked at them gamely, "Don't worry! I'll be okay. It's just that this has been a very, very tough evening. One thing, I can tell you, it's great to see daylight begin to displace the darkness of the night!"

As they settled into the den, Marnie served Kaye a cup of tea. She took a sip, brushed away a tear and turned to Philippe. "Can you please call all my board members? Do this regardless of where they are, or what time it might be for them. I want them to hear this before it becomes public. If you can not get them personally, leave it on their answering machine. Then e-mail the same message to all of them. This is what I want you to say..."

She began to dictate: "The threatening, vulgar and profane calls did resume approximately six months after the first ones had stopped. In the best interests of Kayleen I chose not to make the knowledge of the resumption of these calls public. Instead I secured the services of a private investigator, Mr. Maxwell Kerr of Indianna."

Philippe hastily typed as Kaye spoke.

"Working anonymously with the FBI, it was ascertained, through what the caller had divulged, that he was a serial, sexual killer."

Kaye tilted her head back against the chair, took another swig of tea and resumed her memo, "Mr. Kerr coached me both on what I should say and how to respond to my nightly 3 a.m. caller. I willingly agreed to serve as 'bait' in an attempt to expose this individual. Earlier this week, FBI Agent Mr. Epstein, who had knowledge of my earlier calls, secured permission to tap my phone line, unbeknown by me."

Kaye paused, "This proved to be beneficial, in that the caller was not able to detect any change in my voice and thus be alerted to the surveillance. Mr. Kerr designed a new repertoire for me to goad the caller into action. The attack occurred shortly after 2 a.m., this morning."

At that point, try as hard as she could not to break down, Kaye did. Regaining her composure, she once more continued, "I escaped unharmed to alert authorities. Mr. Kerr was seriously wounded. His injuries were life threatening. However, the Police and FBI arrived, and the predator was killed in the ensuing fray.'

"There is one more important aspect you should know. Based on the early morning investigation being conducted at the deceased's apartment in Morristown , it appears his modus operandi was to become friends with someone close to his intended prey. In my case..." Kaye began to weep.

Marnie handed her some Kleenex.

Kaye blew her nose, took a gulp of air, and shook her head sadly, "In my case, that person proved to be my lovely, beautiful, loyal receptionist, Stephanie."

Alice and Philippe sat in stunned disbelief at what was being revealed. "Oh, no!" Alice eventually blurted.

"Poor Stephanie!" anguished Philippe. "The killer was the boyfriend she was so excited about?"

"Indeed, Philippe," Kaye's eyes brimmed with tears, "So,

please encourage the board, in fact all of Kayleen, to let Steph know about your love for her. Above all, may everyone make an effort to reassure her that no one blames her. Also, to remind her that neither must she blame herself.'

"Stephanie and her parents are to arrive here in Lakeland shortly. The FBI will counsel them, as they will all staff and board members, in the days to come. This way, all of us will have a unified understanding of just how insidious, devious and bizarre this man's thinking was."

Kaye buried her face in her hands, sighed and continued, strain registering in her voice. "A press conference has been scheduled for 8 a.m. here, at Lakeland. I wanted you, my board members, to be informed of what has recently transpired with me, in advance of that conference. My hope is that Philippe or Alice will be able to contact you, personally, by phone, to read my statement to you. If not, I have instructed them to both leave it on your answering machine and then to e-mail it to you."

With her statement finished, Kaye sat back to listen as Philippe re-read her dictation.

Corrections were made, as Epi fine tuned it. Then, Philippe printed off several copies.

One copy, Alice took and headed to the library to begin calling those board members on her designated list.

Kaye asked, "Philippe, before you begin to call your contacts, would you please dial George Cantaro's cell phone first." She leaned forward and handed a number to her aide.

"When he answers, Philippe, let me have the phone. I need to speak personally with George. After I do, I'll give the phone back to you, for you to read the prepared statement." Kaye bit her lip and murmured, "Should George not answer, you tell him that I tried to speak personally with him. Then, just read our statement and invite George to return the call later."

Shortly after 5:30 a.m. Central Time, George was wakened from a deep sleep by the sound of his cell phone's personal ring...appropriately for this occasion anyway, he had chosen 'The Sound of the Light Brigade' as the musical tone. Startled, he fumbled for the phone, desperately trying to shake the cobwebs from his thoughts. He managed to find his voice and croak out a barely audible, *"Hello."*

There was a momentary pause as Philippe handed the receiver to Kaye. George was about to disconnect believing the call to be a wrong number, when a familiar voice spoke his name.

"George?"

"M.K.? What is it?" Sudden alarm gripped him, "Have those calls returned?"

"Yes," was the tired response, "they did!" At this point Kaye began to sob, "Oh George, I lied to you. Please, forgive me."

George held the phone in shocked silence. He quickly rose and exited the room so as not to wake Volante. "M.K., it's okay! Don't cry! What's happened? When did he start calling again? Three months ago! You've got to be kidding."

George had been leaning against the wall, now he slid slowly down to sit on the carpet. He had never heard M.K. so distraught. "Yes, of course, I know you trust me. Yes, I forgive you. I know you, and believe that you must have had a reason why you didn't want anyone else to know about those calls. The main thing is, are you alright now? What has happened?"

Kaye trembled and finally managed to say, "George, Philippe and Alice are phoning all the other board members to fill them in before this morning's press conference. But as always you, my friend, were so perceptive.'

"Since, I did not reply honestly to your genuine concern for me, I wanted to speak personally to you. To let you know how much I do value your perceptivity and compassion. I need Philippe to speak with you to read you my statement. I hope it explains why I did not reveal to you the existence of the calls. I trust you'll also appreciate why I am unable to talk further with you now.'

"I do apologize for waking you so early but the conference is slated for 8 a.m. Eastern Time, and I have to meet now with Stephanie. Give my love to your wife Volante"

With that, she weakly handed the phone to Philippe, who read George the prepared statement.

George sat there quietly in the dark, numbly holding the phone in his hand, long after Philippe had ended their call. His mind struggled to compute all it had been told. At last, he simply nodded his head and sighed, *"At least M.K. is safe, Thank God!"*

Then he began to consider the emotional trauma she must have endured. Anger surged through him. *"How could a person contrive such evil? For what purpose? Nothing but their own gratification!"*

He shuddered to think of the consequences to the business world had this man succeeded. M.K. was a brilliant financial strategist, the loss, not simply to Kayleen but to the world, would have been immense.

He began to smile, "How she had handled it was typical M.K. Keep it quite, suffer alone for the good of Kayleen. Plan and execute a counter attack and like always you delivered." He pumped his fist in the air as he jumped to his feet.

"Yes, you did it again, Girl! Thank Goodness!"

As he turned to go back to his room, he noticed a light coming out from under the door of Frank's study. He thought it funny that Frank would be up so early, and decided to wander down. It even occurred to him that it might be advantageous to let Frank in on his news. He heard muffled voices from inside the room, but since it didn't sound like an argument, George chose to knock on the door.

"Yes?" It was Frank's voice.

"Frank, it's George. I just received some information that might be of interest to you?"

Frank opened the door. Josie was sitting in the chair. She had obviously been crying.

Both were still dressed in their nightclothes.

"Is everything okay?" George asked, suddenly concerned that this may not be the opportune time to share his good news.

Josie smiled weakly, "Yes, George, it's okay. Do come in. I have been awake most of the night."

Frank frowned, obviously troubled. "Jo woke up about 1:30 a.m., feeling like Massimiliano was in difficulty. So, she began to pray for him...tried going back to sleep but just couldn't." He shrugged his shoulders and explained, "when she prays it usually quiets her. Didn't work this time. I thought maybe if we came down here and talked, it might ease her worry." He smiled lamely, "But so far that's not helped either."

Frank walked over to his wife gently laying a hand on her shoulder. "Seems you couldn't sleep either, George. Come in and join us. Maybe your news is more encouraging than our fears."

George smiled at them, "Well, my news is rather shocking, but ultimately it is good news." He paused a moment and looked intently at Mrs. Carron.

"What is it George?" she asked, a little anxious as she observed the sudden change in his expression.

"Well, it occurred to me just now, Mrs. C., that sometimes God wakes people up to pray for others. Sometimes, it is to pray for people they don't even know. Maybe there is a connection between my news and your waking and praying, after all?"

If nothing else, his remarks had served to grab the attention of both Carrons. Frank even sat down on the arm of his wife's chair. He motioned for George to pull up another one.

So George began, "I kept feeling M.K. McDonald wasn't being honest with me about her late night calls. I even called her last night, again asking if the calls had resumed. Once more, she denied it."

At that the grandfather clock in Frank's office began to chime. George ran his hand through his black hair and continued, "My cell rang a half hour ago. Startled me, thought there might be a problem back home with one of our daughters. Initially when I answered, no one responded. I was about to hang up when M.K. spoke." George shook his head, "Frank, I've never ever heard her so distraught!'

"She confessed those calls had indeed returned...started about three months ago. To avoid untoward publicity for Kayleen, she secretly arranged for her own private investigator." George leaned forward. He had tented his hands together and so pointed both forefingers at Josephine Carron. " M.K. called her private eye 'Max.' Mrs. C. isn't Massimiliano, Maximilian in English?"

Josephine wrinkled her brow and said, "I believe that is so, George."

Frank raised a skeptical eyebrow, his body language clearly betrayed his thought. *"What the hell, does the similarity of the name of that broad's private dick, to our son's name got to do with anything?"* He did note, however that at the mention of their son's name, his wife appeared to be listening more intently to Cantaro.

"Anyway," George said, "this private investigator secretly listened in on those calls and began to suspect the individual might be a serial killer. The caller began to reveal specifics of previous conquests. Anonymously, they fired the information to the FBI who confirmed these were real homicides, details of which would be only known by the murderer. In a nutshell, M.K. allowed herself to be bait to try and lure this perp out into the open. The guy attacked early this morning. She escaped unharmed. The private eye did stop the killer but was nearly killed himself. He's in the hospital fighting for his life."

George paused, "Do you think, Mrs. C., that maybe he could be the Max, you were awakened to pray for? I mean it happened about the time you were awakened and from what M.K. said he was pretty badly hurt."

Frank started to roll his eyes but then he looked at

Jo. She was slowly nodding, obviously very attentive to George's words. This spiritual, supernatural stuff was way beyond Frank's comprehension level and most definitely, way out of his comfort zone. However, Josie seemed to be comforted by what George was saying.

It even looked to Frank that she was accepting the possibility that her early morning fears for their son were nothing more than God wanting her to pray for this private eye. He could see the fear that he'd been unable to disperse from his wife slowly receding. Empathy for McDonald and concern for her Max was definitely taking Josie's mind off of her own fear for Massimiliano.

Anything that could do that, Frank was willing to support. He even consented to pray with George and Josie for the health of this Max guy. Bowing his head in prayer, outside of Mass and table grace, was something he'd never done in his life. But he figured he could add his 'Amen' to theirs. After all, if saying one little word brought peace to his wife, he was for it! Because if Josie was at peace, he got peace.

After the prayer, Josie turned to him, all smiles. *"Uh-huh..."* he thought, *"I'll have to remember that tactic."*

He looked at George with new admiration. "Why don't you get your house coat, George and join us in the family room? I'll put on the T.V. and we'll watch that press conference."

So by 7 a.m. the early risers caught the breaking news on CNN. At Lakeland, her official residence, Ms. McDonald made a brief appearance at the press conference. This morning, the world did not glimpse the usually polished and beautiful CEO of Kayleen Enterprises.

It was, instead, a very exhausted, fragile looking young woman who stood before the cameras. Dressed in a plain jogging suit, she leaned heavily against the FBI agent who stood beside her. "I need to express my deepest concern for the well being of Mr. Kerr."

She paused as tears welled up in her eyes, swallowing

hard she added, "My receptionist is as much a victim of this man's callous plans, as I."

Then, for the first time M.K. looked directly at the camera, her face bathed in grief, as she said. "My deepest, deepest sympathy and prayers go out to the families and friends of all Henry Glaxton's other victims. I only hope the exposure of this man's vile activities and his demise brings some degree of closure to them."

At that point, Philippe came and escorted Ms. McDonald from the media interview. Agent Epstein then took over. Jaw taut, he stated, "I reiterate what Ms. McDonald has already said. Her receptionist was duped into taking the man into her confidence. She too is a victim of Glaxton's devious intrigue. Although still early in our investigation, it appears the man's method of operation was to manipulate a friend of his intended victim, to unwittingly divulge personal details about his potential prey. Glaxton would use this knowledge to harass and eventually capture and kill the hapless person."

Epstein commented, "Both Ms. McDonald and her receptionist will undergo therapeutic counseling and a leave of absence from work to recover psychologically from their trauma. Mr. Kerr is, at this time, undergoing surgery to repair extensive damage that Glaxton inflicted when Kerr intervened to save Ms. Mc Donald's life. It is hoped he will have a full physical recovery."

Then Epi switched to describing the horrific details of some of the other crimes that Glaxton had committed, alluding to the fact that as the investigation proceeded they anticipated further cases would be uncovered.

He stared grimly at the camera. "Lately, in his late night calls to Ms. Mc Donald, Glaxton outlined specifics of crimes that only the killer would have known. His murderous spree crossed many state borders. He even would set up his crime to implicate others. In Arkansas he tortured and raped the woman in front of her husband. Then killed both making it look convincingly like a murder/suicide of a jealous husband. In Ohio, he designed the crime so that a relative of the victim was charged and convicted. We suspect that individual has been jailed falsely for a murder Glaxton committed."

True to Epi's original prediction media attention quickly switched from M.K. and onto this serial killer, or more precisely onto the stories behind his victims.

As the conference ended, Josie wiped a tear from her eye and exclaimed, "Poor, poor, Dear, what a horrid ordeal she had to endure. I'm glad I was awakened to pray."

Frank whispered to George, "She may be a dame, but she sure has balls to let herself be used as bait!"

George grinned, "I'll take that as a compliment, Frank."

The older man grunted, "Yeah, but I'm not so sure you should pass it on to your Ms. McDonald." He laughed, "She might not receive it that way."

Chapter Forty

Max's last confession – the one that involved Kaye – occurred seconds before Dr. Ralph slid his stool beside Jack's.

"Well done, Judge, well done!"

The doctor's pronouncement knocked Jack further off balance and appeared also to unsettle Max.

Simultaneously, the two replied, "You heard?"

Ralph actually had a smile on his face, "You bet I did!"

Max just stared. Jack closed his eyes, but before either man could respond, Ralph gushed, "The surgeon just gave the thumbs up! Said that she's confident the bone will set and heal! You'll be able to walk again, Bud. Great news isn't it, Max?'

"By the way whatever you guys discussed under that drape sure worked. Got your temperature, EKG and blood pressure all back into the normal range, Max. Given the state you entered this hospital that, Sir, is quite an accomplishment! Quite honestly, with the degree of injury and blood loss you sustained, I would have given you a less than a 40% chance of making it. Let alone having a surgeon here that was capable of stabilizing your fractured femur."

Ralph clapped Jack on the back, "You are lucky, Max, that this guy's more than a Judge. He's a real man of the cloth and let me tell you, the Man upstairs sure had to be listening."

Ralph was genuinely elated and so it appeared was the whole O.R. team as they began their final check of all the monitors and the vital flow to Max's lower left leg.

A petite, dark skinned woman, approached them. She whipped off her surgical mask, revealing lines of fatigue etched on her face. "So, this is the one who belongs to the mangled leg?" She said nodding at Max. "You look a lot more appealing than your leg, I must say, even unshaven!"

Both Max and Jack stared at her, like deer caught in the headlights! She eyed their shocked looks as she snapped off her surgical gloves. An impish grin graced her face, placing her hands on her hips, she declared, "Sweethearts, if you men persist gettin' in front of them bullets and presenting me with your messed up body parts, I reserve the right to assess the remainder of your anatomy." She broke out laughing, "So, Honey, you got a name?"

"Max," was all he could croak.

"And, you, Lover?" she cocked her head toward Jack and extended her hand.

"Jack," he said but as he shook her hand, he couldn't stop thinking *"What a brazen nurse!"*

"Sorry for the mess, Jack." she replied gesturing to her blood stained surgical gown. She jerked her thumb at Max. "He was a tad bloody!"

Jack glanced at Ralph, he was beaming at this woman like she was the greatest thing since sliced bread.

As if on cue, Ralph turned and exclaimed "Great job, Doctor! Fellows, this is Dr. Chandrah, she's a big part of your miracle! We don't want you to publicize this, but Dr. Chandrah is one of the army's top combat surgeons. She's exploring the possibility of retiring from the military to enter civilian life. She just happened to be with us this weekend...looking over our facility. We hope she'll decide to be our new Chief of Surgery."

Ralph eyed Max intently, "Max, if it had been any other weekend you wouldn't have had the surgical expertise you got tonight!"

Dr. Chandrah's dark brown eyes twinkled mischievously, "All along you two thought I was a nurse, didn't you?"

One look at the two, revealed she'd hit that nail on the head.

"No worries, Boys, it's a common misperception." She

winked, "Being black and female, it's one I like to have fun with, whenever I sense the opportunity to do so. Trust me, as a surgeon in the military, those opportunities are quite frequent!"

She laughed good naturedly, but then her face became quite serious. She turned to Max and asked, "I'm curious, Max, how much did the hospital pay you to let them shoot you? I knew they were anxious to convince me that I could find challenge in their O.R. but I never imagined the extent to which they would go to prove it!"

At her last crack, everyone around burst out laughing – even Jack and Max cracked a smile.

Ralph then introduced Jack, as His Honor, Justice Jack Walters, but went on to tell her that Jack was also a lay pastor at the Summerside Community Church.

Chandrah looked at Max and commented, "Now, Sir, I am not joking! With the extent of your injuries, having a praying man in your corner was an absolute necessity. You had one nasty wound! Even to come through this surgery alive is a miracle, and to come through it with your leg still attached an even bigger one! You'll need more miracles as you traverse the healing and rehab fields, I can assure you." Turning to Jack she added, "So, keep on doing what you started, Your Honor."

Max nodded. The surgery completed, the absence of pain because of the epidural and the doctor's initial frivolity had all managed to take his mind of the seriousness of his condition. With her last words, however, that reality returned. At the same time, he felt a glimmer of hope, deep within himself, that all might turn out okay...just like Kaye's Bible verse promised.

Dr. Chandrah turned to Ralph, "Doctor, would you see that Max is settled in recovery and please keep the epidural running. Judge Walters, could I impose upon you to sit a little longer with your friend? The last six and a half hours has been very intense, both for me and the team. As I suspect, it has been for the two of you."

Smiling at Max, she quipped, "I'd like to get out of my O.R. garb...Max, your blood really did mess with my ensemble." Then she added, "I'll meet you in Recovery, in 30 to 40 minutes, to discuss our post-operative strategy." With that she was gone.

Ralph and the nurses began to move Max and all the necessary paraphernalia to the recovery room, detaching all extraneous tubes and wires.

Jack followed obediently along...on the outside looking like any man might, who had undergone the rigors of the last eight hours. Inside, however, was an entirely different scenario. It could perhaps, best be described as how one might feel if one was watching an avalanche bear down upon one's self.

Never, had he felt so conflicted over his two identities as judge and pastor. Heading for the recovery room he suddenly spied an out. Tapping Ralph on the shoulder he indicated his need to visit the men's room. When he opened the door to the washroom, he was grateful no one else was present!

He slammed his forehead with the palm of his hand and literally spun around. "Man of the cloth? Man of prayer? What a joke!" He shook his fist at the ceiling, "You know I wanted to kill him! What are you doing to me? You heard what he said! You know Kaye is like a kid sister to me! This isn't fair! You know what Jacob's boys did when their sister was raped!"

Tears stung his eyes, "Lord, you know that I have had few if any rants in all the years of my relationship with you, but boy is this ever one now!"

He kicked at one of the doors, swinging around just as one of the male nurses stepped into the washroom.

The man smiled at Jack, "Yeah, Judge, we do that all the time. It gets pretty intense when it's a life or death situation like you just came through."

He put his hand on Jack's shoulder and continued, "It really does help to flail your arms around...Gets your own

409

blood pumping again."

Jack nodded curtly and tried to force a smile mumbling "Thanks for the encouragement, it did feel good to stretch." He smiled sheepishly and added, "Actually, I think I do need to use the cubicle now."

As he sat down, Jack realized that his temper tantrum on top of everything else had really zapped his energy. He hung his head. *"Lord, I really don't know what to do. Please, Jesus, I need you. Other than strangling Max, I have no other options for him."*

He sucked in his breath, *"And Lord, that option I don't think would be appreciated by the O.R. staff, or Kaye nor would it benefit Marnie. So, Lord, save me!"* he sighed, *"Oh Lord, grant me success."*

He bowed his head and silently began to pray The Lord's Prayer – slowly – petition by petition. *"I really do need your will to be done, regarding Kaye's relationship with this man. From my perspective, Lord, there's no way Carron is husband material for her!'*

Jack scowled, *"Oh and as for forgiveness? You forgive me everything. I want to forgive others the same way, but he just confessed to attempting to rape Kaye! That's pretty hard for me to swallow, Lord. I need your help just to go back and face the man! So help me, please to pronounce your forgiveness to him. "*

Jack hung his head and sighed, *"How I wished your Kingdom was here already and I had the bread of your Day. Then I wouldn't be tempted to repay evil with evil,"* he groused, *"I and everyone I dealt with...even Carron, would be delivered from harming others."*

That last reflection provoked another disquieting thought, *"What if he really didn't do what I sentenced him for? What if he took a fall for someone else?"* Jack scratched his head, *"Well, if he opted to take a drug trafficking charge for another dealer that's his choice. He's accountable for that!"* Jack shrugged, *"True, but you*

Walters did real shabby bench work just to expedite your own circumstances, and for that I am accountable!"

As he washed his hands and prepared to go to the recovery room, he heaved another great sigh and added, "Thank God life is all about You and not about me!"

"Here he is, Max!... Here is your buddy!"

Jack gritted his teeth. Outwardly, he smiled pleasantly. Inwardly he thought, "Shut up, Ralph! He is not my buddy, and I don't need your goody, goody pep talk!"

Both men watched Ralph leave and both men had the same thing on their mind... Resume where they had been interrupted. Only each had a slightly different agenda.

Max wanted a priestly pronouncement of forgiveness.

Jack wanted details and he got the first word in. "How many times?" He tried not to hiss the question but sound appropriately probing, as he thought a priest ought to sound.

Max looked stunned. He blinked his eyes, "Once!" Then he added, "That's bad enough!"

Now, it was Jack's turn to be taken aback, "You mean the rest was consensual?"

Max frowned, "There was no rest."

"So, when did you attempt to rape her?"

Max gave a sad sigh, "When I first saw her."

Jack was astounded and let his astonishment show, "that would have been almost three months ago?"

"Right, but it's still a sin! I told Kaye that I was sorry and she forgave me. But I never confessed it to a priest before. I know the Doc says that I'll likely live but I want a clean slate anyway."

"Okay, Max, fine...but if I do the priestly stuff, can I ask you some more questions?"

Jack's demeanor was now generating suspicious, unpleasant thoughts in Max.

"Maybe."

"Maybe?"

"Yeah, maybe. It depends on why you want to ask them

and what you want to ask."

"Okay, that's fair enough, so let me first do the Pastor/ Priest thing. Then I'll ask my questions and if you want you can answer."

So Jack began the absolution expressing it in simple terms. He said, "Because Jesus forgives us unconditionally, it doesn't matter the nature of our sin. Whether it is lying, stealing, dishonoring, sexual sin or even murder. Jesus died to set us free from our bondage to sin. You have turned to him to be forgiven, Max, and on the basis of the Word of God I can declare to you that all your sins are forgiven. Amen"

"Thank you, Jesus! And thanks, Jack, for stepping in to be a priest for me, when I needed one."

Suddenly, Max became very solemn, "Jack, I just remembered I shot that perp. Would Jesus consider that murder? Should I confess that?"

"No, it was not murder. It was self defense!"

"Yeah, that's what I thought. It's a good thing you ducked when I yelled, or both of us could have died."

"You were shooting at him?"

"You think I was shooting at you and missed?" For the first time, Max appeared visibly angry.

"For your information, when I shoot, I don't miss!" He added for clarification.

"Thanks for the explanation. Just checking."

Jack found himself actually grinning and meaning it. This he discovered seemed to relax Max making him receptive to answering the questions that still plagued Jack.

"How come you attempted to rape Kaye when you first saw her, but never touched her afterward?"

Max looked at Jack like he had two heads, "Sheesh, Jack, that's a no brainer. When I first saw her she wasn't wearing anything, and I lost it. It happened just before that guy called.'

"She thought that I was the perp so she was really terrified. After he called she knew I wasn't. However, I heard him and I knew he was real. She also knew I broke two laws – first I broke into her house and ..."

"...Then you attempted to rape her." Jack interjected.

"Yeah, and I knew she was right." Max continued, "So she said I had three options:

a) I could kill her and add murder to the above list;

b) I could run, but she had seen my face. She promised she'd see I got caught and pay the piper; or

c) I could help her catch the perp and she wouldn't press any charges

So, I chose Option C"

"Sounds like that was the best legal choice," Jack nodded. "Professor Brown said you had the best legal mind of any of his students."

Max looked genuinely surprised, "He said that, no kidding?"

"Yeah, he said that. So, you and Kaye had a business deal going?" Jack was starting to feel a little better about everything.

"Well yeah, that was sort of it. And to keep it that way, she wore not particularly sexy clothes. Just like baggy PJs that your kid sister might wear. That helped. Then I took cold showers before going to bed and I also prayed that Jesus would help me."

Jack's jaw dropped, "You took cold showers?"

"Yes, trust me. They really diminish any passion, in fact even thinking about taking them helped me."

"So your relationship was plutonic, option C only?"

"Oh yeah, I mean initially she was pretty intimidating. In fact the night you showed her my mug shot and said who I was, she came flying home from your house spitting mad. Said she didn't want me there anymore. I was to get out, not come anywhere near you, just go home and she'd not press charges."

Jack was shocked, "She said that?" Max simply nodded.

"Why didn't you go?"

"I did. I mean I couldn't reason with her, so in the middle of the night, after the perp's call, I left. I took the trail down the ravine. There was a terrific thunder storm, something inside of me kept telling me I should stay. However, she had ranted on something fierce about me going, so I figured I had to. I stopped at the bottom to collect my thoughts, when a crack of lightening toppled a big tree right in front of me.'

"If I had kept walking, I'd have been dead. Kaye said that those quiet thoughts inside you, people should pay attention to because that's how The Holy Spirit talks to you.'

"Anyway because of the paper I wrote for Professor Brown, I was getting very concerned that her caller might be a serial killer."

Max shrugged, "So, I thought I don't care what you think I am, Kaye, or why you think I'm here. I need to go back so I did." Even the thought of Kaye's rejection brought tears to his eyes.

Max continued, "I emptied my gun on the counter and waited for her to come down. I wanted her to call Dave. He could arrest me. She could charge me...But he needed to know that those calls had started up again. He also needed to know why I believed this guy posed a real threat to Kaye. I figured Professor Brown would tell him of my paper and that I knew what I was talking about."

"You were willing to go back to prison if it would help her?"

"Of course, Jack. After all, just look at who the guy turned out to be! Shortly after I began listening to those calls, I just felt in my gut he was really bad news. I couldn't walk out on a person and leave them to something like that!"

Jack raised his eyebrows, "Why didn't Kaye call Dave?"

Max shook his head, "She changed her mind. I guess dolls do that? I don't have a whole lot of experience with ladies, only my mother and sister. Mama usually meant what she said. Sis always changed her mind. Anyway Dave came to tell Kaye to look after Rufie.'

"You were going to a ball game. She pushed him out of the door before I realized who she was talking to...I ran to get him, but..." Max closed his eyes and bit his lip a little embarrassed to continue.

"But what?"

"She had her briefcase and I was charging full tilt for the door. She swung a round and accidentally nailed me."

Max squinted, "You ever been hit like that? Man, it hurts! Almost, but not quite as bad as tonight. It is a different shock to the system. Anyway, long story short we redid our pact and I stayed."

"Was everything then business as usual?"

"Started out that way, but somewhere along the way... I don't know where or when. Maybe Kaye does? I started to really like her. She said the same for me."

"And there was nothing?" Jack asked.

Max actually blushed, like a teenager, "We kissed a bit, but I really couldn't, Jack."

He swallowed hard, "I mean, I kept thinking how I had lost it when I first saw her. I had always thought I could control myself in all circumstances. Now, I knew for certain I couldn't!"

"But Max, you both are adults. She had allowed you to stay in her house. What was the problem? Did you figure you couldn't trust her to keep her end of the bargain?"

"Course, I trust her. She's a real lady."

Jack smiled, "Yes, Max, she is indeed."

"Jack, you are a judge, do you not yet get the picture?" Max sounded a tad annoyed.

"We knew by then, that this creep killed people. He even feigned one as a murder suicide. Cops believed the guy was a jealous lover because an autopsy on the woman had revealed the existence of two different semen types. This perp was really devious. I wanted to catch the bastard, not give him any grounds to confuse the evidence."

Jack was now seeing clearly, very clearly indeed. He was definitely appreciating Brownie's assessment of this man's character.

But, before Jack could say anything, Max spoke, "Kaye, is a wonderful lady. I'd really like to marry her." He shook his head, "Wow! I'd be so proud to be her husband."

His expression grew serious, as he added, "I know I messed up real bad by what I nearly did when I first saw her. But you pronouncing Jesus' forgiveness, like a priest does. And Kaye forgiving me, it all helps me to forgive myself.'

"As I figure it, the Bible tells us that Jesus' blood has the power to wash away all sin. If I can't accept his forgiveness for myself, that is really unbelief in God's Word. Don't you think?"

Jack nodded to the affirmative, deeply impressed with the sincerity of faith that shone before him.

Max pressed on, "I am so grateful to God for his gift of forgiveness. Like the Bible says, 'in Christ we are a new creation.' So, if I end up lucky enough that Kaye chooses to marry me, I'm going to be pleased that I was able to treat her with the respect she deserves and waited until we are married and..."

Max paused, "...if I'm not the one, she wants to marry. I'll have the satisfaction of knowing that I didn't defile another man's wife!" A little tear trickled down the side of his face.

Jack sat back on the stool quietly studying the one before him. Given all that he'd listened to he couldn't help thinking, *"After all I've heard, I believe the Carron's misnamed their son. It should have been Forest. If ever I've met a living 'Forest Gump', it has to be this one!"*

Slowly Jack leaned toward Max's ear, then he reached down and squeezed his hand.

To Jack's surprise, he heard himself whisper, "Max, want you to know, I'll be in your corner rooting for you."

416

Chapter Forty-One

The drive with Dave and Marnie from Lakeland back to Summerside was one big blur for Kaye. In fact the whole first half of this day appeared surreal.

She leaned her head back on the seat. The anguish on young Stephanie's face as Epi tried to convey the truth about her wonderful miracle boyfriend, Henry Glaxton, was seared into Kaye's memory. Initially Stephanie had been in defiant denial.

Kaye had watched the realization dawn on Mr. and Mrs. Baxter of the devastation that this truth would bring to their daughter. She closed her eyes recalling the sheer terror Steph's parents had exhibited when they realized that the Bureau might be investigating their daughter as an accomplice to Glaxton's crime. A wisp of a smile appeared as Kaye recollected the parents' relief as Epi emphatically assured them "No! your daughter is as much a victim as Ms. McDonald."

The Baxters were on an emotional roller coaster, just as Kaye herself had initially been when she realized the identity of her attacker. "Yeah," she mused, "shock, disbelief, anguish, fear and eventually rage, raced through them too...When they suddenly grasped how this "monster", as Mrs. Baxter put it, had manipulated their daughter. He had disrespected Stephanie's very person by his lying façade."

Tears glistened in Kaye's eyes, as in her mind's eye, she 'saw' their loving embrace of their daughter, while the three listened to Epi outline the nearly two dozen suspected victims of this man's perverted fantasies.

They had heard how the preliminary findings thus far, were revealing that Glaxton's method of operation was to befriend a close friend, co-worker or family member of his intended prey. This way he gained personal information that eventually would provide him fatal access to his victim.

Kaye herself had been equally stunned at the Bureau's revelations. The more she thought about it the more she could not fathom how one human being would choose to perpetrate such evil on another.

As she watched the Baxter's struggle with their emotional anguish, there was no question in her mind that this man had victimized countless others, besides those he had murdered. Unlike the Baxters, most of these 'walking wounded,' at the time of the murder of their loved one, would have had no realization of their own duplicity. Only now, with Glaxton's demise, would these people learn that like Stephanie, they too had been manipulated.

Kaye literally shuddered at the pain about to descend upon these already hurting people. *"Dear Jesus,"* she prayed, *"please ensure each person has all the support systems in place that they need, when they face the horrible facts of this man's crimes!"*

As Dave raced towards Summerside District Hospital, Kaye's thoughts continued to focus on Stephanie. Kaye had left the Baxters in the parlor with Marnie, while she made a brief appearance at the press conference in her Lakeland living-room.

When she returned Stephanie was huddled beside her mother trembling. Kaye had gone and knelt in front of the girl, who moaned "Oh, Ms. McDonald, I'm so sorry...so very, very, sorry. Can you ever forgive me? I was so stupid to think he loved me." With that Stephanie had begun to sob.

Kaye had clasped Stephanie's hands in hers and commanded Steph to look at her. The ring of authority in Kaye's voice so shocked the young woman, that momentarily she had stopped her sobbing. "Stephanie," Kaye had said emphatically, "There is absolutely nothing to forgive. You did nothing, absolutely nothing wrong!"

"Oh, but I did, Ms. McDonald. I don't know how? But he must have gotten your personal phone number from my desk...And, I know I told him when you were away on trips."

She then began to wail, her shoulders violently convulsing with each sob.

"And I told him of your retreat house in Summerside, where you mostly live. I'm so sorry!"

Kaye had moved to sit beside Stephanie and put her arm around the heart-broken girl. Not only did Stephanie need to face the fact that she had never been loved by this man, a man she had given her heart to...Stephanie also had to accept that in her blind love for him, she had failed to protect her employer. Kaye had smiled at Steph and said, "Stephanie, listen to me, I value you as one of my most conscientious employees. You are an excellent receptionist, Steph, because of that warm caring heart...And so many people are blessed by the gentle way their inquiries at Kayleen are handled."

Kaye had paused to let her words sink in, then she said firmly, "Stephanie, that man abused all your good qualities. He, and not you, is the one at fault. Agent Epstein spoke the truth, you are as much a victim as me!"

Kaye's voice had then softened, "Be assured, Stephanie, that I most definitely forgive anything you think you may have done. Make sure you forgive yourself in the same way!'

"Now, Stephanie," she had continued, "I want you and your parents to take a well earned holiday. You choose...a two-week cruise or tropical vacation. Kayleen will pay. Bring a friend with you, if you wish. Work out all the details with Alice and Philippe."

At that point, she had turned to her two aides, "Philippe, Alice, please, do take care of all the arrangements for the

Baxters. Make sure both Stephanie and her parents have adequate spending money, to relax and enjoy themselves." Kaye sighed as she remembered Stephanie's reaction to what she next said.

"Steph, when you get home, I want you to visit our company psychologist and grief counselor. Let them assess when you are ready to come back to work. For myself, I know I will need a couple of weeks rest. This has been a major ordeal for us both."

Stephanie had just sat and stared at Kaye. She didn't believe what she had just heard. Just thinking about it warmed Kaye's heart and brought a smile to her face.

Stephanie had said, "You mean you want me back?"

"Of course," Kaye had replied.

She was shocked actually that Steph could have thought otherwise. She had flown into Kaye's arms weeping her heart out. The Baxters also hugged and thanked Kaye. Everyone else in the room was crying.

As Philippe escorted the family to a private apartment in the compound, away from prying media eyes, Alice mouthed to Kaye, "All the office staff will have a big welcome back when she returns!"

Kaye heaved a deep sigh, *"This is what I had strived for! Yes, I want to develop Kayleen as a formidable financial giant because that will honor Daddy. Equally important, to me though, is for Kayleen to be recognized as a company that cares for its employees, and clients like family."* A gentle smile swept across her face, *" Today has been a real test – a test Kayleen has passed with Honors!"*

For most of the trip, Kaye's mind had been mercifully preoccupied with the recent events at Lakeland. Now as Dave drew close to Summerside's city limits, all other thoughts were suddenly pushed aside. Foremost in her mind was the one question she dreaded to face, *"Did Max die?"*

She began to shake as she remembered his pain, the blood and above all else how cold he had felt when she had kissed him good-bye. *"Good Bye? Oh! Dear God, No! Please,"* she silently pleaded as tears began trickling down her cheeks.

Instinctively, she reached over and grabbed Marnie's hand, holding it as if in a death grip. Kaye felt like she imagined a drowning person might feel. She honestly could not imagine how she could cope if he were gone. His parents flashed into her mind, especially his mother. Six years she had waited to see her son. *"And I shanghaied him,"* Kaye thought back ruefully to their first meeting, *"When I demanded he help me expose that caller and stop those calls. I had no idea it would be such a daunting and violent task!"*

The car came to an abrupt stop. They had arrived. It was Marnie who posed the question first. "Why are we at the hospital's service entrance?"

"Because Marnie," Dave replied wearily, "I am not up to meeting even one newspaper reporter. Not one! Let's go girls and find Jack and Max." He too secretly dreaded what they would find. He was under no delusions as to the gravity of the man's wounds.

Kaye walked between her two friends desperately clinging to both. The glass doors opened as they approached. As they entered the hospital, a deep chill went through Kaye.

She looked at Dave and whispered hoarsely, "The morgue's here, isn't it?"

"Kaye," Dave reprimanded, "let's not think negatively, okay? If he's dead, he is dead, but cross that bridge only if you have to. Right now, let's just pray that he made it."

As they made their way down the granite corridor to the elevator, the door opened and Dr. Ralph emerged.

"Sorry, let me catch it for you," he said, as he absent-mindedly jammed open the door.

Ralph, like Dave was exhausted. It was barely noon and he'd already done more than a day's work. He didn't need to run into anyone else with problems!

He groused to himself, *"That's why I opted for the rear elevator, to avoid people, yet here they are!"*

Almost as an afterthought, he glanced at the three, and was surprised to see church friends. "Why, Chief, Marnie, Ms. McDonald, I'm sorry, I wasn't paying attention. I didn't realize that it was you." He immediately stepped away from the elevator door, allowing it to close.

"Listen, I was heading outside for a breath of fresh air, but that can wait. Let me take you to Jack," he paused looking at Dave, "and it's Max, isn't it?"

Kaye's heart froze, *"he's going to take us to the morgue! I remember it's down this hall."*

Her mind flashed back to that dreadful day, now nearly seven years ago. She was lead in to identify the scant remains retrieved from the airline's crash. Remains that emphatically revealed her mother and father were dead."

Instinctively Kaye wanted to run, but Dave and Marnie held her firmly.

Then Dave posed the question, whose answer she feared, "Did he make it?"

Ralph shook his head, "It was a rough go."

Kaye thought she would faint.

Ralph continued, "As luck would have it, we had a visiting surgeon who's being interviewed as our new Surgical Chief of Staff."

Kaye looked at him in disbelief thinking, *"Why don't doctors ever give a straight answer?"*

Fortunately, Marnie in her gentle but firm way interjected, "Ralph, is the man still alive?"

"Absolutely, at least he's past the first hurdle anyway."

Kaye gasped, "He's not dead then?"

Ralph smiled compassionately, "No, very much alive, Ms. McDonald. Thanks to our Surgeon, Dr. Chandrah. I'd have to say Marnie, your husband was also instrumental in that too. He clamped off the femoral vein initially, and then here in the hospital, he stayed with Max. He prayed and talked with him as we operated."

Kaye's eyes were wide, "You mean he was conscious when you operated on him?" Her stomach turned as she looked frantically for a washroom.

Fortunately for her, Ralph was oblivious to her misinterpretation of his words. He simply continued, "Why, Ms. McDonald, the man would never have survived a general anesthetic. However, I managed to get an epidural into him."

He smiled patronizingly at the two women, "It's like we do with the ladies when they are giving birth. So the gentleman, with his pain blocked and several units of blood smacked into him, had his vital signs improve drastically."

Ralph had shared this information almost matter-of-factly. Now, he became very passionate, "And guess what, in our search for a new surgical head we were interviewing a Major with significant military combat experience.'

"She stepped right in and headed up our O.R. team. Everyone was impressed with her work and how well she worked with us. Horrific fracture that gunshot caused, but truly, the repair was state of the art," he concluded with obvious professional satisfaction. He paused in front of another set of elevators.

"This one will take you to our O.R. recovery area on four," he added as he pushed the button.

In the elevator, for the first time in hours, Kaye felt hope surge through her body. The chill began to dissipate.

Ralph glanced at his watch as the elevator neared its destination, He turned to Marnie, "I expect you're here to pick up Jack? He agreed to stay with Max, so our team could take a much needed break. In about fifteen or twenty minutes, Dr. Chandrah will be back to discuss with Max and the medical staff, the treatment regime she'd like to initiate. So, I'd guess Jack will be free to go home within the hour."

When they stepped out of the elevator, Ralph pointed to doors half way down the corridor. "The recovery room, where Jack and Max are, is through those doors."

Kaye fairly flew down the hall and through the doors. Then she stopped dead in her tracks, unprepared for what she saw.

Max was in a hospital bed, trussed up like a chicken. His left leg was supported in what appeared to be a sling at about a 120 degree angle from his body. I.V. poles and monitors surrounded the bed. Jack sat beside Max's head. Neither had seen her enter.

A nurse intercepted all three. Ralph had indicated approval for their presence, but the nurse firmly informed them, "Only two at the bedside at one time, Recovery Room rules, Doctor!" as she gave Ralph a dour look.

Dave and Marnie stepped back and Kaye walked slowly towards the two men. When she drew near, she could easily see that Max was conscious and speaking. The color had returned to his face. The tears began to flow uncontrollably. Simultaneously, the two men turned their heads toward her and uttered one word: "Kaye!"

Jack stood up and embraced her. She collapsed in his arms. He kissed her forehead gently and guided her to his stool. As he placed her hand on Max's, he gave her a little hug, "The two of you take a few moments alone, okay?" He then turned and strode out of the room to join Marnie and Dave.

Kaye leaned over kissing Max passionately, both were crying unashamedly.

"I hope there's some Kleenex here," she blubbered.

Spying a box near by, she took one and tenderly wiped his tears. "Max," she sadly shook her head, "I had no idea it would end like this. I'm so sorry, please forgive me."

"You mean, you'd rather I was dead?" he quipped.

His response caught her off guard, but not for long. "You, Sir, had better be careful. I note your two hands have been immobilized, and with your leg strung up like this, you my friend, are at my mercy!"

She tried to laugh, but as she gazed into his eyes all she could remember was the excruciating agony those eyes had registered barely eight hours ago. She just wanted to touch him, to caress his face, to tell him how much he meant to her. She leaned forward, her face resting on his hand softly, she rubbed her cheek against the back of his hand.

"Max, you are the most wonderful man, I have ever met. I love you so much." She closed her eyes, "I thank God that you are alive. I don't know what I would have done if you weren't!" Her eyes brimmed with tears.

He looked at her and grinned. She was so beautiful, even in her exhaustion. He stared at her hair, the red hues simply fascinated him.

"Mr. Carron?"

Her formal use of his name snapped his reverie. He started to react and then he saw those green eyes twinkling and knew something was up.

"I didn't think you could stay mushy for much longer, McDonald," he teased.

She didn't miss a beat, "If me memory serves me well, Mr. Carron, ye asked me a question back in yonder bedroom. Does ye remember the question? And, Sir," she paused, "do ye have recall of me answer?"

"I recall both," was the quiet response.

"So, I take it that the arrangement is still viable?"

He wanted to come up with a wise crack but nothing surfaced so he simply replied, "For my part, Kaye, nothing has changed."

"Nor has it for me," she responded. Again her lips found his. Her lips were moist and warm upon his. She sighed and whispered in his ear, "God is good!"

"All the time," he murmured.

Kaye smiled and nodded, "all the time!"

"God is good!" came the emphatic reply.

She sat quietly beside him. A soft smile gently graced her face as she stroked his forehead.

"Max, do you remember the two childhood vows the Holy Spirit revealed?"

He nodded, "About not loving another girl and never crying? Yeah, I remember," he gave her hand a playful squeeze, "I'm glad I renounced them!"

"The thought occurred to me how really important it was for Holy Spirit to bring that memory of little Katie to you. For then we could include it in our prayers for help."

"How so?" was the puzzled response.

"Well, I don't think you could have set up our trap without it. I mean little Katie ran back into danger. You kept stressing over and over to me not to run back. That drill you orchestrated was really important. With out your repeated instructions, when I heard that first shot, I would have turned back. The drill voice kept silently pleading 'No! No! Keep running to Jack's.'"

"You did come back."

"Yes, but only after I had called 911, and Jack had called Dave. Then Jack ran ahead and I saw the men running from Dave's."

"Amazing Grace," he said softly. "I don't suppose you remember, Kaye, but the very first night I saw you...You were humming 'Amazing Grace'?"

"And our relationship has indeed been 'Amazing Grace,' Max."

"Excuse us," a pleasant female voice broke in, "but we need to interrupt you two love birds."

Kaye turned and smiled sweetly, "Max, this is Marnie, Jack's wife."

"Pleased to meet you, Mr. Kerr, we all are so grateful that you could help out our Kaye."

Marnie's gaze now shifted to Kaye, "Dr. Chandrah wishes to speak to both of you concerning the treatment regime she wishes to follow. I'll let her know you are ready."

As Marnie left to call Dr. Chandrah, Kaye quickly revealed, "Epi identified you as Mr. Maxwell Kerr, a private investigator from Indiana."

"Why?"

"He thought it might allow you and I a few more weeks

of privacy, while we, well particularly you, recover from this past night. Professor Brown suggested the name. He recalled that you had told him, that had Maxwell Kerr been your name, you wouldn't have received the sentence you did. But should you wish, Epi will give the media your correct identity now."

"No, let's leave it the way he has it. At least, until I get more mobile."

"As you wish, Mr. Kerr," she gave him a peck on the nose just as Dr. Chandrah arrived with her medical team. She had brought Max's X-ray. Even those with no medical background could see how badly the bullet had shattered Max's left femur. In fact, Max confessed later that when he first saw the X-ray, he momentarily lost all hope of ever walking again.

Dr. Chandrah explained how critical it would be that absolutely no movement occur in the initial stages of healing. This was the dilemma. They needed to discontinue the epidural.

Pain killers would be needed especially in the first couple of weeks of healing. However, people could hallucinate with these types of medications, thereby increasing the risk of movement. In the Military she had one or two cases that presented like Max. In those cases, she had opted to use a general anesthesia. Basically it produced a medical coma, for a week to ten days. This ensured the patient was pain free and that motion would not interfere with the healing of the broken limb.

Jack eyed the doctors and asked, "Is it possible given the unusual circumstances of this case, for all of us, to take turns staying with Max, until he is brought back to consciousness?" He turned and gestured towards the others. "It would include Kaye, of course, and my wife, Marnie and Chief Dave here. Dave's wife Sue is a nurse practitioner, I'm sure she'd help. Don't you think, Dave? Their son Matt would too. He's a police officer."

Dr. Chandrah smiled, "Well, Sleeping Beauty, looks like you've got lots of friends willing to watch over you. Personally, I think it is a good idea to have someone in your room while you are anesthetized. It's just not feasible for our medical staff to be always there. You okay with these arrangements?"

Max nodded his acceptance of Dr.Chandrah's plan for healing. He was relieved that someone would always be in his room when he was unconscious. Particularly when that someone would often be Kaye.

"Okay everybody, this is what will happen!" Dr. Chandra, now sounded like the Major she was. "We'll transfer Max to a private room, close to emergency support, just in case it's needed. Dr. Ralph, you'll ensure that someone from the Anesthesiology Department is on call 24/7. As for the residents of Independence Drive, you work out your own rotation, so someone will be with Max 24/7. The hospital will accommodate your schedules, allowing you to come and go as you have need."

With that, the epidural was removed, the general anesthesia administered and so began what Jack would later dub, "The Max Vigil!"

Chapter Forty-Two

Each resident of Independence Drive was one hundred percent on board with the 'Max Vigil'. However, their motivation for doing so was as far flung as the North Pole is from the South. For Kaye, it was love.

For Marnie and Sue, it was simply romantic. Both were so excited that, at long last, their Kaye had finally noticed the opposite sex. For them, it was a bonus not only that the man was handsome but that he had courageously risked his life to save hers. Each were determined to do their utmost to ensure Max not only survived this injury but had two legs so he could stand before a preacher and say "I do."

When Sue returned home from her Convention that Sunday to discover all the neighborhood excitement that she had missed, she did confide to Marnie that there was one real plus in all of it.

"What is that?" Marnie had asked, truly perplexed.

With out cracking a smile, Sue had replied, "A man with a broken leg can't run that fast so as to elude the marriage trap!"

The two had a good laugh, then made a pact to be part of the "Max Vigil." Only both had in mind a vigil that included much more than ensuring there would be no compromises to his physical health. Their vigil was to assess his "groom" potentiality.

As for Matt, he had observed Max's physique, judged him to be younger than either his father or Jack, and so had sized Max up as a potential neighborhood sport buddy. Perhaps, when his leg healed, he'd be a good jogging partner? Not only that, his Dad had intimated that Kaye was going to build an indoor pool to help Max's therapy. Matt figured he could probably do laps with the guy.

These last three citizens of Independence Drive, all knew this sleeping beauty, over whom they had volunteered to keep watch, as Maxwell Kerr from Indiana. A private investigator, who Kaye had hired. All of them had either failed to remember the mug shot they'd seen over three months ago, or were unable to draw the similarities between the one in the photo and the one in the hospital bed. In his defense, Matt had been absent when the other officers at their house had been briefed on Max's true identity. Those gentlemen, in turn, had agreed to Dave's decree not to reveal the truth to anyone at this point in time.

The other two residents of Independence Drive were committed to ensuring that sleeping Max suffered no wrong doings during his anesthetic naptime for a variety of conflicting reasons. For starters, both felt the Carron family would be much more amicable to receiving a live son rather than a dead one. In addition, it appeared that there had developed a mutual admiration society between Max and Kaye. They genuinely wanted to see Kaye happy. It was also true that both perceived Kaye as a kid sister, a very attractive, kid sister, whose beauty and wealth drew suitors like a light bulb draws moths.

Thus far, all potential suitors had been to them as undesirable as moths would be.

In contrast, Max held a lot of promise. He'd proven himself as a trustworthy and capable protector. Problematic for them, however was the fact that he was a convicted felon. Worse still it had been Jack who had convicted him. Then there was the matter of the Italian, more specifically Sicilian connection.

Dave and Jack were sincere, upright and very committed law makers, not law breakers. All their careers they had strove intentionally to distance themselves, as far as east is from the west, from anyone remotely with the background Max possessed. If all this was not bad enough, even more disquieting to the two was the reality that they were committed members of Christ's family. They now had undisputable evidence that so was Max!

Regardless of their motives and conflicts, night and day for 264 hours, 11 days and 11 nights, Independence Drive citizenry kept dutiful vigil over Max. They oversaw all aspects of his care and in the process became friendly with all the hospital staff...housekeeping, nursing, therapists, Docs, everyone involved with Max.

Dr. Chandrah did end up accepting the post of Chief of Surgery. As her military career wound down, her Washington posting allowed her to make weekly assessments of Max's healing progress. Every one was watching for evidence of infection.

"Praise God," Kaye exclaimed, "none happened!"

The bone fragments were showing evidence of knitting together well. The skin sutures healed unremarkably. Dr. Chandrah had elected to keep Max anesthetized an extra day so removal of the sutures from his rather extensive incision would not cause undo discomfort.

She called an Independence Drive "family conference" the day before she planned to wake him up. "No, I can't tell you just when he will awaken. It's variable between patients. But when Dr. Ralph removes the anesthesia, Max's arms and legs will need to be restrained. It is essential that his left leg experience no movement whatsoever!"

"But you have it securely in that pulley sling contraption," Kaye had protested.

"Oh yes," Chandra said, "but your friend is a strong man. We've had many such men, able to yank out tubes, slings, pulleys, you name it. Trust me, unrestrained they will do it! It's not that they would do so consciously. It's just as they awaken, their bodies are experiencing withdrawal of powerful drugs. In some it causes dreams, nightmares, hallucinations and people do react."

"But, if we are there, we could stop him," Dave interjected.

"Perhaps, but often by the time you react the damage is already done," replied Dr. Ralph.

He added, "We simply can't take that chance."

"So, how long do the restraints have to be left on?" queried Jack, knowing full well that Max would not be able to tolerate them.

Dr. Chandrah smiled warmly at the group, "When he has regained full consciousness for perhaps an hour or so, we must assess his comprehension level. He needs to know that he cannot move and understand fully why. For the restraints to be removed, we have to be assured that the patient is working with us."

Then she continued, "also, after they are removed in the daytime we will put them back on loosely at nights, or if he chooses to sleep in the daytime. It's for his protection and of course with his co-operation. I suspect that all of you will have relived and reviewed that traumatic Saturday night, over and over, in your minds?"

She received affirmative nods through out the room. "Well, Max will just begin to consciously process what has happened when the anesthetic is withdrawn. Likewise, he will still have need of pain medication. We have to experiment as to which drug and which dose best suits him. This is why when he sleeps, we need to use restraints for probably another week. You can help him by repeatedly reminding him of the reasons for the restraints...after all medication can make our minds fuzzy."

"Doctor, can you give us a progressive time line of how you see treatment evolving? Like when we could expect that sling to be removed?" Sue inquired.

"Oh, yes," Jack thought, *"that's exactly what we need. Way to go Sue!"*

So, Dr. Chandrah began outlining a possible healing framework, stressing that she could only speak in generalities. "Each case is after all unique. After we remove the anesthetic, we need to stabilize his pain meds. This might take upwards to four weeks or as little as one.'

"I would hope that after four weeks both the bone and incision will have healed sufficient to change the leg support from sling to metal brace. That is assuming no infection has reared its ugly head. With the metal brace he could be moved to a rehab hospital, even home, if there was good nursing care."

Chandrah paused, and asked, "Any questions so far?"

Receiving none, she continued, "The Radiology Department will help us monitor the bone healing. I anticipate that sometime, probably around the end of October, we can remove the metal brace and put on a less cumbersome support. Max would still not be able to bear weight on that leg but, with the help of crutches, he could at least be mobile. Physio could then initiate water therapy."

"So a pool could be beneficial?" Kaye asked tentatively.

"Absolutely but it would need to be heated, and in this climate, definitely indoors."

Kaye grinned, "I thought it might. I've arranged to have one installed."

"Yes!" said Matt to himself, *"Oh Yes! Will I ever be willing to volunteer to be his pool buddy!"*

"What about a whirlpool?" asked Sue.

"Eventually yes," Dr. Chandra stated, "but certainly, not initially. A lot of bone growth first needs to take place."

"Later tomorrow, I'll begin weaning Max off the anesthetic," Dr. Ralph ventured.

As she stood up, Kaye commented, "Tomorrow, Marnie and I are on to 11 p.m.. Then Jack said he'd do the nightshift, while we go home to get some sleep. I'll be back at 7 a.m. to spend the following day."

With tears in her eyes, she turned to face both doctors, "Everyone in this hospital has been so wonderful! I can't thank you enough!"

"Believe me, Kaye," Ralph replied, "when families step up, like you folk have done, it really encourages the staff. I think I can speak for all of us, to have a very, very bad situation reversed brings joy to everyone!"

The next evening, as Kaye and Marnie sat beside Max, they watched with interest Dr. Ralph's process of slowly reversing the anesthetic. Kaye sat cross-legged in her white jump suit. Even though it was summer she had a pretty hand knit shawl draped over her shoulder, after all hospitals were air conditioned.

Through this vigil Kaye finally had the opportunity to discuss Max with Marnie and Sue. At Jack and Dave's request, she always stopped short of revealing his true identity.

She fairly bubbled, her green eyes sparkling as she shared about their dance date. "Marn, Max never dated anyone before. He said he was always too busy chaperoning his younger sister. So when he cleared away my gym equipment, got dressed in his suit and invited me to dance, I thought he was bluffing." Kaye's eyes were like emerald saucers. "But could the guy dance! He is a fabulous dancer. Turns out he entered dance competitions with his sister." Kaye paused, "One thing that endears me to him is his humility. He is very gifted in so many ways. Yes, the dancing, but look how he planned my defense against Glaxton...absolutely brilliant. Professor Brown told Jack how astute Max is legally. But when you talk with Max he's just so unassuming. There's just not one arrogant bone in his body!"

Kaye began to giggle, "Marnie, I can't wait until he wakes up and you can talk to him. He may be good looking but the man is painfully shy with women!"

Marnie listened attentively and smiled. She had seen Kaye this animated before but never, ever was the focus of conversation a man. "You know, Kaye, love is very becoming on you."

Kaye went crimson, "Does it show that much?"

"Of course, it does and it should! My prayer, for both of you, is that you will be able to carry this into a long lasting marriage."

Kaye got up and gave Marnie a great big hug. "You have no idea how much, what you just said, means to me!"

She carried a chair over to Max's bed, and sat down beside him.

She touched his arm lovingly, running her hand down to the restraint. Grasping his limp hand in hers, she gave it a gentle squeeze and murmured, "Oh Max, how I long to hear your voice again. I love you so much!"

Unashamedly she reached over and kissed him. Max stirred slightly but did not waken much to Kaye's disappointment.

It seemed no time at all when Jack arrived. Both he and Marnie enfolded Kaye in their arms.

"We know it means so much to you to be here when he wakes, but Kaye you need to get your rest. Keep to the schedule," Marnie whispered, as she gave her friend a hug and a kiss.

"Go home, Love, and get your sleep. You'll need it when Prince Charming awakens. He'll want to know all that's transpired in Epi's investigation,." Jack quipped as he gave her a gentle swat on the behind.

Kaye crossed the room and kissed Max softly on the forehead, "Good night, Darling, I'll see you in the morning." Grabbing her purse, she turned and hurried to catch Marnie at the elevator.

Jack walked over and looked at the restraints. "This will not go over well, or my name is not Jack Walters!"

He pulled out the hide away bed and decided that tonight it might be wise to place it close to Max's bed.

"With my luck, I'm sure to be the one present when he wakes up, and probably with a hangover too!" he grumbled.

Jack placed the little night light they had bought on the opposite side of the room and turned it on. By the time he had readied himself for bed, it was almost midnight.

Jack opened his Bible to do his daily reading. As he looked over at Max, he gave a long sigh.

"Well, Lord, you delivered Kaye from the hands of both the Devil and death and this one has been your instrument of mercy. Your Word declares that, with you, all things are possible. So, I give you these two and their relationship with you and with each other.'

"Humanly, I know it just isn't do-able! Kaye said that Max thought his sister and Tony's relationship was like 'Romeo and Juliet'. They couldn't hold a candle to the differences these two face! We all are in need of your 'Amazing Grace,' that is for sure!"

Jack stared glumly at the one, he now had to admit, he had grudgingly come to respect.

"How could I have allowed myself to hold so much disdain for Carron? Through out my football career, I often faced unscrupulous opponents, some were even downright dirty players." He rubbed his chin pensively. *"Yet, I can't recall loathing them like I did Max.'*

"Well sport is sport, not lawlessness," he mused.

However, as he reflected on the many men and women that he had dealt with both in his law firm and as judge, if he were honest with himself, emotionally none had triggered his contempt as much as Max had.

Jack looked at the Bible in his hands and prayed, *"You tell us, Lord, in your Word not to lean to our own understanding, but in all our ways to acknowledge you."*

Setting the Bible down, Jack drew his hand across his face, thoughtfully resting his chin in the palm of his hand. *"Did I fail to do that at Max's trial? Possible I suppose, but I do remember Marnie praying that scripture with me before I even accepted the appointment to the bench."*

He frowned, *"But, what if I had not sentenced Max in my bias? What then? What would have been the outcome for Kaye?"* He smiled wryly as he remembered Joseph's words to his brothers, years after they had sold him into slavery.

"Yeah, he told them that while they had chosen to do evil, God had intended it for good. I guess those words could apply to me now, couldn't they? Even if Max did what he was charged with, the sentence was too harsh. This I will confess to you, Lord, and ask your forgiveness."

Jack bowed his head, *"I thank you, Jesus, for that forgiveness. Lord, I really need your wisdom to know what you would have me do now."*

Calming his heart with the prayer, he turned out the light, crawled into bed and soon was fast asleep.

Max opened his eyes. They felt so heavy that he closed them again. This process repeated itself over several minutes. Each time, he struggled to complete the sentence that formed in his mind.

"Where am I? What happened?"

But try as he might, he failed. His eyelids simply got heavy and closed. At one point in this fog, it occurred to his blurry mind that he might be able to think better if he first scratched his head.

To his horror, his hands would not move, nor his legs. Fear gripped his heart. *"I'm paralyzed!"* The harder he tried to move his limbs the less they would obey.

Somehow, the struggle above and beside him, penetrated Jack's slumbering mind. He drew his hand over his face as he tried to waken. *"Right! Your luck, Walters, just like you figured, Prince Charming wakes on your watch!"*

In fact, simultaneously both men awoke to reality.

"Damn!" Max exploded, tears flooding his eyes. "I'm in restraints." He turned his head and found himself staring directly at Jack.

"You, Bastard, I confessed to you as a pastor. This is the second time that you have done me in!" he snarled.

Jack was now standing over the bed. "Shut up!" he hissed, "Keep your voice down. Those are medical restraints–not legal!"

Confusion flooded Max's mind. "What?" was all that managed to escape.

Jack spoke slowly and clearly, "Remember what we agreed to, including you? You were to be anesthetized to allow time for healing to set in, and to let the doctors make sure that no infection was present."

Max blinked his eyes. Somewhere in the recesses of his mind a distant memory was surfacing.

"You've actually been anesthetized for eleven days. Early this evening Dr. Ralph started to wean you off the anesthetic." Jack glanced at his watch. "It's 3 a.m., Max. They have you in medical restraints so you can't move and undo the healing that has already taken place. Max, do you understand what I am saying?"

"My nose is itchy. Undo me, so I can scratch it."

Jack laughed, "No can do, Bud. I can scratch it for you but I can't undo the restraints until Dr. Chandrah gives the okay. Nice try."

Max scowled.

"So, is it really itchy?"

"No!"

"Max, there's so very much to tell you that has transpired over the past several days. While I'd love to, you need to wait. Kaye will be in at 7 a.m.. She deserves the right to bring you up to speed."

"There are no charges then?"

"Absolutely not, Max! Absolutely not!" Jack said firmly. "You are the hero...Not the villain!"

Max drew a long shuddered breath, "How long was I asleep?"

"Eleven days, the good news is that your stitches are out and there is no infection. The bone healing is progressing well. Max, the doctors will work with you on the pain medication. They know you will need them for awhile. Dr. Chandrah has told us that this sling, your leg is in, can likely be replaced with a metal brace in a couple of weeks."

"And?"

"Then you can be released for Rehab. She figured that by sometime in October even the brace can be removed.

While you won't be able to weight bear for several months after that, you will be able to begin physiotherapy and water exercise to regain your muscle mass."

"So I got everything?"

Jack looked puzzled, "everything?"

"My two legs and everything,"

Finally, Jack grasped Max's concern, "Yeah, everything! It is just that what feels funny is the tubes. You know the catheter, to drain your bladder. Soon it'll be removed. The process has begun. Step by step you'll start to regain control over your body."

Max bit his lip. Jack noted a tear trickling down Max's face and gently wiped it away...Max closed his eyes and dozed off.

Chapter Forty Three

Jack drove home slowly. He was struggling trying to analyze the emotions he felt as he witnessed the interaction between Kaye and Max. One thing he knew for certain they weren't the emotions of a detached neighbor. What he couldn't discern was whether his feelings were those of an elder brother delighted at the happiness of a kid sister. Or were they more paternal in nature.

At last he blurted out loud to no one but himself, "I guess it doesn't really matter? What is relevant is that the sentiments those two were exhibiting were not those of an employer with an employee!"

He chuckled, "For all Max's bravado with me, as soon as Kaye entered the room all façade evaporated. The man immediately relaxed and tolerated the restraints. I could even trust that they wouldn't remove them before Dr. Chandrah's okay.'

"They both were able to grasp how important it is to have absolutely no movement of those bone fragments before new bone forms. So Jack, Old Boy, those two have now presented you with a new dilemma," a frown fell over his countenance, "one dilemma? It will probably end up as several!"

Jack not only went home and fell asleep, but for the first time in nearly two weeks it was a deep sound sleep. When he awoke he looked at his watch, "Wow! Five o'clock, I've been sleeping for over eight hours. I didn't realize how exhausted I was."

He rolled over on his back, and to his surprise noted

that Marnie was in bed beside him. Not only that, glancing out the window he realized everything was dark. *"Surely I haven't slept all this time?"* But in fact, he had. It was 5 a.m.!

"Man, it has been years since I'd crash like this...only after exams or big games!" Now wide awake he got up cautiously so as not to disturb his wife. He also chose to use the main upstairs bathroom rather than the ensuite so the running water wouldn't wake her.

He found himself invigorated by the hot shower and by the time he finished breakfast his mind was made up. It was time to head back to his Washington office.

He had booked the last two weeks off, utilizing both some sick leave and lieu time. Now, it was time to get back. Back to deal with what he now referred to as "the thorn in his flesh." It was time to again touch base with Epi.

Returning to the bedroom he discovered that Marnie was already awake. "Hon, I'm thinking that I should get back to the office for a few days."

She looked at him and smiled, "Now, Jack Walters, why does this pronouncement not surprise me?" She started to laugh, "I'm amazed you lasted this long! Anyway, while you slept the day away, I stopped in to see Max. He and Kaye look like two little love birds.'

"He has the restraints off when he's awake. Neither does he fuss about them being reapplied when he wants to sleep."

"Well, if every thing is okay on the home front, I should be able to be away for a few days. You think?" He bent over and gave his wife a kiss.

"Jack, I've been thinking..."

"Oh, oh, danger zone ahead," he quipped.

"Well, Kaye is staying here with us while her house is being renovated. When Max is able to be released, why don't we bring him here to recuperate?"

Jack just stared at his wife. He admitted later that he should have seen it coming, but the truth was, he didn't.

"Marnie, you don't know what you are suggesting!"

He quickly stopped, short of divulging why it was not a good idea. Instead he cleared his throat and began, "Hon, Kaye is with us. The two of them are obviously into something much more than an employer-employee relationship, which I'm sure you noted?"

"Of course, Silly, that's why I suggested it."

"But that's not fair to them. I mean to be under the same roof and..."

"Why, Jack, you old prude!" She threw her arms around his neck and gave him a peck on the cheek. "Get real! Kaye will be upstairs. Max will be downstairs immobilized in a steel brace."

"So, where do you propose putting him?"

"I thought we could move the dinning room table, rent a hospital bed and transform the dining room into a rehab room."

Jack closed his eyes. When Marnie spoke like this she had already thought through all the potentialities except one, a major one, which he was not yet ready to tell her.

"All I ask," Marnie continued, "is that you promise to think about it."

"Fine," he said resignedly, "I promise. By the way, since you are awake, if you have time could you drop me off at the train station? I think I can catch the 7 a.m. commuter."

She had and she did. As Jack collapsed into his train seat, he groaned inwardly, *My dilemmas just keep mushrooming!*

The familiarity of his office somehow brought order into his life. It was a welcomed relief from the chaos of the past two weeks. A quiet and much welcomed peace descended upon him. He put a call into Epi and got his answering machine. After the customary 'beep' Jack said "Hi Ep, it's Jack. Wednesday morning. I will be here the rest of the week. Is it possible for you and me to get together to discuss that special case?"

He was glad Mrs. Stuart had indicated she would be late arriving, as she had a dental appointment. He wanted to head to the archives to retrieve a specific case. Had his secretary been present she would have insisted that an aide obtain it. This case however he wanted to secure for himself...alone.

Returning to the office an hour later, he found Mrs. Stuart busy at her desk. She beamed when she saw him. "Oh, Judge Walters, it is so good to see you again. Are you alright? Is everything okay?" she inquired anxiously. "Remember, the last time I saw you, was when you left so abruptly with Professor Brown."

"Indeed, I do remember, Mrs. Stuart! Indeed, I do!" he thought quietly.

Fortunately for Jack, Mrs. Stuart just raced on, "And then when we heard about that atrocious crime attempted on your friend, Ms. McDonald...Why everyone in the building was concerned both for you and her."

"Yes, Mrs. Stuart, I can assure you these past few weeks have been very tense. We all are most grateful for the favorable outcome of that situation. I wish to thank you and everyone else for their kind thoughts and prayers."

Jack managed a smile, "Now, I'd like to ask you to blank out some private space for me on my schedule today and tomorrow. I need to be by myself to collect my thoughts, so to speak, and to get back into my routine.'

"However, should Chief Justice Douglas drop by, please have him come in...And, oh yes, Agent Epstein might call. I'd like to speak with him. But aside from those individuals, and of course my family or Chief Davidson, I will be unavailable."

"I understand, Judge Walters, and Judge, it is so nice to have you back!" Mrs. Stuart smiled warmly.

The more Jack poured over the transcript of Massimiliano Carron's trial, the more unsettled he became. He read the police reports, most of which never got to the trial.

Neither the prosecution nor the defense had introduced them.

"Obvious why the prosecutor chose not to," Jack grunted. "He would have lost. But why would the defense refrain?'

"Therein lies the enigma. All Max's attorney did was stress his client's clean record, pushing for a lenient sentence. Other than that there was no defense...why?" Jack frowned.

"Pretty shabby judicial work on your part, Walters. The questions you are asking now should have been asked seven years ago." He sighed, "I know why I didn't then but my reason is absolutely no excuse! What on earth was the defense attorney doing? Was he incompetent or was he covering something up?"

Jack made a mental note to follow up on both prosecutor and defense attorney.

"I wonder what has happened to their careers?" he mused.

Jack now had before him one very glaring dilemma. It was like a flashing neon sign. He had all the evidence before him to declare a mistrial.

"But then what? If Max's father or brother-in-law were involved in something declaring a mistrial just reopens the case, exposing them to prosecution. That will only bring additional pain to Max. Six years of imprisonment, for what?"

Jack slumped back in his chair, "and if the mob is behind this can of worms, opening it up will be very detrimental to Kaye's relationship with Max." He found himself chewing the stem of his glasses.

"Lord, I really do need to talk to Malc Douglas. I hope, if he hears I'm in, he'll pop by my office."

Malcolm Douglas was Chief Justice not only in rank but also in the respect his fellow colleagues afforded him. He was affectionately known as Malc by his associates.

Just thinking of Chief Justice Douglas, brought a smile to Jack's face. " Heavens, he's got to be the tiniest justice we have. He's even shorter than Justice Roberta Mercadi. But what you lack in physical size, Malc, is sure well compensated by your mental acuity!"

Jack locked his hands behind his head and leaned back in his chair. "Gosh, we all consider Malc to be the most perceptive justice among us!. He's just so darn intuitive, when it comes to ferreting out any quandary we might be experiencing, whether professional or personal...And right now I have a very big quandary!'

"It's pretty clear, Walters, that there has been a gross miscarriage of justice here and unwittingly you have been a pawn in the process. I morally can't sweep this under the carpet. That would not be your will, Lord Jesus. But how and what to do, I am at a loss."

Jack bowed his head, "Lord, I need your wisdom and I need your creative Spirit to direct my steps. Grant me the courage to obediently follow your directives!"

He had just said "Amen" when Mrs. Stuart announced that Chief Justice Douglas had arrived.

Jack rolled his eyes upwards, and silently mouthed, *"Thank you, Lord!"*

To his secretary, Jack responded, "Please send him in, Mrs. Stuart."

Under his breath, he muttered, *"If any one can help me sort out this mess, it's bound to be Malc!"* Jack sighed, *"As important as your mental agility is to me, Justice Douglas, even more important right now is your compassionate heart which I've learned I can rely on."*

As Douglas stepped into his office Jack rose, gratefully shook his hand and said, "Thanks for dropping by, Malc, I really appreciate it!"

As Jack sat back down in his chair, he expected Malc to do likewise. Instead the man strode over to Jack's desk and threw his leg over the end. He sat perched there staring at Jack.

"Good Lord, Jack, I came by to welcome you back and express hope that all was well. However, one look, at you, tells me it's not!"

"That obvious, huh?"

"That obvious! How can I help?"

Sheepishly Jack confided, "Malc, I really am in a very conflicted state!"

Douglas stood up retrieved another chair and pulled it alongside Jack's. Then he sat back to listen. So began what turned out to be a very prolonged two hour conference, which stretched into three when Special Agent Bernard Epstein showed up.

Malc admitted, "Initially, when I saw how haggard you look, Jack, I thought perhaps Ms. McDonald's perp had been through your court room. That the guy was released for lack of evidence."

"Not so," Jack smiled lamely, "much worse!" So to the utter amazement of Douglas, Jack began unveiling the truth. The private Investigator from Indiana was neither a private eye nor from Indiana. Instead it was Massimiliano Carron from Illinois.

"Whom you sentenced to six years in the pen for drug trafficking?" interrupted Malc.

"The same," Jack acknowledged.

"What was he doing in Ms. McDonald's house?"

"Coming to see me," Jack responded.

Malc raised his eyebrow, "Intending to harm you?"

Jack gave a hollow laugh, "In the beginning, I did think so, but now I don't. He wanted to know why I had nailed him for six years. Since he had no prior convictions of any sort, even parking violations, he thought I'd been bribed."

"Were you?"

Jack looked at Malc askance, "What do you think?"

"No!" laughed Malc, "but how did Carron get connected to Ms. McDonald?"

"He broke into her house."

"He didn't know where you lived?"

"He knew!"

"So?"

Jack exhaled slowly. He took off his glasses and rubbed the bridge of his nose. "I believe that God directed Carron there because he held the solution to what proved to be her very lethal night time caller."

"But M.K. didn't know his identity?" Douglas queried.

"Not at the beginning, but later she did."

"Jack, after all that transpired with that serial killer, you can't be serious about charging either of them? Can you?" Malcolm asked incredulously.

"No, of course not!"

"So, Jack, what is your dilemma? I can see by your face, there obviously is one?"

"Malc, it is not one dilemma. There are several. I haven't been smart enough to sort them out. Thus, I haven't been able to set in motion plans to unravel them."

"Why don't you start trying to name them. You can prioritize later." Douglas offered.

Jack shrugged, "Good idea! So for starters Carron is in love with M.K., or Kaye as she is known to us."

Malc's eyes widened, "Is it reciprocal?"

"Oh, yes!" Jack sighed.

Douglas ran his hand through his massive, mane of sandy hair, now peppered with white, and commented. "As best as I can recall, both are well over the age of majority and single. Obviously, their romantic inclination, in and of itself, is not the issue. Continue delineating your dilemmas."

"True, but it is from their romance that all other dilemmas are rooted. So for starters, Max appears to have been falsely accused and tried."

"You sound sure of this?"

"I am positive, Malc," Jack shook his head sadly as he said, "I should have caught it six and a half years ago at the trial. It is so blatant, but then had I done so Carron wouldn't have wound up in Kaye's house."

Jack leaned forward, and added, "Malc, had he not done so, I'm equally certain Kaye, not Glaxton would be dead. However, I think you know me well enough, Malc, to know I am not excusing my shabby bench work by that fact?"

Douglas eyed his colleague, and remarked. "I also know you well enough, to know that you wish to correct the error.

Am I right?"

Jack nodded affirmatively.

"Well, you as the trial judge can declare a mistrial. Or you can wait for the prosecution or defense to challenge the court ruling." Douglas stated bluntly.

Jack snorted, "Neither will do so, of that I'm convinced. The prosecution's motives are obvious, personal advancement. The defense's motives to me appear murkier. Being Carron is Sicilian, the mob's shadow always looms in the background as a possibility. Malc, could there be another option? Other than another trial? I guess I'm asking other than a court solution?"

Malcolm stretched out his legs, "The one I can think of is if the original offenders stepped up and confessed and exonerated Carron." He laughed and continued, "which, while possible, Jack, I think you realize would be the most unlikely scenario."

Douglas pursed his lips, "I can also give you a third option."

Jack's demeanor suddenly perked up. "What's that, Malc?"

"Leave it all alone. Let bygones be bygones. You seem to indicate that both you and Carron believe God used the error to save M.K. McDonald's life. It was his ability and knowledge that took out this serial killer. So in the first instance, the man was in the wrong place at the wrong time. Nearly seven years later, he finds himself in the right place at the right time."

It was just before this point was made, that Special Agent Epstein had joined their conversation.

In fact, it was Epi who delineated the problem with Malc's solution. "M.K. in her role as CEO of Kayleen, travels extensively abroad. She attends state dinners and high-profile functions all the time.'

"As a convicted felon, Max won't get a passport. Nor will he even be allowed to escort his wife at state functions in our country. Yet, in many situations, it is expected that she be escorted." Epi paused, "We do it all the time now. Either one of our agents or CIA is discreetly dubbed in as the escort. How well do you think that's going to sit with Carron?"

Now, it was Douglas' turn to exhale deeply. He sat back, pinching his nose, as he pondered his reply. "Yes, I see! Well, gentlemen, that certainly does present itself as a formidable dilemma. Jack, I gather your relationship with Ms. McDonald is... "

Jack groaned, "not entirely sure, Malc, but it appears to be half way between elder brother and father,"

"So your desire is for her to be happy in her romance?"

"Absolutely!" Jack sighed.

"As I look at you, I surmise that there is at least one more dilemma?"

Jack's jaw tensed, as he replied. "Yes, Malc, there is! It is the one that causes me to believe I need to resign from the bench."

This revelation visibly jarred Douglas, startled he queried. "Whatever do you mean, Jack? You have become one of our most trusted and knowledgeable members and this, Sir, I can assure you, is not flattery!"

"Well, Malc, in my limited yet very intense exposure to Max, I judge the man to deeply care for his family...The Carrons and the Marconis. Neither family has formally been linked to the Mafia..."

"But," Epi interjected, "they have definite friends, associates even some family members who either are known Mafia figures or suspected mobsters."

"Jack, let me replay what I think I hear you saying. M.K. McDonald is like family to your family. Thus through her romance with Max, he becomes part of your family? Is my understanding correct? " Douglas questioned.

"And the corollary is that I become part of his," added Jack glumly. "As a supreme court justice this puts me in a very questionable light. One I, with all integrity, cannot agree to."

"In that case, Jack," Malcolm smiled, "As I see it, your dilemma becomes my dilemma."

"Even if I resign?" gasped Jack.

"Jack, my dilemma is losing you, period."

Malc sat hands tented together, his thin forefingers pointing upward forming a triangle. As he raised his hands and bent his head forward, his mouth rested on his forefingers. He sat there silent and pensive for several minutes.

Finally, he began to speak, ever so slowly. "In the fairytales that I read my grandchildren, the stories always end, 'and they lived happily ever after' ..."

Jack and Epi exchanged quizzical glances with each other. Then focused their gaze on Chief Justice Douglas, as he continued, "My point, gentlemen, is although a psychopathic killer has been eliminated, as a direct result of Mr. Carron's self-sacrificing act of bravery, the loose ends of this story have yet to be tied together.'

"I also believe, Mr. Epstein, that your agency, through the apprehension of Henry Glaxton, was able to solve several interstate homicides, which brings closure, albeit tragic, to many families. Not only that, you were able to release from prison a man who had been falsely convicted of one of those murders. Is this not correct, Mr. Epstein?"

"Yes," Epi replied thoroughly perplexed by the Justice's line of questioning.

"Thus, with regard to all these cases, not only have these families and individuals experienced some degree of 'happily ever after' so has the Bureau?"

Epi nodded affirmatively looking at Jack, who merely shrugged his shoulders equally puzzled.

"And, Jack," Douglas continued, "I perceive it would have been a very unhappily ever after for you and the Davidsons had you awoke one morning to discover that right under your nose, a neighbor whom you cherish as a kid sister, even a daughter, had been horribly brutalized and murdered. Am I correct?"

Jack's color drained. The mere thought, of what Malcolm was expressing, was too terrible for him to even entertain. Numbly, he murmured, "Yes."

Malcolm resumed his line of reasoning. "Therefore, can I not conclude that with Ms. McDonald very much alive after this terrifying ordeal, both you and the Davidsons have likewise experienced a significant degree of 'happily ever after'?"

"Most definitely," Jack whispered.

"As a result of what you two have shared, I am persuaded that had M.K. McDonald's life been tragically and prematurely snuffed out, the consequences to Kayleen Enterprises would have been dire.'

"The repercussions of that would have been felt not solely in the company but in the business world itself. Thus the business community could have experienced a very 'unhappily ever after.' Instead, as a result of Carron and M.K.'s ingenuity and courage, both Kayleen and the business world are also experiencing a degree of 'happily ever after.' Am I correct again?"

Both men nodded, totally at a lost as to where they were being lead.

"What I am getting at, gentlemen, is two people made self-sacrificing choices to allow our society to be free from one bent only on harming others. That individual's demise brought a happy ever after scenario to our society.'

"Now, those two people, through whom that scenario came, have a dark cloud hanging over their own happiness.'

"Thus, in the interest of both justice and dare I say, mercy, could not a little out of the ordinary effort, such as they put forth, be expended on their behalf?"

Epi and Jack stared at Douglas with blank expressions on their faces.

Douglas chuckled, "Gentlemen, it is my belief that the two of you possess the ability to provide that 'out of the ordinary' effort.'

"Furthermore, Jack, I think you have the desire to at least try and end this story on the best 'happily ever after' note, for our two lovebirds?'

"For my part, I will throw in my influence along side your ability and desire to see what can be done.'

"Consequently, Jack, I'm reassigning you, temporarily, to justice issues of Homeland Security. That should alleviate some of your current conflict of interest concerns. Also, I will speak with your supervisor, Epstein, and ask him to temporarily deploy you to Homeland Security. That way you can officially work with Justice Walters.'

"By the way, Jack, you are right about an injustice in Carron's trial. If you examine the archive records you will note I reviewed them myself last week."

Jack was stunned. All he could do was stammer, "What? Why?"

"Professor Brown filled me in on Carron's research. It is good! If Brownie thinks someone has the best legal mind that he's seen, I take note! Better it be on our side than the other...Right, Epstein?"

"You bet!" Epi smiled wryly.

Douglas stood and headed for the door. He stopped and turned.

"Well, Jack, you still have dilemmas but at least you are authorized to pursue solutions. Trust me, gentlemen, my gut tells me this story is not yet over. My hope is that the two of you will be able to bring it to a more favorable closure for all parties, including our two star-crossed lovers. Well, good luck, everyone. This will be a challenging assignment, but I'm sure you are capable."

And, on that note, Malcolm Douglas departed.

CPSIA information can be obtained at www.ICGtesting.com
232893LV00001B/1/P